SLOW DANCING *at* SUNRISE

JO McNALLY

HQN™

HQN™

ISBN-13: 978-1-335-00677-6

Slow Dancing at Sunrise

Copyright © 2019 by Jo McNally

Recycling programs
for this product may
not exist in your area.

This edition published by arrangement with Harlequin Books S.A.

For questions and comments about the quality of this book, please contact us at CustomerService@Harlequin.com.

® and TM are trademarks of Harlequin Enterprises Limited or its corporate affiliates. Trademarks indicated with ® are registered in the United States Patent and Trademark Office, the Canadian Intellectual Property Office and in other countries.

www.HQNBooks.com

Printed in U.S.A.

To my brother, Steve, and my sis-in-love, Linda.
I couldn't have asked for a better big brother, and
you couldn't have picked a better bride. Love you both.

Acknowledgments

Special thanks to my brother, Steve, and his wife, Linda (to whom this book is dedicated), for helping me with details and resources for the Finger Lakes wine region of New York, where they live. To my forever love, John— thank you for being my real-life romance hero and partner. Thank you to my amazing friends who helped inspire the feisty Rendezvous Falls Book Club—an eclectic band of seniors who are more likely to be causing trouble than sitting around knitting in a rocking chair (although some of them can knit and cause trouble with equal expertise). Here's to my dear friends Dianne, Kate, Joy, Laura, Liz and Linda, and all smart, sassy women everywhere! To my globe-trotting mom and her sister, Darlene and Shirley, who redefine *old age* for anyone who can keep up with them. Thank you to freelance editor Anna J. Stewart for her help as I was putting this story together. Many thanks to my agent, Veronica Park of Corvisiero Literary Agency. As usual, I couldn't have done it without your guidance, encouragement and occasional kick in the pants. Thanks for always knowing which one I need at any particular time.

Hurricane Florence came roaring through my city of New Bern, North Carolina, as I was writing this book last year, leaving a path of devastation in her wake. I'd like to offer special thanks to the heroic first responders, utility workers and nonprofit volunteers who rushed in to help our community recover. And thank you to my editor, Michele Bidelspach, for being so understanding as we dealt with the storm chaos right at deadline time!

Dear Reader,

Welcome to Rendezvous Falls—a fictional town set on the shores of Seneca Lake in New York's Finger Lakes region. The area is famous for its award-winning wines and beautiful waterfalls, but that's just the tip of the iceberg.

Rendezvous Falls is also known for its festivals and fanciful Victorian homes—each one with more gingerbread trim and wild color combinations than the last. As Whitney, the heroine of this book describes it, the town is "a kaleidoscope marriage of history museum and Disney World, and somehow...it works."

This series was inspired by my fierce, bawdy, smart, loving (did I mention bawdy?) friends. They're far more likely to flip each other a middle finger than call each other "dearie." These ladies gave me the idea for an eclectic senior book club whose members decide to play matchmaker to the younger crowd in this scenic college town. The matches they come up with don't always (okay...never) work out the way they intend, but love always finds a way to bring the right people together in the end.

In *Slow Dancing at Sunrise*, they try to find accounting executive Whitney Foster a "nice, professional young man" while she's visiting Rendezvous Falls. No one, least of all Whitney, suspects she'll fall for the sullen, plaid-clad winery manager working for her aunt. But that's all part of the delicious fun!

Enjoy!

Jo McNally

CHAPTER ONE

WHITNEY FOSTER was stuck in a traffic jam.

On a Thursday afternoon.

In the middle of nowhere.

She thought she'd left this particular problem in Chicago. But here she was, moving at a snail's pace on a two-lane country road. She sat fourth in line behind a monstrous green farm machine. The road was twisty, so attempting to pass risked a fate far worse than slowing down for a few miles.

At least the view was nice. Seneca Lake stretched out below her, narrow and brilliantly blue. Farmland and vineyards sloped down to the water, and on the other side, rose gently to the horizon. A glance at the GPS told Whitney she was only a few miles away from one of the happiest places she'd ever known as a child. A little traffic backup wouldn't spoil her anticipation.

The three-day drive from Chicago to upstate New York was the longest road trip her hybrid SUV had ever seen. It usually just took her to work and back on those rare days she didn't take the train. The fun-yet-practical bright red vehicle had been a rare impulse purchase last year after she'd received her bonus. It was great on gas. And she'd managed to pack a surprising amount of her life into the small cargo area. Her *former* life, that is.

No more bonuses now. No more job. And all because

she'd trusted the wrong man. Wrong *men*. Silly her for assuming the senior partners would do the right thing when she found discrepancies in an audit done by the CEO's nephew. Instead, they'd patted her on the head and told her not to worry, then made her the scapegoat when it all blew up in their faces. They took her job *and* her reputation. Good times.

Brake lights flashed red in front of her as the agricultural machine slowed to a near stop, then mercifully pulled into a farm on the right, raising a cloud of dust as it rumbled up the driveway and past the blue, green and yellow farmhouse. As frustrated as she was by the delay, the scene made her smile. She'd been around too much pavement and cement the past few years. The increasing number of Victorian houses she passed, painted in bright rainbow colors, were a mainstay of Rendezvous Falls.

Aunt Helen had told her the story often. Some famous architect—Whitney drummed her fingers on the steering wheel trying to remember his name—came home to the town after the Civil War. Looking to forget the terrible things he'd seen, the architect started building houses decked out with fanciful gingerbread trim, painted in wild color combinations. People laughed at first. But it wasn't long before everyone wanted the most intricate, most incredible, most colorful house in town. These days, people traveled from all over to see the Crazy Victorian "Painted Ladies" of Rendezvous Falls. Naturally, an influx of visitors led to the meeting of many different worlds. And, as Aunt Helen used to say, the meeting of hearts. "People don't realize what they're missing until they find it," she would say with a wink.

Maybe that was why Whitney couldn't think of any-where else to run to but the Finger Lakes. Just like when she came here as a little girl, she knew she was miss-ing…something. Whitney's mom had been trying to "make it" in Las Vegas back then, and rarely had time for actual parenting. Visiting her aunt and uncle here almost every summer gave Whitney the sense of *home* she'd needed. It was an escape to a magical place, as far removed from Vegas in atmosphere as it was in miles.

Route 14 grazed the edge of Rendezvous Falls. Whit-ney didn't take time to detour through the neighbor-hoods that led down to the water, but the town hadn't changed much. The houses stood out from the bucolic scenery as boldly as ever. American flags waved from old-fashioned lampposts lining the streets. It was still postcard pretty, and indeed, there was a sign proudly proclaiming Voted One of America's Prettiest Towns.

A large home sat on one corner with a for sale sign in front of it. It sported two round turrets, and was painted black, with bright orange-and-yellow trim. Whitney shook her head. It looked like an homage to candy corn. As a little girl, the eclectic paint schemes made her feel like she'd stepped into a fairy tale where anything was possible. As an adult, they seemed…silly. Indulgent. Impractical. They were just houses now, not portals to a storybook wonderland. Because fairy tales weren't real.

Uncomfortable confronting her own cynicism, Whit-ney pulled her shoulders back and tried to loosen her death grip on the steering wheel. She wasn't here to be-lieve in magic. She was here to regroup and figure out what to do next. She chewed on her lip, trying to ignore the roiling of her stomach. Everything would be fine. She just needed a plan.

Mind back on the matter at hand, she turned onto Falls Road and headed up the hill away from town, toward Falls Legend Winery. A smile played at her lips. Okay, there was *one* fairy tale she believed in. Uncle Tony had passed away almost two years ago, but until then, he and Aunt Helen had lived a charmed life together.

Whitney had heard *that* story many times, too, and she'd never tired of it. The scrappy son of an immigrant who fell for the most beautiful girl in town. Despite the odds, he won her heart. They bought a rundown farm with one of the earliest Victorian houses on it, and eventually turned it into a successful winery and party venue. Uncle Tony made the wine and built whatever was needed, and Aunt Helen was a Martha Stewart–level hostess—without that pesky trip to prison, of course. Tony and Helen's marriage had been a statistically rare perfect partnership.

She turned onto Lakeview Road, which hugged the hillside instead of climbing it, giving the car a welcome break. Whitney hadn't seen the house in almost four years. Her smile disappeared. She hadn't come to Tony's funeral. Her boss had made it clear at the time that leaving in the middle of the London audit for someone who "wasn't immediate family" would slow her progress to becoming partner. She didn't know how to explain that Uncle Tony was the only stable male role model in her life. That she loved him like a father, since she'd never known her own. Her boss wasn't interested in any of that.

Guilt poked at her before she pushed it away. Guilt was unproductive. Becoming the youngest female partner at one of the world's fastest-growing accounting firms required a pricey personal toll, and one of the first things she'd had to sacrifice was vacation time. Aunt Helen and Uncle Tony always assured her they understood when she couldn't visit, and they'd all stayed in touch with phone calls and video chats. But it wasn't the same, and she knew it.

Whitney recognized the rise in the road ahead, and her heart jumped a little. Right around that curve was the reason this was called Lakeview Road. She didn't bother stopping at the scenic overlook that jutted out alongside the road, knowing she was less than a mile from Aunt Helen's. Uncle Tony used to walk down here with her from the house, her soft little hand held in his huge, rough one. He'd tell her of the moonlit night he brought Aunt Helen to that very overlook to propose to her.

At the time, Whitney had hung on every word, staring into her uncle's warm, dark eyes and wishing she would grow up to live in a place just like this, with a love just like theirs. But she was an adult now, and she knew the odds of that happening were approximately a million to one. No, wait. Her brain spun through the numbers quickly. With six billion people on earth, a million-to-one chance actually meant something *was* likely to happen. That's not what she was going for. A *billion* to one was more accurate, although people rarely said that…

She was so busy running the calculations, she almost missed the driveway. It didn't help that the grass was so high it nearly covered the faded wooden sign for Falls Legend Winery. A hand-lettered board had been nailed across the bottom, reading Open Saturdays Only.

Saturdays only? That was…strange. Tony had always

opened the wine-tasting room every day, because "You never know who might stop by, Whitney-girl. Maybe some nice person will drive through town on a Tuesday and buy five cases. You just never know."

The driveway was bumpier than she remembered. Whitney frowned. Tony had done most of the physical work around the place, but Helen told her they'd had some guy working for them who'd stayed on after Tony died. She vaguely remembered seeing a dark-haired teen following Tony around the vineyard when she'd come here as a girl. Obviously, Tony could never be replaced, but…she still didn't expect to see this level of neglect. Maybe the hired man had left?

At the crest of the knoll, the driveway opened into a large level parking area. Thin weeds grew up through the gravel in spots. She parked her car in front of the carriage house to the right that functioned as a tasting room and wine shop. It had the same gingerbread trim and rounded turret as the main house, but in miniature. The only variance on the Victorian styling was the limestone porch pillars, a nod to Uncle Tony's beloved Italy. The paint, once bright and cheerful, was peeling. Sections of siding were missing. A pile of lumber was off to the side, showing the small promise of intended improvement.

Whitney exchanged her practical driving flats for her favorite navy pumps and got out of the car. Looking up at the main house across the lot, she swallowed hard, feeling like a stone was lodged in her throat. It was still a life-sized dollhouse, painted dark green with burgundy and ivory trim as Tony's way of honoring the Italian flag. But now it was…tired. Forgotten. The paint wasn't peeling as badly as the carriage house, but there was no *life* to the place. The curtains were drawn tight on all the windows. Flower boxes still lined the porch railing, but they sat empty. The big rocking chairs that were always on the porch were gone. When she was little, this had been her own special Secret Garden, but even Aunt Helen's precious roses were an overgrown mess.

Why hadn't Helen told her things had fallen apart like this? She dug the toe of her shoe into the loose soil. Helen had been sad and withdrawn when they spoke recently, but that was normal for a woman who'd lost the love of her life, right? Whitney had, as usual, been busy and rushed on those calls. But she *had* asked how things were going at the winery. Helen always said things were fine. Whitney hadn't realized "I'm fine" was the age-old cry for help.

A movement caught her eye near the corner of the long fermentation barn farther up the hill. A man came out of the smaller door, a worn leather bag slung over his shoulder, and a brown dog trotting at his side. His head was down and his strides were long and sure—a man on a mission. She could see the shadow of a dark beard along a strong jawline. He ran his hand through his longish hair, then rubbed the back of his neck as he walked, as if trying to solve some complex equation. Cargo shorts hung low on his hips and a dark T-shirt clung to sweaty skin. Was he some super-hot vagrant just wandering through? Was he looking to rob the place? What had he been doing in Aunt Helen's barn?

The dog saw her first, and let out a sharp bark. The man looked up and spotted her car parked by the carriage house. He came to such an abrupt halt the canvas bag swung forward and smacked him in the elbow. He grimaced in its direction, his scowl deepening when he spotted her. Whitney returned the expression, plus tax.

"We're closed." He lobbed the words at her from across the parking lot. Didn't even bother walking toward her. *We're* closed. *We?*

"And who," she asked, crisply, "might 'we' be?"

The man cocked his head toward the Falls Legend Winery sign above the door.

"We," he replied, as if speaking to a small child, "are the proprietors of this winery, and we are not currently accepting customers." Whitney couldn't help wondering how many customers showed up here wearing Armani, with a car full of luggage. He glanced at her car, then back at her, towing his eyes up and down her body. "No wine for sale here today. No drinks to be had. That is what 'we' mean by 'closed.'"

Her fingers twitched. Whitney had dealt with men like this for years. Coasters. Lurking losers who stayed under the radar and collected a paycheck for basically just showing up. They acted as though their lack of accomplishment somehow meant they were smarter than the rest of the world. As if the fact they were pulling one over on their bosses made them more worthy.

Whitney propped one hand on her hip and gestured around the property with her other.

"Yes, I can see how you may be put off by unexpected visitors. Are you actually expecting *any* customers, at *any* point in the near future?" she said, matching his condescending tone.

"Excuse me?" He let the battered leather bag slide off his shoulder, catching the strap in his hand at the last second. The dog, with white and tan trim on its face and legs, sat at his side, watching them curiously.

"Look, I don't know what your issue is, but you're going to want to take your Random Thursday Day Drinking somewhere else. This is a family-owned place, and I've got things to do."

At the mention of family, Whitney bristled, breaking her own "stay cool" rule.

"Wow, that is…quite the customer service approach." She started across the parking lot, struggling to walk on heels that weren't meant for crushed stone. "Fortunately for the *actual* proprietor, I'm not here to buy wine. But I can't help wondering how many customers you've chased away with that attitude."

As she got closer, his jawline hardened. Already square beneath the scruffy beard, it was now set firmly in anger. If she had to guess, she'd say he was only a few years older than her. His dark hair was long enough to show thick, sweat-soaked curls. His skin was tanned and ruddy from the sun, and the layer of grime on his neck almost made her recoil in disgust. But she didn't stop walking until she heard a low growl coming from the dog at his side.

"Molly, hush." His voice was low and even, at odds with the muscle she could see ticking dangerously in his cheek. "This 'lady' isn't a threat."

He set the bag on the ground with a heavy thud. Metal clanked against metal…and a memory surfaced. That was Uncle Tony's old tool bag. She'd often watched Tony trudge between the house and wine barn with that same bag, always fixing something. He'd taken the time to explain what each tool was for and what he was doing. As a little girl craving attention, having someone talk to her like a grown-up was beyond special. Handed down through generations of Russos, those tools had built half the structures on this property.

What was this man doing, handling something so precious with so little regard? Was this…was this jerk *stealing* from Helen as well as taking advantage of her? Whitney's fingers curled into fists.

Ignoring her started objection, he continued, "Look, if you're not here for wine, you'll have to go. We're not buying whatever you might be selling. If you're looking for Mrs. Russo, she's not home." He stared hard at her to make sure she got his point. "And *she's* not buying anything, either."

At that, he reached down to lift the tool bag, dismissing her.

Before the thought had even fully formed in her mind, Whitney was reaching for the strap on the tool bag. As the man went to throw it back over his shoulder, she pulled, setting the weight off balance, which caused him to let go. The bag was much heavier than she anticipated, and as it came swinging toward her hip, she braced herself. This was going to leave one hell of a bruise. But at the last second, the bag jerked, tools clanking loudly as it jostled between them. He'd caught it just in time, but Whitney didn't feel grateful. And he clearly wasn't feeling chivalrous.

"What the hell are you doing, lady?" Anger turned to incredulity, his brown eyes widening in surprise, before quickly morphing back to anger. "Are you insane? Let go of my tool bag!"

"It's not *your* bag," Whitney corrected him, still clutching the strap. "And I don't appreciate you acting like you have the authority to tell me—or anyone, for that matter—who can or cannot do business with *this* company. As you said, it's family-owned, and I happen—"

Before Whitney could continue her lecture, which wasn't at all as articulate as she wanted, the crunch of gravel stole the attention of them both.

A dusty blue Subaru rolled up and parked beside the house. Was Aunt Helen still driving that old thing? Whitney's nervousness about facing her aunt after being away so long evaporated as soon as the short— and just a little round—woman got out of the car. Whitney needed an Aunt Helen hug in the worst way. She turned toward her, temporarily forgetting she was in the middle of a tug-of-war with a hired hand who smelled like a wild moose. His hand landing firmly on her arm was a sharp reminder.

Whitney snapped her attention back in his direction, realizing she was still clutching the tool bag. They were closer than she'd thought. So close she could almost make out her own reflection in his dark eyes. His voice took on a new tone, hard and urgent.

"Listen, Crazy. Whatever your problem is, take it somewhere else. I'm not gonna let you hassle that woman. You need to go. *Now.*"

It took all of Whitney's self-control not to slap him right in the face. Despite her spectacular downfall recently at the hands of arrogant men, she'd never been tempted toward physical violence. But this man's touch sparked something new and dangerous inside her. Not flight, but fight. Her voice went ice-cold.

"Take your hands. Off of me."

He did so immediately Now on firmer mental ground, she faced him again, barely registering the sound of the car door closing behind her. For a few seconds, their eyes locked in a silent battle of wills. He didn't back away, or let go of the bag. Neither did she. She gave it a tug. He tugged back with a smirk. It was the smirk that did it. She leaned forward and hissed at him.

"If I have anything to say about it, and I'm guessing I will, you're about to be fired." She knew it was foolish, but she tried again to yank the bag away. "And when you pack up to leave this place, this bag will not be among the things you take."

Amusement flashed briefly in his eyes, and he opened his mouth to reply. She braced herself, wary of the grim set of his jaw.

"Whitney! You're early! What a wonderful surprise! Come here and let me look at you!" Aunt Helen's words caused a sudden and violent shift in his expression. For the first time, Whitney saw a shadow of discomfort. Even, perhaps, a bit of dread. Finally releasing the bag, Whitney shot him a smile of victory before turning into her aunt's warm embrace. The clank of the tools hitting his leg made her smile turn into laughter.

"Aunt Helen, I'm *so* glad to see you!"

AUNT HELEN?

Luke Rutledge closed his eyes to ward off a sudden pain in his temple. *Aw, crap.* Helen told him her niece was coming this weekend for some last-minute visit. It never crossed his mind this raven-haired woman in full-on city bitch mode could possibly be related to sweet little Helen Russo.

He rewound their encounter in his head. It wasn't good. Judging from her appearance, with the ridiculous shoes, the news anchor haircut, and the sleek business attire—snug blue ankle-length trousers and a matching jacket over some silky bright green confection… Well, he'd assumed she was one of those early weekenders hoping to start off her trip with a daytime buzz and a bottle or two of chardonnay "for her and the girls" on their way to some B&B. It happened from time to time, and usually he'd be all for the extra sales. But not today. He was already behind on his to-do list, and he'd learned from experience that spoiled city types had little respect for anyone else's time.

…you're about to be fired…

Luke couldn't stop his grin. Need to apologize, maybe. Even though it would grind his last nerve to do it. Get *fired*? Not happening.

"And you've already met Luke!" Helen and her niece turned in his direction. "My two favorite people in the world!"

The brunette scowled at him over her aunt's head. It wasn't hard, considering Helen wasn't much over five feet tall, and her niece was only a few inches shy of six. But it was the look on Helen's face that struck him momentarily silent. He hadn't seen her smile like that in ages. Not since before Tony's fatal heart attack twenty months ago. The weight of her grief was lifted from her shoulders, at least for the moment, and she was beaming. She'd helped save him years ago, and her happiness mattered. A lot. Luke regrouped.

"We hadn't exchanged names yet, Helen. Your niece just got here, and started… Well, it's a funny story." He rubbed his thigh where the tool bag had smacked him, trying his best not to shoot the woman a blame-filled glare. "I thought she was selling something."

Helen laughed. "That makes sense. Why else would someone drive up here on a Thursday?"

Luke forced a lighthearted chuckle, walking a fine line between upsetting Helen—which would be bad—and upsetting her niece…which could be fun. He held out his hands in innocence, ignoring the evil look he was getting from the brunette.

"That's what *I* thought, but I couldn't get rid of her. And believe me, I tried!" He smiled through every word, and Helen bought his act, laughing so hard she had to wipe her eye.

"Oh, I'm sure you couldn't! This girl has a mind of her own!" She looked up at her niece, who quickly smoothed on a smile. "Whitney, this is Luke Rutledge. Luke, this is my niece, Whitney Foster. You may have seen each other here through the years, but I don't know that you've ever met. Luke is running the place for me."

"*With* you," Luke corrected her gently. Helen had been through a hell of a rough couple of years, but she was finally starting to show an interest in the business again. He was grateful not to feel alone in caring about the winery, but he knew Helen's recovery was still fragile. Whitney reached out and shook his hand as Helen answered.

"Oh, Luke, all I do is show up with cookies on Saturdays. You're the one doing the *actual* work."

"Really?" Whitney's brow arched sharply, leaving Luke no doubts about what she meant. She released his hand as quickly as possible.

Helen rambled on, oblivious to her niece's sarcasm. "Oh, yes! Luke does everything now. Making the wine, running the vineyard, taking care of the place…" Whitney's brow upped the ante and disappeared completely under a lock of dark hair that fell across her forehead. She looked toward the house, and he knew damn well what she saw. The overgrown garden. The empty porch. The ragged weeds. She wasn't even close to knowing the story behind it, and she probably didn't care. Another one of those judge-at-first-sight people. Having carried the Rutledge name his entire life, he was used to being on the receiving end of snap judgments from people like her. It still rankled.

"I do what I can, Helen." If only he could figure out a way to survive with no sleep. Until then, he needed to get that damned mower fixed before the grass got tall enough to bale. He also had to be at the bar to start his shift by seven. He bent to pick up the weathered tool bag, giving Molly a scratch on the ear while he was down there. He straightened, nodding as respectfully as he could manage. "I'd better get working on that mower. Welcome to Falls Legend, Whitney. I hope you enjoy your little visit."

"Oh, this is more than a *little* visit." Still beaming, Helen slid her arm around Whitney's waist. "Whitney took a sabbatical from her job to spend a month or two with us. I know the poor girl works with numbers every day, but I'm hoping I can entice her to take a look at *our* books while she's here."

A chill slid down Luke's spine. He didn't know this woman, and he sure as hell didn't need anyone poking around in their business. Things were tight enough around here without someone new sticking their nose in. Whitney's eyes went wide with surprise, but it passed. She tucked her shining dark hair behind her ear.

"I'd be happy to help in any way I can, Aunt Helen." She glanced in his direction and the corner of her mouth tipped up, like a cat toying with a mouse. "I'd especially like to dig into the expenditures and see if there's anything that can be trimmed."

So that's how it was going to be. He met her gaze straight on.

"Dig away, Miss Foster. In the meantime, I'll be out here getting actual work done."

There was a determined glint in Whitney's tip-tilted golden brown eyes, and a definite smirk factor to her smile.

"Really? Trying to turn over a new leaf?"

CHAPTER TWO

HELEN RUSSO WAS FLUSTERED. It felt good. It was one step closer to feeling alive again. But the sensation was a lot like walking into a bright room from the darkness, making a person blink and shield their eyes from the light. That's the thing about wallowing around in self-pity for almost two years—she hadn't had to deal with pesky emotions.

Sounds and colors had been muted, problems easily pushed aside for another day. The sensation was a lot like floating. Drifting peacefully where the currents took her. Until finally, she realized she'd been adrift far too long.

She pulled the dessert plates from the kitchen and took them out to the event room behind the tasting room. Tony laughed twenty years ago when she suggested using what was then storage space for events. But they'd always trusted each other's instincts, and he got to work on making it happen. That was her Tony in a nutshell—a hardworking man with a ready laugh who loved and trusted her. Facing life without him was the hardest thing she'd ever done.

She put the plates on the table with a broken sigh. Little did either of them know it would become a nice source of income as well as an area for customers to sit and enjoy a glass of wine. Once Tony finished the

remodel and added a wide deck with a breathtaking
view of the lake below, they'd started booking parties
and meetings. The room held only sixty people, but
in a small town like Rendezvous Falls, that was just
right. People had the college and the golf club for bigger events, but this room was in use several days a week
nearly year-round. Or at least it *had* been, before the
heart attack that stole Tony from her life.

White linen napkins were folded into the shape of
swans, forming an elegant circle in the center of the single table by the wall of windows. Helen smoothed the
lace tablecloth and told herself it was only a book club
meeting. If she thought of it that way, instead of as the
first time the room had been used since Tony's funeral
luncheon, she could keep moving and not break down
into tears for the third time today.

When she'd finally caved to Rick's nagging and
agreed to start hosting the club's meetings at the winery again, she hadn't known her niece would arrive this
same week. She'd had to make a choice—get the event
room ready, or get the house ready for unexpected company. In the end, Helen figured Whitney was family,
so she could deal with a little clutter in the house. But
to have her friends in the Rendezvous Falls Book Club
see the famous event room a mess would not do at all.

Tonight, the crystal sparkled, the wood floor
gleamed, the table was beautiful and several bottles of
Falls Legend's finest wines were open on the sideboard.
Her chin rose. It was important that her friends, even
the fussiest ones, saw her tonight as having everything
under control. Fake it till you make it, right? Even Victoria Pendergast, with all her beloved etiquette rules

and high airs, would find nothing to criticize when she walked in tonight.

"Yoo-hoo! Helen? We're he-ere!"

"Come on back, Vickie. Everything's ready." Or at least, as ready as it was going to be. She wiped her palms on her cotton skirt. Women's voices and laughter echoed in the hallway, accented with a deep male voice joining in. Helen put her hand over her heart and took a deep breath. Tony loved the sound of laughter. He used to repeat an old Italian saying *"Il riso fa buon sangue."* The first time he translated it for her, she'd been appalled. *Laughter makes good blood.* But Tony explained it was the Italian equivalent of "laughter is the best medicine." It had been a long time since there'd been laughter in this place. Tony would have said it was long overdue. Her heart warmed at the idea of Tony giving her one of his "I told you so" winks.

There were lots of oohs and ahhs and look-at-that-views as everyone came into the room. Vickie, in Chanel and pearls as usual, gave her a quick, light embrace, with air kisses over each shoulder for dramatic effect. "You look lovely, Helen!"

"Beyond lovely. Radiant." Huge hoop earrings jingling alongside her smile, Lena Fox gave Helen an incense-scented squeeze and went right to the sideboard for a glass of wine. As if it hadn't been ages since Helen had hosted—or attended—a book club meeting. Lena's hair had been worn in long intricate braids then, but now she wore it short and natural, with a dusting of silver in the mix. The trim look highlighted the artist's high cheekbones, just as her gold earrings accented her dark skin.

Cecile Harris, dressed head-to-toe in bright pink,

squealed with excitement and hugged the air out of Helen's lungs before heading to the food. Cecile was definitely Helen's...*bounciest*...friend. Her blond hair bounced. Her step bounced. Even her voice was bouncy.

Rick Thomas, unfiltered as always, waved off a hug and muttered in his whiskey voice that it was "about damn time" Helen got "off her ass and did something." Rick's private wink was his only admission of how happy he was to be there. Helen gave him a nod in return. He was her pushiest friend, but in the most loving way.

He turned to introduce the unfamiliar woman beside him—a new face to Helen. Her dark hair was swept back into an elegant twist. Her clothes were expensive, but understated. "This is my neighbor, Dr. Jayla Maloof. She moved here a few months ago, and I've finally convinced her to get out of the house and meet some people."

Helen greeted Jayla with a handshake, and liked her right away for the eye roll she gave Rick. The man loved to take credit anytime he managed to browbeat someone into doing something. To be fair, it *was* his incessant nagging that had pushed Helen to host this meeting. Rick was one of the few friends who refused to take the hint and leave Helen alone after Tony died. He never gave up on her, even when she'd given up on herself.

Jayla's voice was rich and warm, her words formal. It wasn't exactly an accent, but she had a very precise way of speaking. "Your winery is beautiful, Helen. Thank you for having us here."

"I called Iris and offered her a ride," Rick said, "but she was too tired to make it. That's two meetings in a row she's missed. That woman is way too old to be run-ning that bed-and-breakfast alone."

"Ha!" Vickie laughed. "Don't ever let *her* hear you use the *o*-word. And I thought she had that young woman next door helping her now? The one with the kids?"

Rick shrugged. "That's what I'd heard, but I'm guess-ing Iris isn't about to give up too much control."

Iris Taggart was the club's founding member. She was a bawdy, opinionated bulldozer of a woman, and Helen was sorry to hear she wasn't coming tonight.

"Oh, my god, Helen—these shrimp toast things are incredible!" Cecile had filled her plate with snacks from the side table. "And you made your pignoli cookies, too! There goes the diet!"

Ignoring the fact that Cecile, as short and curvy as Helen was, constantly bemoaned her "diet," Helen nod-ded. "I knew those were your favorite. The wine is open, everyone. Tonight we're trying our three-year-old cabernet blend and last year's chardonnay. The chard is one of the first products of the new stainless steel tanks. The cab blend…" She stopped, facing the wave of grief head on. That's how it happened these days. One minute she was fine, the next she had tears burn-ing behind her eyes. The cab blend was from Tony's final harvest. He'd have been so proud of it. She took a deep breath and smiled brightly. "We've named it our Legacy blend. We're entering both wines in the Bless-ing of the Grapes Festival this year."

After a bustle of conversation while the wine was poured, they all settled at the table with their paper-backs and tablets.

"The book was…interesting," Vickie started cautiously. Considering she'd selected the Edith Wharton novel for the group to read, it was far from glowing praise.

"Interesting?" Lena, the club's second-most-senior member at seventy-three, tossed her Kindle onto the table. *"House of Mirth* my ass. I trudged through the first chapter, jumped to the last chapter and wasn't even surprised. Total crap."

"Now, Lena, we agreed to read the entire book each month." Cecile shook her head in censure, sending her blond curls bouncing. "But I'll admit I was disappointed. I thought it was going to be a romance, but it was all just so...sad."

Rick snorted. "This must be what inspired that Sparks guy to write those tearjerkers. None of the characters had any redeeming qualities, and if they developed any, they died. Honestly, Vick, what were you thinking with this book?"

"I figured we should read some classics, and this was a classic written by a *woman* who won a *Pulitzer,* but..." Vickie shrugged, then smoothed her hands over her ice-blue silk blouse. "Yeah, it was pretty hard to read. Sorry."

Helen sat back in her chair in relief. "I thought it was just me. This story was so melodramatic. When did you decide to go for the classics?"

"We didn't," Rick replied. "Victoria was mad because I picked a political book last month, so she decided to torture us with this Gilded Era nonsense." Rick knew full well it irked Vickie when he used her full name, especially with his emphasis on the middle syllable. Vic-*TOR*-ia.

"Enough, Rick." Helen's voice held enough warning

that Rick's mouth snapped shut. Helen and Rick went way back. Jayla, who'd been quietly observing the group dynamics, seemed to enjoy seeing her steamroller of a neighbor get shut down with two words and a sharp look. "I think we agree the book was depressing. The main character missed far too many opportunities to be happy because she was looking for a rich husband instead of a loving one."

Cecile nodded. "And the perfect man, the man who loved her through everything, was right there the whole time. Such a tragedy."

Lena made a huff of disgust. "If he loved her so much, he should have said something before she offed herself."

"I thought you said you didn't read the book?" Cecile asked pointedly.

"Bah!" Lena waved her ring-clad fingers. "Who'd want to admit reading this sappy nonsense?"

Helen bit back a laugh. She'd missed this banter. She'd missed her friends.

Cecile turned toward Rick. "Well, it should have been right up Rick's alley, with all his cynicism about love."

He rolled his eyes. "Yeah, yeah, Cecile, we know you believe in cupids and rainbows and unicorns. But here in the real world, life ain't like that." The two were quite a contrast—Rick's tall, lanky frame, all angles and sharp edges, against Cecile's fluffy hair, fluffy figure and fluffy outlook on life.

Cecile wasn't deterred. "It is for me. Charlie and I are a living, breathing romance novel. After forty years of marriage, we still know how to keep things…fresh." Her cheeks colored, and Helen wondered what all the blushing was about. It wasn't the first time she'd wondered what Charlie and Cecile were up to behind closed doors. Cecile turned to Lena. "You and Jerome were madly in love, too, weren't you?"

Lena scoffed. "Yeah, fat load of good it did us. He dropped dead and left me to raise two little girls on my own." She chuckled humorlessly. "I'm a living, breathing three-hanky movie. Fall in love, then right away someone dies."

Helen stared into her wine glass, only half listening. She and Tony had over three decades together, and he was still gone much too soon. She flinched when Rick put his hand on her arm.

"I doubt talking about dead husbands is what Helen needs tonight, ladies." Everyone's face fell.

"Oh, damn. Sorry, Helen."

"Yeah, sorry, honey."

"We all miss Tony, Helen."

She nodded, not trusting her voice enough to speak. People used to joke that the winery should have been named Happily Ever After because she and Tony had such a fairy-tale life. Every couple had their problems, of course. She and Tony could really do battle back in their day. But now, in hindsight...

"Is that your niece's car outside with the Illinois plates?" Vickie changed the subject, earning herself a good number of friend points. Helen gladly grabbed for the new topic.

"Yes! Whitney arrived yesterday. She's taking a sabbatical or something from her job in Chicago. She called me out of the blue last week and asked if she could come for an extended visit, and of course I said yes." Helen wasn't sure what was behind Whitney's decision to come here for the first time in years, but she was pretty sure it wasn't a social call. Especially when Whitney said she wanted to stay for "a month or two." She hadn't visited for more than a few days at a time since growing up. Something had happened in Chicago. And it wasn't something good.

"She should have joined us!" Cecile said, refilling her wine glass.

Lena laughed. "Yeah, like some twenty-something is going to want to sit around with a bunch of old folks talking about a depressing book."

"She's actually in her thirties now," Helen said. "And I *did* invite her. But she wanted to get started on a little project I gave her. I asked her to help organize our bookkeeping so it's easier for me to manage. She's a CPA for some fancy international firm. The girl is pure ambition."

Helen tried not to think of the look of horror on Whitney's face when she'd first seen Tony's desk that afternoon, piled high with receipts and statements. Boxes filled with more papers were scattered around the room. Around the whole house, really. Helen had let things get away from her after Tony died. None of it had been important at the time, but at least she'd been smart enough not to throw anything away. All Whitney had to do was sort through and organize things. So they'd have some idea if they were making any money, or if they'd ever make enough to pay off the debts Tony and Luke had incurred when they'd remodeled the fermenting barn. Judging from Whitney's reaction earlier, it might take a little more work than Helen thought.

"Well, if she's going to be here that long, she needs to get out and meet people, even if it's a bunch of old farts like us. Right, Jayla? Aren't you glad I brought you to book club?" Rick nudged his neighbor. Helen felt a stab of sympathy for the quiet, composed woman, thrown into this noisy bunch of friends who all had history with each other.

"She needs to meet people her *own* age," Cecile said. "Maybe we can introduce her to a few guys in town."

Rick frowned. "Why do you automatically assume she's interested in guys?"

Cecile considered that for a moment, resting her hand on the book in front of her. "I didn't mean it like that, but you're right—we should find out if she likes men or women. Then we'll see if we can give her more luck than the poor girl had in this dreadful book."

Helen shook her head. "I don't think Whitney needs any help getting dates. And yes, the last I knew, she dates men, just like you, Rick. She's tall and beautiful, with thick, dark hair like Tony's. If Whitney wants a guy, trust me, she'll get one. Besides, she's not staying."

"But wouldn't you like her to?" Cecile asked. "If she found a good local man, she might stay and keep you company…"

Ah. That's what this was about. They wanted Whitney to stay to take care of Helen. Sweet, but not happening. She leveled a stern look at Cecile. "She's got a job in Chicago. She's not going to give that up to come babysit me. And I wouldn't want her to. If Whitney wants a social life in Rendezvous Falls, she'll figure out how to find one."

"But how?" Cecile ruffled the pages of her book absently. "The college bars are dead this time of year. And the Purple Shamrock is hit or miss these days. Where else is she going to meet a nice man if we don't help? Sometimes it only takes a little nudge."

"What about Luke Rutledge?" Lena asked. "He works here. He's single. I was talking to him the other day…"

Vickie leaned forward and dropped her voice, as if Luke might be standing outside the door listening. "The last thing she needs is to get tangled up with a Rutledge. No offense, Helen."

Cecile nodded sagely. "You're probably right. That family…"

"Oh, for heaven's sake!" Lena slapped the table with her hand. "That boy is as honest as the day is long. He came down and fixed my steps so I won't break my neck this winter, and now he's working on my patio."

"It doesn't matter." Helen knew all about the rumors that swirled around the Rutledge family. But Luke had been like a son to her and Tony, and she wasn't going to tolerate gossip about him. "Whitney and Luke didn't exactly hit it off when they met yesterday." She smiled, remembering the sight of them both tugging on the strap of Tony's old tool bag. "I'm not sure yet if they'll be *friends*, much less anything more. Besides, they're polar opposites. Whitney's city-girl ambitious, all about climbing the corporate ladder. Luke just wants to make a good bottle of wine and be left alone." Helen couldn't remember the last time she'd seen him with a woman.

"Well," Cecile said, "I still think we could come up with some names and maybe set up a few dates for the poor girl while she's here. All we've done lately is argue about the books we've picked. Setting Whitney up on a couple of dates would give us something *fun* to do!"

Rick scoffed. "We're a book club, not a dating service. Leave the girl alone." He finished his glass of water—he was designated driver for the evening—and stood. "Come on, matchmakers, it's time to head home. And speaking of arguments, who picks the next book?"

Cecile's hand shot into the air. "I do! But I'm stuck between a suspense and a romantic comedy. I'll email everyone with my decision."

Lena groaned. "I could use a break from reading about men and women chasing each other around like teenagers."

Cecile leaned over and gave Lena a quick hug. "Men and women chasing each other is what makes the world go round." She glanced at Rick. "Or men chasing men, or whatever. But I'll take your vote under consideration. I promise no one will die in this romance." She glanced at Helen. "Oh, damn it…sorry."

WHITNEY COULDN'T FIND her coffee cup. She'd come into the office with one that morning, but damned if she could find it now. That's how high the stacks of paper were in Uncle Tony's small office.

Her uncle hadn't been compulsively neat, but she remembered him as being at least somewhat organized. This mess? This was all on Helen. Or maybe Luke What's-His-Name who looked more like a wilderness guide than a bookkeeper. Whitney sighed. He was a jerk, with the half-grown beard and the brown dog, and she was pretty sure he was taking advantage of Helen. But she doubted he was managing the money directly. Still, why hadn't he jumped in to help?

Helen's gray tabby cat, Boots, wandered among the piles of paper and mail stacked on the floor. The desk was just the beginning of this disaster. There were bills and bank statements and catalogs and God-knows-what piled *everywhere*. Boots sat and licked the white front paws that gave him his name, as if he was washing his hands of the mess.

"Yeah, I know how you feel, Bootsy."

She moved an armful of unopened mail from the chair to the floor and sagged into the seat, which put her at the right height to spot her coffee cup on the desk. She grabbed for it. If Helen couldn't handle the bills, why hadn't she hired someone? She glanced at the unopened envelopes she'd shoved to the floor and took a long sip of coffee. This level of disorganization made her twitchy. Was the winery in trouble? They were open only one day a week. Income had to be way down. Things were in disrepair. And if Helen hadn't been paying the bills...

Her throat tightened. If she was looking to place blame, she didn't have to look far. If she'd been here after Tony's death. If she'd come when Helen asked her to at Christmastime. But no, she'd been too focused on her own career to ever imagine this was happening. She could have fixed it...if she'd been here.

"Oh, here you are!" Helen appeared in the doorway, a bright smile on her face. "I wasn't sure where you went after breakfast. I see Boots is keeping you company." The cat leaped over a pile of paper to get to his mistress and rub against her leg. "How's it going in here?"

Eight years of working at KTM Accounting, dealing not only with clueless clients but, more recently, clueless senior partners, had given Whitney the ability to keep a straight face at Helen's question. But just barely. *How's it going?* Was Helen looking at the same room Whitney was?

"Well, Aunt Helen, at this point I'm trying to come up with a plan of attack. It's a bit…overwhelming." Yeah, that was the word for everything right now. Her employer had tossed her aside, while her aunt—her *rock*—had been quietly falling apart.

Helen's smile trembled for a moment. "I know it looks bad, but I'll help you…"

"No!" Whitney caught herself. As appalled as she was at the idea of Helen creating any more havoc with the paperwork, the last thing she wanted to do was hurt her feelings. "I mean… I don't think it would be productive for both of us to try to sort through…this…" She gestured to the buried desk. "I need to find a spot where I'll have room to spread out, so I can start prioritizing things."

"If we put the extra leaves in the dining table, that thing's about a mile long. Would that work?" Her aunt was so desperate to help. Whitney didn't have the heart to remind her the dining table was covered with newspapers, magazines and junk mail. She'd made that discovery last night while Helen was with her book club. There was hardly a surface in this house that *didn't* have a pile of something on it. But, unless Helen had turned into a true hoarder who was emotionally incapable of parting with things, the clutter on the dining table didn't appear to be business related, so it should be fairly easy to discard. It would give Helen a way to be a part of the process.

"Yes, I think it will. Let's try to clear it today, and then we'll put the leaves in."

"Oh, I can't today. The tasting room opens in an hour and I still have to get the food ready." For years, Helen had served snacks and sweets to people who stopped by for wine tasting on Saturdays. Hors d'oeuvres, cheese trays, desserts. Some of it was bagged up for sale, and some was set out on fancy platters for customers to enjoy. Sadly, Whitney hadn't inherited her aunt's cooking skills.

It would be far more productive if Whitney sorted through the dining room clutter on her own anyway. "No problem, Helen. I'll get a start on it by myself."

"Well, be sure to take a break to come to the tasting room and try some wine later. Our Legacy blend is going to be a huge seller."

"Um…speaking of sales, where do you keep your sales records? Are they on this computer?" The computer that could barely be seen behind all the papers.

Helen waved her hand. "I don't have the patience to punch numbers into some computer program. Luke has some reports on the computer out in the store, though. He takes care of the reports to the state and the ATF for alcohol sales, inventory and all that. I'm sure he'd print them out for you."

Whitney's fingers tightened on her coffee mug. Luke would *definitely* be printing them out for her. On second thought, Luke would be giving her access so she could print the reports herself.

"Is Luke the only person who has access to your sales reports?" He could be falsifying records in a dozen different ways. "He's handling the money *and* controlling the books? Aunt Helen…"

Helen held her hand up. "Stop right there. Don't finish that thought. This place wouldn't have survived without Luke. He hardly gets a paycheck most months, other than free rent on the apartment, and he works nonstop. I know people talk about the Rutledge family, but…"

"Hold on. Free rent on *what* apartment?"

"In the carriage house, above the tasting room." Helen reached up and smoothed the collar of her shirt, her fingers fussing with it longer than necessary. "Luke and Tony converted it to a living space four or five years ago when Luke needed a place to stay. With him doing so much work here, it made sense." She swallowed hard, glancing away for a quick moment. "It wasn't always free, if that's what you're wondering. Luke paid rent until after Tony… Well, he paid rent until things got… difficult…financially. I won't accept rent from a man I can't afford to pay."

Whitney pressed her lips together tightly. She had so many questions. So many doubts about this Luke guy. But this wasn't the time to scold her aunt for giving a shady character a free place to live. They would definitely be discussing it at some point, though, and Whitney would make sure Luke started paying his rent or moved. Preferably the latter.

"What do you mean, 'people talk'? What are they talking about?"

"Oh, never mind that." Helen checked her watch. "I have to finish those cookies. Come on out to the tasting room later, and—" her eyes went around the cluttered office "—don't work too hard."

Whitney held in her laughter at that last comment. Good thing she loved a challenge.

CHAPTER THREE

LUKE WATCHED HELEN rearrange the empty wine glasses on the tasting counter for the third time. It was a bright, sunny Saturday in July. It was perfect boating or picnic weather, which meant it wasn't a great day for wine tasting. The limo and bus tours were still running throughout the Finger Lakes, but Falls Legend wasn't a regular stop anymore. That would change this fall, but at this point, they weren't ready to handle busloads of people.

It broke his heart to see Helen look up at every sound to see if they had a customer. He was relieved she was working her way out of the fog of her depression, but that meant she was fully aware of how slow business was these days.

"It's the weather, Helen. Beautiful days like today are not our friend. People are off doing other stuff."

She looked out at the brilliant sunshine and nodded reluctantly. "I suppose you're right." Helen nibbled absently at a cookie, then smiled. "But when business picks up this fall, we'll have some award-winning wines to share, won't we?"

"Damn right we will. A gold medal winner last winter, two silvers and a bronze." He held up a bottle of their award-winning pinot noir as if to toast Helen. "We still have the festival competition coming up in September, so hopefully we'll have even more to brag about."

"You and Tony had a vision, Luke, and you made it happen. It was quite an investment, but…"

"It will be worth it, Helen. I promise." His chest tightened as she turned away to dust the sales counter again. He shouldn't keep making promises, but he couldn't stand to see her worry. Helen was more of a mother than his own had ever been, and he wasn't about to let her down.

She and Tony had practically raised him from the time he was a teen. They helped him feed his siblings when his father's drinking took up the grocery budget. He had to figure out a way to hold on until September, when they'd be back on the official wine trail and buyers would be back on their doorstep. The first vintage they'd bottled from the new stainless steel tanks was sensational, and there was more coming. Falls Legend Winery was poised to make a comeback.

But comebacks weren't cheap, and the winery was running on fumes. Or at least, it appeared that way. Helen's recordkeeping was so disorganized that he wasn't sure *what* their situation was. His own paychecks had been few and far between. But that didn't mean there wasn't any money. Helen had refused all his offers of help with the books, telling him everything was fine. Everything was definitely *not* fine, but he hadn't wanted to upset her, so hadn't pushed. Maybe he should have.

He hadn't seen Helen's niece since their tug-of-war on Thursday, but Helen said Whitney was setting up shop in the dining room to "fix things." Helen had been going on and on about Saint Whitney ever since she'd arrived. Would have been nice if Little Miss Perfect had shown up to help before now. He vaguely remembered seeing her around when he was a teen, a little girl play-

ing on the porch. Helen said she'd visited a few times
as an adult, but never for more than a day or two, and
it had been years. Would have been nice if she'd bothered to show up for Tony's funeral. Helen had explained
that she was off working in Europe then, but she could
have grabbed a flight if she'd really cared. He slid a re-
volving display of gift bags across the floor to make
the cash register more accessible.

What was Whitney's angle? She'd arrived at the winery like some avenging angel, hostile and practically
accusing him outright of stealing from Helen. He wasn't
new to accusations. That's what happened when your
father lived in prison. But how would *she* know that?

Why had she suddenly decided to show up *now*?
Helen said the visit was a surprise. That Whitney was
on some sort of sabbatical from her fancy Chicago job.
That didn't make sense, though. Sabbaticals were usually for studying, weren't they? How the hell would
he know—it had taken him almost five years to finish his associate degree. Luke stepped back and studied the display.

But he had the street smarts, and strong cynicism,
of a Rutledge. If Whitney was so indispensable to her
bosses, why would they let her take so much time off
to help an aunt she hadn't seen in years? Did she think
there was something she could take advantage of here
at the winery? Some untapped inheritance from Tony
she could get her paws on? He almost laughed out loud.
Good luck with that one.

"Well, look at this! Our first customer is my favorite
customer!" Helen's enthusiastic greeting had Luke turning toward the door. But *his* enthusiasm popped like a
soap bubble. Whitney Foster stood there looking around

the shop. She was dressed pretty fancy for a Saturday in Rendezvous Falls. The ruby red silky top fluttered over her trim black capris. At least her shoes were more practical than on Thursday—simple leather flats. She smiled at her aunt, and Luke blinked. The woman knew how to work a smile, that's for sure. And Helen was falling for it, almost preening under her niece's warm gaze. Whitney quickly shifted into investigator mode.

"It's two o'clock in the afternoon, Aunt Helen. Am I really the first customer?" She turned to Luke, her voice taking on a decidedly sharper edge. "Maybe you should be out fixing something instead of standing around doing nothing."

Something inside Luke snapped.

"Lucky for me, I don't work for you, lady." He caught Helen's quick frown, and dialed it back. "I mean, I don't work for you, Whitney. Just because you saw me carrying a tool bag the other day…"

"My *uncle's* tool bag," she corrected him. As if he didn't know. As if Tony hadn't taught him how to use and care for every hand tool in there.

"Correct. Seeing me carry your *uncle's* tool bag does not mean I'm just the handyman."

She raised her chin and fixed him with a hard glare. "It's pretty clear this place doesn't have a handyman at all."

Helen's laugh sounded forced. "Okay, back to your own corners, you two! I know you had a little squabble the other day, but there will be no sparring this afternoon." She looked between him and Whitney, a little furrow appearing between her brows. Her voice dropped, as if talking to herself. "You're both so important to me…"

A touch of color bloomed on Whitney's cheeks, and she brushed her hair over her shoulder.

"We weren't sparring, Helen. And we didn't have a squabble, either. That was just good-natured fun, like today. Right, Luke? I was teasing him about his minimal handyman abilities." He appreciated her trying to make Helen feel better, but not at his expense. Whitney glanced his way, and her smile had a hint of steel to it. "But then, we all have things we're not very good at, don't we?"

The woman somehow managed to push buttons he didn't even know he had. He usually shrugged off people's preconceived opinions of him, but she made him want to fight back. "The thing is, I haven't found *your* weakness yet, Whitney. I'm at a disadvantage in all this 'fun' we're having. Can you help me out, Helen? Is there anything your niece *isn't* good at?"

Helen wasn't buying their routine for a minute. Her eyes lit up with amusement. "Well, I love her to death, but it's no secret that she's not very outdoorsy. When she used to visit, she'd spend more time in the house than out around the vineyards. That's probably why your paths never crossed. I think it had something to do with a little old snake…"

Whitney's face paled, highlighting the bright spots of pink still on her cheeks. "Aunt Helen, you're supposed to be on my side! And by the way, there was nothing *little* about that snake. I hardly think being spatially aware of dangerous animals is a shortfall. It seems very prudent to me."

Luke winked at Helen. "Since only a tiny percentage of snakes around here are venomous, they're not really dangerous animals."

"And what do you consider a 'tiny percentage'? When it comes to venomous snakes, what risk ratio is acceptable to you?" A small shudder went through her body, and she waved her hand in dismissal. "Never mind. We're done talking about that. I'm sure you have somewhere else to be, Luke."

She wasn't going to get rid of him that easily. He folded his arms on his chest and rocked back on his heels.

"You think the winemaker should be somewhere other than the wine-tasting room? Where would you suggest I...?"

He knew it was a mistake as soon as the words left his mouth, and she pounced.

"Are you asking me to suggest where you should go? Hmm, let's see..." She cupped her chin with her hand, tapping her finger on the side of her face. She was sassy, and he liked that a lot more than he should.

Helen giggled. Luke couldn't remember the last time he'd heard her laugh as much as she had in the past few days. "My god, it's like having a pair of toddlers in the room. Whitney, I know you're a hot shot at a fancy company in the big city and you're used to being the boss, but this is a family business. We work as a team, don't we, Luke?"

Something happened when Helen mentioned Whitney being a "hot shot." She visibly recoiled at the words, and a shadow flickered across her face.

Helen didn't seem to notice. "And teams work *together*. Why don't you two stop 'teasing' each other—" Helen made air quotes with her fingers "—and make peace with a handshake?"

Whitney opened her mouth to argue, then snapped

it shut and flashed that smile of hers at Helen. She extended her hand toward Luke and he took it. An unexpected hum of…something…buzzed under his skin at the first touch. Her fingers wrapped around his and she did a quick, professional handshake, as if she was eager to get it over with.

But Luke, now enjoying her discomfort, held on longer. Just to see what would happen. She gave a little tug, but he didn't release her. There was a determined, confident gleam in her eyes. *You're not going to rattle me that easily*, her expression said.

He gave her hand a quick squeeze. Not enough to hurt, but enough to send a message of his own. *Bring it on, I can take you.*

Luke wasn't sure how long their silent wrestling match lasted before Helen broke the moment.

"Well, that was good for a start, I guess. Luke, why don't you take Whitney on a tour… Luke?"

He blinked away and reluctantly released Whitney's hand, conceding the stalemate. For now.

"A tour? Um, yeah…"

Whitney waved off the offer. "Don't bother. I know where everything is. I used to crawl around on the wine barrel racks during the summers, remember?"

Helen winked at Luke. "Oh, I think you'll find things have changed, honey. Let Luke show you around so you have a better understanding of the business before you start working on the ledgers. Then come back here and have a glass of wine with me so I can at least say I poured one sample today."

WHITNEY FOLLOWED LUKE OUTDOORS, unable to come up with a plausible reason to refuse. She hurried to catch up with Luke's long strides as he marched toward the wine barn. At least he didn't look like a vagrant today, wearing relatively unwrinkled chinos and a dark green Falls Legend Winery polo shirt. His dog appeared out of nowhere, and was happily jogging at his side, ignoring Whitney completely. She wondered if Luke had taught the dog that trick. Whitney had to scamper again to keep up with him. He didn't want to be doing this any more than she did.

"Look, I didn't want to upset my aunt by arguing, but a tour isn't…"

He got to the barn and turned to face her, his hand gripping the handle of the door. "Helen wants you to have a tour, so you'll get a tour." His lips pressed flat. "Helen wants us to get along, so we'll get along. At least when she's around."

"What does *that* mean?"

He looked at her as if she was asking if the moon was made of cheese. "It means when Helen is around, you and I will play nice. When Helen's *not* around, there's no need to pretend to be friends."

"What—we're enemies?"

He gave a harsh laugh. "That would require me to give a damn about what you're doing here, and I don't. You keep yourself busy in the house, and I'll take care of the wine making. Our paths won't cross much, and when they do, we'll smile for Helen's sake and keep on moving."

Without waiting for a response, he yanked the sliding barn door open. This was not the fermentation barn she remembered. Instead of a cool, dark place with wooden racks of oak barrels stacked to the rafters, the barn was now bright, shining and open. The polished cement floors gleamed, but nowhere near as much as the huge stainless steel tanks which had replaced the barrels. Pipes and hoses and electronic panels gave the barn a futuristic feel, so different from the pungent atmosphere created by the old oak barrels.

"What is all this? Where's the wine?"

Luke nodded at the nearest steel tank. "The wine's in there." She stepped inside, and he followed, standing close enough behind her to make her restless. Not nervous. Just…restless. If he was trying to intimidate her, he was in for a surprise.

"But wine's made in barrels…"

"Not *all* wine. We're still doing some of the reds in oak. They're along the back."

Uncle Tony used to go on and on about the sanctity of his precious French oak barrels for making premium wines. He'd told her how the barrels were carefully assembled, then toasted over an open flame. The amount of toasting impacted the taste of the wine. How on earth could you get that unique oaky flavor from a cold stainless steel tank hooked up to hoses and computers?

"Uncle Tony *wanted* this?" She stepped away from Luke and the uncomfortable energy he exuded. The mountains of bills on Tony's desk came to mind. "How much did this all cost?"

He avoided her eyes, sliding his hands into his pockets. "Well, it was a big investment. Tony was reluctant at first, but…"

Yeah, she imagined Tony *would* be reluctant. Had her uncle hooked up with some kind of con man in Luke?

"But *you* talked him into it, right? That 'big investment' didn't come out of *your* pocket, did it?" The whole thing felt wrong. She couldn't connect how the purchase of the metal tanks would benefit Luke exactly, but she couldn't shake the conviction that it had. Maybe he got a kickback from the seller? One thing was sure—it wasn't like her uncle to make a drastic change that could put the winery at financial risk.

Luke gestured around the barn. "My livelihood depends on the success of this winery. If we fail, I don't have a job."

"Or a roof over your head, right? Helen told me you've been living here for free."

"Jesus, why do you have to *twist* everything?" Luke jammed his fingers through his hair and spun away from her. "Not only did I help *build* that damn apartment with my own two hands, I pay my rent every freakin' month."

"That's not what Helen said."

His head snapped up, and he slowly turned to face her again, his mouth open.

"Helen *told* you I don't pay rent?" He studied the floor. "When she tried to refuse my payment last year, I deposited the money directly in the account. Every month. I had to take a second job to do it, but no way would I not pay her." His voice fell. "Did she really say I don't pay? She's never tried to return any of the payments, so why…"

Whitney hesitated, thinking of all that unopened mail in the house. "She may not have seen the deposits."

"How could she not…" Luke's eyes went wide. "Are you saying she's not looking at the bank statements?"

She didn't know this guy. She definitely didn't trust him. If Luke Rutledge *was* taking advantage of Helen, she didn't want to give him any more ammunition.

"I did not say that. And the state of her finances is none of your business."

"That's not exactly true." He opened the door to the office, which hadn't changed much since the last time Whitney had been here. There were small stacks of papers all over the desk, but they appeared to at least be in some semblance of order.

"Are these statements all for the winery?" Could it be this simple? Could the bookkeeping mess be solved right here?

"No, these are my records on the wine making—dates, mixtures, the results for different tanks. Tony used to do a lot of the business work out here, but after he passed, Helen insisted I bring all the mail to her in the house so she could…um…keep track of it." He glanced at her. "You're going to have quite a challenge if you're trying to put it all together."

That was the understatement of the century. And she should get back to it. It had taken her almost four hours to clear the dining room table, and she still hadn't touched the magazines and junk mail stacked on the chairs and sideboard. They headed down toward the carriage house. There was a small red convertible parked there. Whitney hoped it was a customer.

She glanced up at the dormered upper floor of the carriage-house-turned-wine-shop, with its tiny round turret and multipaned windows. Luke Rutledge *lived* there. He followed her gaze and arched a brow.

"You want a tour of that, too?"

Whitney shook her head. "Not today." She'd had enough contact with the man without stepping into his living space. She passed a pile of lumber clearly intended for repairs to the buildings. Her curiosity got the best of her. "What *happened* to this place?"

Luke looked around. His voice softened, and a little bit of his guard softened, too. "Look, I don't know how often you and your aunt spoke after Tony died, but she...she sort of clocked out for a while." He looked up at the main house with its empty porch. "A long while."

Whitney's stomach soured. "What do you mean 'clocked out'?"

"She slept all the time, didn't care what happened. Couldn't make a decision. Wouldn't accept any help." Luke sighed, sounding as if he was trying to convince himself of his own words. "I did the best I could to keep things going. And she's been getting better these past few months. She went to see a doctor and got some medication." A smile played on his lips. "It's like watching someone wake up out of a coma or something—the old Helen is coming back a little at a time."

Whitney pushed back at the guilt that rose up inside her. She should have called more often. She should have paid more attention when she did call. But should-haves were unproductive.

Luke stopped her with a light touch to her arm before they reached the door to the tasting room. He pulled his fingers back, muttering what sounded like an apology under his breath. His eyes met hers.

"I was inside the house last month when Helen had a problem with the washing machine. The door to Tony's office was open. It looked pretty bad. How much trouble are we in?"

Before she could decide how to respond, the door to the tasting room opened and an older couple came out, clutching two bags that obviously held wine bottles. They were smiling, and waved back into the shop.

"Thanks, Helen! Tony would have been proud of this chardonnay! Great to see you!"

The two nodded at Luke and Whitney, got into their sports car and drove off. At least they'd made one sale today. How could they possibly survive on that kind of income? What was their overhead? Were there financial liabilities or loans she wasn't aware of? Did a P&L report exist anywhere? What was the expected ROI on those steel wine tanks? Did the asset value outweigh the expense? Had they even paid their taxes this year? Her heart ached at the thought of how bad things might be for Aunt Helen.

The answers were somewhere in the massive pile of paperwork in the house. Whitney was going to have to play detective to figure it out. This might be her most challenging audit yet.

"It's a bit…disorganized. I've seen worse." No, she hadn't. "Believe me, I won't have any problem getting things sorted out so I can see exactly what's been going on here." That was probably a lie, too.

His expression hardened at her implication, but it couldn't be helped. She had a job to do. She'd originally intended this summer to be a much-needed escape from the implosion of her career. It was an audit gone bad that led to her downfall. She came here to *escape* that. To spend time with her aunt and revisit some comforting childhood memories. A mindless break to help her recharge before she picked up the tattered remains of her professional reputation and started job hunting.

Luke turned to walk away. "If you're trying to scare

me, you're not. Tell Helen I'll be back to close up. I don't feel like pretending you and I are friends right now."

He stalked back toward the barn, his brown-and-white dog close by his heels. Things were turning out to be a lot more complicated here in Rendezvous Falls than she'd anticipated.

CHAPTER FOUR

THE ROAR OF the mower blades whirling was one of the sweetest sounds Luke had heard in a while. He'd hated the way the place looked last weekend, but there was nothing he could do about it. He was spending his own money on the mower parts, and he couldn't afford to rush the shipment. The parts had finally come in, and went on this morning with barely a hitch. He rolled the mower off the makeshift repair ramp and shut it off.

He wiped his brow, grimacing at the thick oil on his hands. Great—he was probably wearing it on his face now. He'd lain in the dirt for hours getting the mower fixed and the labyrinth of a belt reattached. Dark clouds scuttled over the hills. There might be time to grab a much-needed gallon of water and a quick bite of lunch before he started mowing. With any luck, he'd have it done before the rain arrived.

Molly leaped to her feet and trotted along at his side. The red Australian shepherd was his constant shadow. He'd never had a dog—his folks couldn't afford to feed the four *kids* they had, much less a pet. And after he came to Falls Legend with Tony and Helen, getting a dog never crossed his mind. He was busy. He lived in a tiny converted carriage house hayloft. And Tony and Helen always had cats.

But when he'd walked into Matt Harrison's basement

three years ago to look at Matt's home wine-making set-up, he'd discovered twelve bouncing balls of fluff. Actually, Aussie puppies were more like cubes than balls—as wide as they were long as they were tall, on stubby little legs, often with no tails. Molly was the first one he picked up, her auburn fur trimmed with tan and white on her face and feet. He set her down to check out the others. Every time he looked down, there was Molly, sitting quietly at his feet and staring up at him as if to say, "Why are you wasting your time with these other dogs?"

Sure enough, he'd driven home that night with a brown fluff cube under his coat. Molly bumped his leg just then, as if she knew he was thinking about her. The dog was eerily psychic like that, and he'd accused her of being an omniscient alien life form more than once. She gave a short growl, the sort she gave as a heads-up that someone was coming and she hadn't decided if they were friend or foe. Aussies were territorial as hell. The winery was her turf, and she had to approve all activities.

A battered green pickup came up the driveway and continued past the house, up the hill and into the vineyard. Steve Jenkins waved as he drove by, but didn't slow. They could no longer afford a full-time vineyard manager, so they used Steve on a part-time basis. He was responsible for the vines at three different wineries around Seneca Lake. The man was a grape savant, and they were lucky to have him.

Luke followed the truck up the hill on foot, trotting between two rows of vines to catch up. Steve, stocky and heavily bearded, slid out of the truck.

"Damn, boy, if I'd known you wanted to come up I'd have stopped for you."

"We both know that's a lie."

Steve laughed. "Yeah, probably. What's up?"

"That's what I was going to ask," Luke responded. "How do things look? Should I start trimming off some of the leaves yet to let the sun get to the berries?"

Steve squinted at the darkening sky. "We definitely want to do some canopy removal, but I'd hold off. We're supposed to have a hot spell after this week. You don't want to sunburn the grapes." He looked down the head-high walls of green. "We might want to start trimming those overaggressive young shoots, though."

Luke nodded. Grape vines sometimes wanted to grow more vine than grapes. The summer months were a constant battle to maintain balance.

Steve took out his ever-present pruning shears and clipped a few young shoots. "You guys skipped the Glens Falls festival, huh?"

"Yeah." Luke had hoped they could get to the popular summer event, but he was only one man and there was too much to do. "We'll be at the Rendezvous Falls festival in September."

"Glad to hear it. How *are* things at the winery?" Steve asked. "Business picking up any?"

Luke shrugged. "Not much. We gotta get the tours back and expand our hours before we see more sales, and we're not ready. We need to get into some restaurants and liquor stores again, too." He frowned down the hill at the dark green house with its conical tower. "All I need to do is figure out how to be five places at once."

Steve grunted. "I feel that way sometimes, too. One thing at a time, kid. You can only do one thing at a time." Steve studied Luke for a minute and grinned. "Although you could take time to shower in between."

"Sorry, man. I finally got that old mower working today. I was heading in to clean up and eat when you came through." Luke glanced up at the clouds. "But I think lunch'll have to wait. If I don't get the grass cleaned up around the front of the place we won't have any customers at all."

Steve reached into the truck and tossed Luke a power bar. "Here. Linda makes me keep them on hand in case my blood sugar gets low."

Luke studied the brightly wrapped meal-in-a-bar. "Thanks."

"No problem. I've got plenty. I'm going to check out the pinot gris grapes farther up the hill." Distant thunder rumbled overhead. "It's supposed to rain heavy the next couple days. Good thing you and Tony invested in that underground drainage system." The two of them had spent months laying the black flexible piping under the vines ten years ago, but it was worth it. Water was much less likely to run down the surface of the soil now, washing away valuable nutrients and exposing fragile roots.

"Whoa. Who's that?"

Luke followed Steve's gaze. Whitney was walking up the far edge of the vineyard, toward the path to the falls. It was a twenty-minute hike from here, with rain moving in. He'd bet money that girl was gonna get wet. He still hadn't answered Steve's question.

"Helen's niece. She's visiting from Chicago for a while."

Steve gave Luke a wink. "She's a looker."

Whitney moved up the hill with long, smooth strides,

wearing dark shorts and some sort of fluttery pink top. Even from here, he could see her legs were shapely and strong. He'd assumed a city girl like Whitney would be soft, but he may have misjudged her, at least as far as fitness went.

"She's not bad," Luke replied. Steve chuckled and turned back to his truck.

"Not bad, huh? You're either lying or you need your eyes checked."

"She's from the city." Luke said it as if it was explanation enough, but Steve just laughed again and drove on up the hill. Luke watched Whitney until she disappeared into the trees, following the path leading to the top of the waterfall that gave the town its name. He could follow her, and warn her there was weather moving in.

But she wasn't his problem, and he had work to do. He turned away and headed back to the mower, hoping to get as much grass cut as possible before the rain hit.

WHITNEY STOPPED ALONG the wooded path to inhale the rich scent of summer and lush growth. She'd spent much of her time this week inside the dusty, cluttered farmhouse with Helen and the nosy cat who insisted on knocking over every pile of paper she'd organized. This morning she'd pushed it all aside and walked out with a quick wave to her aunt in the kitchen. That bright yellow kitchen was one of the few rooms downstairs that *wasn't* cluttered with junk. It was spacious and bright, with lots of natural light from several windows.

Helen had called out something about the weather, but Whitney didn't even slow down. She had to escape. Yes, it was overcast, but that just meant she didn't need sunglasses. Before she realized it, she was headed up the hill toward the waterfall.

She hadn't walked to the falls in years. The last time had been shortly after she graduated college and came to visit for a long weekend. She and Uncle Tony had followed the trail to the top of Rendezvous Falls—the actual falls, not the town—and they'd sat up there and talked about her plans to take the accounting world by storm. Tony had been supportive, but cautionary.

"Careful, Whitney-girl. There's more to life than numbers. You're *good* at numbers, but don't forget to be good at other things, too."

At the time, it had been sweet advice from a beloved old man. Of course, back then she'd known *so* much better than Tony what she'd needed. But now? She continued walking. Now she wondered if Uncle Tony hadn't been on to something. All those years she'd spent chasing numbers and playing the corporate game at KTM, and what did it get her? A fancy title and nice bonuses, sure. But all of that had vanished when she got thrown under a career-killing bus.

The sound of the waterfall through the trees made her smile. How many times had Tony told her the legend through the years? The great Iroquois Confederacy of Native American tribes had existed peacefully for generations in upstate New York, with vast orchards and storehouses of furs. But the tribes were torn apart during the American Revolution, when some sided with the British, and some with the Colonists. The legend told of two star-crossed lovers from now-warring tribes, who met at the falls to declare their undying love for each other. An Iroquois goddess saw their tears and turned them into a stag and doe so they could run away and be together forever. Tony told her their song could still be heard in the water that tumbled over the granite cliff.

A few more minutes of walking and she was there, at the top of the falls. A steep trail went down alongside the water to the small pool where the water gathered before going down the hill toward the lake. In the pool of water was a large boulder, smoothed by centuries of rushing water. Legend had it that any couple who stood on that rock and declared their love would be together forever. Hopefully without turning into deer.

There was a smooth wide path approaching the falls from the opposite side. That was the walking path from the small public parking area below. The falls were preserved as a county park these days, but Whitney figured there wouldn't be many visitors on a Thursday in July, and she was right. She sat on a rock—not *the* rock—and tried to let the sound of the tumbling water wash her mind clean.

There were no stacks of years-old paperwork here in the secluded hollow. No piles of unopened bills and bank statements. No dusty clutter that invaded Whitney's dreams at night, in between nightmares of what her future might look like if she didn't get back out there and find a job.

She was tired. Instead of spending time reconnecting with Helen and soaking up some of her homespun wisdom and comfort, Rendezvous Falls was turning into a steaming pile of accounting dung she was going to have to dig her way out of.

Great decision to come back here, Whitney.

She leaned back, propping herself on her elbows, and did her best to refocus on the sound of the water.

Come on, mind—cleanse yourself, damn it!

Probably not the most Zen approach to relaxing. KTM had offered stress management classes a few years ago, and Whitney tried to remember what the instructor had said. She'd only attended to look like a team player and support the corporate program, as a good little future partner should. At the time, the idea of reducing stress seemed ludicrous. Stress was what made a person an intense competitor. Stress kept a person sharp. Focused. On point. Relaxation was for losers and retirees, not for people like Whitney.

She wasn't going places anymore, though, was she? The instructor had talked about taking art classes, or picking up a new hobby unrelated to numbers and accounting. Whitney suspected playing sudoku, as she used to do on the train, would not have been an approved hobby in the instructor's eyes. Maybe she could learn more about wine making.

No. That would require more time with Luke Rutledge, which would do nothing to reduce her stress levels. They hadn't spoken since Saturday, but she'd seen him working around the winery through the dining room bay window. Walking with that easy, laid-back stride that made him look both confident and entirely unconcerned if anyone thought he looked confident or not. His dark hair always looked as though someone had just run their fingers through it in an elevator on the way to a penthouse somewhere.

Wait. *What?* That was a disturbingly specific image, and it had no business in Whitney's head. Sure, Luke was good-looking, but not in a penthouse suite sort of way. More like a walk-on-the-wild-side sort of way, which was a path Whitney carefully avoided. The few relationships she'd managed to squeeze into her busy schedule had been safe. And boring. Who had time for drama and…passion? That stuff never lasted. It certainly never had for her mother, and Whitney *never* wanted to live like that.

Besides, she still suspected Luke was taking advantage of Aunt Helen, even if she hadn't figured out how yet. Despite his denial, Helen said she'd given him free rent. It didn't add up. She didn't like it when things didn't add up.

A bird sang nearby, and Whitney opened her eyes. She was surprised to realize she *had* relaxed a little, even with all that thinking about drama and passion and…Luke. Her neck and shoulders moved more easily as she rolled her head, and her chest was no longer constricted. She took a deep breath. Rendezvous Falls had worked its magic. Above the falls, though, the overcast sky was growing darker. She should get back to the house before she got caught in a downpour, which would *not* be relaxing at all.

Whitney stood and brushed dirt from her backside with a grimace. Helen's house was so damn hot to work in during this week's heat wave, and this outfit was about as close to warm-weather-casual as Whitney got. She'd bought the pink silk top in the cruise-wear section of an upscale Chicago boutique last year, but never took time off for a cruise.

Her aunt explained she was conserving energy by not turning the air-conditioning on, insisting the "valley breeze" kept the house cool enough. Whitney had a feeling Helen was more worried that she couldn't afford it. So Whitney put on her pretty cruise wear and dealt with it. Maybe it was time to go shopping for something more practical.

She heard a rumble of thunder as she climbed the path back to the summit of the falls. She picked up her pace when she got to the trail heading back to the vineyard. Getting caught in a rain shower was one thing. Being caught on this hill dodging lightning bolts was entirely another.

A few more rumbles and she'd started jogging, thankful it had been only a few weeks since her last visit to a gym. But running on a treadmill was not the same as jogging a rutted path in canvas flats. She caught her toe on a tree root and landed hard on her knees and hands, air whooshing out of her lungs. She scrambled back up and checked for damage. A little broken skin on one palm and one knee. Nothing to worry about.

The wind now whipping through the treetops? The steady, nonstop roar of approaching thunder? The swishy sound of what was definitely approaching rain moving through the trees? *That* was enough to make her worry. Maybe she should have listened to whatever it was Helen was trying to tell her before she'd bolted out of the house.

The vineyard was just ahead. Which begged a new question. Should she hug the tree line during the storm, or take her chances in the open vineyard? Trees were bad, but so was being the tallest thing standing in a clearing. The rain caught up to her at the exact same time she saw something moving quickly up the hill. The silver pickup truck turned and stopped right at the end of the path. Whitney started to slow, but the rain was hitting her as if shot out of a firehose, so she wasn't going to question the gift of a dry vehicle to jump into.

Until she realized Luke Rutledge was sitting behind the wheel.

CHAPTER FIVE

LUKE SMILED WHEN Whitney stopped abruptly, standing in the heavy rain and staring at his truck as if it were some kind of trap. He reached over with a sigh and opened the passenger door.

"Come on, get in!"

Whatever she'd been wearing before the rain started was soaking wet and basically plastered to her now, so it was no surprise when his body reacted. Strongly. He reminded himself who this was. Whitney Foster. A stuck-up city snob who clearly held him in contempt. And even if she didn't, she was Helen's niece, which meant hands-off. His voice was more gruff than he intended when he shouted above the pounding of the rain on the truck's roof.

"If you'd rather walk, just say so."

She blinked against the rain hitting her face, started to move, then hesitated again. Lightning streaked across the sky and thunder shook the air. Whitney landed in the truck cab as if launched by a catapult.

"Smart move." He did his best to hide his grin. "Close the door, genius."

She slammed the door shut and glared at him. "What are you doing here?"

The rain was so heavy he could barely make out the main house. He shook his head and gave her some side-eye. "I'm pretty sure I'm saving your ass. You're welcome."

Her dark brows knitted together and her voice lost a little of its perpetual challenge. "I meant…how did you know? And…" Her mouth twisted as if the words were pickle juice. "Thank you."

Luke put the truck into Drive and started down the hill. "A farmer always watches the sky. I hadn't seen you come back before the rain started, so I figured you might need a ride."

The edge of the vineyard wasn't designed to be a highway, and the ground was rough and rutted. The truck bounced and dipped, forcing Whitney to grab the door with one hand and the dash with her other.

"I'd have thought the idea of me getting caught in a rainstorm would make your day."

He gave her a quick glance. Just because she was off-limits didn't mean he was blind.

"Trust me, it did." Luke slowed the truck and reached behind the seat to grab his zippered hoodie hanging there. Whitney looked down and her cheeks flamed when she realized how her clothes were clinging to her. She snatched the hoodie from his hand before he could give it to her, and thrust her arms into it without offering any thanks. Even the zipper sounded pissed off when she yanked it closed.

"Perfect. Another guy with more testosterone than manners. Nice to know it's not just a Chicago thing. Assholes are everywhere."

Luke frowned. He'd been having fun at her expense, figuring she'd give it right back to him as she had before. But her words hinted at a story that didn't reflect well on men in general. She'd been hurt. He shouldn't care. But that quick dimming of fight in her eyes made him feel ashamed. *That* was a new experience.

A flash of lightning made her flinch. But the thunder didn't follow as quickly as the last time. The storm was moving off. He drove from the vineyard into the parking lot and over to the main house. The sound of the rain on the roof was less angry. But Whitney wasn't. She was clutching his sweatshirt around herself, her knuckles white. From anger? Embarrassment? Both? Luke shook his head.

"Look, I thought I was doing the right thing, driving up there." He rubbed the back of his neck and grimaced, remembering how sweaty and filthy he still was. "It's not my fault you walked out of the woods soaking wet. I mean, I try not to be an asshole, but I'm still a man. And I *did* offer my hoodie."

Whitney's chin pointed up toward the second floor of the main house. Her neck was long and graceful. There was a vein pulsing at the base of it. She blinked a few times, and for a horrifying moment, he thought there might be tears shimmering there in her eyes. *Damn it.* The last thing he needed was to have Helen's niece *crying* in his truck. He opened his mouth to say something—anything—but she beat him to it.

"I'll concede I wasn't prepared for rain." Her mouth barely moved, her words forced through clenched teeth. "But a gentleman would have looked away or…something."

His low laughter was enough to crack that brittle shell of hers. She turned to face him, eyes wide.

"See, Whitney, that's where you made your biggest mistake." He shrugged. "It wasn't going out for a day hike with a storm coming." He talked over her attempted objection. "Your *biggest* mistake was thinking I'm any kind of gentleman."

The corner of her mouth tipped up into an almost smile. "But you said you weren't an asshole."

"There's a hell of a lot of real estate between asshole and gentleman, babe."

Her half smile faltered, then returned. That familiar spark appeared in her eyes. The crack in her veneer had been repaired, and the sharp edge returned to her voice. Any other guy might have been annoyed, but Luke was oddly relieved to see Whitney back in fighting form.

"The fact that you just referred to me as 'babe' tells me you're a lot closer to asshole than you think."

He lifted his shoulder. "I never told you which end of the spectrum I fell on."

The rain had slowed to a steady drizzle. She reached for the door handle, looking over her shoulder with a smirk.

"Actually, I'm pretty sure you just did."

She hurried up the steps to the covered porch. He waited, but she didn't look back before going into the house. Her energy still filled the cab of the truck, and so did her scent. Spicy, woodsy, rain soaked. Finally coming to his senses, he threw the truck into Reverse and headed back toward the carriage house. He needed a long shower. A long *cold* one.

"I'm telling you, Helen, my neighbor's grandson would be perfect for your niece." Vickie took a sip of her tea, carefully pursing her lips so she left minimum lipstick marks on the fancy teacup. Her short champagne blond hair was carefully styled to look casual, as if she'd rolled out of bed looking like that instead of spending an hour in front of the mirror. "Mark is quiet and bookish and he's an *accountant*, like Whitney. He's not terribly tall, but he's cute and polite and just generally adorable."

The two women were sitting on the porch of the Taggart Inn, waiting on the founding member of the book club, Iris Taggart, to join them. Iris was a spry eighty years of age, and she was still treated as their grand matron, even if she didn't get to as many meetings as she used to.

Every afternoon, tea and snacks were served at the inn, following the English tradition Iris grew up with as the daughter of an expat member of Britain's peerage. Coffee and real lemonade were provided for those who didn't embrace Iris's love of all things British, but indulging in those outlier beverages would always earn a sideways glance of disdain from the white-haired hostess.

"I don't know," Helen said. "She hasn't said what happened in Chicago, but I have the feeling Whitney isn't interested in dating."

Whitney had been at Falls Legend for a week now, and last night she said she'd probably need six to eight more *weeks* to sort out the finances of the winery. Helen's response had been a mixture of relief and embarrassment. She knew she'd let things slide after Tony's death, but it wasn't until Whitney started dragging boxes of papers from Tony's office to the dining room that Helen understood the mess she'd made. Dealing with that guilt had kept her from talking to her niece much. Usually, all they *did* was talk when together. Tony used to call them his "cackling hens." Whitney was the closest thing to a daughter Helen would ever have, and Whitney called her a second mom.

Vickie sat back and sighed with her typical sense of drama. "Regardless, the poor girl can't stare at spreadsheets all day long. It's unhealthy."

"But she loves numbers. She loves her job."

"What job is that, exactly?" Vickie lifted one shoulder, half innocent shrug and half artful insinuation. "What kind of job allows employees to take an entire summer off? She's an accountant, not an elementary school teacher. And you said she's a *partner*, so…"

"What exactly are you saying?" Helen liked Vickie, but her theatrics could be tiresome, especially when she was beating around the bush like this.

Vickie took another sip of tea. "Look, I serve on a lot of boards with a lot of executives, including several up in Rochester, and I've never heard one of those professionals say they're taking a couple months off, unless they're between jobs."

Helen frowned. "Are you saying Whitney is lying?"

Vickie's shoulder made that strange, circular motion again.

"No-o. I'm saying it sounds…unusual." Another precise sip of tea. "And if she's under some kind of job stress on top of working at your place, then the girl needs a night out on the town. Even if the town is Rendezvous Falls. And Mark would be a lovely match for her." Vickie looked up and smiled brightly. "Iris, darling! We're over here!"

The smiling older woman stopped at a table where guests were sitting. She was in full-on hostess mode, asking them how they were enjoying the summer afternoon on the porch and laughing lightly in response to something that was said, before turning to Vickie and Helen.

"Hello, ladies." Iris's sharp blue eyes settled on Helen, her voice loud enough for everyone to hear. "How nice to see you getting out and about again, Helen." Iris settled into her chair, tucking her snow-white bob behind her ear and smoothing the ruffled pink apron across her lap. She leaned forward and dropped her voice. "It's about damn time, don't you think?"

No offense was meant or taken. Iris was right—it *was* about time Helen started living again. While many friends had tiptoed around her, it was Iris who'd insisted Helen visit Dr. Lupine and get some medical help to kick her depression to the curb. Besides, taking offense would be a waste of time with Iris. The octogenarian simply didn't care.

She played the part of sweet-little-old-grandmother-fresh-from-baking-bread to charm her guests. In reality, Iris Taggart was a shrewd businesswoman. She bought the inn fifty years ago when it was a run-down old mansion with peeling red paint and a dangerously sagging porch. Her divorce—a fairly scandalous thing back then—left her with some money, and she poured it all into the big house, along with her sweat equity. Iris had done much of the work herself, putting her young son to work right alongside her. Never a follower, Iris defied the colorful tradition of Rendezvous Falls and painted the exterior bright white. She surely knew being the only white house in town made the place stand out.

As her business improved, she'd strong-armed her neighbors into fixing up their homes, too. She took over the Rendezvous Falls Business Owners Association like McArthur storming the beaches. Much of the town's current success was due to the formidable personality of the "sweet little grandma" sitting across from Helen.

Helen lifted her tea in a mock toast. "Thanks for the warm welcome, Iris."

Iris barked out a laugh, then glanced at the guests two tables away and quickly reverted to more grand-motherly light, musical laughter. She reached over to pat Helen's hand. "You know I'm happy to see you, girl. You look good." Iris glanced at Vickie, who was dressed in her Sunday best on a Friday afternoon. "And you look overdressed, as always."

Vickie waved her hand in dismissal. "My mother taught me there's no such thing as overdressed."

Iris snorted. "You've told that story so often you've started to believe it yourself. That was your first—or was it second?—wealthy mother-*in-law* who taught you that. Your *mother* was a waitress at the old Gem Diner up on Route 14, remember?"

Vickie's cheeks went pink for a moment, then she reached up to scratch her nose. With her middle finger extended. Everyone knew what they were getting into when they stepped into Iris's no-bullshit zone, and Vickie and Iris had been friends-slash-rivals for decades. Helen's heart warmed as the two women sniped playfully at each other. She'd missed this.

The coneflowers below the porch were blooming, tall and pink. The stalks swayed in the warm breeze. What the inn lacked in paint color, Iris made up for with her vibrant flower beds. Helen pictured her own garden and cringed. It had once been her pride and joy. Now it was overgrown and chaotic, screaming for attention. Maybe she'd get out there this weekend with some trimming shears...

"Helen? Did you hear me?" Vickie tapped Helen's

arm, causing her to startle. "Which book are we supposed to be reading this month?"

"Oh…uh…the mystery. Cecile sent an email. I can't
remember the title, but I've already put it on my Kindle."

Vickie nodded. "That's right. I was telling Iris we're
trying to set your niece up on a few dates while she's here."

Helen squirmed. She doubted Whitney would be in-
terested. She always said she had no time for dating.
But if she didn't start *making* time, she'd end up alone.
Iris tsked.

"It's too bad I can't get that grandson of mine back
here. Logan needs to put down some roots." Iris looked
up at the lacy gingerbread trim around the porch.
"Someone else is going to need to run this place sooner
or later."

Vickie winked at Helen over the top of her teacup.
"Come on, Iris. You're a tough old broad. You'll be running this inn for another twenty years."

"Until I'm a hundred?" Iris scoffed. "I don't mind
living that long, but I sure as hell don't want to be *working* until then. But I've got a few good years left in me."
She turned to Helen. "I've met Mark Hudson. Your
niece could do worse."

Helen ate the last of her cookie. "I just don't think
she's interested in being set up on a blind date."

Iris tipped her head for a minute, then gave a devil-
ish grin. "So don't tell her. Figure out a way to get them
both in the same place, then let nature take its course."

Vickie leaned forward. "Yes! That would be perfect!
I could ask Mark to drive me to the winery to pick up
a bottle of wine—"

Iris nodded. "And Helen can make sure Whitney's
in the tasting room to sell it to him!"

Helen raised her hands in protest. "No! She's doing my accounting records, not working in the tasting room. Besides, Luke would be in there."

"Helen, you own the place," Iris said. "*You* decide where people work. Figure it out." She slapped her hand on the table. "Now we need a camera in there so we can see what happens."

"I am *not* recording Whitney on her date!"

"Ah-*ha*!" Vickie pounced. "But you just agreed she was getting a date!"

Helen stammered a few times, then snapped her mouth shut. Why was she even *considering* this? She was out of practice dealing with her strong-willed friends, especially when two of them ganged up on her. And Whitney *had* been spending too much time indoors with invoices and statements. The poor girl— the one time she'd headed outside for a walk this week, she'd been caught in a storm and came back to the house soaked to the skin. She must have grabbed one of Luke's sweatshirts from the barn on her way back, and she'd held it tight around her as she stomped upstairs to change. She'd been on edge since she'd arrived. Maybe it wouldn't hurt to introduce her to some people here.

"Fine," Helen sighed. "We'll arrange for them to meet each other, but that's *all* we do. If Mark just buys wine and goes, that's it. I'm not locking them in the storeroom or anything. They hit it off or they don't. Period."

Vickie nodded. "Agreed. Good thing Cecile isn't here, though, or she'd be pushing for some kind of romance novel meet-cute in a locked storeroom for sure. I'll call Mark as soon as I get home and see if he's free tomorrow." She looked at Helen. "You're still only open on Saturdays, right?"

"Yes, for now." Luke had a few more repairs to do around the place, and they had to bottle a few new vintages. Then they'd be able to send press releases announcing that Falls Legend Winery was open for business again, starting right after the festival. "Let me know what time, and I'll figure out how to get Luke out of there and Whitney in."

If the two of them weren't at each other's throats all the time, she might try to get Whitney interested in Luke. But no. They had nothing in common other than an instant dislike for each other.

CHAPTER SIX

THE LAST OF the unopened mail from Tony's office had now been opened. There were two blue recycling bins out on the porch overflowing with discarded envelopes. Whitney wiped her brow and stared at the mahogany dining table. Actually, she couldn't *see* the dining table anymore—not the top of it, anyway. Every inch was covered with semiorganized stacks of paper. Bills, sorted by company or utility—paid or unpaid, who knew?—occupied more than half the table. Bank statements and miscellaneous mail that might be official, but she wasn't sure, covered the other half. And there were three stacks of papers from the Department of Agriculture and Markets, referring to permits and licenses and other things Whitney didn't understand. Not yet. But she would.

Helen's records were a *disaster*, but Whitney was determined to make things balance somehow. She had no idea if her aunt was a pauper, a millionaire or somewhere in between. Her chest tightened. She had to determine if the winery could survive or not, and what role Luke Rutledge had in its success or failure. If she was going to give her aunt sound financial advice, she had to know that man's cost-benefit ratio for the business.

She frowned at the magazines and catalogs stacked high on the dining chairs. Helen had promised to sort through them and save whatever might be in there that she wanted, but it hadn't happened yet, leaving few seating options in here. It wasn't all bad that she was spending so much time on her feet. At least it was exercise of some kind. She glanced out the window to the vineyard sloping up behind the carriage house. She hadn't tried *outdoor* exercise since the storm incident. Whitney lifted a heavy stack of catalogs, most from last Christmas, and dropped them on the floor with a thump. She plopped down on the now-vacant chair, her scowl deepening.

Luke let her get into his truck that day looking like a drowned rat. She picked up a bank statement and let it flutter back onto the stack. There'd been so much emotion in his chocolate-colored eyes. It wasn't until she'd finally looked down at herself that she realized why.

That silk top clinging to her...ugh. The way Luke's heated gaze quickly traveled up and down, leaving trails of sizzling skin behind, left her feeling exposed in more ways than one. But then he'd given her something to cover herself up with and launched into that gentleman versus asshole conversation. The whole incident left her feeling confused, awkward and sexy all at the same time.

When she'd set the recycling bins outside the door yesterday, Luke had been walking across the driveway toward the barn with his dog. Even from across the drive, she felt the heat of his eyes. She saw the half smile he always seemed to wear around her. The smile that made it seem he knew some secret about her, and couldn't decide if he found it amusing, annoying or arousing.

Whitney straightened. *Stop it*. The last thing she

wanted to think about was Luke Rutledge being aroused in response to *anyone*, especially her. She wasn't hiding from him. She was just…busy. Inside the house. Where he never was.

She stood and grabbed the bank statements again. Time to stop thinking about her aunt's employee and start thinking about how to sort this mess by date. If she sorted each pile chronologically, she should be able to start working her way backward—or forward from Tony's death, she hadn't decided yet which way would make the most sense—to see where the money was or wasn't.

"Oh, good! You're here!" Helen swept through the doorway, surprising Whitney. Her aunt usually stayed in the tasting room on Saturdays. "I came up to grab some more cookies, but I remembered that I'm…um…supposed to call…Iris…from my book club. Would you be a doll and go watch the shop for me?"

"What? Me?"

Whitney had no idea how to sell wine. Helen's fingers toyed with the collar of her blouse anxiously as she nodded.

"Yes, you!" Her voice was bright. "If you can run a calculator, you can run the cash register."

"Where's Luke?" Wasn't he supposed to be running the place?

Helen stammered, then gave an odd giggle. "Oh, I sent Luke into town to pick up some sugar for me, so I can bake more cookies."

"You're baking more cookies today? It's already afternoon." Whitney looked out the window. There wasn't a single car parked at the carriage house.

"For next week! I'll freeze them." Helen's cheeks

had two high spots of color. "It's slow, and I figured Luke was bored, so I asked him to go. Just to…keep him busy, you know?"

No. Whitney did not know.

"Helen, are you okay?"

"What? Oh, yes. Well…a bit tired, I guess. Please, Whitney, go cover the tasting room for a bit so I can put my feet up and rest, okay?"

But what about that phone call she had to make? Or the cookies to be baked? If she was having a stressful day, Whitney wasn't going to pressure her. Luke said Helen had "clocked out" for months after Tony's death, and Whitney didn't want to make it worse. Besides, it might be nice to get out of the house for a Luke-free change of scenery.

The dark green tasting room smelled of wood and wine. The tasting counter was in the back and the cash register toward the front corner, so customers had to walk through the whole store to do business, passing temptations along the way. Uncle Tony had built the wooden aisle racks himself, sanding out the grooves that held the bottles securely. Along both side walls deeper shelves stretched to the ceiling, loaded with loose bottles on one side and cases of wine on the other.

Whitney probably shouldn't be happy that the place was deserted, but it was nice to be able to walk around on her own and get familiar with things. She wandered down the hall that led to the event room in back, with its large windows, wraparound deck, and spectacular views of Seneca Lake and the long narrow valley. Small tables were set near the windows, and she knew the idea was for customers to come back here to enjoy their wines. If only they could find some customers.

The tinkling of the bell over the front door made Whitney jump. *Damn it.* She had no idea what she was doing, and if that was someone looking to taste wine, she'd have to fetch Aunt Helen from the house. She hurried up the short hallway and into the tasting room. Maybe it was her aunt coming out to relieve her. But no.

An older woman, meticulously dressed and carrying that season's Dooney & Bourke leather bag, walked around one of the islands of wine racks. A man Whitney's age followed quietly. His brows were gathered together and he looked around as if he had no idea what he was doing there. He was attractive, with sandy hair and kind blue eyes. An inch or two shorter than Whitney, but that wasn't all that rare at her height. He smiled when he saw her, and gently touched the older woman's arm.

"Mrs. Pendergast? Here's an employee. Maybe she can help you remember the wine you wanted so badly for tonight."

The woman smiled at Whitney, giving her an odd up-and-down glance as if taking her measure. Whitney was used to that in the corporate world, especially among women—the way they viewed every other woman as a rival for the few executive offices available to them. But why would someone be assessing her like that in the winery? Could the woman tell at a glance that Whitney didn't belong? She silently thanked herself for pulling her hair back into a neat twist and changing into white capris and a tailored blue-and-white top before coming down here.

A slow, satisfied smile formed on the woman's carefully painted matte lips, as if Whitney had passed some unknown test.

"You must be Helen's niece, Whitney, here to visit Rendezvous Falls for a few months…all by yourself. I'm Helen's friend, Vickie Pendergast. Helen says you've been busy with her accounting work…" Vickie made a little gasping sound. "Oh! That's right, you're an *accountant*! And my neighbor here, Mark Hudson, is an accountant, too! What a strange coincidence!"

It wasn't as if accounting was some never-heard-of career like professional lion tamer. There were basically accountants on every corner, nearly as common as attorneys. Mark gave Whitney an I-don't-know-what-she's-talking-about shrug from behind the woman.

"Yeah, Mrs. Pendergast. Very strange." Mark stepped forward and extended his hand. "Nice to meet you, Whitney." It was a friendly, business-like handshake, if a bit hurried. She had the impression there were a hundred other places he'd rather be than here. "My neighbor is determined to find a specific bottle of wine for a dinner party tonight, and enlisted me to drive her."

Now it was Whitney's turn to give the head-to-feet examination of Vickie. The woman was around Helen's age. Her health seemed as sharp as her fashion sense, so why couldn't she drive herself? Her mental faculties seemed pretty sharp, too, as she rushed to answer Whitney's unasked question, making a point to rest her hand on Mark's arm.

"My doctor has me on medication right now that makes it impossible to drive, but I knew a *single* guy like Mark would be available to run me on an errand today."

Mark's face twisted. His neighbor had basically said the man had no life. Judging from the well-defined muscles on his arms and the way his shirt stretched across his chest, Whitney had a feeling this guy didn't make a habit of sitting around with nothing to do. Taking pity on him, she tried to move the conversation along before Vickie embarrassed him any further.

"I'm not very familiar with where things are in here, but if you give me the name of the wine, I'm sure I can find it for you so you can go prepare for your party."

Vickie gave her a blank look. "What party?"

Was the woman experiencing early dementia? Whitney softened her tone.

"Your dinner party? You wanted something specific for a dinner party?"

Color flamed Vickie's cheeks. "Oh! Yes! Of course! My dinner party!" She glanced away, smoothing her hands down the front of her linen skirt. "Yes…that's right…"

The poor lady. "Do you remember the name of the wine? I'll find it for you."

Vickie blinked, then stepped back, seeming affronted. "Of course I remember it, I'm not stupid." She looked between Mark and Whitney. "I mean…you know what? I should go up to the house and ask Helen. She'll know what I'm talking about."

Whitney met Mark's baffled gaze.

"Helen is resting right now—"

"Oh, it's okay. I called her before we left. She's expecting me. Just a quick visit." She headed to the door, but stopped when she realized Mark was following her. "No, dear, you stay here with Whitney. I'll only be a few minutes."

"Mrs. Pendergast…" The words sounded like a plea.

"Oh, call me Vickie, Mark. You're all grown up now. And you two have so much to talk about! You just moved back here, she's visiting, you're both young, single, attractive accountants. You probably have all sorts of other things in common."

Something clicked, but Whitney didn't want to believe it. Helen wouldn't be part of such a foolish plan, would she? Vickie was out the door in a flash. Medication, her ass. That woman was perfectly fine, and up to something. Whitney had a sinking feeling her aunt was involved. Helen, who had suddenly needed an odd midday *rest*.

Mark hadn't caught up with what was going on. They both watched out the window as Vickie hurried across the lot to the house. Sure enough, there was her aunt, standing on the porch smiling at her co-conspirator. *Busted, Aunt Helen.* Mark looked so confused it made her laugh. Glancing outside and back again, he shook his head.

"What the hell just happened?"

"Does your neighbor often ask you to drive her around town?"

He threw up his hands. "*Never!* The woman has a Mercedes convertible she drives like she's on the race-track at Glens Falls. She hasn't said more than two words to me in the month that I've been back with my grandparents. Then she calls me today and gives me this story about doctors and pills and parties and her desperate need for a bottle of wine from this specific winery and I'm the only one who can get her here." He scratched the back of his head. "I don't get it."

"I didn't, either, until that last thing she said."

He looked down at the floor, then shrugged. "I must be missing something…"

"She worked awfully hard to make sure two—" she held up her fingers into quote marks "'—young, single, attractive accountants' were left alone together, don't you think?"

He frowned, mulling her words until the truth dawned and his eyes went wide. He nearly shouted the words.

"She's trying to set us up? Because we're *accountants*?" An incredulous grin spread on his face. "She barely *knows* me!" He slowly scrubbed his hands down his face and groaned loudly. "I'm so sorry. I have no idea what made her do such a thing."

"Oh, I have a pretty good idea." Whitney shook her head. "She and my aunt have clearly been talking, and somehow they decided we both needed companionship. Because everyone knows accountants only date other accountants, right?"

He chuckled. "Yeah, because we live and breathe numbers so we can't wait to talk about them on our dates." He started to laugh harder. "You want to hear the funny part? I'm *not* an accountant. I mean, I have a degree in accounting, but I quit my job. My passion is art. I guess that little fact appalls my grandmother so much she never mentioned it to Mrs. Pendergast." His smile faded.

Whitney had zero interest in dating him—or anyone else—but Mark seemed like a genuinely nice guy. She hooked her arm through his and leaned in to nudge his shoulder.

"I may not know much about the winery business, but I do know there have to be open bottles of the stuff back at the tasting counter. Interested?"

He tipped his head back and closed his eyes. "Thank Christ. Lead the way."

LUKE DIDN'T RECOGNIZE the compact car parked in front of the tasting room, but he wasn't surprised to hear loud laughter when he got out of his truck. People often had a good time driving from winery to winery for samples. But he didn't like the idea of Helen being alone with a group of drunken dipsticks. He hurried inside.

Helen wasn't behind the tasting counter, and he panicked for a moment, thinking she'd taken ill or maybe been a victim of some crime. He eyed the baseball bat Tony had always kept by the cash register and moved in that direction.

"Luke!" The female voice was familiar. "Come on back and tell us about this stuff we're drinking!" He turned, and his jaw went slack.

Whitney Foster was sitting at the counter with some guy. There were six bottles lined up, and an untold number of wine glasses. She was sporting a wide, slightly crooked smile while holding up a bottle, then flipping it upside down. Luke flinched, but only a drop came out. It was empty, and he had a pretty good idea where most of it had gone.

"Lu-u-uke, come taste wine with us." She looked at the other guy, who seemed vaguely familiar. That didn't make Luke like him. "With Mark and I. Mark and me? I can never keep that straight. Us. Come drink with us. This is Mark, by the way. Mark, this is Luke. He thinks he runs the place."

Luke bit back his annoyance at that remark. Mark, short but solidly built, just nodded, smiling at Whitney. Like he *knew* her. And where was Helen? Luke started to ask that very question, but Mark cut him off.

"Yup. I'm Mark. And she's Whitney. And you're obviously Luke." He snapped his fingers. "Wait… Luke Rutledge, right?" Luke braced himself. His last name brought out the worst in people. But Mark extended his hand. "I went to school with your sister, Jessie. Is she still in the area?"

Luke's eyes narrowed in suspicion. Jessie graduated with a visible baby bump under her robe, and never did admit who the father was. Luke shook his head. No way was he telling this guy she'd left Rendezvous Falls and never returned. Luke turned back to Whitney.

"Where's Helen?"

She threw her head back and laughed so loud it echoed in the empty shop. He'd heard a few of her controlled laughs, the ones tinged with contempt for him, but this was the first time he heard a true, uninhibited belly laugh from Whitney. He had a feeling she didn't let go of her control very often. This laugh looked damned good on her. Her eyes were shining. Her cheeks were pink. She winked at him. *Damn.* She was really something when she kicked back like this. She should do it more often. Kick back, that is. Not get drunk.

"My aunt? You mean the co-conspirator?" she asked. Mark laughed at that, and Luke had no idea what was so damn funny. "She's probably up at the house celebrating, or maybe plotting some other little surprise."

The other bottles on the counter still had plenty of wine in them. She hadn't had *that* much to drink. Mostly the chardonnay.

"No more drinking our profits. Clean up this mess. I'm going up to the house."

"What're you going to do, tattle on me? This is all her fault! Her and Vickie. It's part of the master plan."

Mark straightened, his eyes getting more clear and sober by the minute. "We'll clean up, man. Sorry." He took Whitney's arm and helped her off the counter. "This has been more laughs than I've had since I moved back, Whitney, but I need to get Vickie home and get out to my studio. The art festival's next month and I have some pieces I need to finish, including that mural downtown."

Whitney's eyes went wide. "Hey, I could model for you!"

Mark looked Luke's way. "Uh, no. I do landscapes, remember?" He lowered his voice after Whitney shrugged and walked away. "Dude, I didn't know she'd get that tipsy off a little wine. I swear we're just friends."

Luke wondered how they'd become "just friends" in the eight or nine days since Whitney's arrival, especially since Whitney had hardly left the house, but that was none of his business. *She* was none of his business.

So it made no sense that Luke's hands were clenched into fists when he walked away.

CHAPTER SEVEN

HELEN WAS APPROPRIATELY chagrined and apologetic the next morning. Whitney wasn't sure what was worse—that her aunt and her friend had arranged a double-secret blind date for her, or that Luke had seen her acting a little tipsy. She'd always been a lightweight, and alcohol on an empty stomach was *never* a good idea for her. The combination of amusement and disapproval on Luke's face wandered through her dreams all night.

"Seriously, Helen, what were you thinking?" Whitney set her coffee mug down with a thunk on the table, sloshing a little onto her fingers. "You and your friend go through this elaborate scheme to get me to meet someone, and you leave me alone with him for almost two hours. You didn't even *know* Mark. What if he'd been some sleazy stalker?"

Helen finished cleaning the pan she'd cooked scrambled eggs in and turned to face Whitney. "I *said* I was sorry. And Vickie knew Mark—he wasn't some random stranger we plucked off the sidewalk. We came down to check on things after half an hour, and heard you two laughing together inside, so we left you alone to have some fun." Helen put a fresh saucer of milk down for Boots. "You haven't laughed like that since you got here, Whitney. It didn't occur to me it was because you two were drinking in the shop during business hours."

Whitney didn't like having the tables turned on her self-righteous anger. But Helen was right. It had been irresponsible and unprofessional. *Very* un-Whitney behavior. So was arguing with her aunt. Helen sat next to her at the table, putting her hands over Whitney's.

"I don't want to fight with you, Whitney. And I *am* sorry. It's just…" Helen gave her hands a squeeze. "You've locked yourself up with all that paperwork and haven't left the house, and I feel like that's my fault. I thought you might be lonely. Maybe I came at the problem the wrong way with Mark, but I thought maybe you'd talk to someone your own age, because you're sure not talking to me. Why are you really in Rendezvous Falls?"

Whitney blinked away from Helen, swallowing hard and staring out the window over the sink. She and her aunt had always shared *everything*. Helen had helped her make her most major decisions through the years. But discovering her aunt's troubles made her reluctant to share her own.

"I told you why. I took a sabbatical from work and wanted to come see you." She gave Helen a sincere smile. She didn't have to lie about this part of her story. "I've missed you, and I felt bad for being so busy these past few years. I didn't even make it to Uncle Tony's…" Tears suddenly clogged her throat. "I'm sorry. I was focused on making partner, and I lost perspective for a while." And it was all for nothing, since she was no longer a partner, or an employee, for that matter. "I needed a break, and the company…agreed."

A long break. A forever break.

Helen's eyes shone with unshed tears. "Oh, honey, we knew how busy you were building your career. Tony and I would talk about how hard *we* worked those first years here, when we didn't know if we'd ever get the winery off the ground. It took all of our energy and time. And you were in *Europe* when Tony passed—it would have cost you a fortune to fly back."

Her aunt was trying to make her feel better, but each sentence twisted the guilt blade deeper. It wasn't the money that had kept her from catching a flight from London. It was the censure in Harold Carmichael's voice when she'd asked for a few days off in the middle of the audit. The client had already given their blessing, but Harold grumbled about her "priorities." He insinuated she'd be letting the client and the company down by leaving mid audit, even for only a few days. That a *man* trying to make partner would never do such a thing. And she'd caved, canceling her plans and finishing the audit.

As if reading her mind, Helen spoke again. "That's why you haven't come back since then, isn't it? You felt too guilty to face me?"

Whitney walked to the sink, suddenly needing to be busy. She grabbed a dishrag and started wiping down the gold-flecked vinyl countertop. The kitchen was quiet, the only sound the muted tones of the wind chimes out on the porch. She finally took a deep breath and faced her aunt.

"I could have been here. And I *should* have been here. I let my boss talk me out of it. My ex-boss. I'm not on sabbatical, Helen. I quit. It was that or be fired."

Helen sat speechless for a moment. "Because of Tony's funeral?"

"No, not really." That was when she should have known it wasn't the job for her, but she'd been too wrapped up in chasing a partnership to see it. She was determined to be a star at KTM. But she'd failed. "It was…a lot of things. A client did something illegal, and one of our accountants covered it up. I took it to the senior partners, and they laughed it off. When the SEC started investigating, they tried to make it my fault. As the only female partner, they figured I was expendable." She stared out the window, the dishrag cold in her hand. Carmichael had started a whisper campaign that painted her as incompetent, even though she'd tried to warn them. She wiped her nose with the back of her hand, swallowing her tears. She turned to Helen. "All I could think about was coming here, to you."

"Does your mother know?"

Whitney gave a short huff of laughter as she brushed some crumbs off the table and into her hand, turning to step on the old metal trash can to open it and deposit them there. "You're the first person I've told. Mom's too wrapped up in setting up house with Boyfriend Number Two Hundred Sixty-Five to be concerned about me, anyway. Did you hear this one works at the Bellagio? Maybe she'll finally get that big career break she's been chasing…" Her own words spun around and slapped her. "Oh, my god. I've turned into my mother! Chasing career unicorns and ignoring my family! *She* didn't come to Tony's funeral, either, did she?" Her laughter quickly turned to hot tears. "How could I let that happen?"

Helen stood, tugging Whitney into her arms. And, for the first time since losing her job, she wept. She'd always teased that Helen's height made her a perfect headrest, and she put it to use now, laying her head on Helen's and letting the tears flow. Helen's arms were tight around her waist and she made sweet, soothing sounds. She finally looked up at Whitney. "Baby, you are *not* your mother! You're here *now*, aren't you? And your career was no damn unicorn—you studied and worked hard and you got what you wanted. You made partner! And you *chose* to walk away. I guarantee you that's something your mom would never be able to do. Frannie has always been too proud to admit a mistake, when it's our mistakes that make us human."

Whitney hiccupped, wiping tears from her cheeks as she looked down at her aunt. "Don't ever let her hear you calling her Frannie. She hates that."

Helen grabbed a box of tissues from the counter. "The odds of your mother hearing me say anything are pretty slim, especially now that her big brother, Tony, is gone. She and I were never all that close."

Helen was as different from her sister-in-law as she could be. A hardworking wife and partner who always saw the best in people and situations, where Francesca Russo's compulsive desire was for fame above all else. As if having her name in spotlights would make her life meaningful, even if it meant leaving her young daughter to take on grown-up duties at home. Whitney's father died in a car crash soon after she was born. It had always been her and Mom and whatever man Mom was dating. And she was *always* dating someone. Thankfully, Mom had never objected to Whitney's summer visits to the winery and her aunt and uncle's happy, normal home.

Helen directed Whitney back to the table to sit. They started emptying the tissue box one by one. "Besides, Tony always called your mom Frannie. I think that was his way of trying to keep Francesca's feet on terra firma. Not that it ever worked."

"Nope. Walking on lowly planet Earth with all the other pedestrians will never be enough for Mom. Oh, Helen, what a mess I've made."

Now it was Helen's turn to bark out a sharp laugh. "You and me both! You came here to catch a break, and I threw you right into *my* mess."

They'd had enough soul baring for one morning, and Whitney's emotions were still right at the surface, begging for release. She needed to stuff them back where they belonged. Where they could be controlled. She gave her aunt a bright smile.

"The good news is I have all the time in the world to work on that project, Helen."

Helen tipped her head to the side. "You'll have to make some career decisions eventually, but yes, you should stay the summer and be part of the great revival of Falls Legend Winery. I could really use your help, and Luke probably could, too."

And just like that, Whitney's little bubble of maybe-things-aren't-so-bad burst. She'd like to help Luke Rutledge right off the property, but she needed to understand his role in the winery, and in its possible demise, before she made a move.

"I don't think Luke wants any help from me, Helen." Especially after seeing her act like a spoiled drunk coed yesterday. During business hours. If any actual customers had arrived…she sobered at the thought. She may not like the man, or trust him, but she owed him an apology.

Helen tsked. "I don't know what it is between you two, but you need to figure out how to get along. If we're not back on our feet by the Blessing of the Grapes Festival in September, we won't have another good chance until next year." Helen glanced toward the cluttered dining room. "Next year might be too late. It'll take all three of us to turn this place around." She patted Whitney's arm. "Besides, I don't want you spending every day inside this house. That's how I got in this trouble. I turned into a hermit. You need to make friends here."

"Helen, I'm not staying permanently."

"Friends don't have to be permanent. But you need people to have fun with."

Whitney remembered sitting in the human resources office at KTM a few years ago, listening to the HR manager lecture her on making friends. Apparently, Whitney had a reputation as a "loner" and that wasn't good for partners. She was advised it would be good for her career to build a network within the company. Maybe if Whitney had found some friends outside of work, they wouldn't have all dropped her like a hot rock when she left KTM. She had to admit, she'd isolated herself since coming here.

"No more surprise blind dates." Her voice was firmer than she intended. "No more secret setups. I don't mind having coffee with someone, but *I* get to choose who I hang out with."

Helen blinked a few times, then nodded. "Agreed. And who knows, you might meet someone you really like. It wouldn't hurt to have a little summer fling as long as you're here."

"A summer fling? Aunt Helen!" Whitney got up with a laugh. "This isn't *Grease*. I'm not looking for a summer boyfriend."

But maybe a little "fling" *was* what she needed. Lord knows, it had been a while. Nah, that was a really bad idea. Tempting, but bad. Or, at least…ill-advised. Poorly timed. Meeting over coffee was enough. No flinging with anyone. Helen made a suspiciously noncommittal sound as she got up from the table.

"What you're *looking for* and what you *need* could be two very different things."

LUKE SLID THE stainless steel paddle through the bung-hole on top of the barrel and moved it around to stir up the sediment from the bottom, bringing more flavor into last year's pinot noir. He put the plug, or bung, back into the hole and moved on to the next barrel. Before stirring, he extracted a bit of wine with a wine thief, which was basically a large suction dropper, and put the wine in a glass to taste it. Wine was always trying to become vinegar, and sometimes a barrel would just go bad, no matter how careful they were. He could usually tell from the smell, but it took a taste to know if the pH balance was off.

He was savoring a sip—damn this was a good batch of pinot—when Molly levitated out of a sound sleep at his feet and bolted toward the door, barking fiercely. He hadn't even heard the door open, but Whitney stood there, eyes locked on his snarling dog.

"Molly!" His voice snapped and echoed in the barn. "No! She's okay." Molly stopped barking, but gave Whitney one last woof before turning to trot back to his side. Her stub of a tail was wagging, making her whole butt wiggle. Aussies were like that—snapping, snarling terrors one minute, goofy family dogs the next. Once someone was approved to enter their territory, an Aussie's job was done.

Whitney's brow arched slightly, gesturing to Molly. The edge was back in her voice today.

"Does a dog like that belong on a winery that's open to the public?"

"The winery isn't open to the public today. Unlike *yesterday*, when you and your new pal were getting shit-faced during business hours." He figured she'd snap back at him with a sharp retort. That had pretty much become their thing. Instead, her face paled and she looked away, her shoulders falling in defeat. That bothered him more than it should have.

"Um…yeah. That was bad." She ran her tongue along her upper lip, causing something in his chest to jump. "That's why I'm here. Can I come in?" Technically, she was already in, but her eyes were on Molly.

"Once I tell her you're okay, you're okay. If you scratch her belly, you'll be okay every time you come up here." Molly sat by his side, looking from him to the brunette cautiously approaching. The dog's mouth was open in a happy, tongue-lolling grin, and Luke worried for a moment that he might be wearing the same expression.

Whitney was in tight dark jeans and a cropped yellow top that made her eyes look more golden than usual. A narrow band of skin peeked out from beneath the top, pulling his eyes to her narrow waist. She pushed all his buttons, alright. Including some that hadn't been pushed in a long time. Buttons he didn't have the time or energy to acknowledge. Buttons that made him think about moonlit nights and tangled sheets.

Holy shit…knock that off, Rutledge!

He shuddered, earning a worried look from his dog.

Whitney looked at the dog, sounding skeptical. "A belly rub, huh?"

He swallowed hard. "Yup. That's all it takes to win Molly's heart."

"I'm not used to being around dogs."

Hmm. A rare admission of vulnerability from Miss Foster. She didn't look afraid, just…uncertain. He should enjoy the rare moment when she wasn't bossing him around, but there was something unsettling about it. She looked off her game today. Her eyes were puffy, as if she'd been crying. Again—none of his business. He nodded at the dog.

"Hold your hand down to her. Open, not fisted. Once she sniffs and sees I'm not concerned about you, she'll probably hit her back for you."

Whitney carefully did as he suggested, and sure enough, Molly lay down and rolled over, legs in the air, and waited. He nodded at Whitney.

"Go ahead. Scratch her belly. Make a forever friend."

Whitney kneeled on one knee and touched Molly lightly, her voice low and soft. "Helen thinks I need more friends."

Had he heard that right? Before he could ask, Molly let out a moan and extended one leg up in the air. Whitney laughed and started rubbing more aggressively. Molly's eyes rolled back and she let out a doggy sigh of pure contentment. Luke tried his best not to feel jealous.

"I think Helen got her wish." He had to spell it out when Whitney looked up, confused. "You just made a friend for life."

Whitney checked Molly's expression and chuckled as she stood up. "I think you're right."

"Why does Helen think you need friends? Don't you have friends back in Chicago?" There he went again, asking about stuff he didn't care about. Whitney didn't seem to take offense to the personal question, though. She tipped her head and considered for a minute before answering, sounding thoughtful.

"I didn't have time for a lot of friends outside of work, and work friends are…well…things change, and work friendships tend to change with them." Her expression was distant, and her voice dropped to nearly a whisper. "Friendships follow power."

Luke was no expert on friendship—it wasn't something that came naturally to him, either. But he knew that wasn't how it was supposed to work.

"People follow power," he said firmly. "Friends don't. Friends stick."

Whitney shook her head. "Maybe I should have made better friends, then." She drew her shoulders back, her voice brisk. "But that's not why I'm here. I came up to apologize for yesterday."

She looked him straight in the eye when she said it, and he felt a grudging respect. He wasn't her favorite person. She'd made it clear right from the start she didn't trust him. She'd also made it clear she wouldn't hesitate to cause trouble for him with Helen. And then, of course, there was the rain incident. This apology had to be tough for her, but she'd given it to him straight up.

"Are you talking about all your wine tasting yesterday?"

Her cheeks flushed, her gaze breaking away from his.

"Yes." She huffed out a deep breath before rushing into an explanation. "I was upset, and I hadn't had anything to eat since breakfast, and that was just a bowl of sugary cereal, and I swigged down that first glass of wine in two gulps and it hit my system like…pow.

The second one went down fast, too, and then I was… feeling no pain. In the middle of the afternoon. With a complete stranger."

Luke frowned. They'd seemed pretty chummy yesterday. "You said you and Mark were friends."

She laughed, rolling her eyes up to the ceiling. But there was no humor in her voice. "Our friendship was not of our own planning."

What the hell did that mean? He turned away to put the plug back in the barrel, telling himself he didn't care.

"You lost me."

She told him how Helen and Vickie had set up an elaborate scheme to get Mark and Whitney together. How, after Mark and she realized what was going on and recovered from their embarrassment, they'd decided to raid the tasting counter. It wasn't like Helen to concoct something like that, but he sure wouldn't put it past Victoria Pendergast.

That woman, much like Whitney, *also* disliked Luke. But her dislike had nothing to do with him personally. She held a general disdain for the entire Rutledge family. It started when Victoria's second husband, the district attorney, sent Luke's father to prison eighteen years ago. Not that the old man didn't deserve it, but Luke didn't have a lot of warm fuzzies for Pendergast. He was doubly annoyed Vickie had taken it upon herself to set Whitney up on some date. And that it had apparently worked out okay. After all, he'd found the two of them laughing up a storm in the shop.

"You gotta admit," he pointed out, "you guys hit it off."

Whitney shrugged. "It wasn't the romantic meet-cute they intended, just two people stuck in the same humiliating situation and commiserating with each other. Mark's a good guy, but…"

"But what?"

She thought for a few seconds, then gave him a smile. Damn, this woman had a great smile when she cut the edge off it. "But good guys never seem to be my type." She laughed. "I guess I inherited my mother's inability to fall for a good one." There was definitely a story or two behind *that* comment, but this wasn't the time to chase after it. Whitney shrugged. "So, anyway, that was a really long-winded way of saying…I'm sorry."

She wasn't the one who should be giving apologies. She'd been set up.

"Have you heard those words from Helen and Vickie?"

Her eyes widened. "From Helen, yes. We talked it out this morning before she went to church."

"Helen went to Mass today?" Luke wondered how Father Joe would deal with that little surprise. Helen hadn't exactly been a regular since Joe's arrival at St. Vincent's last year.

"Yes. Why do you sound surprised? She and Tony always went."

"Yeah. Of course." Molly stretched and yawned at their feet. "Hey, about yesterday…don't be too upset with your aunt. I'm sure Vickie strong-armed her into it. She likes to think she's the great mastermind behind a lot of things. And if you were drinking on an empty stomach, that explains…a lot."

It explained the bright shine she'd had in her eyes, and the pretty giggle on her lips. It probably explained the way she'd sassed him playfully, instead of with her usual sharpness. It did *not* explain how much he'd enjoyed those things, despite his annoyance with her. It also didn't explain the burn of anger he'd felt when he'd heard the way her light laughter mingled with that of another man.

"So… I'm forgiven?"

He couldn't resist yanking her chain one more time.

"I wouldn't go that far…" He relented when her eyes narrowed dangerously. "It's all good. Forget about it, okay?"

She nodded, apparently satisfied, looking around the wine barn. "What are you doing up here? It's Sunday, right?"

"This wine ferments every day, so I'm here every day."

"But what are you *doing*?"

Making her feel better about what happened was one thing. Letting Whitney get involved in his *work* was another. "Why do you care? Don't you have numbers to crunch somewhere?"

"What I *care* about is my family's winery." The familiar snap returned to her voice, and her hands hit her hips. "I'm trying to learn about the business."

He turned his back on her and headed for the large tank in the back corner, stepping over cables and drains, checking gauges and recording the numbers in his notepad. Just as he'd feared when she arrived, she was after something. She was staking her claim as Helen's family. Fine. *He* was staking his claim as the guy in charge. Not her. Whitney hurried behind him, watching every move he made.

"I'm *serious*!" She was a little out of breath from trying to keep up. "Helen is my…"

He spun before she could talk herself into some really dangerous territory.

"I know who Helen Russo is." He gestured in the direction of the main house. "The last I knew, hers was the only name on the deed to this place. Hers is the only name on my paychecks." When he got a paycheck. "And everything I do here is for *her*. So before you start throwing the word *family* around... I've been more family to that woman since Tony died than anyone, especially you. Don't try to set yourself up as some heir apparent. It ain't happening."

He could see it in her eyes—his words had hit home, and he couldn't decide if she was feeling offended or guilty. Maybe a bit of both. She stepped up so close he could see the individual flecks of gold in her eyes. Her finger waggled threateningly under his nose.

"I'm not 'setting myself up' as the heir apparent..." Each word came at him like a bullet. "I *am* the heir apparent. I'm the closest blood relative Helen has." He liked to think it didn't matter, but blood was blood. He was *like* family to Helen, but he wasn't *actual* family. If Whitney wanted to, she could make things uncomfortable for him here.

She moved up against him, her eyes boring into his. Her woodsy, mossy perfume curled around his nostrils. "But I'm not here to steal the winery from her. I'm here to help her *save* it, you idiot. And if this Blessing of the Grapes thing can do that, then you and I will be seeing a lot more of each other. And you're going to teach me the wine business."

She stalked off, and Luke wondered what the hell just happened. She had a way of making down seem up and in seem out. Being around her was like riding the world's scariest amusement park ride.

You and I will be seeing a lot more of each other...

Luke's mouth went dry. She could make things uncomfortable for him in more ways than one.

CHAPTER EIGHT

As DAYS WENT by and temperatures climbed, Whitney needed something other than office clothes and cruise wear. She took a much-needed break from the paper avalanche in the dining room and went shopping.

Helen gave her a list of supplies needed from the box store up in Geneva, then gave Whitney a stern command to go into Rendezvous Falls on the way home to check the shops there. Whitney protested that she wasn't looking to buy vacation souvenirs, but Helen didn't let up until she promised.

It was just as well, since she was starving by the time she got back to town. The back of her SUV was packed with bags containing practical shorts, jeans, T-shirts, work shoes, and various house and yard supplies. She turned off Route 14 at the corner with the big black-and-orange Victorian, and drove into the town center.

Flags fluttered from every old-timey lamppost on Main Street, probably left over from the Americana festival, which had taken place over Independence Day weekend. Whitney remembered going to see the fireworks as a child. Helen said there was a festival of some kind in Rendezvous Falls every month these days. The Americana festival was still their largest, with parades, fireworks and a giant antique show.

She parked in front of a small restaurant named

simply The Spot. The bright colors in town were even wilder than she remembered as a child. Most of the buildings were clapboard, with Victorian gingerbread trim and sharp peaks. Even the brick ones had colorful painted doors and window frames. Pink, green, blue, yellow, red—it was like walking through an explosion of paint samples at a home store. The town's over-the-top homage to all things bright and fanciful made Whitney smile. No wonder the place had become such a popular tourist destination. It was a kaleidoscope marriage of history museum and Disney World, and…it worked.

The Spot had neon orange benches outside the cornflower blue building, with white lace cafe curtains inside the window. Gold leaf outlined the white lettering on the windows. An older couple came out the door, and the delicious smell of something grilling propelled Whitney inside. She sat at the counter that ran down the right side, rather than sit at one of the booths alone.

"Be right with you, hon!" A large woman with salt-and-pepper hair was at the far end of the counter, wiping the surface with a towel and chatting with an older man eating the biggest piece of cherry pie Whitney had ever seen.

"I got it, Mama!" A woman closer to Whitney's age, maybe younger, with a figure that had enough curves to stop traffic, came out of the kitchen and nodded in Whitney's direction. "Coffee? Iced tea? Soda?"

"Iced tea sounds perfect. No sugar."

The woman slapped a glass down in front of Whitney, along with a menu encased in heavy plastic. Her name tag identified her as Evie. There was a bright pink streak in her thick dark hair which was pulled back in a

messy knot under a hairnet. A tattooed flock of small
birds wound its way up her left arm from her wrist
to disappear under the rolled-up sleeve of her shirt.
Another unidentifiable tat peeked out from under her
collar. She pointed to the blackboard above the cash
register. "Those are today's specials, but we're out of
the salmon melt. We can make one with tuna, though,
and honestly, it's just as good. If you're vegan, we have
a soy burger melt with fake cheese, and if you like
your protein on the hoof, we've got beef patty melts
with cheddar and onion. I don't know what's up with
our cook, but everything's melting in this place today.
What can I getcha?"

"A beef melt sounds great."

Evie nodded in approval. "A meat eater like me.
These days it feels like we're the minority, right?" She
turned and tucked the order slip in an old-fashioned
metal carousel in the opening in the wall, spinning it
toward the kitchen and rapping her knuckles on the
metal counter. She turned back to Whitney. "I swear,
eighty percent of the tourists these days don't eat any
real food. It's a pain in the—"

"Evelyn!" The older woman stood nearby, arms
folded, glaring at Evie. "We don't discuss personal
opinions with customers."

"Sorry, Mama." The waitress looked down in cha-
grin, turning so only Whitney saw her wicked wink.
Whitney fought to keep a straight face so "Mama"
wouldn't know she was being disrespected.

Evie's mother, whose name tag read "Evelyn"…
wait… Evie caught the look and grimaced.

"Yup. That's my mom, Evelyn, and I'm her daughter,
also Evelyn. But she's the only one who calls me that."

Her mom frowned. "I call you Evelyn because that's your name, *mija*. And my name, and your *abuela*'s name, and *her* mother's name. You're the first one to ever be embarrassed by it."

"I'm not embarrassed by it. I just prefer my more modern version." Evie folded her own arms to mirror her mother's pose. "And *now* who's sharing personal opinions in front of customers?"

Evelyn harrumphed and stomped away. Whitney should have come into town sooner—she'd been missing all this entertainment!

Evie grabbed Whitney's order from the cook and set the plate in front of her. "Sorry for the family squabble. It's been one of those days, but Mama's right. We shouldn't bother tourists and I talk too much. Enjoy your lunch."

She started to turn away, but Whitney reached out to stop her. She liked the smart-mouthed, quick-witted waitress. And she hadn't enjoyed a good girl talk in ages.

"I'm not a tourist." She rushed on when Evie gave Whitney's expensive linen suit an arched look. "I know, I know—I'm overdressed. I'm working on that. My name's Whitney, and I'm visiting my aunt, Helen Russ—"

"Helen Russo?" Evie rested her arms on the counter and smiled.

Whitney nodded as she picked up her sandwich, which smelled too good to ignore, and took a bite.

"How is Helen?" Evie asked. "We've missed her since Tony died. They used to sit in that booth right there for breakfast a couple times a week."

Whitney glanced over at the booth. Something

caught in her throat, and she blinked a few times. Luke had said Helen "clocked out" after Tony's death. If she was going to help the winery get back on its feet, she should help Helen do the same.

"What else did Helen used to do?"

Evie considered for a minute while Whitney ate.

"When I think of Helen, I always think of Tony and Helen together. Those two were practically joined at the hip, you know? Always holding hands and stuff like that, which is super cute in older couples. I even saw them kissing on the sidewalk—you gotta love senior citizen PDA! Helen used to come in with her gal friends, too. Haven't seen her with them lately, though. They have a book club or something. Iris Taggart at the inn started it, and let's see..." Evie tapped the counter with bright green fingernails. "Victoria Pendergast is in it, of course. And everyone's favorite grandma, Cecile... Oh, and Lena Fox. She's an artist, and she makes these amazing tribal masks. And that Rick guy who teaches at the college."

Whitney stifled a laugh at the matter-of-fact way Evie described everyone. She seemed pretty well connected in this little town.

"I met Vickie Pendergast over the weekend. What's her story?"

Evie straightened with a laugh. "You saw her on a weekend, huh? Let me guess—her hair was perfect, her makeup was flawless and she was wearing Gucci sunglasses. Her accent was somewhere between eastern Connecticut and London. Did she happen to mention any of her three or four husbands?"

Whitney laughed. "No mention of husbands, but you

get an A on all the rest. She was trying to hook me up with her neighbor, Mark Hudson."

Evie went still. "*Mark?* Mark's back in Rendezvous Falls?"

"Yes. Do you know him?"

Wiping the counter with sudden vigor, Evie shrugged, all laughter gone from her voice. "I thought I did. A long time ago. But I was wrong." There was a beat of silence before Evie gave her a sardonic smile. "Anyone else you want to know about?"

Luke Rutledge's name was on the tip of her tongue, but she held it back. She'd asked for enough local gossip for one conversation.

"My aunt's been alone a lot. If I wanted to get her back out and active in town again, where would you suggest I start?"

Evie turned to look at a colorful July calendar on the wall near the front window. It had a close-up photo of a bright pink-and-white Victorian turret, with scalloped shingles.

"Well, you missed Americana Days, but the summer ArtFest is coming up. I don't know if Helen was ever big into art, but she's friends with Lena Fox, and Lena runs the thing, so she'd probably like to go."

"Oh, yes. That must be the one Mark was talking about."

"Mark was talking about *art*?" Evie's eyes were wide, and her grip tightened on the blue dishcloth in her hand until droplets of water hit the counter.

"Yeah, he quit accounting and paints landscapes or something."

Evie stared off toward the windows, but Whitney was pretty sure she wasn't seeing anything but memories. A soft smile played on Evie's lips, and she made a small sound of pleasure.

"His grandmother must be having a cow. Good for Mark."

Whitney pulled her wallet from her bag. "I have to get back to the winery. But if you think of anything else Helen might enjoy, or that I might enjoy for that matter, let me know, okay? Here's my card…" She pulled out one of her old business cards and scratched a big X across the KTM Accounting information. "I don't suppose you'd know where a gal can go for some night life around here?"

Evie chuckled. "In the summer, everything's geared to the tourists. There's a decent place on the waterfront by the marina. And, of course, there's the Purple Shamrock. That's the townie bar. The music is hit-or-miss these days, but you won't have some married asshat from Indiana laying bad pickup lines on you."

Whitney laughed. "I know what you mean. I always avoided the tourist bars in Chicago. But I'd feel like a fraud going to a townie bar. Especially alone. Want to join me?"

Evie nodded. "It's not like I've got anything else to do. I'll meet you there tomorrow at eight. It's up on the highway."

LUKE WINCED WHEN the "band" started warming up. He wouldn't be surprised if this was the first gig the four pimple-faced teens ever had. If Patrick McKinnon were still alive, he'd never have signed these guys, especially during the summer when there was no hope of drawing college students in. Luke lugged another case of beer out and finished stocking the ice-filled cooler behind the bar at the Purple Shamrock Pub. The name was supposed to be a nod to the grape growers in the area. Luke's two or three nights bartending every week helped cover his rent with Helen and added a little to the rainy-day fund Tony had set up years ago. And the tips put spare change in his pockets.

The guitar player turned to face the amplifier while he tuned up, causing an ear-splitting screech of feedback. Luke motioned with his hand for the kid to turn around. If only all problems were that easy to solve.

Sam Vrabel from the wine trail commission had called today. The commission was working on their website for the fall, and Sam was skeptical the winery could meet their stated goals.

"I drove up there on Wednesday," Sam said, "hoping to see you or Helen, but the place looked deserted. There was a huge pile of stone in the middle of the driveway, and the tasting room needs paint, at the very least." The older man's disapproval came through loud and clear. "Tony Russo never would have let people see the place looking like that."

Sam wasn't wrong there, but what the hell was Luke supposed to do? He started stacking glasses on the shelves behind the bar. He was one man, working two real jobs and half a dozen under-the-table ones to make ends meet. He'd explained to Sam, as calmly as possible, that the crushed stone was just delivered on Tuesday, and would be used to repair and expand the parking lot. He had the paint for the carriage house, and was waiting until he had the time to use it. The winery would be open six days a week by the time the festival arrived in September, and it would once again proudly join the ranks of Seneca Lake's finest wineries. He did his best to sound convincing, and Vrabel, with a few grumbles, had agreed to put Falls Legend on the organization's fall calendar for the wine trail.

He served a few drinks to the customers starting to file in for tonight's so-called "music." This was a younger crowd than Patrick McKinnon went after when he was alive. His daughter, Bridget, was working the kitchen tonight, filling in for yet another cook who'd quit under her hypercritical watch. Bridget hadn't figured out yet that this wasn't the fancy restaurant she'd left behind in Boston. This was strictly a wings-and-fries crowd.

The Purple Shamrock wasn't his concern, though. Falls Legend Winery was his life's work, and he was going to have to figure out a way to get that stone spread and the buildings repaired, the landscaping fixed, and the wine made. All while he balanced *this* job and his other odd jobs.

Lena Fox had Luke working on her outdoor studio, leveling paving stones so she could have classes in the fresh air. He had to finish adding the last layer of binding sand this weekend. Couldn't do it tomorrow—Saturday was the winery's only open day. Maybe he could spread some of the driveway stone between greeting customers. He pulled another glass of dark beer from the tap. That wouldn't work. He couldn't be all sweaty and dirty while trying to sell wine. If only there was someone else to pick up the slack once in a while.

Golden eyes and mahogany hair spun through his mind. Yeah, he needed the help, but what help could Whitney possibly be when she didn't know anything about the business? He sure as hell didn't have time to teach her.

The bar was filling up. Todd was checking IDs at the door the best he could, but Luke started doing his own checking when orders were placed. The last thing they needed was to get slapped for serving to minors. He checked the driver's license of a young blond before handing over a flight of party shots, then headed down to the far end of the bar to take orders.

He came to an abrupt halt halfway there. Whitney Foster was sitting at the bar, head bobbing to the band's halfway decent cover of a Bruno Mars song. Evie Rosario turned, her glass held high.

"Can I get a refill? Oh, hey, Luke! How are you?"

Ignoring the crazy train of emotions going across Whitney's face, he nodded at yet another of his sister Jessie's high school classmates. He should get her home for a reunion.

"Hey, Evie. Whatcha drinkin'?"

"Corona Light. And my friend here wants a...a gin and tonic, right, Whitney? Luke, this is Whit— oh, wait." Evie's eyes went wide. "I don't need to introduce you two—you're working together at Helen's place, right?"

Luke's "Not exactly" was said simultaneously with Whitney's "Yes."

Evie laughed. "O-kay. I'm gonna leave that one alone. Luke, you be a good boy and fetch us our drinks. And a plate of curly fries to munch on, too. I'm starving. Whitney wanted to know how to have a good time in Rendezvous Falls."

As she said it, the band ripped into a shaky cover of a Linkin Park hit. The driving drum beat and the chops on the lead guitarist were the only thing keeping the youthful crowd hooked. The dance floor filled with girls in crop tops and short skirts, hands high in the air, while the country boys stood along the far wall and watched, too cool to admit they had no clue how to dance to this stuff.

Whitney wanted to know how to have a good time...

None of his business. But the words rattled around in his head until Evie slapped the bar with her hand.

"Yo! Luke! Hungry, thirsty women here!"

"Yeah, okay. Be right back."

The two women talked nonstop while they drank. Evie was way ahead of Whitney, who was pacing herself. Smart girl. He headed back to the kitchen, dodging Bridget's outrage—and the spatula she threw—when he grabbed a plate piled high with curly fries intended for someone else.

Evie looked up in surprise when he set it in front of Whitney. "That was fast."

He met Whitney's gaze. "I didn't want you drinking on an empty stomach."

Her cheeks flushed deep red, and her jaw had a dangerous set to it.

"How considerate, Luke. Thank you."

The fire in her eyes made it clear she was mentally putting a very different word in front of "you."

He chuckled. "You're welcome, Miss Foster. Are you planning on helping yourself... I mean, helping *out* in the tasting room again this weekend?"

Evie let out a dramatic groan, missing the look of death Whitney was giving him. "I am *so* jealous! I get leftover donuts and french fries at the end of my shift at the diner, which is the last thing I need." She patted her hips. "But you guys? You get leftover *wine* at the end of the day!"

Whitney rushed to speak before he did, probably anticipating where he was going. She came in hot, clearly a scorched-earth kind of fighter. He smiled to himself. He didn't expect anything less.

"If I were going to do any 'helping out' tomorrow, it would be in the parking lot, where a mountain of stone was delivered days ago."

He hoped to get the siding repaired on the carriage house next week so he could paint. After he finished Lena's patio. "I can't spread stone when there are customers there."

"We don't have customers on weekdays. As if the place doesn't look ragged enough—"

"Ragged?" She'd pushed the wrong damn button. He leaned across the bar, but she didn't flinch. "What about that so-called garden that's overgrown up at the house? Or the dead hanging baskets on the porch? You've been here for weeks and haven't lifted a finger to do anything about *that*, have you?"

Her eyes went wide. "I don't know anything about gardening!"

"I'm pretty sure you don't know anything about parking lots, either, but it doesn't stop you from having opinions, does it?"

She started to point a finger at him when a new voice, gentle but firm, broke into the conversation.

"Luke, can I trouble you for a spot o' Guinness, lad?"

"Father Joe…" Luke closed his eyes in self-censure, remembering the priest didn't like being "outed" in public if he wasn't wearing his collar. Tonight he was wearing a rugby shirt and jeans. "Of course, Joe. Gimme a minute—"

"Ah, Luke, I've worked up a powerful thirst." Joe's

brogue made the word sound like "turst." The father gave a pointed look at the way Luke was still leaning toward Whitney. "You wouldn't want me going wid'out, would you?"

Luke straightened. Message received. "Of course not, Joe. Let me get that draft right now." He turned to the two women. "Excuse me, ladies. Duty calls."

Joe's arrival had effectively ended the conversation. Catholic or not, the man didn't abide strife in his parish. But Whitney didn't know that. Still raring to go, she folded her arms on her chest.

"Funny how you pay attention to your duties at *this* job, but not—"

"Evening, ladies," Father Joe interrupted, his voice smooth and his accent heavier than ever. "Evie, love, it's good t'see you. Tell your mum we missed her at Mass last week. And I don't t'ink I've had the pleasure." He turned to Whitney. "I'm Father Joseph Brennan, but please call me Joe tonight." He leaned in and spoke in a stage whisper. "People act funny if they know they're hanging out with a priest."

Whitney's eyes went soft. Father Joe's Irish charm had won again. She took his hand. "I'm Whitney Foster, Fath… I mean, Joe. I'm—"

"Ah, yes," Joe said. "You're Helen's niece from Chicago, the accountant here to help her out this summer. It's grand t'meet you."

Luke shook his head as he waited for the dark stout to settle in the glass before he finished the pour. He was no longer surprised by how much information Joe knew. It wasn't just the confessional that fed him news—the man had a knack for getting people to talk to him. Or the Good Man Upstairs was sharing it with him in dreams.

Whitney, of course, assumed Luke had talked. He could see it in the way her eyes sliced his direction before she nodded at Joe.

"Yes, that's right, Joe. Things are a bit of a mess there and I plan on finding out why."

Luke grunted, then slid a perfect pint of Guinness to Joe. He had a dozen good comebacks for her, but he wasn't going there with the good priest in earshot. He didn't need the lecture the next time he went to mow the lawn at the rectory.

Whitney studied him with a frown, as if waiting for the response she'd poked him for. Evie finally distracted her, pointing at a some twenty-year-olds grinding together on the dance floor. Everyone's phones were up, recording the pub porn to gather internet clicks. Joe didn't even look. Whatever everyone else felt they had to capture on video would hold no interest for him. He watched Luke pouring drinks for a few minutes before speaking up.

"Helen came to Mass on Sunday. Did you have anything to do with that?"

Luke shook his head. "I was as surprised as you were. But she's been doing better lately, so maybe she figured it's time. Maybe she forgave you for—"

Joe chuckled. "For not being Father Lorenzo?"

Luke poured another flight of shots. They were a hot seller tonight. After he made change, he turned back to Joe. The man was in his fifties, but looked ten years younger. Short and lean, he was often spotted on his high-tech racing bike, peddling up and down the hills around town. Sandy hair fell across Joe's forehead, and his blue eyes were always bright with laughter and wisdom. He was basically impossible not to like.

"I never understood why Helen blamed you for that."

Joe shrugged. "I was the new young buck who showed up after her husband died. The priest they knew and loved for years was retired and gone. She resented me for being one more change in her life. I told you she'd come around." The priest winked. "I think I won that bet, boy-o."

When Helen was at her lowest, Luke told Joe he didn't think she'd ever go back to church. Hell, she *told* him she wouldn't. But Joe had been unconcerned when they'd made their friendly wager. Luke didn't need another task on his to-do list, but a bet was a bet. And you didn't renege on a priest. As usual, Joe read his mind.

"Those hedges have been overgrown for years, Luke. Another few months won't hurt."

"Thanks, Joe, but pruning in the fall is a bad idea. I'll get it done. No problem." Yeah, sure. No problem. Maybe he could use floodlights and trim hedges at night.

A burst of female laughter brought his eyes back to Evie and Whitney. They were watching the dance floor antics, and Evie was pointing to someone and shaking her head. Luke followed her finger. Doug Canfield. Yeah, he was definitely a no-go. Doug had two DUIs and a misdemeanor assault conviction for punching a bouncer at a bar in Watkins Glen. The guy was a hot mess on a downward spiral.

Todd was already heading toward Doug. Luke would join in if needed, but there was bad blood between the Canfields and the Rutledges. He didn't want to stir that up if he could avoid it. After a brief, angry exchange, Doug and his buddies headed out the front door. Evie was directing Whitney's attention elsewhere—in the direction of Owen Isaacs. Damn it. There wasn't a damn thing wrong with Owen. He was a good, hardworking dairy farmer. Luke started to smile. Owen was boring as hell. Whitney would eat him alive.

His smile faded. She could do the same to him if he wasn't careful. Instead of feeling concerned about it, he felt oddly…energized. He was more than ready for whatever Whitney Foster was going to throw at him. At least he hoped he was.

CHAPTER NINE

HELEN HAD NO idea how she was going to tell Whitney about these extra boxes of bank statements and other mail. She'd forgotten all about stuffing them in her bedroom closet months ago. She lifted the lid on one, then quickly closed it again. Confronting the mistakes she'd made was so damn painful.

After watching Whitney sort and resort papers in the dining room for days on end, Helen was overwhelmed with guilt. If her niece could work that hard every day, it was time for Helen to do the same. She'd started this week by sorting through the magazines and catalogs that lined the walls of the dining room. After an afternoon spent trying to determine what was so important in each one that she'd saved it, she realized there was no acceptable answer to the question. They all had to go.

Luke hadn't said a word when she asked him to remove everything from the chairs and floors downstairs. He'd boxed it all in the back of his truck and hauled it to the county recycling center. Then she'd cleaned and reorganized the living room. She'd flipped the cushions on the sofa—one was pancaked from where she'd spent months after Tony's death sitting and staring at the television with no idea what she was watching. At one point during her darkest days, there'd been a pile of crumpled tissues and empty tissue boxes as high as the arm of the sofa.

"Aunt Helen? Are you in here?" Whitney appeared in the doorway to the bedroom.

Helen scooted back out of the closet and closed the door. There was no need to tell Whitney about the additional paperwork in those boxes right this very minute. It could wait. And besides, she hadn't finished cleaning the rest of the bedroom. She should do that first, in case there were any more surprises in here. Made perfect sense, right? She turned to smile at Whitney.

"Yes. I'm here!"

"Don't you have your friends coming over tonight? It's almost six o'clock."

"Oh, shitcakes, I didn't realize it was that late!" She was still in her dusty shorts and T-shirt. The event room was set up for the book club, but she needed to get the food out there and open the wine. "Whitney, can you preheat the oven for me? Those little quiches just need to be warmed up. I'm going to shower and change real quick." She wiped her brow. "This cleaning business is exhausting!"

Whitney gave her a surprise hug. "Aunt Helen, you don't have to do it all at once. Pace yourself."

Helen laughed. "I guess you're right. After all, it took me months to create this mess." Her laughter faded, and she took both of Whitney's hands in hers. "I don't know what I would have done without you coming home this summer. There's no way I could have tackled that paperwork…"

"I haven't exactly tackled it yet," Whitney sighed. "It feels like I'm just shuffling things from place to place without accomplishing anything. There's something missing, but I can't figure out where the gap is."

Helen cringed, glancing at the closet door, but Whitney was already walking away, still talking. "I won't give up, though. And Helen…" She turned at the doorway. "One day we need to talk about what happened after Tony died. I need to know you can handle the books after I go."

"Sure, sure. But you've been working too hard. You came here to relax and I ruined that for you."

When Whitney announced she wanted to learn more about the wine business, she hadn't been kidding. When she wasn't pouring over wine magazines and websites, she was grilling Helen on everything from the types of grapes they were growing to the layout of the tasting room. Helen tried to steer her toward working with Luke, since he was the real expert. But the two of them were still like fire and gasoline.

"You didn't ruin anything, Helen." Whitney reached out and tamed a wayward lock of Helen's hair. "I'm used to working sixty-hour weeks. Go get ready for your friends. I'm not much of a chef, but I think I can handle warming up appetizers."

When the book club arrived forty-five minutes later, Helen had managed to scrape the burnt sections from the mini quiches, salvaging most of them, even if they didn't look very pretty. Whitney saying she wasn't much of a chef was a vast understatement. It was hardly a surprise with the upbringing she had—her mother was always on the road or singing in some bar at night, so Whitney had been left with babysitters and frozen meals. The girl could operate a microwave and a can opener, but that was about her limit in the kitchen.

Helen was wondering how she could help her and almost missed what Rick was saying.

"So you and Vickie tried your hand at matchmaking, even after we agreed not to?"

Vickie rolled her eyes. "*You* agreed not to, but there wasn't a vote or anything. And it was too perfect, with Mark coming back to town and being an accountant and all."

"And how did that work out?"

Helen met Vickie's look from across the table. When they'd tiptoed down to the carriage house that afternoon and heard the happy laughter inside, they'd congratulated themselves on a successful match. They'd had no idea the two knuckleheads had decided to raid the tasting counter. Somehow, Mark and Whitney figured out their scheme. She turned to Rick and smiled.

"They became friends, so that's something. But there wasn't any romantic spark there."

Cecile sighed. "Ah, yes. You have to have that spark. That's where the magic comes from. When Charlie and I met forty-two years ago, those sparks were like fireworks going off. We knew right away—"

"There's no such thing as love-at-first-sight," Rick scoffed. "And you can't convince me otherwise, no matter how many romances you try to make us read."

Cecile didn't lose her dreamy smile. "I didn't say anything about love. That came later. But trust me, *sparks* can happen in the blink of an eye. Haven't you ever looked at another guy and wished you could whisk him away to…do…whatever?"

Rick shifted in his chair, suddenly having a great deal of interest in the paperback in his hands. Jayla watched him with a sharply arched brow. She wasn't about to let him ignore the question.

"Well, Rick? Have you ever seen a man and felt instant sparks?"

"Yeah, okay. Attraction can happen fast, but that doesn't mean anything if it isn't followed by an emotional connection. Without that, it's just a fun backseat romp that leaves you feeling empty after."

Lena burst out laughing. "A 'backseat romp'? Where are you meeting people, Rick? The Shamrock?"

"The Purple Shamrock isn't my kind of crowd." Rick shook off whatever memory had made him melancholy. "But I will say Patrick's daughter can really cook."

Vickie shook her head, frowning at the crispy quiche in her hand. "We're veering off course here. The idea is to find someone for Whitney. Mark wasn't a disaster." She leaned forward, her voice dropping for dramatic effect. "Besides, I hear Mark only has eyes for his high school flame, Evie Rosario. His grandmother is fit to be tied. How were we supposed to know?"

"I still say this is a bad idea," Rick said, turning to Helen. "Do you honestly think your niece needs us meddling in her love life?"

Helen had been against it at first, but now… Whitney was working so hard, and she hardly ever got out of the house, except for the time she was spending with—interestingly enough—Evie Rosario.

"Whitney wasn't happy about the Mark situation, but her main complaint was that it was what she called a 'double blind' blind date. Neither party knew what was happening beforehand and it was…a bit much." Whitney had been *furious*, but Helen didn't want to give Rick the satisfaction of hearing that. "I think I might be able to convince her to meet some nice young men as friends, as long as we don't trick her into it. But how do people meet up these days?"

Cecile waved her hand, showing her phone screen to everyone. "There are all kinds of apps, like Tinder and stuff, where people hook up, or pick up a partner for a threesome, or..."

"Whoa!" Rick grabbed her phone. "That was a pretty specific example, Cecile. Where did *that* come from?" He looked at the screen. "And why do you have one of those apps on your phone?"

Heads swiveled to Cecile. It wasn't the first time she'd hinted she and Charlie had a different sort of sex life. Cecile's cheeks went pink, matching her cardigan. She snatched back her phone. "Anyway, if people make a match online—" she gave Rick a pointed look "—I've *heard* they often meet somewhere public the first time, usually just for a drink or even coffee. They don't commit to more than that unless they know they hit it off."

Vickie rested her chin in her hand, tapping her cheek with a manicured finger. "Cecile, darling, one of these days you and I need to talk about your marriage. But for now, let's focus. If Helen can convince Whitney to agree to some innocent coffee dates, all we'd have to do is find some fellas we think would be a good fit. College-educated professionals, like her. Successful. Well-mannered." Her brows furrowed. "Who do we know that fits that bill? Let's start a list..."

Lena frowned. "Do you *really* think this is a good idea, Helen? I mean, who are we to decide what kind of man she needs? And let's not forget that she doesn't *need* a man at all…" Lena had marched in the '60s and still considered herself a social justice warrior.

Cecile interrupted what was sure to be a women's rights lecture. "But if she finds someone, she might stay with Helen a little bit longer."

Lena looked over to Helen. "Is that what you want?" Helen didn't answer right away, imagining how nice it would be to have Whitney nearby. Lena smiled knowingly. "I see."

They soon had a short list of Whitney-eligible bachelors. Even Rick pitched in after a while, naming a fellow professor from the college.

"Leonard might be a little old for her, though." Rick took a sip of pinot noir. "I think he's in his midforties, but he teaches economics, so they could talk numbers for *days*." He glanced at his smart watch. "Ladies, it's after nine, and I have a tee time in the morning."

"I still can't wrap my head around the idea of you taking up golf." Lena stood and starting cleaning up the plates and napkins.

Rick shrugged. "It's all about the networking. I'm on the endowment committee now, and the best place to talk rich guys out of their money is on the golf course. Besides, I can wear the silliest clothes and no one bats an eye." He turned to Helen. "Are we really doing this matchmaking thing? Do I need to ask the drama department to perform *Fiddler on the Roof* next semester?" He started humming the melody to the matchmaker song from the musical.

Helen stared at the list of five names scribbled onto a napkin in front of her. It *would* be nice if Whitney stayed longer. "We *only* do this if Whitney agrees to it, and it's *only* for coffee."

WHITNEY SAT AT The Spot, drumming her fingers on the table. Evie giggled from behind the counter. Again. *Not helping*. But who could blame her? This was a ridiculous, juvenile, desperate thing Whitney had agreed to do. She was cringing in embarrassment before her "date" even arrived.

A shudder went through her at the thought of Helen's so-called book club—a bunch of senior citizens who apparently had nothing better to do—dissecting her love life as if she was their latest novel. The *nerve*, especially after the debacle of Vickie and Helen setting her up with Mark. And yet here she was, in her white capris and cheery blue top, which Evie had assured her was neither too racy nor too prudish. Waiting for a college professor named Leonard.

Why had she said yes?

Because she couldn't say no to Aunt Helen. They were both struggling this summer, but there was no comparison between losing a job and losing the love of your life. Helen had finally confessed how she'd been almost catatonic with grief after Tony's sudden death. She told Whitney she craved a sense of romance and fun, even if was vicariously through Whitney. And what harm was there in it? Making Helen smile was worth a couple weird coffee dates.

Besides, Helen had made another fair point. Whitney *had* been sorting papers and creating spreadsheets for too many hours. She was starting to crave human interaction. Evie was a great friend, but Mark Hudson was occupying a lot of Evie's free time these days.

Whitney's hours tagging along behind Luke didn't count, since he was barely human to her, and ignored her questions about the winery more often than not. He thought she was trying to trip him up and prove he was doing something nefarious. And she was, in a sense. She didn't have a shred of proof, but her suspicion that he knew more about the finances than he was letting on wouldn't go away. She hadn't found any sign of the rent he claimed he'd paid, and there were gaps in the records that still had no explanation.

What Luke didn't get was that she *also* wanted to understand the business. That was part of an auditor's job—understanding standard operating procedures and putting them together with the numbers to see what lined up and what needed to be investigated or changed. And she honestly wanted to know more about the business her aunt and uncle had built. As a child, Falls Legend had been a farm that happened to grow grapes. A pretty place with a pretty house and pretty gardens near a magical little town full of other pretty houses. But she wasn't a child now, and she was curious to know more about the successful winery Tony had created with Helen's—and apparently Luke's—help.

The tinkle of the brass bell over the restaurant door made her jump. She looked up to see an older gentleman in pressed jeans and a tidy oxford shirt buttoned nearly to the collar. He wasn't geriatric or anything, but Helen's friends had been way off when they said he was "around forty." He had to be at least twenty years her senior. His eyes met hers and he gave her a tentative smile.

"Whitney?"

She stood and extended her hand, trying not to make this too much like a business meeting. Behind the counter, Evie was practically swallowing her dishrag trying not to laugh out loud.

"Leonard? Nice to meet you. Won't you join me?"

Oh, god, it was *just* like a business meeting. She heard Evie choking, probably thinking the same thing.

That feeling didn't change as their conversation continued over blueberry muffins and coffee. Leonard was a nice man, and dedicated to his study of economics. *Very* dedicated. It was apparently the only subject he was comfortable discussing. At one point, Whitney said something about the campus's enviable location on the lakeshore, and Leonard was affronted, claiming the town had squandered valuable waterfront property over a century ago when they bequeathed it to the college.

"Having an institution of education on a lake provides no value to that institution, and robs the community of the potential tourist dollars that propel our economic engine."

"But doesn't the college bring a lot of revenue to Rendezvous Falls?" Her mind was growing numb.

"Of course! But the college doesn't need to be taking up space on the waterfront to do that." He pushed his plate aside, warming up to the subject. "If the town could entice the school to move to a different property, the campus property could be converted to commercial use and create a substantial tax revenue."

Whitney had a hard time imagining a move like that ever happening. "Have you discussed this with anyone at the school? Or in Rendezvous Falls?"

He waved his hand in dismissal, slumping back in his seat. "No one has any vision here. The college board laughed, and the mayor wasn't any better. He reacted as if I'd suggested he give up a limb."

Whitney could imagine so. Leonard's numbers made sense on face value, which normally would appeal to her, but he was missing the cultural essence of the com-

munity. She couldn't believe she was spending brain
cells on this plan that would *never* happen. She popped
the last bite of muffin into her mouth and smiled at
earnest-faced Leonard.

"My aunt is expecting me back at the winery before
three." That was a lie. "We have to go over some papers together." Not quite a lie. There *were* mountains
of papers still to be sorted. But she didn't want her
aunt anywhere near them. "It's been a pleasure chatting
with you, Leonard." A *pleasure* might be a stretch. He
jumped to his feet when she moved to stand.

"Oh! Okay. Um…yes. It was a lovely time, wasn't
it?" She didn't answer, for fear of going to hell if she
stretched the truth one more time today. He reached for
his wallet. "I'll take care of the tab."

"Only for yourself. I took care of mine before you
arrived."

She could pay her own way, thank you very much.
Leonard's eyes widened again, then he nodded, mumbling something about changing times before shaking
her hand and saying goodbye. He didn't ask to see her
again, saving them both an awkward conversation.

Aunt Helen and her nosy book club pals were pretty
bad matchmakers so far. Mark was nice, but it turned
out he was still crazy about his high school sweetheart,
Evie. And Leonard was old enough to be her father. She
waved goodbye to a still-laughing Evie, ignoring her
"sugar daddy" comments, and headed out to her car.
She was doing this to make Helen happy and get out of
the house. She was *not* looking for a soul mate in Rendezvous Falls. They hadn't set her up with an ax murderer or anything, so their lack of skill was harmless.

CHAPTER TEN

LUKE WAS COMING OUT of the barn to finish spreading the last of the gravel, Molly close at his heels, when he saw Helen weeding her flower garden. Wait. She was *what*? He stopped so fast Molly ran into his leg, then gave him a WTF? expression. Helen hadn't shown interest in the once beautiful rose garden since losing Tony. She smiled from where she was kneeling when he walked over, shielding the sun from her eyes.

"Where's your garden hat?" Luke asked. She used to wear a huge, floppy-brimmed straw hat Tony had bought her on one of their trips to Italy. A wide strip of colorful fabric had wound around and through it to tie in a big bow. Helen often tied it off to the side, telling Tony it made her feel like Sophia Loren. Tony always had the same answer: *Sophia's got nothing on you, tesoro mia.* Helen had always been Tony's "treasure."

The wave of loss hit Luke hard. He'd been forced to keep a tight lid on his grief over Tony once he'd realized Helen was falling apart. She'd been proud and strong through those first difficult days. But when the funeral luncheon was over and everyone had left, she'd barely made it to the front porch before collapsing. That's when he knew he had to be the one standing strong for her.

But Tony's sudden death from a heart attack at the top of the vineyard had gutted Luke. The man had been everything to him—father, mentor, boss, friend. And in an instant, he was gone. It left Luke feeling unmoored. Helen's hand on his arm snapped him from his thoughts. He hadn't even noticed she'd stood.

"Luke, I'm sorry. I brought back a bad memory for you…"

He blinked rapidly, then put his hand over hers. They hadn't talked about Tony much. "Not a bad one, Helen. I was thinking of that hat, and how Tony used to tease you…" He stopped, knowing how emotional Helen got when Tony's name came up.

Her eyes shone bright, but clear, as she laughed softly. "My Sophia Loren hat. I remember. I think it's up in my closet, but I haven't worn it in so long I forgot about it." She looked around the garden, about half of it weeded, then nodded, as if in approval of her own hard work. "Most of the roses survived my neglect, but they need attention. And the planters on the porch are still empty in July. I don't know if I'll find many summer plants to buy this time of year, but Sylvia's nursery might have something. Geraniums would be nice, don't you think?"

He grinned down at her. "Red ones? With the little white things hanging down? Tony said it was like the Italian flag." And there he went again, saying Tony's name out loud. But Helen didn't flinch.

"That's right. It might be a little late in the season, but I'll see what Sylvia has. It's been too long since I've paid her a visit." Her voice trailed off. "It's been too long for a lot of things."

He patted her hand, his throat tight. "Can't change the past, Helen. But look at you now—out here in the garden, trimming your roses. Tony would love that."

She nodded slowly, with no sign of the tears he kept bracing for. "He *would* love it. But he wouldn't love the way this place looks. We have to get it cleaned up before the fall tours arrive. And we have to be ready for the festival." She gave his arm a gentle squeeze. "Do you really think we can do it?"

They didn't have a choice. Not if they wanted to be in business next year. There was no way Luke could let Tony's dream fail. Not on his watch. He'd have to find a few extra hours in every day. Maybe give up bartending? No. He'd lose the truck without that job. Hire someone? No money in the budget for that. At least none he knew of. And he didn't think Whitney would be sharing the books with him any time soon.

As if he'd summoned her out of thin air, her red SUV came up the driveway and stopped next to the garden. Whitney jumped out, brushing dark hair over her shoulder, looking between him and Helen.

"What happened? Are you okay, Aunt Helen?"

It took him a few seconds to understand. She wasn't any more used to seeing Helen working in the garden than he was. She'd seen Helen leaning on Luke's arm and panicked. He probably would have done the same. It was the one and only thing they had in common—caring about Helen.

"Nothing's wrong," he assured her. "Helen decided to work in the garden, and she and I were talking about old times."

Helen huffed a soft laugh. "I'm more concerned with *new* times right now." She turned to her niece. "I suddenly realized how much work we have to do here before the festival, and I'm not sure it can be done."

Whitney looked around, then met Luke's eyes. Their

gazes locked, and, without saying a word, they came to an agreement. The fact that they were able to do it so effortlessly sent a shock wave right through him. How could he be on the same wavelength with a woman who spent most of her time irritating the hell out of him?

Whitney took Helen's other hand, showering the woman with one of her breathtaking smiles. He could feel Helen relaxing in the warmth of it. Even more surprising, there was a warmth growing in *his* chest, too. Whitney's eyes flickered to him before returning to Helen.

"We *will* be ready. I'll make sure of it. When is this festival, anyway? What needs to be done?"

"It's next month, honey. September. The garden... the parking lot...the tasting room...setting up a booth at the festival...maybe a float for the parade? Plus we'll be starting harvest. Oh, I don't know..."

Whitney's gaze met his again. She was asking for his help. He couldn't come up with anything to say. Her brow quirked in amusement at his stunned expression, and she reassured Helen again.

"We'll make it happen. Luke and I can work together. Right, Luke?"

His first impulse was to give her a sarcastic insult and walk away. That was the safe thing to do. The expected thing. The smart thing.

Instead, he found his head bobbing in agreement.

"Absolutely. We'll figure it out." He had no freaking idea how, but he was in it now, and he couldn't let Helen down.

Helen smiled brightly, her shoulders visibly relaxing. "You two make me think we might just do that." She reached up and patted her dark gray hair. "Sorry

for panicking. I think the garden overwhelmed me…"
She looked at the half that was still choked in weeds.

"I'll tell you what," Whitney said. "Let me change
and I'll come out and help you with the rest of this."

"Wonderful!" Helen stopped. "Oh! I almost forgot
to ask you about your date. How was it?"

Ice water hit Luke's veins. *Date?* Who the hell was
Whitney *dating*? Had Mark Hudson moved out of the
friend zone? Had she gone out with him last night? His
jaw tightened, then he noticed Whitney's face. Judging
from her expression, the date hadn't been a showstopper.

"Leonard's a nice man."

Leonard? Leonard who?

Helen chuckled. "Ouch. A 'nice man,' huh?"

Whitney shrugged. "There wasn't anything *bad*
about him. He's quite a bit older than me. We had a nice
conversation over coffee, but…" She shrugged again.

Luke's curiosity got the best of him. "You had a coffee date? Today? With who?"

Whitney gave him a sharp look. He was pretty sure
she'd forgotten he was standing there. Her voice got
its edge back.

"Yes, I met someone for coffee. The 'with who' is
none of your business."

Her eyes raked up and down his body, making him
sharply aware of his dirty cargo shorts and torn T-shirt.
He'd been headed to spread crushed stone and level the
driveway, not have tea and crumpets.

"Whatever. A boring afternoon coffee date just
seems a little tame for someone like you."

He walked away without bothering to listen to her
muttered response, but he was pretty sure there were a
few curse words in there.

Two DAYS LATER, Whitney scowled at the wine display, blinking away her exhaustion. She'd spent an hour reorganizing the bottles by the color of the labels, creating a rainbow effect along the left wall of the tasting room. It looked good, but now she wondered if she shouldn't create *diagonal* lines of color instead of vertical. She glanced outside. The sun was just rising over the far side of the Seneca Valley.

She'd tossed and turned last night, trying to figure out the best way to tackle turning this place around. Helen had gone on and on about the importance of the Blessing of the Grapes Festival. The festival coincided with the beginning of the grape harvest. There was a fierce wine competition there among the Seneca Lake wineries.

The festival was held in the center of town, with booths and rides, and even a parade. Many wineries put floats, or at least vehicles of some kind, in the parade. Wineries also had wine-tasting booths, which was a great way to get new people to try the different wines available.

Falls Legend Winery hadn't participated in two years. Helen said they *needed* to be a part of it this year. They had to show the public, as well as the other vintners, that the winery was alive and well. That they deserved to be taken seriously again, and not be the object of everyone's pity. Or a target for vultures.

"I saw it in their eyes when I went to the quarterly growers meeting in May," Helen told her last night, as they sat in the kitchen after dinner. "Luke had been going on his own, but he convinced me I should get back in the swing of things. When I walked in, all I saw was pity. Not just for me, but for this winery. Herb Daniels even asked if I was ready to sell yet. It was right then, when I saw everyone leaning toward us to hear my answer, that I knew we had to put this place back together. For Tony's sake. He'd never want me selling, especially to a guy like Daniels."

Whitney had reached over to take Helen's hand. "You can't change the past, Helen, but we can go forward from where we are."

Helen had laughed at that. "Luke said the same thing to me the other day. You two are just what I need to make this work. The three of us will make a great team."

Whitney hadn't responded. There were still too many gaps in the bookkeeping records for her to be willing to completely trust Luke as a teammate. Yes, Helen created the mess, but there was something…off…in the bank records. Things didn't jive and she couldn't figure it out. But they needed his expertise to make repairs and handle this year's harvest and festival. After that, she'd have to figure out if he had any role in the mystery. According to Tony's records from before his death, there should be a lot more money somewhere. She frowned at the wall display again. Diagonal colors would be more eye-catching.

She'd given up on sleep hours earlier, and started typing ideas into her laptop. She'd split her time between the books and getting ready for the festival. And first on her list? Using consumer research to change the shop around and make it more appealing. Marketing in general was a little too "smoke and mirrors" for her analytical mind, but she liked the research and analytics part of it. She'd taken enough marketing classes in college to know what consumers responded to.

Freshly energized, she'd pulled on a yellow tank top,

a pair of shorts and a pair of flip-flops. She'd taken the key off the hook by the kitchen door and had snuck into the wine shop while it was still dark. Uncomfortably aware that Luke's apartment was directly overhead, she'd been as quiet as possible while juggling wine bottles and rearranging them. She did her best not to think about the brooding winemaker in bed, but it was a tough image to dispel.

He irritated her to no end. She wasn't sure he was trustworthy. And yet, there was a little buzz under her skin when he was around that was more than simply irritation. More like attraction. She huffed at herself—that was her mother coming out in her. Always attracted to the worst guys. She heard a muffled bark, but, after holding her breath and freezing in place with one foot suspended in air for longer than she imagined possible, silence returned.

She had to shift only a few dozen more bottles to get her diagonal design, but that was a few dozen more than her body was apparently willing to handle, considering she'd already moved every bottle on this wall at least once. The final bottle of the red blend slipped from her fingers as she set it on the top shelf. It crashed to the terracotta floor neck first, smashing to a million slivers of glass and sending bloodred wine everywhere.

Damn it! She unconsciously went to her tiptoes in her flip-flops, trying to stay dry.

"Don't move!"

Whitney let out a squeak of surprise at the barked-out command from behind her. She spun around, feeling the swish of sharp glass slicing the skin on the side of her foot. It was one of those nasty cuts—clean, deep and straight. It didn't even hurt at first, but she knew without looking that she was bleeding.

"Jesus. Do you always listen that well?" Luke was stepping off the staircase, giving his dog a hand signal that clearly meant *stay*. Molly was twitching to follow, but there was broken glass everywhere. Luke's voice was emphatic. "Don't move, either one of you."

Whitney was still trying to wrap her head around his sudden appearance, dressed in low-slung jeans that didn't appear to be buttoned, a pair of tattered sneakers and nothing else. The cut on her foot was starting to burn, but she was too mesmerized by Luke's slow, careful approach to care.

"Where did you…?"

Luke grabbed a bundle of kitchen towels from a display. They had pithy sayings on them, like "How low will you merlot?" and "Is it wine-o'clock yet?" Before she could protest the destruction of sales merchandise, he'd removed her flip-flop and wrapped one of the towels loosely around her left foot, ignoring her hiss of pain. He stood, scooping her into his arms as he did so.

"Hey!"

"Shush." The one-word command worked. She snapped her mouth shut and reluctantly grabbed his shoulders for balance. He was the one wearing actual shoes in a minefield of broken glass. She was not. He deposited her on top of the wine-tasting counter in the back of the store. He held up his hand the same way he had with his dog and said, "Stay."

She was tempted to hop off the counter just to make the point that she wouldn't be bossed around. But her foot hurt like hell, and Luke had already turned his back on her, so the move would be pointless. He went to the closet and pulled out a huge cotton mop and a wheeled bucket that already had water in it.

"Looks like you were prepared." Good little Boy Scout.

He grunted, bending over to pick up the larger pieces of glass with a heavy towel draped over the side of the bucket.

"It's a wine store. With a tile floor. When things drop in here, they break in pretty spectacular fashion."

"Maybe tile wasn't the best choice?"

He glanced over his shoulder as he started mopping. "You think? Tony would have nothing but Italian terracotta floors in here."

"It won't stain?" She hated creating a problem when she'd been trying to help.

Another grunt. "It's sealed."

Whitney had no idea what that meant, but she discovered she couldn't ask for an explanation. In fact, she wasn't sure she could assemble the words to say *anything*. Luke leaned into the mop, swinging it in narrowing circles to pull the glass shards and spilled wine into a smaller area. Every time he swung the mop, the hard muscles in his shoulders bunched and released, sending ripples down his spine, and down Whitney's spine, too. Holy good lord, the man was carved out of granite. By an artist. A really freaking good artist.

And his ass. *Oh, my my my.* Those worn, faded jeans hugged his butt cheeks and made them look…perfect. Whitney sighed. Damn. He was one fine example of the male human form. She barely managed to look away in time when he turned to grab a big squeegee. He glanced her way, seeming surprised she hadn't moved. He had no idea watching *him* was the reason she was frozen in place. He finished cleaning the floor and rolled the bucket back into the closet. He walked toward her, and, as much as she tried, she couldn't control the way her heart started to race.

"How's the foot?" he asked.

"What?" Her cheeks went hot. She'd forgotten all about her bleeding foot wrapped in a dish towel that said Save Water—Drink Wine. "Oh…it's okay. I'm pretty sure the towel is ruined, though."

He grunted again. He did that a lot.

"Can you walk on it, or do I have to carry you upstairs?"

It must have been her lack of sleep, because the idea of a shirtless Luke carrying her anywhere was ridiculously tempting. His dark hair was tousled, with one lock falling across his forehead. She fought off the urge to reach out and touch it. She started to slide off the counter. "I'm fine. I'll go up to the house and put a bandage on it."

"I didn't see any large bits of glass, but there could still be a sliver embedded in there, and you won't be able to find it on your own. Come on. I'll make us some coffee and take a look."

Mmm—coffee. A jolt of caffeine might snap her out of her crazy, lustful thoughts about this guy. Practically speaking, it would be a good excuse to get a look at the place Helen said he was living in rent-free. Going up those stairs could be considered research for auditing purposes, right? Okay, that was a load of hooey, but… coffee and curiosity won out.

Luke wrapped a rock-solid arm around her waist and helped her down off the counter.

"Use the other aisle. I'll come down and vacuum this

one after the water dries to make sure I got all the glass up." She didn't argue, wincing as she tried to walk on her heel. Luke followed her up the wooden stairs, with Molly trotting ahead of them.

The apartment was essentially one large room, taking up the entire top floor of the carriage house. The walls were painted a nondescript beige. Two well-worn leather chairs faced a smallish flat-screen hanging on the wall. The kitchen area was in one corner, with a small butcher block island on wheels. A metal table and two chairs, painted bright blue and obviously meant for use on a patio, sat near a window looking up the hill at the vineyard. And in the opposite corner sat a bed, placed in front of another window that offered a breathtaking view of Seneca Lake below, now shimmering in shades of light blue as the sun rose higher over the hills.

It felt open and inviting. Or at least, it would have with less clutter. Clothes were stacked near the bed, some folded neatly, others hanging on hooks along the wall. A jumble of shoes sat at the foot of the bed. The end tables and coffee table were piled high with papers, magazines and wine supply catalogs. The limited kitchen counter space was barely visible under the dishes, glasses, bread, cans of soup, bags of chips, many wine bottles, and pots and pans. It was all *clean*. But messier than any corner of Helen's house.

No wonder those two got along so well.

Luke brushed past her, pointing to the blue kitchen table. He noted her expression and shrugged.

"I wasn't expecting company. This is basically just a place to sleep. Sit down and I'll look at that foot."

In the vineyard outside the window, the vines marched

up the hill in perfectly straight rows, neatly pruned and tidy. The apartment was the exact opposite.

"But it could be so much more. You've got great views up here. With some paint and some shelves for storage and a nice rug and curtains and maybe a *dresser*—" she gave the clothes in the corner a pointed look "—this could be a charming little apartment."

Luke was opening the door to what she assumed was a bathroom in the far corner. He turned to look at her, his mouth slanting into an amused smirk.

"Do I look like a 'charming little apartment' sort of guy?" She tried not to give his half-naked body another perusal, and failed. He looked like *something*, that's for sure. She cleared her throat.

"I'm only saying a little more…order…up here would make it a more restful place to be."

He flipped on the bathroom light, and then rummaged through the small medicine cabinet on the wall. "By the end of most days, I'm so tired a bed of nails would be restful. And I'd have been well rested this morning if the motion sensor in the tasting room hadn't woken me up at five o'clock." He was walking toward where she sat, making no attempt to hide his scowl. Now that he mentioned it, he *did* have dark circles under his eyes and a drawn expression.

He set a box of gauze on the table and kneeled in front of her before making eye contact. "After getting to bed at two."

She started to bristle. He made her feel like she constantly had to be on guard. Like her heart might be in danger around him. As if he could end up provoking far more than her temper, which was always sharpest when he was around.

"Maybe you should get to bed earlier."

He was slowly untying the towel around her foot now, and studied her face through thick, dark lashes. "I was *working*. I closed up the bar last night. Tonight. Whatever."

Of course. She forgot he worked at the Shamrock, too. And she'd disrupted what little time for sleep he'd had. There was something about having Luke Rutledge on one knee, cradling her foot in his hand, that fried her brain. It was agitating, but in the sweetest, sharpest way. Her confusion put even more of an edge to her voice.

"Maybe you should focus on the job my aunt gave you, instead of hedging your bets by starting a second career serving drinks."

He didn't deserve that, and she knew it. Snarking was their normal shtick, but, for the first time, she wished things were somehow different. She was always such a bitch around him, and she didn't understand why.

Luke's fingers were far more gentle on her unwrapped foot than either of their moods at the moment. He was still examining the cut when he answered.

"Maybe we should both stop talking for a few minutes. You concentrate on how you'd redecorate the place while I get this glass sliver out of your foot." He produced a pair of tweezers from somewhere, and she quickly looked away.

This wasn't the time to lecture him on his work habits or tell him he lived like a slob. The guy was a hard worker, putting in long hours at the winery and then at a second job. And he was helping her. Yes, she had suspicions about him, but her heart was starting to whisper that maybe she'd been making him a scapegoat for her own anger and guilt. An unfair target for her frustration with herself and all the male asshats at KTM who pulled the rug out from under her plans and dreams.

Being in Luke's home made her see him more fully as a person. Something in her softened, just a little. Something else whispered that she still needed to be careful.

CHAPTER ELEVEN

WHITNEY FLINCHED AND let out a hiss when Luke plucked the sliver from the ball of her foot. She let out a lot more than that when he wiped that spot and the half-inch cut on the side of her foot with an alcohol pad.

"Ow! Shit! What the hell are you doing?" She jerked her foot out of his hand, but he calmly took hold of her heel again, reaching for the gauze pads.

"What I'm doing is dressing the injury you gave yourself while breaking and entering."

Luke had *not* been happy when the chime of the security camera went off a few short hours after he'd fallen asleep. He'd grabbed his phone and had to rub the crust of sleep from his eyes to focus on the image. Their so-called security system was a smattering of digital surveillance cameras that sent alerts to his phone when triggered. It wasn't high-end by any means, but it was what he could afford out of his own funds.

Whitney sounded miffed. "It's not breaking and entering if you use a key."

Luke grunted in response. When he'd seen the dark-haired figure unlocking the front door, he couldn't believe it. She'd walked in and flipped on the lights, and sure enough, it was Whitney. She was dressed in a simple tank top and shorts. Wide awake at that point, he'd sat up and watched in fascination as she emptied the entire wall of bottles, then restocked them. At first he thought she might be having some sort of sleepwalking episode. Then he'd realized what she was doing— arranging by *color*. No one did that. Wine should be arranged by vintage or variety. White wines together. Reds together. That's how everyone did it. But damn if the wall didn't look pretty decent when she was done.

Of course, she hadn't been satisfied with it. Big surprise. He'd learned the woman was rarely satisfied. She'd stared hard at the shelves, hands on her hips, scowling. Then she attacked it again, creating angled lines of color. The angles made it look like the wall was in motion. She was almost finished when a bottle toppled from the highest shelf, barely missing her head and exploding on that tile floor Tony had loved so much.

"You do that a lot," Whitney said.

He finished taping the gauze and made the mistake of looking up. Kneeling at her feet left him on eye level with her breasts. He stilled, her foot in his hand. It was all he could do to resist running his hand up her long, shapely calf. Damn, he was losing it. He'd been too long without a woman. He needed to fix that and get this urge out of his system.

"Do…what?"

She studied the bandaging job and found nothing to complain about with her neatly wrapped foot. He wondered if she was disappointed.

"You do that grunting thing when you don't want to say what you really think. Or when you don't think a question deserves an answer." An edge of playful challenge hit her voice as he stood. "Or maybe it's the best you got."

Luke stared down at her, forcing himself not to grunt

in response. He wasn't used to people psychoanalyzing him—with the possible exception of Father Joe—and he sure wasn't used to someone cutting so close to the truth. He glanced down at her foot and back up again.

"You're welcome."

Her mouth opened, but no sound came out. One corner of it slid up, and she nodded.

"Thank you." She lifted her leg and examined the bandage again. "Such a nice, neat job." Her gaze swept around the apartment.

He got her point. The place was messy. At least, it *looked* messy. But he knew where everything was—most of the time—and he was the only person who ever saw the place. He'd never been comfortable bringing a woman back to the winery. It would be too weird. On the rare occasions he hooked up with someone, they went to *her* place. Hotel room. Rental cottage. Maybe even a boat.

He preferred tourists to locals. Something always went sideways with local women. Their friends or families would eventually have something to say, whispering warnings that he was "a Rutledge." He'd get mad. The woman would get upset, and that was that. Not once had a woman ever stood shoulder to shoulder with him against the gossip. They always caved.

This apartment served a limited but functional purpose, and it worked fine for him just the way it was. He'd grown up in worse, sharing a single-wide with three siblings. But having Whitney here gave him a sudden urge to straighten up the place. It was annoying.

"Yeah, yeah," he said, turning away. "It's a man cave. I get it. But it's *my* man cave, and I like it. Did you want coffee?"

A soft sigh moved across her lips and hit him hard right in the chest. "I'd *kill* for a cup of strong black coffee."

"You got it." He filled the basket with ten scoops of grounds and filled the water reservoir with eight cups of water. That should make it strong enough for her. He still had his back to her when she started asking questions. There was no accusation to her voice, just curiosity.

"How did you know I was downstairs? Oh…you said there are motion sensors."

He nodded, reaching for a couple small plates and a box of day-old raspberry Danish. "The floor is pretty well insulated, so I doubt I would have heard you. That's why we have a security system and cameras down there. I got the alert when you opened the front door and started your redecorating project."

That set her back a bit. "Wait, you were *watching* me?"

He grunted in answer, cutting and plating two slices of the Danish. Her fingers tapped idly on the table.

"You could have at least come down to help instead of sitting up here like some stalker."

He handed her a plate. "I figured if you wanted help, you wouldn't have snuck into the place alone at five o'clock in the morning."

She took a bite of the Danish, and Luke forced himself to look away as she moaned in delight. She was killing him. Having her sitting here in his kitchen and carrying on a civil, almost lighthearted, conversation was too surreal.

"Oh, this is good!" She took a second bite and gave him a soft smile. *Killing him…* "I'm sorry for waking you. I didn't know about the security system. I'm surprised the service didn't send the cops."

Luke filled two mugs with coffee, setting one on the table next to Whitney. "*I'm* the service. It's designed to be a residential security system, and it sends an alert and the camera feed to my phone. Low budget but effective. What got you up and out of bed so early anyway?"

She downed half her mug of coffee while he was still adding sugar to his. "Helen's worried about the winery and this festival coming up. After looking at the mess the books are in, I'm worried, too. I've taken some marketing classes, and I started writing ideas down. I was too excited to sleep, so…here I am." She looked down at her foot and grimaced. "It *would* have been a nice surprise for Helen if I hadn't dropped that damn bottle and wrecked the place."

He sat across from her with his coffee. "You didn't wreck anything other than a bottle and your foot. And my sleep, of course."

She winced. "Sorry."

"It's okay." He took a bite of his Danish, doing his best to sound unconcerned. "Sleep is overrated."

"Why *do* you work two jobs?"

"Two? Try three, or maybe four, depending on the week." He saw the question in her eyes and explained himself. For once, he didn't feel like he *had* to. He *wanted* to. "I mow the lawn at the Catholic church during the warm weather, and shovel the sidewalks in the winter. And I pick up the occasional odd job around town."

Whitney looked out at the vineyard, her forehead furrowed. "But…why? This place seems like it should be a full-time job."

Luke stared out at the vines. They needed rain, but there wasn't any in the forecast for the next few days. He needed to get up to the pinot gris block at the top of the hill and trim the roots and shoots. Today he'd be in the tasting room most of the day, but maybe tomorrow.

"Is it some big dark secret?"

He met her gaze in surprise. "What?"

"The *jobs*." She waved her hand in the hair. "Why do you have them?"

He gave her a pointed look. "You've been working on the books. You tell me."

Her mouth thinned. "You're saying you're not getting paid?"

"Not with any consistency. After what you said about Helen thinking I'm not paying rent, it makes more sense. Helen probably thinks this apartment is acting as my salary, but I can't pay my bills with it. And I *have* been depositing rent into her account."

Whitney shifted in her chair. She pushed her hair behind her ear, then did it again when a strand fell free. She crossed her long, lean legs. Those short shorts didn't leave much to the imagination. Neither did the little top she was wearing, with those tiny strings holding it up. This woman had to be bad for his heart. *Had* to be. She frowned, but it wasn't her usual angry frown. When she spoke, she sounded worried. Apologetic.

"I'm still digging my way through all the bank records. It's a mess. I'm still missing stuff, but it's hard to know exactly *what*. I'd like to see you get paid for the work you do, Luke. That's only right. But…I still don't know if Helen can afford it or not."

Something gray and hollow settled in Luke's stomach. "It's really that bad?"

Her voice sharpened. "I just said I don't know." She blew out a long breath, tracing her finger around the rim of the coffee mug. "It doesn't look good. Is this wine festival as make-or-break as Helen makes it sound?"

Luke ran his hand through his hair, rubbing the back of his neck absently. It was weird having a beautiful woman—*any* woman—sitting at this table, much less discussing the winery with him over coffee and Danish. He hadn't talked about the business with anyone, with the possible exception of Steve Jenkins, in an effort to keep the gossipmongers away. There were enough rumors floating around out there as it was, although Helen had helped dispel a few of them by showing up at the quarterly owners' meeting in May. Some of the owners had fed into a whisper campaign, suggesting she was selling the place, or perhaps even letting it slide into bankruptcy. Luke couldn't let either happen.

"It's the biggest event of the year in this area, and it kicks off the biggest season. Fall is harvest time, and that's when the tourists want to come to the wineries. Add in the pretty fall views around the Finger Lakes, and it gets crazy busy. All the wineries depend on a good fall season for survival, and we've missed *two*." He stared into his coffee cup, almost forgetting Whitney was there. "If we miss another, our reputation will be toast. We've gathered a few awards this year, but we haven't marketed that news the way we should have. We're not sold in many restaurants anymore, or even liquor stores. The world is going to forget we exist if we don't make a big statement at the festival and after."

"What needs to happen to make that statement?"

He didn't completely trust her, but then again, no one else was showing an interest, and his back was against the wall. His imagination briefly took a trip to imagine *Whitney's* back against the wall, legs around his hips… Uh, no. Bad idea. He managed to push the enticing image aside.

He looked around the admittedly cluttered apartment. "Marketing, for one thing. And commercial sales. I'm not good at the fluffy stuff. And I don't have any time to learn it."

He'd laid his weaknesses on the table in front of a woman who generally pounced on them, but instead, she went silent. Her brows furrowed, and she took a sip of her coffee. Finally, she looked at him and gave a sharp nod, as if in agreement to some question he hadn't asked.

"I'm not artistic—that's using the wrong side of the brain for me—but I understand marketing theory and what appeals to consumers. I was never in sales, but I can negotiate a deal. Okay, let's do this."

Luke stared at her in confusion. "Do what?"

"The *festival*! Let's go big. We'll get some new marketing materials. Do a float for the parade. We'll let everyone know that Falls Legend Winery is back in business."

Luke sat back in his chair. "Who's this 'we' you keep talking about?"

"*Us!* You and me. And Helen, of course." There was a sparkle in Whitney's eyes he hadn't seen before now. She was excited, and…happy? It was a damn good look on her. She lifted her chin. "You're in charge of making the wine. I'll project manage. We can do this!"

He shook his head. "We can do *what* exactly?"

Her brows knit together. "Come on, Luke—we can bring this place back, maybe make it better than ever!

We need to make a splash…" Her eyes lit up with laughter. "Ha! Splash…wine…get it?"

"I'm sorry, but…" Maybe it was his lack of sleep making him fuzzy. He splayed his hands. "I don't get *any* of it."

She leaned forward. "Luke, do you think we have a chance of winning anything in the wine competition?"

"Of course. The chard is nearly perfect, and the pinot has already won a few awards."

"Okay, let's be ready to capitalize on that." She looked out to the vineyard. "This place has a wonderful story—Tony and Helen's story. And stories *sell*. We need to tell people why this place exists, and make them want to be part of it. We have a website, right?"

He winced. Tony used to take care of that. "Yeah, but…it's not great."

"No problem. I can update it. And we should create some marketing pieces to hand out at the festival. Maybe little booklets telling the story of Falls Legend Winery." Her enthusiasm was contagious. Maybe they *could* use the festival to turn things around. If they worked together. He and Whitney. He gulped.

"Tony kept journals about the winery from the very start. They're in his office up in the barn. There could be something interesting you could…"

"Oh, Luke!" She reached out and took his hand, sending a sizzle of heat straight to his chest. "That would be great. I could put pictures of the old journal pages on the website." She chewed her lip. "I know I said you just had to make the wine, but…the place is looking…"

He nodded, feeling even more tired than he did before. "I know. It needs work. My plan is to have everything done before the festival, but…"

"I'll help." He looked up in surprise.

"You'll…help…"

She scrunched her face. "Well…maybe not with the repairs, but I'll do as much of the other stuff as I can. I'll learn about the wines, help in the tasting room, make plans for the festival."

It was tempting. But this could be one of those "slippery slopes" people always talked about. One wrong step would send him sliding downhill toward a fate he couldn't see waiting for him. And Whitney was tied into that fate somehow.

"Will you still be around next month?" It was a fair question. He didn't need Little Miss City Girl messing around with Helen's hopes, or the winery's future, and then vanishing the minute she got bored. But he also didn't want to see the light in Whitney's eyes dim the way it did just now.

"Why wouldn't I be here?" She pushed her coffee cup aside.

He needed to keep things real. For Helen's sake. It had nothing to do with him, or how he felt having coffee with Whitney in his kitchen early on a summer morning.

"Won't your bosses want you back in your fancy Chicago office to count more beans pretty soon?"

Her face paled, and she pressed her lips together again. It was a tell—she did that when she was struggling with what to say. Her voice went flat.

"There's no job to go back to." She glanced at the clock on the microwave as if she hadn't just dropped a bombshell. And he let her do it, getting the strong sense she did *not* want to discuss it. "I should get up to the house before Helen comes down for breakfast. Thanks for the coffee, and the first aid." She stood, wincing as she looked down at her bandaged foot. "I'll talk to Helen and put a task list together. Once we have that, we can break down assignments by individual and set some due dates."

Back in charge again. Rather than ask about Chicago, he slid into their usual poking and prodding mode. They kept each other sharp that way.

"Due dates, huh? Where am I going to fit *your* due dates in with what I'm already doing?"

She swept her eyes around the apartment. "The same way I'll fit them in around doing my audit of Helen's books. It's called compartmentalization and multitasking. We're all going to have to get good at it if this plan is going to work."

Compartmentalization and multitasking?

He watched her descend the stairs to the tasting room, with those shorts hugging her swaying hips. As if he wasn't already juggling enough tasks? As if he wasn't already stuffing his attraction to dark-haired, serpent-tongued Whitney Foster into a very tight *compartment* in his head? And now she wanted them to work as some kind of *team*?

Luke wasn't sure he had a compartment strong enough to hold his thoughts about that idea.

"OKAY. LET ME SEE if I've got this now." Whitney set the bottle down after pouring a small amount of dark wine into her glass. "The three-year-old pinot has notes of dark berries, caramel and fresh earth. And saying wine tastes like dirt is a *compliment*." She carefully swirled the wine around her glass, without sending it flying over the edge like she had earlier in the day. She raised the glass to her nose and took a sniff. She tried not to do it like a beagle hot on a rabbit's trail, which Helen had accused her of earlier. It was more of a *gentle* sniff, but she still drew enough of the aroma in to form an opinion.

It smelled like red wine.

She was getting better at telling the difference between the varieties, but between the vintages of the same variety? All the pinots smelled the same to her.

Helen laughed. "You've stuck your nose in too many wine glasses today. No wonder you're confused. You can't become a wine expert in six hours, Whitney."

"But I need to know enough to *sound* like an expert if I'm going to be able to sell Falls Legend wines to stores and restaurants, and..." Whitney took another sip. She held up her finger to put that thought on hold. One more sip, holding it in her mouth as Helen had suggested, then swallowing. "Wait! I taste dirt! I mean, I taste *earth*! Like fresh earth—the scent of earth after a summer rain. And...there's the hint of caramel at the end. What do you call it? The finish? It finishes like melted caramel. Oh, Helen, I taste it now!" One more sip. Or more of a gulp. "That's amazing! No wonder this vintage won a medal this year."

Helen poured herself a small amount of the wine and tasted it. "We're entering it in the Blessing of the Grapes competition, along with the Legacy blend and the unoaked chardonnay you like. That's the one that has the buttery finish. Luke did a great job with it."

That brought up a question that had been bugging Whitney. "Was it Luke's idea to buy the steel tanks and do the 'unoaked' thing?"

Helen nodded. "Yes, but it didn't take much to convince Tony to go for it."

"Wasn't it expensive?"

Helen's eyes narrowed on Whitney, as if she knew where she was going with this. "Sure. But so are French oak barrels. Those have to be replaced every few years, you know." Helen leaned back in her seat. "French oak is becoming harder to find, and white oak just doesn't have the same tannins. The tanks last forever, and make great wine. Like the chardonnay."

It gave Whitney an odd sense of relief to cross off the steel tanks as a possible reason to suspect Luke of taking advantage of Tony and Helen. All she had to do now was figure out the gaps in the bookkeeping records, and hopefully clear his name in her mind for good. For some reason, that was becoming important to her.

She turned the bottle in front of her to check the vintage. The winery labels all carried a variation of the bold Russo family crest, with its bright red lion and suit of armor. The background color of the label varied by wine variety, but the logo had been the same for decades.

"Aunt Helen, have you ever considered updating the labels and branding for the winery?"

Helen hesitated, her glass at her lips, before she took a sip and carefully set it back on the counter. "As a matter of fact, we did. Tony talked to my friend Lena about a new logo, but then he…well…"

An idea was taking shape, but only if Helen was open to it. Whitney waited, knowing her aunt was sifting through her emotions.

"What was the new logo like?" she asked gently.

"I don't really know." Helen stared straight ahead at the wall. "I'm not even sure Lena created one. I know she and Tony had a couple meetings, but then he passed and…" Helen's shoulders rose and fell with her deep sigh. "I never thought about it again."

Whitney hated causing her aunt more pain, but Helen wanted Falls Legend Winery to make a big, bold statement at the festival.

"Helen, if you want to get people talking about the winery this fall, what better way than to rebrand the business?" She hesitated when Helen's brows gathered together. "It would *still* be honoring Tony. We'd be finishing a job he started." Helen nodded, still unconvinced. Whitney leaned forward. "We'll create press releases about the 'new' Falls Legend Winery." She warmed up to the idea as she thought out loud. "Maybe unveil a new logo at the festival, so everyone would want to come to our booth to see it."

Helen swirled the remaining wine in her glass, staring into it as if she could see the future there. Or perhaps it was the past she was looking for. Was Tony speaking to her from inside that glass? About the time Whitney thought her aunt wasn't going to respond at all, Helen slowly nodded, her lips pursed. She gave Whitney a slow smile.

"I didn't care what our image was after Tony was gone. I was determined not to change a single thing, because I saw Tony in all of it." She reached out to take Whitney's hand, her eyes brightening. "Maybe we *should* shake things up a bit."

"That's what I was thinking, Helen. We'll give Rendezvous Falls something they'll never expect!"

It was only fair, since the town had already delivered a few surprises to Whitney. Including a scruffy-but-sexy winemaker who wouldn't leave her dreams at night.

CHAPTER TWELVE

HELEN CALLED A special meeting of the book club as soon as Whitney and Lena were ready to reveal the new Falls Legend logo. Rick and Jayla were the last to arrive, and Jayla rushed to apologize.

"I'm *so* sorry! My husband called from our condo in Boca Raton." She blinked. "I mean, my *ex*-husband called from *his* condo in Boca. 'Jayla, how do I set the thermostat?' 'Jayla, where should I order dinner from?'" She sat down with a heavy sigh, showing more emotion than Helen had seen from the normally reserved doctor. "Honestly, it's like the man has never been there before, and we've owned the place for ten years! It was extremely satisfying to tell him he'd have to figure it out for himself." Jayla noticed Whitney sitting at the table. "Oh, hi—I didn't know we had a guest. I'm sorry for just barging in here and venting."

Cecile laughed. "That's the most words I've ever heard you say in one sitting, Jayla! I'm impressed!"

"That's nothing," Rick said. "I've been listening to this tirade all the way here. She hasn't stopped for a breath since she got into my car." He leaned in with a conspiratorial wink. "I suspect there are some unresolved issues from the divorce."

Jayla put her hands to her cheeks and closed her eyes. "Argh! The man infuriates me. He never appreciated the way I took care of things when we were married, and now he thinks I'm going to *keep* doing it? He has another thing coming if—"

"Jayla and Rick, this is my niece, Whitney. She's already met everyone else." Helen attempted to bring the gathering back on track. "She and Lena have been working on some marketing designs this week and would like our feedback."

Jayla gathered herself together and extended a hand to Whitney with a warm smile. "Pay no attention to me tonight. I'm Dr. Jayla Maloof, and it's wonderful to finally meet you. Helen has told us so much about you."

Whitney gave a short laugh. "So I gathered, since you're all determined to help my love life along."

Helen shifted in her chair. She knew Whitney wasn't thrilled with the whole matchmaking deal, but she was being a good sport about it. "The reason Whitney's here tonight is because she thought our marketing image needed an update. Tony had the same idea before he…" Helen wondered if she'd ever be able to speak of his loss without it hitting her heart like a sledgehammer. "Tony and Lena were working up some designs a couple years ago, so here we are for the unveiling of a new Falls Legend Winery logo. They'd like our thoughts on a few details."

Lena walked to the easel near the window. Her arms, as always, jangled with gold and silver bracelets. She wore a flowing caftan of soft yellow, which glowed against her dark skin. Lena put her hand on the white cloth draping the easel.

"I'm more into tactile arts like pottery than graphic design. But I was honored when Tony asked for my help with a new logo. He already had the concept. I just put it on paper. It was nearly done—" she glanced at Helen "—when he left us. He loved the initial sketches. Whitney suggested doing the logo in brush and ink to make it more contemporary, and I agreed. So...what do you think?"

She pulled the cloth away with a magician's flourish, and everyone let out a little gasp. Cecile started to applaud. Helen had already seen it, of course, but she studied it afresh. It was Rendezvous Falls—the waterfall, not the town. A solid swoosh of water came over the edge of the cliff, with tall trees on the far side of the pond. On the near side were the outlines of two deer—a large stag and a doe—standing side by side and looking at the water. The ground beneath them was drawn to look like a feather, giving a nod to the legend's Native American origin.

Vickie was the first to speak. "It's perfect, Helen. I mean, this is Falls Legend Winery, and now your logo shows the legend of the falls right there. Great job, Lena!"

"You should pick up a brush more often." Rick rocked back in his chair. "That's damn good."

Whitney looked relieved. "Thanks, everyone. Now we need your ideas on colors. We printed up some mock labels for the bottles. Which colors do you like best? Do you like the winery name over or under the logo? Don't be shy—you're the only marketing research we've got."

Whitney tossed color prints onto the table and everyone started talking at once, laughing as they argued over which was best. But Helen already knew which one would be used. Tony told Lena he wanted shades of blue to reflect the water of the falls and of Seneca Lake. When Whitney first showed her the soft blue label with a silver foil edge, Helen knew it was the one. Lena explained that the silver foil would add expense to the labels, but Helen didn't care. Tony would have loved that hint of bling on his bottles, and she'd find the money somewhere.

Fortunately, her friends agreed the blue was the prettiest. They'd use different shades for the different varieties—darker on the white wines and lighter on the dark for contrast. Cecile picked up a bottle of pinot noir and frowned.

"Are you sure you're okay with losing the Russo crest?"

Whitney replied before Helen could. "The crest will be on the back label." She handed Cecile a sample label. "See it there in the background? It's a watermark behind the printed words. We didn't want to lose Uncle Tony's love of his family legacy."

"That's right," Helen said. "We've renamed our cabernet-merlot blend 'Legacy Red' to honor Tony." That had actually been Luke's idea a few months ago, when he'd been trying to cheer her up. God bless Luke, who'd worked so hard to keep this place afloat. He'd been less than enthusiastic about the logo change, but mainly because of the extra work it would create.

"Okay." Whitney scooped up all the color prints from the table. "We have a winner. Blue it is." She glanced around the table with a sly smile. "It's nice to see you all using your powers for good instead of…well, you know."

Rick barked out a laugh. "Be patient, Whitney, we're new at this matchmaking business. I tried to tell them it was a bad idea."

Vickie arched a brow in his direction. "Maybe so,

but weren't *you* the guy who set her up with that crazy old coot Leonard Milroy? Is he still trying to convince the college to spend millions on moving the campus?"

Rick winced and nodded. "I honestly thought he was younger than that. Sorry."

Whitney waved him off. "He's a nice man. You guys may not be the greatest Cupids in town, but that's okay, since I'm not really looking for romance."

Cecile looked around the table. "Does anyone have any new prospects?"

Whitney recoiled at the word choice, but Jayla jumped in. "One of my lab techs broke up with his girlfriend last month, and I think he's starting to date again. Kyle's around your age, and he's a very pleasant man. Let me ask him if he'd like to meet someone."

Helen worried that "pleasant" was too close to the "nice man" description her niece had used for Leonard, but Whitney gave Jayla a game smile.

"I'd be happy to meet him. I need a break from staring at spreadsheets, and coffee with a pleasant man sounds nice." She met Helen's gaze and gave her a wink. It was clear Whitney was doing this only for her. Whitney wagged a finger at the book club members in warning. "But don't get your hopes up, guys. I'm not in the market for a soul mate."

LUKE STOOD AND STRETCHED, groaning a little as he did, soaking up the warmth of the sun on his back. This wasn't easy work, checking for new roots from the grafted vines that were always trying to connect with the earth rather than rely on their host roots. Then again, none of the work here was easy. He and Steve had worked on trimming the canopy leaves for the past two days to bring more sun to the cab franc berries. At the same time, they'd cut away any smaller berry clusters that might pull too much energy from the more productive vines.

A movement caught his eye. Whitney was walking in his direction. He sighed. She'd been a royal pain in his ass this week. Helen had taught her just enough about wine to make her hungry for *more* knowledge. Knowledge he didn't have time to impart. She and Helen had shown the new logo to him a few days ago. What did he know about color and font? The deer were pretty.

He'd said as much, thinking it was a compliment. But Whitney had rolled her eyes in disgust. Were those deer going to sell more wine? Probably not. But if they made Helen happy, then he was happy. End of story. With Whitney, though, there was *never* an end of story. She was tenacious. To her credit, though, she was working hard to try to help her aunt. Two days ago she'd rearranged the utility closet in the tasting room. The day before, she'd raked the lawn that stretched down to the road. She might be a pain, but he wasn't so proud that he'd turn down an extra set of hands around here. And hey—she was easy on the eyes.

As she got closer, he could see she'd been doing more manual labor today. Her hair was pulled into a low ponytail, and she was dressed in denim shorts and a dark red Falls Legend T-shirt knotted on the side, showing off a narrow expanse of skin at her midriff. She had on sturdy work shoes and carried leather work gloves in one hand and two bottles of water in the other. She tossed a bottle of water his way.

"Helen thought you could use something to drink."

"Helen was right. Thanks." He drained half the bottle in one swig and wiped his mouth with a satisfied sigh.

"What are you doing up here?" Here came the twenty questions. He'd never met someone so eager to absorb information.

"Are you always this curious about everything?"

Her eyes went wide, and she thought about it. "Well, yeah. I like to know things. That's what makes me good at my job. I decipher fact from fiction." She smiled. "Besides, we're a team now, remember? Helen said so."

Right. *Compartmentalization and multitasking.* He needed to compartmentalize his physical attraction to her and focus on the task at hand.

"I'm trimming vines." He saw a random woody root growth stretching for the ground and bent over to snip it off with the small razor-sharp pruner from his pocket.

"Those look more like roots. Aren't roots good?"

Answering one question with this woman always led to another question. "Remember how I told you the vines are European varietals grafted onto native roots?"

Whitney took a drink of water and wiped her forehead, then scratched her arm absently. "The European grapes are the vinifera ones, right? They get some disease from American soil that kills them, so the vineyards started grafting them onto roots of native grape vines, and it worked. The roots act as host plants for the grapes."

He was impressed, but he did his best not to show it. She had enough ego as it was. "Exactly. The problem is, those vinifera vines *want* to take root here. If they connect, it could kill the vine. So I cut them off before they can."

Whitney was scratching at some red lines on her

stomach, then reached around to scratch her back. "Seems like you spend more time cutting things off the vines than growing them."

"Yup. Vineyard management is basically deciding what to cut and what to save. This is where wine is really made—right here on the vine. Every decision can make or ruin a vintage." He lifted a bunch of grapes gently and checked for any signs of problems. "This feels like a battlefield sometimes. The vines want to kill themselves. The wine wants to be vinegar. It's my job to keep everything going in the right direction."

She was scratching her forearm again, but she didn't seem to notice, looking around at the vines. "That's quite a speech for you, Luke. I'm not used to you speaking in multiple sentences."

He ignored the barb, not wanting to examine why he opened up to her more than anyone else. She was leaving red marks on her skin from her fingernails digging in. "What have you been doing?"

"Helen wanted to clean things up around the carriage house, so I tackled that mess along the driveway side. There were vines crawling up the trees." She reached up to scratch her neck, but Luke grabbed her hand.

"Did you pull those vines down? Dressed like that?"

Her eyes narrowed. "Is there a particular dress code for doing yard work?"

Luke took off, tugging her behind him toward the wine barn. "There is if the yard work involves poison ivy vines."

Cleaning those vines out—carefully—was one of those things that kept sliding down his to-do list. It's not like customers walked near that side. It never occurred to him Little Miss Tasky here would wade in with all that skin exposed and start pulling on freaking *poison ivy*.

He was practically dragging her down the hill now, ignoring her protests. Time was of the essence. And he felt responsible.

"How long ago did you handle the vines?"

"A couple hours maybe?" She was jogging to keep up with him. "I trimmed the bushes and raked after that. God, am I going to die or something?"

He pulled her inside the barn, to the hose that was coiled on the wall for cleaning the tanks. A large drain grate was in the floor a few feet away.

"You won't die, but you might want to if your skin is covered with oozing blisters of pus." He grabbed the hose. Whitney's eyes went wide and her mouth dropped open. He had her attention now. He turned on the hose, set to lukewarm. "You need to wash the oil off your skin, Whitney, and the faster the better. I know what I'm doing. Let me help you, okay?"

"Okay, *fine*."

She let out a yelp when the water hit her, though. He grabbed her hand, knowing the water would be cool at first. It was a little like washing Molly, holding on and aiming the hose at her like a firefighter on a mission.

"Holy... Does it have to be freaking ice-cold?"

"It'll warm up. Close your eyes." She surprised him by complying right before he sprayed her in the face. Having her eyes closed didn't do anything to improve her temper. The curses she hurled his way were impressive. He slapped a bar of soap in her hand and released her.

"Lather up." She stared at the soap blankly, blinking away the water. He'd turned the hose to the side, leaving it running to warm it up. "Tick tock, Whit. You only have a small window of time to get that oil off your skin."

That got her moving. She started scrubbing every inch. She skipped over her wet shirt, and he shook his head. "Soap it all up. The oil could be on your clothes, too. I should probably make you strip..."

She sudsed up her shirt and shorts furiously, kicking her work boots toward the door as her eyes slammed into his. She let out a sharp, angry snort.

"Yeah, I bet you'd love that, wouldn't you?" She glared at him through strands of dark, wet hair.

He didn't trust himself to answer that question. "You ready for a rinse? The water should be warm by now."

Whitney straightened, stoic and silent, closing her eyes and holding her arms straight out. He started at her head and worked down, hoping for her sake the oils from the poison ivy were washing away with the soapy water that swirled around the drain. She turned without being asked, and he continued with the hose until he'd drenched every shapely inch of her. Nope. Not gonna think about her gentle curves and all that glistening wet skin. Not gonna do it. This was strictly a humanitarian mission. He turned off the water and grabbed a roll of paper towels from the shelf. After yanking four or five feet of it for himself, he handed the roll to Whitney.

"It's the closest thing to towels I have out here. Don't rub—just pat yourself dry." He started drying her upper arms while she tore off a length of paper towels and patted her chest. *Really not helping.* "You should go to the house and take a real shower. Throw those clothes in the wash." He inspected her forearm. "Looks like you have some scratches there that could turn into a rash.

Helen probably has some calamine lotion to control the itch. Don't you know what poison ivy looks like?"

"Uh, no. My tenth-floor apartment didn't have any ivy issues of *any* kind, so excuse me if my horticulture skills are lacking."

The comment was an unwelcome, but healthy, reminder that any attraction to Whitney was wasted. She was way out of his league, with her fancy former job and tenth-floor apartment. She stopped patting her stomach and looked to where her arm rested in his hand. Her gaze rose to meet his, and he realized how close they were standing. So close he could see the gold flecks in her brown eyes. So close he could see those eyes go dark and wide. Her lips parted, the tip of her tongue tracing her top lip.

His voice was raspy in his own ears. "You should... um...dry off...and..."

Too close. They were much too close. But he was caught up in her gravity field now, and couldn't step away. He took the wadded-up towels in his hand and touched them to her waist, allowing his fingers to trace across her skin.

Stupid move. Really stupid move.

He did it again.

He wasn't sure how, but now they were standing even closer than before. Her eyes dilated to pure black, and her pulse fluttered at the base of her neck, where her skin was soft and white. Her voice turned soft and breathy.

"I thought you were supposed to pat it dry."

He blinked, his fingers moving on her skin again, as if he had no control of them.

"What?"

Her mouth slanted into a grin. "Aren't you supposed to be *patting* me dry?"

"Oh…yeah…" And damn if his hand didn't trace another circle on her waist. Her lips parted.

His hand slid around her back and flattened against her warm, wet skin. He tugged her against him, and she didn't resist. Her eyes fell to his lips, telling him they were both on the same page. It was a very *bad* page, filled with very *bad* ideas. But he had no more control over what happened next than he did over the spinning of the planets. His head dropped, her face turned up to meet him and their lips touched. She made a soft, contented sound from deep in her throat, like she was purring. And Luke lost his mind and kissed her.

He'd kissed plenty of women. It was the traditional preamble to more…vigorous…activities. Kissing was alright in general, but it had never been Luke's end goal. It had never stopped him in his tracks and made him think he might want to slow down and spend an hour or two just kissing somebody. Until now. Until Whitney.

A jolt of electricity shot from his scalp to his toes the moment his lips brushed against hers. Soft. Sweet. Warm. He brushed them again, almost afraid to do more. Whitney took the decision out of his hands, standing up on her toes to press the length of her body against his, pressing her lips firmly on his. He was still trying to understand what was happening when her tongue ran across his mouth.

Sweet holy gift of God…

His arms wrapped tight around her, and he growled when her fingers slid through his hair. Determined not to cede complete control, he pushed past her tongue to enter her mouth first. She made a little noise of surrender, and his world went white-hot when their tongues touched. How the hell could a *kiss* make him feel like this? She finally fought past him to return the pleasure, and the feel of her tongue inside him was nothing short of intoxicating. His fingers tightened on her, and…

A truck door slammed right outside the barn. He tried to set her away from him, but Whitney was oblivious, murmuring a soft "don't…" when he lifted his head.

"Someone's here." He slid his mouth along her jaw, as reluctant as she was to stop. He repeated the words near her ear, as much for himself as for her. "Someone's here."

Whitney jumped back once the words sank in, covering her mouth with her hands and looking around. Luke found it a little easier to breathe with some space between them. But he wanted to pull her back. To hell with breathing. To hell with whoever was out there.

"Who? Where?"

"Outside. Probably Steve Jenkins. He said he might stop today. He'll probably head to the vineyard first." Luke scrubbed his hands down his face. Blood was starting to flow to the places where it belonged. That was a close call. Too close. He never should have kissed her, and he never would have stopped if they hadn't been interrupted. Her eyes reflected the same realization. She blew out a long breath and moved farther away. He was both relieved and filled with regret at the move. Damn, his brain was twisted—none of this made any sense.

"Okay. Okay." Her voice was brisk, as she started patting herself down with the towels again. She carefully avoided looking his way. "I don't know what that was, but it is *not* going to happen again." Was she talking to him or herself?

He nodded. "Agreed." She was right, of course. That couldn't happen again. But acknowledging that left a sharp jab of regret in his chest. He swallowed hard. "Go out the side door and down to the house. I'll go catch Steve. No one will be the wiser."

She gave a jerking nod of her head and turned for the door. He still hadn't seen her eyes. He needed to know she was okay. He called out her name as she grabbed the doorknob, then waited until she looked reluctantly over her shoulder. Her eyes were clouded. Troubled. Uncertain. He couldn't let her leave like that. He gave her a sly smile.

"Just because it can't happen again doesn't mean I regret it. That was one hell of a kiss."

Her face softened from its panicked state. The corner of her mouth lifted.

"It really was, wasn't it?"

And she was gone.

CHAPTER THIRTEEN

A FEW DAYS LATER, a small patch of tiny blisters on her forearm was the only visible result of Whitney's poison ivy adventure. The chalky pink calamine lotion kept the itching under control. If only there was a magic lotion she could apply to her lips to erase the memory of kissing Luke Rutledge.

She'd kissed him. He'd kissed her. They'd kissed. Her and Luke. Kissed.

How the hell had that happened? And *now* what?

She glared at her reflection in the bathroom mirror as she jammed her hairbrush through her hair Friday morning. Now *nothing*. That could not happen again. Not ever. Even if Luke had accurately declared it "one hell of a kiss."

The kiss was…amazing. Delicious. Shocking. Indulgent. Riveting. Intoxicating. She'd thought about it nearly nonstop since Wednesday, but she still couldn't pinpoint how it happened. One minute she'd been somewhere between angry and frantic. Angry that he'd dragged her down the hill and doused her with cold hose water. Frantic because she knew he was right about the poison ivy—she'd have ended up with a rash head to toe if he hadn't acted. And then, somehow—they were kissing.

She yanked a white cotton top over her head. Was

it the warm water that had mellowed her into letting her guard down? Or maybe the fact that they'd gotten way too close to each other without realizing it? When she'd looked up to see his coffee-colored eyes looking down at her, with his fingers brushing her stomach… was that the moment? She'd probably had the same surprised expression on her face that he did. But the surprise hadn't stopped them from moving even closer. It hadn't stopped Luke from lowering his head and briefly touching his lips to hers. It hadn't stopped her from going on her toes to meet him.

Who'd have guessed Luke Rutledge could kiss like that? She shoved her feet into a pair of sneakers. Sure, the guy was built like sex-on-a-stick for any woman who might be interested, but Whitney was *not* interested, not even for a one-night stand. And if his kiss was any indication, a one-night stand would never be enough.

Giving in to her attraction to the man was not only unprofessional, it was pointless. It's not like she was staying in Rendezvous Falls. And there were still unanswered questions in the paperwork piled on the dining room table. To be honest, she was having a hard time suspecting Luke anymore, though. He might be a grumpus, but he clearly cared deeply about Helen and worked hard to run this place single-handedly. She stomped her way down the stairs. See? This was why you didn't get personally involved with someone during an audit. It was clouding her judgment. She needed to stay away from…

"Good morning, Whitney! Look who decided to join us for breakfast."

And there sat the man she'd just vowed to avoid. His eyes raked over her as he raised his coffee to his mouth.

That mouth that had kissed her so well. A wave of heat crawled up her neck.

"Good morning, Whitney." His voice was morning rough, and it moved across her skin like flames. Oh, damn, she was in trouble. Best to make it clear that nothing had changed between them.

"Good morning." She gave Luke a narrow look. "Shouldn't you be working on getting that siding repaired instead of lounging around eating free food?"

Helen started to protest, but Luke's sharp bark of laughter cut her off. He made a point to slather strawberry jam on another slice of toast.

"So that's how it's gonna be, huh? I was actually thinking about finishing the job you started a few days ago, clearing all those weeds. Unless you want to do it?" He bit into the toast with way too much humor in his eyes.

"Luke!" Helen scolded. "You know those weeds are full of poison ivy and poison oak. She got an awful rash working in there Wednesday. You should spray that stuff with weed killer after breakfast."

"Oh, I'm sorry. You got a rash?" One brow arched high, his voice oh-so-innocent. "You have to be careful with poison ivy, you know. Did you wash it right away?" Fake concern dripped from his words. "I'm sorry I missed it. Must have been when Steve stopped by. That guy is always interrupting something."

Helen looked back and forth between them, confused. "Steve Jenkins? What are you talking about— interrupting?"

Whitney made the mistake of locking eyes with Luke. He was thinking the same thing she was. If that Jenkins guy hadn't interrupted their kiss, who knew how far they would have gone? And what would that have been like? *No.* It was a One. Time. Thing. If he thought they had some kind of bond between them now, he was mistaken. She knew how to set him straight, turning back to Helen.

"Kyle called yesterday, Helen. We're all set for our date tonight."

Her aunt beamed. "That's wonderful! You're meeting for dinner, right?"

Whitney nodded. Luke scowled. Message delivered.

"Yes, I'm meeting him at the Psychedelic Grape at seven."

Luke cleared his throat, standing to put his dishes in the sink. "Dinner at the Grape? Hope you like greasy burgers. I thought you only did *coffee* dates?"

He had a point. That *was* her policy. But Kyle Sanders seemed like such a nice guy when he'd called—even if he did keep bringing up his ex-girlfriend—that she'd agreed to meet him for dinner. To be fair, kissing Luke may have had something to do with it. Maybe she was trying to prove to herself she was so unaffected by their kiss that she'd gladly have dinner with a stranger. She gave Luke a flippant shrug.

"I never said I *only* do coffee dates. I'm a free woman, Luke. I do what I please."

His mouth curled into a smile as he brushed past her on his way out, popping the last of the toast into his mouth.

"Yes, I'd say you do."

She barely resisted the urge to flip both middle fingers at his back.

Helen handed Whitney a mug of coffee. "Okay, what am I missing?"

"Not a thing." She filled a bowl with cereal and pulled the milk from the refrigerator. "I'm going to work on Evelyn Rosario's business statements today. I'll leave the poisonous plants to the hired help."

Helen chuckled. "I heard Bridget from the Purple Shamrock might become a client, too. And Vickie said the wine festival committee needs an auditor after the event wraps up. Pretty soon we'll have to hang a shingle for you."

Yeah, and wasn't that just a kicker? Evie's mom asked for Whitney's help with the diner's books. They were in decent shape, not a mess like Helen's, so she'd agreed to set up a system for them to track revenue and inventory more easily. Then Mrs. Rosario talked to the woman running the bar Luke worked for, but they'd been playing phone tag so far. It was only filler work while she was in Rendezvous Falls. Nothing long-term.

"No shingle necessary, Helen. It's just a few temporary accounting gigs while I'm in town."

"Would it be so bad if it *wasn't* temporary?"

Stay in Rendezvous Falls? Was that an option? Sure, she could probably pick up some small jobs. Maybe even do some higher-level consulting via the internet. Of course, that meant never being a partner in a prestigious firm like she'd dreamed of. But maybe owning her own firm would be better. If only she and Luke hadn't kissed, the decision might be easier. Staying would mean remaining in his orbit permanently. Not a good idea.

"I've already started sending résumés, Helen. My career may be toast in Chicago, but I'll find a firm that's more open to female partners. That's always been my goal, and I don't see any point in changing it now."

Helen turned to face Whitney with her arms folded. "Don't write off small-town life yet, girl. Life changes. Goals change. Who knows? Tonight might be the night that changes everything." She winked. "A good man would be a great reason to stay."

"A good man?" Whitney scoffed, trying to forget the feeling of being in Luke's arms. "A man of any kind would be the *last* thing that would make me want to stay anywhere!"

"Uh-huh. Easy to say until the right guy comes along." Helen patted her shoulder as she walked by. "You'll never know what hit you."

Whitney finished her breakfast in silence. That's how she'd felt when Luke kissed her. Like she didn't know what had hit her. No way was *he* the right guy, though. She'd have a nice greasy burger with nice-sounding Kyle tonight, and put all those kissing thoughts straight out of her head.

WHITNEY'S HANDS CLENCHED and unclenched the steering wheel as she drove up back to Helen's house that night. It was a miracle there wasn't actual smoke coming from her ears. She was officially *done* with this blind date business. No more matchmaking from that merry band of conspirators in that so-called book club. She parked the car and slammed the door shut. Mr. *Nice* Guy stood her up!

She never should have broken her rule about having a broad daylight coffee date first, but Kyle Sanders had sounded harmless on the phone. And Evie gave him her thumbs-up of approval, so Whitney agreed to meet him at the Psychedelic Grape in town. First, the place was a dive, packed with twenty-somethings dancing to techno-something. Then Kyle sent her a text twenty minutes *after* the time they were supposed to meet, saying he was still in love with his ex-girlfriend and couldn't "cheat on her memory." Perfect.

She thought the night might be saved when Doug Canfield stepped up and offered to buy her a drink. Doug looked normal enough. He even looked familiar, although she couldn't remember from where. She'd accepted his offer of a drink. What the hell—she'd put on makeup and was wearing high heels, even if it was with skinny jeans rather than a dress. Why let it go to waste?

Maybe *she* could do better at this dating business than that stupid book club. Sadly, she forgot how lousy Foster women were at picking men. It didn't take long for her to realize Doug was well on his way to being drunk. She didn't do drunks. She especially didn't do drunks like Doug who stood much too close and purposely brushed against her breast as he reached over to pay for the drinks. Loser.

She drank her gin and tonic as quickly as she could, nodding as he told her how close his family was with the Russos. Doug went on and on about how successful his family's local flooring store was. He definitely wanted to make it clear he was a "big man" in town.

It wasn't until she was trying to leave that she remembered why he seemed familiar. This was the same guy Evie warned her away from that first night at the Purple Shamrock. Said he was nothing but trouble. Sure enough, as soon as she said she had to go, he got pushy, pressing her to stay for one more drink, and maybe a dance, and maybe they could find somewhere else to go together. *Yeah, right.*

When she'd firmly declined and walked away, the

guy had the nerve to wrap his arm around her waist and try to pull her back to the bar. She'd shoved against his chest, hard, and called him some choice names before storming out. A perfect freaking night.

The sound of crunching gravel interrupted her mental rant. A dark red pickup truck pulled to a perpendicular stop behind her car. *Son of a...*

Doug Canfield got out of the passenger door. Some other guy was behind the wheel. Doug held his hands up as soon as he caught Whitney's furious glare.

"I *know*! This looks shitty. I'm *sorry*. I couldn't let you leave thinking that I was 'that guy.' I'm not some creep. I wanted to apologize and see if we could start over." He stopped rambling long enough to glance up at the house. "It's not like I didn't know where you lived, right? I didn't *follow* you, okay? I knew you'd end up here." His eyes went wide, as if he'd just surprised himself with his own brilliance. "And I was right! Here you are. And I didn't drive, because *you* were right, I've had a few drinks. So I'm showing responsibility, okay? I asked my buddy Frank to drive. Smart, right?"

The slight slur to his voice, combined with his nonsensical conversation and slight weaving motion, confirmed his level of inebriation. He'd probably had a few shots since she left the bar. *Perfect.* Handling a handsy drunk in a bar was one thing. She'd had plenty of practice at that in Chicago. But getting this guy and his pal—she didn't like the idea of being outnumbered—to drive away without disturbing Helen would be a challenge. If she told him to fuck off, he'd get pissed, and possibly create a scene. The fact that Whitney was perfectly justified in saying it didn't matter. She didn't want Helen upset.

"I appreciate the apology, Doug." She walked toward him, stopping a few safe feet away and giving him her most sincere look. She was skilled at using her neutral "I hear you" expression with clients and coworkers. "And I accept it. Let's chalk it up to having an off night, okay?"

He nodded for longer than was really necessary, his head bobbing up and down rapidly. Had he heard her? Did he know where he was? Was he about to face-plant in front of her? He weaved to the side and she reached out to steady him. It was a rookie mistake and she knew better. Doug's eyes lit up at her touch, and he grabbed her hand. He gave her a sly grin and put on what he probably thought was his sexiest voice. He sounded like a lecherous drunk.

"We got off to a bad start, but that doesn't mean we can't have a great finish." He tugged on her hand. "Why don't you hop in the truck and we'll go back to the bar? You never gave me that dance I asked for."

And she never would. Whitney settled her weight back so he wouldn't be able to budge her. If he let go right now she'd fall on her ass, but no way in hell was she getting anywhere near that open truck door. Frank was showing plenty of interest in what was happening, and no interest at all in stopping Doug.

Whitney felt her first shiver of apprehension. The guy's fingers were locked tightly around her wrist now. Her worry about upsetting Helen vanished. She opened her mouth and Doug jerked on her arm, causing her to stumble forward against him. She planted the heel of her hand on his chest and shoved, but he twisted her around and slammed her back against the side of the truck. *Shit.*

Her rush of fear was quickly replaced with one of

fury. How *dare* this drunken tool try to manhandle her! She stomped her heel down hard on his foot, and he grunted in pain and surprise. And then he was just... gone. There was a thud, and Doug was on the ground, with Luke Rutledge's boot against his chest.

"Let me go, Rutledge! This ain't none of your business!"

Frank was sliding across the seat of the truck, ready to scramble out and come to his friend's defense. But Luke, still holding Doug down, pointed his finger.

"Stay out of this. One more inch and I'll give you the same beatdown I'm about to give your buddy here. And you know I can do it."

Whitney never knew a person's voice could actually be hard as steel. Luke's words were clipped. Unwavering. Ground out through clenched teeth like nails from a nail gun. He was telling Frank to stay put, but she could see the slightest hint of invitation in his eye, as if daring the other man to make a move. He *wanted* to take them both on. For *her*.

She couldn't take her eyes off him, her hand resting over her chest in a vain attempt to control her heart rate. Luke was a tight bundle of rage. She was fascinated and a little frightened by the fury in the air around him. Her back still against the truck, she watched as Frank considered accepting Luke's invitation to the fight, then decided against it.

He slid back behind the wheel, not making eye contact, and whined, "Let him go, Rutledge."

Luke snorted, and for the first time, the sound meant something other than he wanted to laugh at her, or he was hiding something from her. This was a snort that told both men he wasn't about to take orders from them.

He was in charge of this show. He reached down and grabbed a fistful of Doug's shirt, yanking the man to his feet with one pull. He didn't look at Whitney, but she knew he was talking to her by the way his voice softened.

"Move away from the truck."

She willed her feet to obey, and moved well behind Doug, where Luke could easily see she was safe. His gaze quickly swept from her head to her feet and back again, and she swore she could feel the heat moving across her skin. His mouth was in a grim, straight line.

"You okay?"

Whitney wasn't sure "okay" really summed up the way adrenaline raced through her veins, but she nodded quickly. Luke still had Doug's shirt knotted in his hands, but his shoulders eased somewhat. He'd thought Doug had hurt her. And he'd come running. Maybe later she'd feel offended about some guy playing Prince Charming for her, but right now, his actions filled her with gratitude. His intense gaze made her feel a few other things, too, but she couldn't unpackage all of that while he still held the other man tightly.

She had this crazy urge to run to Luke. Touch him. Kiss him. *Crazy.* It had to be the adrenaline. That was the only explanation for the molten desire burning through her veins. She closed her eyes long enough to get some self-control back.

"Let him go, Luke. I'm fine. Although I'm guessing he's going to be limping for a while from the foot stomp I gave him." She saw the flare of admiration in Luke's eyes when he glanced down at her stiletto-heeled pumps.

A smile tugged at the corner of his mouth, but the

moment was broken when Doug Canfield decided he'd had enough.

"Yeah, Luke. Let me go. She's fine. But I think I have a broken toe, thanks to that b—"

Luke shook Doug like a dog, shutting him up in a hurry. The steel—she pictured polished blue steel impervious to damage from anything—returned to his voice.

"Watch your language around the lady, Doug. Or I'll give you a few broken teeth to match that toe. Here's what's going to happen. You're going to get in that piece of shit truck with your buddy and get off this property, never to return. *Never.* Got it?"

Doug had the audacity to look to Whitney. "What if I'm invited?"

She rolled her eyes. "You won't be."

Luke shoved Doug, sending him stumbling toward the truck. "You heard the lady."

Doug wasn't ready to let go of his pride quite yet. "And if I don't go?"

Luke's hand curled into a tight fist and he took a step toward Doug. Whitney grabbed his arm. Good lord, his *muscles* felt like hardened steel, too. He looked back at her with a mix of confusion and anger. His eyes held hers for a long moment, then he uncurled the fist.

"If you *don't* go, you have two choices. Wait for the cops to get here, or come out behind the barn with me and we'll see which one of us walks away." Luke took a quick step toward Doug, forcing the other man to flinch. Luke had several inches and thirty pounds on the guy. "And right now I'd really like to take you behind the barn, Dougie, so just say the word."

Doug huffed out a forced laugh, backing toward the

truck. "Yeah, I can picture the sheriff taking a call from a *Rutledge*. He'd laugh his ass off. Your daddy's still in prison, ain't he?" Whitney silenced her gasp of surprise. Luke didn't move a muscle. Unless you counted that dangerous one ticking along his jaw. He also didn't deny what Doug said. She stepped up to his side.

"Go home, Doug. And believe me when I say you will *not* be getting any second chances from me, so stay away from my family's vineyard." She bent over and looked into the truck cab. "That goes for you, too, Frank."

Frank raised his hands in protest. "I didn't do anything!"

"Exactly." If possible, Luke's body went even more still next to her, but Frank was clueless to her point.

"But I didn't *do* anything!"

Doug turned toward the truck. "Shut up, Frank. Let's get out of this dump." He looked over his shoulder, unable to resist trying to have the final word. "You might want to keep a tighter leash on your woman, Luke. She was trolling for men at the bar tonight. She's quite the tease—"

Before Whitney had time to blink, much less deny the accusation, Luke grabbed Doug and punched him right in the face. She'd never seen men fight before, and the sound of knuckles connecting with flesh and bone wasn't one she'd soon forget. Doug stumbled back against the truck door, his hand on his face. He started to spring back toward Luke, but Frank leaned out and grabbed the collar of his shirt.

"Get in the truck, you idiot! Everyone knows you don't piss off a Rutledge. One of them already killed your brother, man." She couldn't hold the gasp this time, and Luke's eyes cut to hers. Was his father in prison for killing Doug's brother? How did *Luke* factor into that? Why hadn't Helen ever said he was the son of a felon?

Frank tugged hard enough to half drag Doug into the truck. Doug shook him off, but got in and slammed the door shut, glaring out the open window.

"Screw you, Rutledge, and your little bitch of a girl-friend!"

The tires of the truck spun, and Luke automatically stepped in front of Whitney to protect her from the flying stones. Still in superhero mode. She was surprised how much she liked it. A movement in one of the downstairs windows of the house distracted her, but there was no one there when she looked up. Probably just the cat. Helen's room was in the back of the house, and she was usually there by now, watching her favorite TV shows from bed until she fell asleep.

Luke blew out a long breath and wiggled his hands as if trying to shake off his tension. He flinched when Whitney touched her fingers to his rigid bicep.

"Are you okay?"

He'd punched a guy. For *her*. There was something about the energy rolling off him right now that told her he wasn't happy about it. He turned his head. The movement was robotic. It was a moment before his eyes focused on her.

"I should be asking *you* that."

"You did. Back at the start of all this. I'm okay. I had it under control." She shuddered, the movement coming from out of nowhere. "Until he put me against the truck. That's when you…" She tipped her head. "How…?"

"I heard your car pull in, and then I heard a second vehicle. Doug and Frank had no reason to be here unless they were invited, and it didn't look like you'd invited them."

"Of course not!" She kicked at the stones in the driveway. "You came down to rescue me?"

He made some guttural sound. It was almost a growl, but she wasn't sure who it was aimed at. Sure, her family was unconventional, but they weren't *criminals*. How would she feel if someone blurted out that her father was in prison? She chewed on her lip. She'd feel embarrassed. Exposed. Luke had only come down here to save her. She didn't want him feeling bad about it.

"Is that bottle of whiskey still behind the tasting counter?"

Luke's dark brows bunched together. "How did you know about that?"

"Tony always kept a bottle of top-shelf stuff there to celebrate good days and wash away bad ones." She glanced up at the house. "I'm too agitated to go inside right now, and I get the feeling you're a little agitated, too. Let's go wash it all away, Luke."

He stared at her long and hard before nodding slowly. "Yeah. Agitated." He blew out his cheeks. "One drink."

"Whatever you say." She trotted to catch up with his long, tense strides. It had been a crazy night, and she was getting some crazy ideas. Ideas about Luke Rutledge and his kisses and the power of his arms around her and…well…adrenaline or not, Whitney was feeling reckless.

CHAPTER FOURTEEN

LUKE'S LEFT HAND held a shot glass, which he'd already drained twice. The fingers on his right hand curled into a fist and uncurled again. Over and over. He recognized trouble pretty quickly, and Doug and Frank were nothing but trouble. He'd headed out of the apartment the minute he saw them, making Molly stay behind. If someone was going to take a piece of those two, it was going to be him, not his dog.

They'd bullied his baby brother, Cody, and they were part of the crowd that chased his sister Jessie right out of town after she got pregnant in high school. And then, of course, there was the wreck that left Doug's brother dead, and Luke's brother Zayne badly injured. It had all started with dear old Dad. His actions had made his children targets. Made them hard. Hard enough to take on a couple of townies hassling Whitney.

Luke had been coming around the back of the truck when Doug shoved Whitney against it. Through the red haze of anger that had blurred his vision, he saw Whitney jam that spiked heel into Doug's foot. Clever girl.

Doug Canfield wasn't the type to take a hit without returning it, though, woman or not. Before Doug could even think about retaliating, Luke had him on the ground. He still wasn't sure why he hadn't beaten the guy to a pulp. His fingers curled again.

"For a minute there, I was pretty sure you were going to beat the bejesus out of Doug Canfield."

He blinked and looked at Whitney. She quietly sipped her whiskey, watching him over the rim of her glass as she leaned against the wine-tasting counter. It wasn't bad enough she was under his skin and in his dreams these days—now she was inside his head? His heart thumped an extra beat.

"Why?" He saw the surprise in her eyes at his sharp tone. Good. Anything to make her back off and get out of his head and heart. "Because I'm a Rutledge?"

"You know, I keep hearing 'a Rutledge' used around you like it's some common descriptive noun everyone knows but me." Whitney stepped closer. Wrong direction. "I don't walk around claiming to be 'a Foster.' I'm *Whitney*. And you're *Luke*. I don't know what your last name means to everyone in this town, but your surname doesn't define you." She drained her glass, wiping her mouth with the back of her hand and flashing him a grin that hit him square in the chest. "If it did, I'd be a lounge singer in Vegas."

He couldn't hold back a huff of laughter at that image. Buttoned-up, professional Whitney, sitting on top of a piano in a slinky dress, dark hair tumbling over her shoulders, crooning to the crowd. His laughter died when he realized that image of her, uninhibited and free, was…beautiful. And way too good for a Rutledge. She was out of his league. He reached over to refill his glass, but her fingers touched his hand, stopping him.

"Tell me about this Rutledge name of yours."

Bad idea. He tried to ignore her, forgetting how relentless she could be.

"Is your father really in prison, like Doug said? Did he kill Doug's brother?"

"I don't talk about my family."

She patted his hand. "I get that. I don't talk about mine much, either." She boosted herself up to sit on the counter, crossing her long legs. The combination of skin-tight jeans and spiky heels was hot as hell. There was something about the way she was looking at him. Curious, but not about his name. About *him*. Was she… *flirting* with him? Whitney picked up the bottle and refilled both their glasses. "But this is a weird night, and maybe we should do stuff we don't normally do. Like drink whiskey and share history. Or whatever."

Whatever? What the hell did she mean by "whatever"? And why did it sound so inviting?

He stared at the honey-colored liquid in his glass. She was right—this was a weird night. And she was sending him some serious seduction vibes. Touching him. Sitting up on the counter so close he could smell her perfume. Talking about *whatever* in a voice that curled around him and drew him in. He tried to keep his guard up, reminding himself he'd had women come on to him before *because* of his name. Women who wanted a "bad boy," whatever the hell that meant. They wanted the thrill of danger, but he was a man, not an amusement park ride.

"Let's stick to finishing our whiskey, and then you go back to the house." They should both retire to their prospective beds, in separate buildings, and wait for morning to arrive. Alone. They should *not* stay together here in the tasting room, drinking and talking and flirting. And they should *definitely* not go up to his bed and make love.

Aw, hell.

Where did *that* idea come from? No. That was an awful idea. A horrible idea. The worst.

Whitney's voice was as honey-colored as the whiskey, and just as smooth and tempting.

"Maybe...I don't want to be alone tonight. After all that with Doug, I just... I want to feel connected to someone." The corner of her mouth quirked into a smile as she took another sip of whiskey. "And you refuse to answer my questions, so maybe we need to...connect without using words."

He swallowed hard. "Connect without words, huh?"

She leaned toward him, her voice dropping. "Yeah, you know. Let *other* parts of us do the connecting?"

He should walk away. Walk away right now.

"What exactly are you suggesting, Whitney?"

Her voice was tinged with laughter. "Seriously? Does being 'a Rutledge' mean you can't understand innuendo?"

The reminder of who he was had the same effect as if she'd poured ice water over his body. He welcomed it, because it kept him sane. Or at least as sane as he could expect to be around this woman.

"Being a Rutledge means I know my place. And that place is nowhere near this *whatever* that you're suggesting." He drained his glass, wincing against the sharp burn in his throat as he set it down hard on the counter. "Look, you said it yourself. It's a weird night. You had a scare. I punched a guy. We've had some whiskey. And you're looking for a walk on the wild side with a Rutledge. It's not gonna happen."

He turned away, but Whitney grabbed his arm. Her eyes were dark and angry.

"4 for 4" MINI-SURVEY

We are prepared to **REWARD** you with 4 FREE books and Free Gifts for completing our MINI SURVEY!

NEW YORK TIMES BESTSELLING AUTHOR

DIANA PALMER

ANY MAN *of* MINE

"You just can't do better than a Diana Palmer story to make your heart lighter and smile brighter." —Fresh Fiction on *Wyoming Rugged*

Romance

NEW YORK TIMES BESTSELLING AUTHOR

SHARON SALA

DARK WATER RISING

"A wonderful romance, thriller, and delightful book. It's that will keep you glued to the pages." —USA TO!

Suspense

You'll get up to...

4 FREE BOOKS & FREE GIFTS

FREE Value Over **$20!**

ust for participating in our Mini Survey!

Get Up To 4 Free Books!

Dear Reader,

IT'S A FACT: if you answer 4 quick questions, we'll send you 4 FREE REWARDS from each series you try!

Try **Essential Suspense** featuring spine-tingling suspense and psychological thrillers with many written by today's best-selling authors.

Try **Essential Romance** featuring compelling romance stories with many written by today's best-selling authors.

Or **TRY BOTH!**

I'm not kidding you. As a leading publisher of women's fiction, we value your opinions... and your time. That's why we are prepared to reward you handsomely for completing our mini-survey. In fact, we have 4 Free Rewards for you, including 2 free books and 2 free gifts from each series you try!

Thank you for participating in our survey,

Pam Powers

To get your 4 FREE REWARDS:
Complete the survey below and return the insert today to receive up to 4 FREE BOOKS and FREE GIFTS guaranteed!

"4 for 4" MINI-SURVEY

1 Is reading one of your favorite hobbies?
☐ YES   ☐ NO

2 Do you prefer to read instead of watch TV?
☐ YES   ☐ NO

3 Do you read newspapers and magazines?
☐ YES   ☐ NO

4 Do you enjoy trying new book series with FREE BOOKS?
☐ YES   ☐ NO

Please send me my Free Rewards, consisting of **2 Free Books from each series I select** and **Free Mystery Gifts**. I understand that I am under no obligation to buy anything, as explained on the back of this card.

❑ **Essential Suspense** (191/391 MDL GNQK)
❑ **Essential Romance** (194/394 MDL GNQK)
❑ **Try Both** (191/391/194/394 MDL GNQV)

FIRST NAME	LAST NAME

ADDRESS

APT.#	CITY

STATE/PROV.   ZIP/POSTAL CODE

"We're back to the Rutledge thing again? I still don't know what it means, and I don't care." Her grip loosened. "Maybe it *is* the adrenaline, but Luke...we already know we have chemistry. We're grown-ups who can choose to explore it if we want to. And tonight? Maybe I want to."

He carefully pried her fingers from his arm. How the hell had they reached the point where they were seriously discussing this?

"You're tossing around an awful lot of maybes. You need to be damn sure before we go any further."

Whitney's lips parted slightly, curving into a seductive smile. Her eyes softened and warmed, and something inside of him warmed, too. Her hand slid up his arm to cup his face. And Luke knew he was toast. He'd do whatever she wanted, as long as she'd keep looking at him like this. Touching him like this, with her fingers barely brushing his skin. In a way no one had ever touched him before. Or looked at him before. Like he was something valuable. Worthy. Desired.

"I'm sure, Luke."

He swallowed hard, fighting back a surge of fear and doubt. The most beautiful woman he'd ever seen was sitting on the counter in front of him. Wanting him. *Seducing* him. She uncrossed her legs and he moved to stand between them without a second thought. His hands rested on either side of her hips. He was afraid to touch her. Afraid he was misreading everything. Afraid she'd come to her senses and...

She leaned forward and touched her lips to his.

Sweet Jesus.

Their first kiss had been tentative and brief, full of sweet caution. They'd given into temptation, and they'd been interrupted before it could build any real heat. There was no caution to *this* kiss, though. Her lips were soft but determined, and he gave in without hesitation. He gripped her waist and pulled her against him. Then he slid his hands up her back, twisting his fingers roughly in her hair, pulling it free from the ponytail so it tumbled around her shoulders. Her hands gripped his face as if she was as determined to hang on as he was. He tugged her closer, driving his tongue into her mouth. The taste of whiskey on her completely undid him.

He was on fire. His veins were flowing with gasoline, and her kiss had just lit the fucking match. He yanked her off the counter and spun to put her against the wall. Wine bottles rattled next to them, but they didn't care. Whitney had been in control while sitting above him, and that was fine. But now? Now *he* was taking charge. Small, desperate sounds came from her throat as she kissed him over and over. She dug her fingers into his shoulders. He ground his hardness against her, his shorts against the zipper of her jeans, and her sounds changed. Less whimper. More demand. Her hips moved against his, and damned if things hadn't officially gotten out of hand right there in the tasting room.

He tore his mouth from hers, running kisses down her neck, barely able to keep his lips away long enough to grunt out one word.

"Upstairs?"

Her head hit the wall with a thud, and her back arched to push her breasts into his very willing hands. His mouth moved lower, over the top of her shirt, finding its way to her right breast and nipping through her clothes. They were out of control, but he wasn't moving until she answered him. She cried out, then gasped a breathy reply.

"Upstairs."

WHITNEY HAD NO idea how they got up the steep staircase, seemingly without removing their hands from each other or ending their kiss. She didn't remember the door opening, but she remembered Luke kicking it shut behind him, his mouth firmly on her breast. Wait. When did she lose her shirt? And her *bra*?

Her fingers tugged his hair until he released her nipple and lifted his head to meet her eyes. His pupils were so dilated his eyes looked black in the dim light from the single table lamp. Black with desire. With lust. For her.

A shiver of caution traced up her spine. She'd been looking for a distraction tonight. A scratch to an itch. An exploration of the odd little spark between them. A follow-up to that tender wine barn kiss she couldn't stop replaying in her head. But right now, looking into Luke's fevered eyes, half-naked and feeling reckless, she wondered if they were going to get far more than either of them anticipated. If they were going to *ruin* each other for other lovers. Because there was no doubt that Luke Rutledge had the potential to do just that.

Luke's brow rose as she stared at him. His tight grip relaxed a bit. His voice was gravelly and thick.

"Are you putting on the brakes, babe?" He stroked her skin with his fingers, grinning at the groan she couldn't hold back. He looked mighty proud of himself for making her sound like that, so uninhibited. Hell, he *should* feel proud. She'd been with a few men in her time, but she'd never made that sound before. His gaze cooled with concern. "I need to hear your answer, Whit.

In words, not moans. You can say no anytime, but if you're gonna say it, I'd sure as hell rather you do it before we go any further."

She *should* stop this, for so many valid reasons. And she might have. If only his thumb wasn't gently grazing the small of her back, sending goose bumps across her skin. If only it didn't feel so good to have her bare chest against his. Hey, when did he take *his* shirt off? If only he hadn't kissed her literally senseless downstairs. If only she didn't want this…want *him*…with a hunger she'd never felt before tonight. Considering all the random thoughts weaving in and out of her head, she was surprised how strong her voice was.

"I'm not going to say no, Luke."

She gave a quick glance toward the double bed, which was, of course, totally disheveled. His pillows were thin, and folded in half. The faded blue sheets were untucked and twisted, and the light quilt had been kicked to the foot of the bed, where it tumbled like a waterfall to pool on the floor. Shoes and sneakers were tangled together under the bed, along with some random, mismatched socks. A pile of folded T-shirts was stacked on the floor, side by side with a stack of jeans and shorts. Whitney had stayed in plenty of luxury hotels around the world, and she'd never seen a bed look so inviting.

Luke's lips pressed together and he stared hard at her, as if waiting for her to change her mind. She slowly moved her hands up his chest, letting her thumbs flick across his nipples, causing him to hiss in a sharp breath, his own hands tightening around her waist. He still didn't move, but she could see flames there in his eyes. Flames that surely mirrored her own. She flicked her thumbnails across his chest again, playfully trying to break him out of the trance he'd fallen into.

She'd never played the role of temptress before. But right now? She was a woman going after what she wanted. Not in the boardroom, which was suddenly inconsequential, but in the bedroom. Or, to be more accurate, a studio apartment that included a bed.

"This was *my* idea, remember?" Her hands slid down his ribcage, resting just inside his low-riding jeans. "You need to believe me when I tell you I. Am. Not. Saying. No." She pushed up onto her toes to kiss his cheek, and he closed his eyes. "I'm saying yes, Luke. I'm saying take the rest of my clothes off. The rest of *your* clothes off. I'm saying take me to that bed of yours and—"

Before she could finish, Luke tugged her hard against him. His mouth landed on hers and all hesitation was gone. Buttons came undone. Zippers were unzipped. She kicked her jeans off in one direction across the floor and he kicked his in the opposite.

He said one word sharply. "Bed!"

Whitney laughed. "I think we've already established that."

His teeth nipped at the base of her neck. "Not talking to you. Molly."

Who? Oh, the dog. Molly the *dog*. Whitney rolled her head to give Luke better access and saw the brown dog walking forlornly to the puffy green dog bed by the sofa. *Tough luck, Molly. He's mine tonight.*

Something happened to the space-time continuum when she and Luke kissed. Clothing vanished without warning. Locations changed with no sensation of moving. It was the only way to explain how Whitney came to be lying on Luke's bed. The pillows, top sheet and quilt were nowhere to be seen. It was as if some giant hand had swept the bed clean and placed her there, wearing only her pink lace panties.

Luke stood next to the bed, thumbs hooked into the top of his dark boxer briefs, starting to draw them down, but frozen midway. He looked as surprised to find her there as she was to be there.

Whitney decided to embrace her new brazen side. She nodded at his hands. "What are you waiting for? Keep going."

His smile started in his eyes, and he complied with her demand. The result was…well…the result was a fully naked Luke Rutledge, and she finally got to see what that delicious happy trail of dark hair led to. *Oh, my.* If she'd had any doubt he wanted this to happen, those doubts were long gone now. He was rock hard and ready. She reached for her panties, but Luke stopped her.

"Uh-uh-uh. Those are mine." He kneeled on the edge of the bed, stalking toward her. She opened her mouth, but couldn't form words. His calloused hands caught the edge of the lace and he slowly—oh, so slowly—pulled the pink panties down her legs. As he slid them past her feet, he lifted one foot and kissed her toes, one by one. Could she die from this? From a man kissing her toes? She dropped her head back and closed her eyes, but he was having none of that.

"Eyes on me, Whitney. Eyes on me."

She watched as he kissed his way up her leg, caressing and kneading with his fingers as he went. He kissed the top of her knee, then lifted her leg and licked the tender skin behind it. She cried out so loudly she clamped her hand over her mouth in horror. She wasn't a screamer. She usually had to concentrate to have an orgasm the regular way, so why did she feel like she almost had one just now, as Luke's tongue slid across her skin? Behind her *knee*?

Strong fingers wrapped around her hand and pulled it away from her mouth. She got lost in his eyes, feeling another wave of ecstasy threatening to drown her.

"The sun won't be up for hours, Whit." He smiled, his voice calm and sure. "We have all the time in the world. Don't hold back. For one night, this night, neither one of us needs to hold anything back."

"But I don't want it to be over too soon..." She winced, knowing she was whining. Luke kissed her shoulder, laughing against her skin.

"Well, if that happens, we'll just have to do it again." He ran his nose up her neck, nibbling her earlobe and making her tremble. "And again." His lips brushed the side of her face, kissing her temple. "And again." He kissed her mouth, pulling away before she could return it. "We'll do it as many times as we have to. Or until one of us passes out from the effort. But right now I feel like I could be here with you for hours on end without running out of steam." Another kiss. "How about you?"

His nose was touching hers, his chocolate eyes looking down, filled with desire and promising a night filled with passion and abandon.

"I don't know how to do this..."

Luke frowned, raising his head. "You don't know how...? Whitney, are you...?"

"Oh, my god, Luke!" She didn't know whether to laugh or cry. "No, I'm not a thirty-one-year-old virgin. I know *how* to have sex. I've done it more than once. A lot more."

His face twisted. "Yeah—don't need details. Thanks. What don't you know how to do?"

How could she possibly explain this? Obviously, he'd had plenty of nights where he did things over and over. Goodie for him. And for the lucky women he'd been with. She'd clearly been sleeping with the wrong guys. Or maybe it was her. Maybe *she* was the defective one. Scientifically speaking, if her experiences with men were always something less than randy all-nighters, then the likeliest cause was the common denominator—her. It was only fair to come clean. To lower Luke's expectations.

"My body isn't...wired right, I guess. I'm not an over-and-over-again kind of girl. Just ask any of the men—"

"Again, don't need those details. Not now. Probably not ever." He studied her intently. "You're afraid."

"I am not afraid." She gestured around the apartment. "Again, *my* idea, remember? But I don't want you to be expecting more than I can—"

His kiss silenced her. Hard and insistent. Firm, yet full of tender promise. How did he do that? His hand moved up her side, leaving a ripple of chills on her skin that made her breath catch and her abdomen clench. How did he do *that*? He raised his head and she was horrified to hear a whimper escape her lips. There was a quick spark of humor in his eyes.

"Whitney, if this little meltdown of yours is because you're feeling more turned on than you've ever felt with another man...well, feel free to say that." He kissed her softly, speaking against her lips. "Tell me as often as you like." Another kiss. His hand slid up her neck to cup her face. He stared into her eyes. "But believe me when I tell you I know exactly what you're feeling. I'm a long way from being a virgin myself, and no woman has *ever* made me feel anticipation like this." He dropped his forehead to hers, closing his eyes. His words, rasping and deep, burned into her soul. "I want to taste every inch of you, and I want to take my time doing it. Then I want to taste you all over again, to make sure I didn't miss a spot." His fingers trembled against her skin. "I don't know what's going to happen tomorrow. But if tonight is it for us…if we're both feeling the same weird kind of magic…then let's just…roll with it." His eyes opened again, dark and hooded. "Unless you don't want—"

She put her finger on his lips. "I want. I really, really want."

His mouth curved into a wide smile beneath her finger, and he kissed it.

"Good, 'cause I'm so hard it hurts."

The graphic confession surprised a laugh out of her, and it was exactly what she needed. She relaxed in his arms. She'd deal with tomorrow when tomorrow got here. But right now she was naked in bed with a man who wanted to taste every inch of her. Yeah. She was definitely going to roll with that. She removed her finger from his mouth and kissed him.

Kissing Luke Rutledge was her new favorite thing to do. But she had a feeling having sex with him was about to make a strong fight for first place.

CHAPTER FIFTEEN

LUKE TRIED TO wrap his head around the fact that Whitney Foster was naked. In *his* bed. Under his pulsing body. She wanted him. And she was laughing as she kissed him. And it was the sexiest damn laugh he'd ever heard.

His sexy times with women generally involved a quick release. A one-night stand with some tourist in town long enough to be someone's bridesmaid or see her kid sister graduate college. No expectations. No complications. No feelings.

It was a good plan. And lying naked with Whitney was not. There were complications he couldn't even imagine. And expectations? Hell, his expectations were all over the map. He *expected* this to be the best sex of his life. He *expected* this to be a disaster once the sun rose. He glanced at the bedside clock. Dawn was still six hours away. They could have a hell of a lot of fun in six hours.

He traced his kisses along her chin and behind her ear. Her body arched against his and he could swear she was purring. No matter what he did or where he touched her, it was the right place. The right touch. He wasn't doing anything special. It just…worked…with her. Everything just…worked. He kissed the base of her neck and grinned when she whispered his name.

Luke hadn't lied when he'd told her he wanted to taste her everywhere. But they had all night for that. Right now, he needed to be inside of her. He needed it like he'd never needed anything else. He grabbed at the jeans hanging off the headboard. Whitney made that needy, whimpering sound again, amping his heart rate into the stratosphere. He was pretty sure he had a condom in his wallet…his fingers closed around a thin square of foil. Thank you, God.

He tore the packet open with his teeth and slid the condom on. Bracing his forearms on either side of her head, he kissed Whitney hard and fast. Damn, this woman was more intoxicating than whiskey neat.

"Baby…" He breathed the word more than spoke it as he slid into her. Whitney rose to meet him and he had all he could do not to come right then, the minute he entered her. He tasted blood from where he'd bit the side of his own mouth to control himself. Neither one of them moved, and he knew she was fighting to make this last, too. Fighting just as hard as he was.

He didn't know which one of them finally started to move, but it was pure bliss when it happened. They were in perfect rhythm. Her arms wrapped up around his ribs, her fingers digging into his shoulder blades. His hands cradled her face, and he couldn't look away. Couldn't even blink. They moved together. They breathed together. They sighed each other's names together. They picked up the pace together. And he saw the moment her pupils dilated before she closed her eyes and fell apart around him at the same exact moment his whole world vanished in a flash of white.

"Luke? Luke?"

The word was familiar. A name. His name. Someone was saying his name. He let out a low groan.

"Oh, thank god. I thought I'd lost you for a minute there. I need you to move…"

He shifted, and shook his head, trying to clear the cobwebs. He'd just had earth-shattering sex with Whitney Foster. Hot damn.

"You okay?" He shifted again, putting his weight on his arms.

"You and I need to stop asking each other that."

He looked down at her. Hair splayed out like shadowy flames on his sheets, skin flushed and pink, lips soft and kiss-swollen, eyes a little unfocused but shining with contentment.

Damn straight.

He'd put that look there. A twitch from between his hips told him that his body, although still recovering from the first time, was ready and willing to do it again. He dropped his head to her shoulder.

"I think you almost killed me."

WHITNEY KNEW EXACTLY what Luke meant. If their kisses altered space and time, their sex had managed to bend all laws of science. No one's heart should feel like it was about to burst like that—it couldn't be healthy. Even now, it hammered against the inside of her rib cage. Her skin was chilled and on fire at the same time, twitching randomly with little aftershocks. It was more than a little scary. But boy, had that been fun.

It had been fast. They'd both been holding back, trying to slow down, but it was impossible. Their bodies took control of the situation. No thinking required, thank you very much. Just moving together and letting the flame race down the fuse, leading to an explosion that left her—left them both—senseless for a moment.

Luke groaned, sliding off her to remove the condom. She hadn't even thought to ask about protection in the heat of the moment earlier. She was on the pill, but still…she was always so careful. Instead, it was Mr. Unorganized who not only *had* protection, but knew where it was and used it. Before she could analyze that thought any further, a jolt of electricity went through her. His mouth was on her breast. His fingers were sliding between her thighs, and she remembered his promise.

I want to taste every inch of you…

Yes, please.

Everything was slower this time. He lingered over her breasts until she came, just from that. Well, that and what his fingers were up to. He traced kisses down her stomach to join his magic fingers, and she didn't even try to stifle her cries when he took her over the edge again. And again. How did he *do* that, damn it? What was his secret, that he could make her entire body burn with desire? Pulse with need. Shudder with release. How many times could she do that before her heart quit?

"Luke…?" Worry tainted her voice. Worry that it was too much. That *he* was too much. And then he was over her again, his voice soft and sure.

"Easy, baby. It's okay. I know what you want."

And hey, he *did* know. He filled her, absorbing her moans with a kiss that lasted forever. They moved slowly, completely aware of each other as their hands explored and their mouths never parted. How was she breathing? Who cared? The heat built more slowly this time, but once it flamed, they were both done for. She went first. Luke kissed her tears away, then breathed her name across her skin before joining her.

She woke in a tangle of arms and legs—a pretzel of sated bliss. Luke was asleep, his chest to her back, face nestled into her neck, arms wrapped around her. Their legs were entwined. She was too warm, but she didn't move. Didn't even think about it.

She'd never been one for cuddling after sex. What was the point? Other than in college, none of her relationships had been serious. She'd been too focused on making partner to think about the distraction of a serious relationship, and guys rarely wanted to compete with her career. Her last relationship had been with Pete, a bartender at the Omni Hotel. Pete was funny, outgoing, easy on the eyes. She'd always slipped away from his place as soon as she could. No morning coffee and Danish to complicate things. Pete was looking for more, though, so they'd gone their separate ways. Pete had been inventive in bed and could make her laugh. But he'd never made her scream.

Luke sighed behind her, then pressed his lips on the back of her neck, mumbling against her skin.

"What time is it?"

She stretched to look at the bright blue digital clock. "Oh, it's only one o'clock."

His arms tightened around her as he did a shuddering stretch. "Why do you sound surprised?"

"It feels like I've been asleep for hours." She rarely slept for more than a few hours without waking to check her emails or watch some mindless cooking show on TV to slow her brain down. She had no desire for that tonight.

"Mmm-hmm. We may have invented a new way for

people to get eight hours' worth of sleep in a single hour. Just have stellar sex with someone amazing. Twice. You'll be out like a light."

She chuckled, doing her best to ignore the warm feeling she got at the *someone amazing* part. "We do have a tendency to bring out the narcoleptic in each other, don't we?"

He tugged her back against him, and he was hard and ready.

"Here's an idea." He turned her on her back and brushed his fingers gently through her hair, kneading her scalp and making her want to purr like a contented cat. "Let's do a little experiment. If two rounds of sex give a full night's sleep, imagine what could happen if we go for three? I bet we could get a full *week's* worth of rest after, then we can figure out how to sell it and solve all the productivity problems of the world."

"But if we do that, morning will come more quickly," she pouted. The thought of the sun rising made her sad. Tears-burning-in-her-eyes sad, which made no sense. A shudder went through her.

"Hey, you're shivering." He ran his hands up and down her arms briskly, then sat up. "Let me grab the blanket—"

"No!" She grabbed at him, panicked at the idea of him not touching her. "You're all the heat I need."

Whitney couldn't believe the thought manifested itself into words so quickly. The corner of Luke's mouth tipped up into an arrogant grin. She had to derail this.

"I mean… I mean… Um… I'm not cold. There's no A/C up here, and it's warm. That's what I meant. There's enough heat already. I mean, this bed is hot enough with you in it… Ugh!"

"You make this bed pretty hot yourself." He tried to keep a serious face, but she could see the laughter in his eyes. "If you don't want any more sex with me, just say so."

"No! I mean…yes! I *do* want more sex. With you." She covered her face with her arm, but he gently lifted it up.

"But?"

"Look, I'm barely forming coherent sentences. I need a little more time to get my brain cells back into formation. At the risk of overinflating your ego, that really was…something. I need to get myself back in one piece emotionally, okay?"

"Okay." He slid back onto his side, head propped on one arm, while the other arm draped across her stomach, fingers tracing circles on her skin. This was definitely not helping put her thoughts in order. But it was oh, so good. Her eyes slid closed, all of her focus on those fingers.

"You don't like losing control, do you?"

Her heart skipped a beat. "Where did *that* come from?"

His shoulder lifted and fell. "Just an observation. Am I wrong?"

She chewed on her lower lip. Her mind was already blown to bits from having sex with Luke. That was scary enough. Sharing intimacies while lying naked in the soft shadows of his apartment could be far more dangerous. Sexual vulnerability was one thing. Personal vulnerability? Whitney avoided that at all costs. That's how her mom always got into trouble—letting passion rule and waltzing men into her life with open arms.

Uh-uh. No reason to open that locked and bolted door. Tear down that stone wall. Cross that well-marked line.

Luke waited, watching her without saying a word. His fingers kept moving on her skin, in looping circles that flirted with her breasts, then dove toward her hips, then back again. And again. The action must have hypnotized her, because she heard herself speaking words she didn't intend to say at all.

"I've been in control of my life since I was eleven."

And just like that, the locks fell off the door, the wall tumbled to earth and the line blew away like dust. In their place was...no protection. Just a frightening void. Luke's fingers splayed across her stomach and stilled.

"Tell me what that means."

"That was the age I became the parent. I was a child being raised by a child—a woman who never grew up. My mom is...a dreamer." That put a gentle spin on the truth. Better than saying her mother was an irresponsible, impulsive, borderline manic-depressive allergic to maturity. "She's been chasing fame as a singer all her life. And she falls for every scheme and promise she hears. All a guy has to do is say he's in 'the industry' and she's his. Her money's his. Her home is his. Her bed is his."

Luke's hand pressed down, then released and curled into a fist against her before flattening against her skin. His voice was low and barely controlled.

"Where did that leave you?"

"Answering the phone, mostly." She sighed. "The bill collectors were having a field day. The bank was calling about the mortgage. Her car was repossessed. Mom had a closet full of fancy outfits, but our refrigerator had no food. One day I realized it was up to me. I took over the checkbook and learned to sound older than my age while begging some adult on the phone not to shut our power off. She was actually making decent money waitressing and doing the occasional singing gig. She was spending it like water, though—giving it to some loser to reserve 'studio time' that never materialized, investing in crazy schemes, singing lessons, new 'costumes' that would get her that job she wanted. So I put her on an allowance."

"You put your *mom* on an allowance when you were eleven?"

"Someone had to do it."

He chuckled, and his fingers started their delicious patterns again.

"You've always been good with numbers?"

"Again, someone had to do it. With all the chaos of living in my mom's orbit, controlling numbers was a pretty heady feeling for a kid." When was the last time she'd felt that way about crunching numbers as an adult? She shook it off. That was enough soul baring for one night. Time to shift the focus.

"Okay, I've shared my deep, dark family secret—my mom's an impulsive, overtrusting spendthrift, which is why I'm not any of those things." She pushed on his shoulder, sending him on his back so she could be the one leaning over. Running her fingers across his skin. Chasing his happy trail... No. If they had more sex they'd sleep all night. "How about you? Are you rebelling against overachiever parents who made you put your clothes away one too many times?"

His sharp laugh didn't hold a lot of humor. "Not exactly."

"Oh, that's right. You're 'a Rutledge.' Maybe it's time to finally tell me what that means now that we've—"

"Bed privileges don't automatically lead to sharing childhood nightmares."

Whitney started to protest. "Mine wasn't exactly a nightmare…"

Her face went hot. That's not what he was saying. *Your daddy's still in prison, ain't he?* Luke was saying *his* childhood had been a nightmare. His jaw was rigid, his eyes staring up at the ceiling. They still had hours before dawn, and she didn't want the magic derailed yet.

"You got any food up here?"

His gaze snapped to meet hers, his brows bunched together.

"I'm sorry…what?"

"My so-called 'date' ended before any food was ordered." It wasn't a lie. "I could use a little midnight snack if you have anything around."

"Well, I *live* here, so yes, I have food." He sat up, the previous dark conversational direction forgotten. Mission accomplished. "I've got a turkey breast in the fridge. How about a sandwich? On a brioche roll? With a little cranberry spread?"

First, that sounded delicious. Second…

"You have brioche rolls?"

Luke stood, apparently comfortable walking around naked. Lucky her. He glanced back, one brow raised. "You don't like them? I'm out of croissants, but I have some Amish bread that toasts up nice."

Her mouth dropped open. "You're out of croissants? You're a sloppy single guy living in a sloppy studio apartment." She glanced at the pile of folded clothes on the floor. "I figured you'd offer me a bag of chips, or a frozen pizza. Now you're offering to make me a deli sandwich on my choice of fancy breads? Who *are* you?"

He stood facing her, making it difficult to keep her eyes on his face. And he knew it. She saw the arrogant smirk.

"I'm a guy who likes good food. Do you want the brioche or not?"

Two could play this game. She sat up on the bed, crossing her legs and cupping her chin in her hand. His eyes narrowed, and a vein pulsed at the base of his neck. Something else pulsed, too, but she somehow managed to keep her gaze up on his face. She flashed him a bright smile.

"I'd love the brioche, but I can't eat a whole sandwich at this hour."

He nodded, turning away to open the refrigerator. "I'll split it with you." He leaned over, exposing his very nice butt as he pulled out the food. *Sneaky bastard.*

As Luke prepared the sandwich, they both became a little more aware of their states of undress. Walking around naked wasn't bad, but *eating* naked? Whitney grabbed a T-shirt from what she hoped was the clean pile of clothes. When Luke saw her pulling it over her head, he took a dark red bath towel and wrapped it around his hips. It looked like a kilt, and Whitney's romance novel fantasies took flight.

They sat at the small table where he'd dressed the cut on her foot a few weeks ago. Luke set two glasses of white wine on the table with the sandwich. She lifted her glass in a toast. "Cheers. And thanks—this looks amazing."

He took a bite, wiping his mouth with the back of his hand. He glanced at her, then flushed and grabbed a paper napkin. He tossed her one, too. It was kind of adorable that he suddenly wanted to have good table manners for her. They ate in comfortable silence, which was…odd. He was Luke Rutledge. The man she'd been butting heads with from the moment she got to Rendezvous Falls. They were still mostly naked. The only light in the room was from a small table lamp that looked like a yard sale find from the seventies. The sandwich he'd made tasted like it should be on the menu at the Four Seasons. It was the understatement of the century to say she'd never expected to be sitting here. Like this. With him.

She washed down the last bite with her wine.

"That was delicious. Did you make that cranberry spread? It had a kick to it."

Luke nodded. "There's a little bit of horseradish in there. Offsets the sweetness of the cream cheese." He held up the wine bottle and gave her a questioning look, but she waved it off. When he set it down, she reached out to take his hand. His knuckles were red and starting to bruise and there was a tiny cut on one. From punching Doug. It was a sobering reminder of how the evening had started.

"I don't think I've thanked you for what you did."

He stared at her fingers as she touched his reddened knuckles, swallowing hard. His jaw went rigid again, and so did his voice.

"No big deal. Beating people up is a Rutledge family tradition."

CHAPTER SIXTEEN

LUKE PULLED HIS hand away from Whitney's tender touch. Damn it, the woman had a way of getting him to say and do things he never intended. Like making a sandwich at one o'clock in the morning. With no clothes on. And liking it. But he *never* liked talking about his family history.

Everyone in Rendezvous Falls seemed to have an opinion about his family, and most of those opinions were based on rumors that barely flirted with the truth. He'd given up on setting things straight. People enjoyed perpetuating the myth of the violent Rutledge family from the wrong side of the tracks. Impoverished trailer park losers doomed to a life of crime and failure. It was a tidy box he and his siblings had been shoved into, and he'd long ago stopped giving a damn what people thought. Until he met Whitney. He backtracked on his comment.

"At least, that's what folks in town will tell you."

She stared hard into his eyes. "I only care about what *you* tell me."

When Luke was a child, he'd foolishly leaped off one of the docks at the marina. The day was hot and the water was cool. It seemed like a good idea, even if he'd never been in the lake before. People naturally knew how to swim, right? Before someone dove in to save his

stupid ass, he thought he was going to sink down and
down forever, surrounded by all that soft, warm water,
with the sun shining up above. It was beautiful, even
though he was sinking and doomed. That's how he felt
now, as Whitney Foster looked deep into his soul and
told him she wanted to hear *his* words about *his* story.
Inviting. Safe. Treacherous.

He lifted one shoulder, trying to play it casual, but
her expression said she wasn't buying it. Of course not.
He still wasn't going to go there. But his mouth didn't
get the memo.

"My parents lived a hard life, and we got sucked
into it, no matter how much we tried not to." Her hand
reached for his again. He almost pulled away, but found
he couldn't. Her fingers had intertwined with his. He
was trapped. "Neither one of my parents ever caught a
damn break in their lives. Second or third generation
poverty, with no idea how to change it." He glanced up
and gave her a crooked grin. "Well, I'm sure the idea of
going out and getting actual paying jobs crossed their
minds, but they didn't want to sacrifice their lifestyle."

"And what lifestyle was that?"

"The one where Dad got shitfaced every night, and
Mom tried to hide us kids from him." He could still
smell the stale cigarette smoke that darkened the walls
and ceilings of the single-wide trailer. "Her efforts
didn't seem that noble as I got older, since she was
the one who sold our food stamps so she could buy
Dad's beer every week." The refrigerator was always
empty, other than rows of shiny metal cans. Those never
seemed to run out.

"Why didn't your mom just leave him?"

Luke's head dropped. He'd hoped Whitney would

do more than spout the same answerless questions everyone else asked. Who the hell knew why Joanie Rutledge stayed with a creep like Cliff? He stared out the window, watching clouds scuttle across the face of the nearly full moon. For the first time in a long time, Luke saw some of the answers.

"Like I said, third generation. Her granddaddy beat her grandmomma. Her daddy beat her momma. Mom thought it was just the way of the world. It was her job to do the impossible—try to keep a perpetually angry man from blowing up." The weight of his memories pressed down on him. "But Dad was raised in even worse circumstances than she was, and he spent all his energy raging at the world for the unfairness of it all. The five people sharing a three-bedroom trailer with him were the easiest targets, and Dad loved easy targets."

He swallowed hard. He hadn't wandered down memory lane in a long time. Confronting the hopeless truth behind his parents' choices didn't make him feel any better about what had happened. Understanding didn't always lead to forgiveness.

"But you broke the pattern, Luke."

He'd almost forgotten she was there.

"What?"

Whitney squeezed his hand. "You said your parents were the third generation of a dysfunctional spiral. But you're a strong, decent, hardworking man who's nothing like that."

Luke wasn't accustomed to receiving compliments. He pulled his hand away, holding it up and clenching the fingers tightly to show her the bruised knuckles. "*This* says otherwise. You want to know what it means when people called me 'a Rutledge'? Well, this is exactly what it means. Trouble."

She pulled his fist across the table toward her, and he didn't resist. Couldn't. That's the kind of power she had over him. His heart started thudding against his ribs when she lifted his still-clenched hand to her lips.

"This…" She…damn, she *kissed* his knuckle, her voice calm and sure. "This means you are a gentleman willing to defend a woman's honor. My knight in shining armor."

He had a hard time drawing in his next breath. She saw him as some kind of *hero*? That was a first. She looked up through her long dark lashes, and his heart joined the strike his lungs were on. He felt…exposed… in a way he'd never been before. In danger, but not afraid. She kissed another knuckle. *Son of a…*

"This? This means you're the kind of guy who doesn't sit around and hope everything turns out okay. You're the kind of guy who gets off his ass and walks into trouble to make things right."

No. He *avoided* trouble, if only to confuse all the people who expected it of him. But he wasn't afraid of it. Whitney wasn't finished messing with his head. She kissed the bloodied knuckle. "This says you're strong."

She studied his hand some more and planted a kiss on an old scar. It was from pruning vines last year, when he dropped the clippers and tried to juggle them to keep them from landing in the mud. The result was a slice across the back of his hand. And muddy clippers.

"This says you're not afraid of hard work. You're a do-it-yourselfer who probably could have worked at some other vineyard for a lot more money, but stayed *here* because Helen needed you."

Well, that much was true. He'd do anything for the couple who'd saved him from following the Rutledge family tradition. Whitney saw a truth most people in this town never bothered to look for. How was he supposed to respond when a beautiful woman, wearing only his faded T-shirt, told his fortune? Not from reading his palm, but from reading the marks on the back of his hand. And she wasn't finished stripping him bare.

She tugged his ring finger up straight, exposing a spot of cranberry spread on the tip, giving him the naughtiest of smiles.

"And this? This means no one you care about will ever go hungry." She licked his finger clean. Two images crashed together in his brain. One was of the old Kenmore refrigerator in the trailer, filled with cold beer and all those boxes of frozen fucking fish sticks. The other was of Helen's stovetop, loaded with boiling pots of deliciousness that smelled like salvation to a teenage boy. It had been a glimpse of a better, different world from the one he'd known. A world he'd been destined to live in, right up until that moment when Tony had put his arm around a teenaged Luke's shoulder in the kitchen.

"You can eat all this food yourself," Tony had told him. "Or you can learn how to make it and feed your brothers and sister."

That had been the first time someone had suggested *he* had the power to change things. Some people had given his family free food and clothes out of pity, and he'd hated it. No one until Tony ever told him he could do more than just accept his fate. Tony could have had Luke arrested the first time he caught him stealing tomatoes from his garden. Instead, he and Helen taught him how to grow things. How to cook. How to be a man. He closed his eyes tight, holding back the tears that threatened.

Whitney watched patiently, waiting for him to process her words, that playful smile still on her lips. Thank god she'd run out of things to kiss and praise, because his head was already pounding from trying to reconcile it all. The light cast from that ancient lamp of his mom's was muted by its dark red lampshade. The warm tone made Whitney's skin glow, even in the shadows. Or maybe that was just Whitney. Maybe that glow came from inside her, and not some thrift shop table lamp.

Their fingers were locked together again. He was drawn to her against all odds. There was no sense fighting it. He stood abruptly, pulling her to her feet in front of him. This night had been insane. He'd punched a guy. Drunk whiskey with Whitney. Let her seduce him up into his own damn apartment. Into his bed. The towel around his hips twitched. He tugged Whitney close enough for her to feel him against her. That naughty smile of hers deepened, and she pressed her body against his.

His arms slid around her waist and they started to sway to a silent melody. He was dancing with Whitney Foster. In his kitchen. Her head nestled on his shoulder. He rested his cheek on her head. It was…perfect. Luke's chest swelled with some unfamiliar emotion too frightening to explore.

He brushed his lips across her ear. "I want you again."

She chuckled, looking up at him. "I can tell."

Would "again" be once too often? Would they cross some line that couldn't be uncrossed if they spent the night in his bed? He gave her a chance to choose caution.

"I'll understand if you don't want to. Tomorrow's Saturday. The winery's open. We should get some sleep."

Whitney turned away, taking his hand and heading for the bed. She winked over her shoulder at him.

"I have a friend who says sleep is overrated."

He laughed, feeling the tension from their heavy conversation evaporating with every step they took toward his bed.

"Sounds like a smart friend."

Whitney released his hand and swept the T-shirt off with a flourish before falling onto the bed, her hair falling wildly across her face. She pushed it back and gave him a smile that created a blossom of warmth deep inside his chest. Then she patted the mattress at her side in invitation.

"I don't know about smart," she said. "But he's definitely talented."

SOMETHING WAS BEEPING.

Whitney moaned and threw her arm over her face. What was Aunt Helen doing?

And now the bed was moving.

The bed.

Was moving.

Her eyes snapped open. This wasn't her room. This wasn't her bed. She started to sit up, trying to knock the cobwebs from her brain.

The sharp male voice inches from her head did the trick. "Oh, shit!"

Clarity returned with a rush. She was in *Luke's* bed. She'd been in Luke's arms until the beeping started.

Beep. Beep.

"Luke! Turn off your alarm clock already!"

"Hush! It's not my alarm clock."

She turned to find him sitting on the edge of the bed, staring at his phone. She sat up, trying to see the screen over his shoulder.

"What's wrong?"

"Helen." He ran agitated fingers through his hair.

Whitney started to scramble off the bed. "What's wrong with Helen?"

Luke grabbed her arm, pulling her back onto the mattress.

"Stay *put*, damn it!" His voice was low and tight. "There's nothing wrong with Helen." He held his phone up so she could see it. "Helen is what's wrong. She's downstairs."

The last thing they needed was for Helen to find her and Luke together. She might be upset. Or worse—delighted. They didn't need her romantic notions interfering with whatever was going to happen next.

Whitney watched the security camera feed in horror. Her aunt was moving through the tasting room, rearranging the occasional bottle and picking up a cloth to wipe down the tasting counter. The counter where the whiskey bottle—and both glasses—sat.

"Oh, shit," Whitney whispered. "What is she doing down there? What time is it?"

"It's not seven yet. Sometimes she comes out to putter around if she can't sleep." He glanced her way. "A lot like her niece."

"What are we going to do?"

Luke stood, bending over for a quick kiss and handing her his phone. "You're going to stay right here. I'll go down and see if I can get Helen back up to the house. When we leave, you can sneak out and…"

"And *what*, if you're both in the house?"

"And…figure out how to *quietly* go in the back door and get upstairs to your room. I'll keep her in the kitchen. Then come down like you just woke up in your own bed." He yanked on his jeans, commando style, and it was one of the hottest things Whitney had ever seen. He pulled on a T-shirt and looked back one last time as he headed for the door, his dog following closely. His voice was low, but firm. "Stay there until the coast is clear."

Luke and Molly came into view from the base of the stairs on the camera feed. Helen turned quickly, holding up the bottle of whiskey. She seemed to be laughing. That was a good thing, right? Luke went to Helen and they talked, looking around the tasting room, pointing to various shelves and a display of local hand-made soaps by the cash register. After what seemed like hours, Luke ushered Helen out the front door. As Helen exited, Luke looked directly into the camera and waggled his eyebrows. Whitney covered her mouth to hold in her laughter. It was such a silly, un-Luke sort of thing to do.

Now to make her escape. God, her clothes were *everywhere*. Her panties were on top of a pile of Luke's jeans. Her own jeans were crumpled on the floor at the far end of the sofa. Her bra was… Where was her bra? And her top? And her shoes? One high-heeled pump was by the television. The other was under the dining table. She had a vague memory of arriving in the apartment last night, wrapped in Luke's arms, her lips on his, her bare chest against his skin.

Where was her bra?

Oh, dear god, what if her bra was hanging off a bottle

of wine downstairs, where Helen could see it? Whitney's cheeks flamed. Hell, her whole body flamed. How embarrassing would *that* be? But she hadn't seen Helen twirling any items of clothing on her fingers while she was down there.

She found her bra and top on the top step outside the apartment door, as well as Luke's T-shirt, all rolled into a little mound. Luke probably tripped over the clothes they'd both discarded as they kissed their way up the stairs, and he'd tossed them out of Helen's sight. *Nice save, Luke.*

She left his T-shirt inside the apartment and tugged her own clothes on as she descended the stairs. She ran her fingers through her hair, knowing she was probably making it worse instead of better. She snuck around the main house and across the back porch. The back door would get her to the hallway and the staircase leading to her room.

Luke's voice was unusually loud in the kitchen, and he was laughing. Sort of. The laugh sounded forced to Whitney's ears, now that she'd heard his genuine, soft laugh of pleasure last night. Her abdomen clenched at the memory...

"I know you've shown me how to poach eggs a hundred times, Helen, but I never get it right. And that hollandaise sauce—mine always curdles. I need another lesson. Where's the pan you use with the little cups for the eggs? Is that it over there?"

For one horrifying moment, Whitney was sure all was lost. She was at the bottom of the stairs, ready to dash up and change. But the kitchen doorway was right there, and Luke was at the stove, digging through the broiler drawer where Helen stored the pans she didn't use often. He glanced up and saw Whitney. She had one foot in midair. She was barefoot, her high heels dangling from her fingers. His dark eyes swept up her body and the heated gaze created a highlight film from last night in her mind. He really had tasted every inch of her. She'd tasted more than a few inches of him, too. He straightened, his eyes darting to the unseen corner of the kitchen.

"No, Helen, not that one. What's the pot behind you? Up in the cupboard? Isn't that it? Are you sure?" He didn't look at Whitney again, giving her a hand gesture that said "Go!" And she did, now that she was free from the grip of his eyes.

She flew up the stairs and into her room, shedding clothing almost as fast as she had last night, but not having near as much fun. She tugged on a pair of denim capris and a bright pink cotton top, slipping into her canvas flats and pulling her hair back into a messy bun. Glancing into the mirror after brushing her teeth, she decided she'd pass for a woman who'd just rolled out of bed after a chaste night's sleep.

But there was nothing *chaste* about the dark shine in her eyes, or the slight beard burn on her cheek. Her skin was flushed, her lips swollen. Who was she kidding? She looked like a very satisfied woman who'd had a long night of stellar sex. She grinned, and almost laughed out loud at the seductiveness of her smile. It was her own reflection, damn it. She wasn't supposed to be falling in love with it.

Her eyes went wide. She wasn't supposed to be falling in love with *anything*. Those three words needed to stay out of her vocabulary. Last night was simply two adults having a good time together. A *very* good, maybe even epic, time together.

"Whitney!" Helen's voice startled her from the base of the stairs. "Are you up? Luke and I are making eggs Benedict for breakfast!"

It would have been easier if Luke had left before Whitney went downstairs. Easier on her heart, and easier on her desire not to deceive her aunt. But he'd used a cooking lesson as his excuse to occupy Helen and save Whitney from humiliation, so she was going to have to suck it up and have breakfast with the man. All while knowing he was commando under those jeans.

CHAPTER SEVENTEEN

HELEN WAS BITING her lip so hard to keep from laughing, she was pretty sure she'd drawn blood. Luke had bolted from the kitchen as soon as their bizarre breakfast was finished. Helen asked Whitney to help with dishes. Not because Helen needed help, but because she was having so much fun.

When she'd heard shouting coming from the driveway last night, she'd peeked through the curtains in time to see Doug Canfield grabbing Whitney. Tony's baseball bat still sat by the door, and Helen had turned to grab it. No way was she letting anyone get away with *that*. But when she got to the door and glanced outside again, Doug was on the ground, with Luke standing over him. It wasn't long before Doug was in the truck and gone. And that's when things got interesting.

Luke and Whitney walked into the carriage house together. And never came back out. Helen listened for Whitney to come back up to the house, but she never heard a sound. When she woke this morning, she'd tiptoed upstairs to find Whitney's bed undisturbed. One of two things had happened last night. Luke and Whitney had finally killed each other...or they'd slept together.

Her curiosity had finally gotten the best of her, and she'd headed down to the tasting room to "tidy up" and search for evidence. She didn't have to look very hard.

The stairs to Luke's apartment were near the front of the tasting room. And a lacy pink bra was dangling from the railing. The cute yellow top Whitney had been wearing last night was draped across the stairs. Luke's T-shirt was sprawled on a step farther up. Helen smiled. She and Tony had left their share of similar trails on the way up to their bedroom through the years. Clearly, Luke and Whitney had *not* killed each other. Tony always said there was a fine line between the two passions of love and hate, and her two favorite people in the world had managed to cross it. And Helen never saw it coming. Did they belong together? Was it a one-night stand or would it last? Only God knew those answers.

Luke had appeared before Helen could get back to the house, and that's when things got Keystone-cops funny. He apparently thought she had no peripheral vision and couldn't see him snatching all the clothing from the stairs and throwing it up to the door. Then he tried to say the whiskey was left over from the afternoon before, when Steve had stopped by to check the cab franc grapes for fungus. As if Luke would leave a bottle and dirty glasses sitting out... Oh, who was she kidding? Luke was very likely to do that, because he wasn't the neatest person in the world. It was a workable lie.

Helen had turned to leave when Luke's deception went into overdrive. He took her arm and practically carried her out of the carriage house, insisting he'd forgotten how to make hollandaise sauce and had a "powerful craving" for her eggs Benedict. Luke might be lackadaisical about cleaning up after himself, but he was serious about wine and food. He never forgot a recipe, and he'd been making eggs Benedict for years.

But she went along with the ruse, knowing Whitney was upstairs, missing half her clothes.

No matter how fast and loud Luke spoke in the kitchen, or how many pots he clanged together, she heard the back door squeak and knew Whitney had entered. Helen played along with their game, inviting Whitney to join them for breakfast.

Helen took the last dish from Whitney and dried it, putting it back into the cupboard. Watching their two faces at the kitchen table had been the best entertainment she'd had in years. Working so hard not to look at each other, and failing so miserably. Every time their eyes did meet, it sent a sweet, sharp sense of loss through her. Tony used to look at her the same way Luke was looking at Whitney. With that intoxicating mix of heat and tenderness.

"Helen? Are you alright?" Whitney touched her arm. Helen blinked away and looked out the window, trying to hide the tears that threatened to overflow.

"I'm fine, honey. Just thinking about your uncle."

"Tony loved you so much."

Helen nodded. Yes, Tony had loved her. That's why he'd given her those looks that used to curl her toes. Her eyes went wide. Those looks...like Luke had given Whitney. Looks of *love*? Oh, boy. She cleared her throat.

"You and Luke were quiet this morning. You two aren't fighting again, are you?"

Her niece's cheeks went pink. "Fighting? No. No. Not fighting." She straightened her shoulders. "But we're not...friends...or...anything."

Helen was pretty sure the pair had achieved "anything" last night. Maybe it was just the whiskey and a

full moon. But that look in Luke's eyes this morning…
it was more than "friends" for him.

"Tony thought the world of that boy." They both
watched through the window as Luke and Molly walked
up toward the vineyard.

"I'm surprised I didn't know him back then."

Helen shrugged. "He was working with Tony and
you were usually in the house."

Whitney's voice went soft. "How did Luke wind up
at Falls Legend after the childhood he had?"

"Oh, don't go listening to the gossip about his family. Luke did his best to keep his brothers and sister on
the right track."

"I haven't been listening to any gossip," Whitney
said. She leaned a little to the right to keep her eye on
Luke. "I'm just trying to understand how a kid with
such a hard life and an abusive father ended up here,
making wine."

Helen gave her a sideways glance. "Didn't you say
you weren't listening to gossip?"

"I'm *not*!"

"Then how do you know about his father?" Cliff Rutledge was a cruel-hearted slob of a man who'd rather
drink himself into a stupor than feed his own children.
He didn't have a single redeeming quality as far as
Helen was concerned, other than somehow managing
to sire a good man like Luke.

Whitney was still looking out the window, her answer spoken so softly, Helen almost didn't hear it.

"Luke told me."

Helen kept her lips tightly pressed together, doing
her best to avoid overreacting. It was one thing for Luke
and Whitney to have a little roll in the sack. They were

adults and these things happened. Sparks had flown the minute they'd met, and sometimes sparks—even the adversarial kind—led to fire. The kind of fire that led to bras being thrown over banisters. It had given Helen a good laugh this morning. But this was no longer funny.

Luke had talked about his childhood, about his *father*, with Whitney. Luke didn't talk about his parents. *Ever.* Even when Cliff was sentenced to spend the rest of his life in prison for a botched armed robbery, Luke didn't talk about it. Not even with Tony. And yet, he'd told at least part of the story to Whitney.

Luke and Whitney had been having a tug-of-war for power from the moment she'd arrived and they'd fought over Tony's tool bag. And yet, despite all the book club's efforts to find a good match for Whitney, here she was watching *Luke* move through the vineyard with hunger in her eyes. Helen sighed.

"Luke was a scrawny thirteen-year-old kid the first time he showed up here. Tony caught him stealing tomatoes from the garden." She nodded when Whitney's head spun around. "We'd watched him doing it for nearly a week. He'd come just after dawn, take a couple tomatoes, maybe a zucchini, and, of course, a fistful of blueberries. We knew who he was. Who his parents were." Helen turned away to refill her coffee mug. She held up the pot, but Whitney shook her head.

"What happened when Uncle Tony confronted him?"

"Oh, Tony didn't *confront* him. He went out and gave Luke a sturdy basket so he could carry more produce. We figured he was trying to feed his siblings." Helen sat at the table, staring into her coffee.

Luke had been a sight—long dark hair flopping across those angry, fearful eyes. Clothes hanging off his thin frame. Canvas sneakers with more holes than canvas. He'd pulled back like a feral cat at the sight of Tony approaching, ready to bolt. But Tony pointed to a towering tomato plant and told Luke how to tell when a tomato was ripe for picking. That a bright red tomato was pretty, but might not last as long as a slightly green one that could ripen on a windowsill. Then he'd filled Luke's basket himself, with the boy watching in stunned silence.

"After Tony loaded him down with vegetables, he sent Luke on his way with one request. If the boy was going to reap the harvest, he should help maintain it. There was weeding to be done in the garden and in the vineyard, and if Luke wanted to help with that, he could have all the produce he wanted."

Whitney leaned against the windowsill, still watching Luke with distant eyes.

"Uncle Tony saved Luke's pride."

"He did. And damned if we could get rid of the boy after that. He followed Tony around like a lost puppy who'd been kicked too many times, but still wanted to be loved." She lifted her shoulder. "Luke had a temper, but your uncle had a soft spot for that kid. He even taught him to cook, so Luke could give the other kids at home more than cold tomato sandwiches. He taught him about growing grapes, and, probably younger than he should have, how to make wine. The more Tony gave, the harder Luke worked."

Whitney nodded, looking back out the window. "Because Luke has honor."

"Lord only knows where he got it from, but yes. The boy knew right from wrong, and he always wanted to do right by Tony. And me."

Whitney stared out the window for a while. Suddenly she straightened and turned to Helen.

"I need to finish working on your accounts. I have to find the gap in the bank statements and figure out exactly what's going on."

Helen had a hunch Whitney's focus had changed from hanging blame on Luke to clearing his name. She thought of the boxes up in her closet.

"Before you do that, there's something I need to show you."

WHITNEY HAD SPENT a lot of time staring at this dining room table over the past month or so. But now she could finally see a glimmer of hope. Once she'd recovered from the shock of Helen showing her those boxes in her closet earlier, they'd started a whole-house search for more. Helen insisted she hadn't hidden any others, but they found a box in the laundry room, and two paper bags full in the upstairs linen closet. Those hidden gems went back to the first few months after Tony's death, when Helen had been at her lowest.

"I...panicked, I guess." Helen wouldn't look Whitney in the eye when they found the last of it. "I'm not stupid. I just... I guess I figured if I didn't see it, it wasn't there. I shoved it all out of sight. But then it kept coming. All the bills and statements and solicitations and legal stuff and..." Her shoulders slumped. "I guess I *am* pretty stupid, aren't I?"

While Whitney couldn't imagine doing what her aunt had done, she'd never been through a trauma like Helen's. And she felt partially responsible, because Helen *had* asked her to come to Rendezvous Falls a year ago, and she'd been too busy to realize what a cry for help it was. She could have prevented this if she hadn't been so self-absorbed.

Whitney gave Helen a hard hug. "You were grieving. You were scared. It was self-preservation, and I get it. But we can fix this. *I* can fix this, now that I have all the missing pieces. You go down to the tasting room and get ready to greet customers, and I'll get busy."

It was almost four o'clock now, but she'd emptied the surprise boxes and bags and put everything where it belonged chronologically. Her laptop was set up next to the piles of opened bank statements. Now she could finally start reconciling the accounts.

"Holy…" Luke stood in the doorway, eyes wide and fixed on the table. "How are you ever going to get through all that?"

"The same way I've gotten through every other audit. One line at a time."

But she didn't want to talk about audits. She wanted to talk about the intoxicating scent of outdoors and sweat and wine that swirled into the room ahead of him. She wanted to talk about his tousled hair that was begging her fingers to run through it. The long, lean body she knew was under that shirt and those jeans. Was he still commando?

"Hey, my eyes are up here, lady." There was a light, teasing laughter to his voice. It was something she hadn't heard from Luke until last night. He'd laughed a few times in her presence—usually at her expense. He'd teased a few times—usually to get her riled. But she hadn't heard *lightness* from him. It made her heart hurt to think that very few people had probably ever heard that.

Was this where they were now? A light, teasing

friendship? A light, teasing coworker-with-benefits relationship? A light, teasing...

Luke moved forward and tugged her to her feet and into his arms. She put her hands on his chest in warning.

"Helen..."

"Helen went grocery shopping. She told me you were doing paperwork and that I should come up here to see if you needed any help taking more recyclables outside."

Whitney frowned. That was a little...convenient. Helen had never sent Luke to help her before. She'd generally tried to keep them working in separate parts of the vineyard to avoid what Helen called their "squabbles."

"Do you think she suspects anything about last night?"

He didn't release her, but his grip relaxed.

"I don't know how she could. We covered our tracks pretty well. But would it really be a problem if she did?"

"I don't know. I haven't had time to figure out what it means for *me*, much less how it affects her and you and the business." She couldn't help glancing at the papers, and he took it the wrong way.

He released her like she was on fire, stepping back and hardening his expression.

"Do you think you have a conflict of interest in your investigation now? Are you suggesting I seduced you to distract you from your search for incriminating evidence against me?"

After last night, she understood why his first reaction to anything was to defend himself. Before that, she'd have thought those stormy brown eyes meant he was angry. But it was so much more than that. He was feeling judged. He was *hurt*, and ready to lash out.

"No, Luke. And if you'll recall, I did most of the seducing." She moved closer, and was stung when he tried to back off, but the wall got in his way. This was getting ridiculous. "Look, in order to believe you arranged everything last night, I'd have to believe you set me up with Doug Canfield so he could play grab ass with me so you could come to my rescue and punch him. Then you'd have to know I'd be upset enough to suggest a shot of whiskey, and once that happened, I wouldn't be able to resist dragging you up to your bed." She poked him hard in the chest with her finger. "And, of course, you figured all that great sex would render me incapable of doing my job. That's quite a diabolical scheme you came up with, Luke Rutledge."

They glared at each other in silence, her finger still resting over his heart. His brows were low over his eyes, angry and hard. Wait. Was that a little spark she saw? His cheek twitched. She would not smile. She was angry. She would *not* smile. But when the corner of his mouth quirked upward, hers did the same. He covered her hand with his, raising it up to his mouth and kissing her fingertip. The zap of energy went straight from that fingertip to her belly, which tightened with desire. His eyes softened to gold-flecked chocolate.

"Great sex, huh?"

Her laughter bubbled up.

"You're such a *man*. All those words, and the only two you heard were 'great sex.'"

"No. I also heard you admit *you* seduced *me*. And just so you know—*that* was hot."

Whitney tried not to preen, but in her mind she was sweeping her hair back, brushing off her shoulder haughtily and saying *Hell, yes!*

Behind her, a few bank statements slid from their stack to the table as the cat made his hourly trek across the table. Boots was such a good little helper. Luke's defenses started to rise again, but she grabbed his arm.

"I'm not doing an *investigation*, Luke. I may have acted a little skeptical at first..." She sighed when he arched a brow at her. "Okay, I *was* skeptical at first. Downright suspicious. But not anymore." She glanced over her shoulder at the paperwork. "This is a mess, but I don't think there's anything criminal here. It's just...a mess."

His face lowered toward hers. When he spoke, the lightness had returned to his voice, which made Whitney happier than it probably should have. She shouldn't be so invested in Luke's *lightness*, but it was rare and precious and she cared far more than she realized.

"And you're not saying that because of the great sex we had?"

"No, never." She smiled, her voice dropping to a whisper. "It really was pretty amazing, wasn't it?"

His lips touched hers, and lightness evaporated. Her arms slid around his neck and his arms were hard around her ribs as he pulled her in and turned his head to give himself better access to her mouth. Access she gladly gave him, moaning in a highly unladylike way as her fingers twisted into his hair at last. His hands slid down to cup her buttocks and she could feel him growing hard against her. In Helen's dining room.

"Luke..." She pulled away from his kiss, but he trailed more down her neck. "Luke...we can't... Helen... Wait..."

As soon as she said that last word, he stopped, dropping his forehead to her shoulder.

"Damn, woman. I get within ten feet of you now and I can't not touch you. Breakfast was freaking *torture* this morning." He lifted his head and set her away from him, making her ache for the feel of his body against hers. "You're right, though. Helen doesn't need to know anything until we've figured out what we're doing."

"And what do *you* think we're doing?"

She hoped he'd tell her, because she had no idea.

"I was hoping you could tell *me*."

So much for that plan.

"Well, we've only had one night." She turned away, needing the space. "It's not like it's a relationship or anything."

"True." Looking away hadn't helped. His voice still set her skin tingling with awareness. "I suppose we could call it a one-night stand and let it go at that. We're both adults. We know how the world works. We don't have to get all emotional about it."

Whitney nodded. She'd done it before. An evening romp with a guy, no strings attached. No expectations of a phone call the next day. Luke had been in this town his whole life, and surely he'd had a few hookups along the way. She turned to face him.

"You're not seeing anyone, are you?"

His eyes went wide. "Uh, no. Last night wouldn't have happened if I was. You?"

She shook her head, probably more sharply than necessary. "Nope."

Luke sighed. "Okay, that's one set of complications out of the way. Look, we don't have to figure this out right now. I've got to get to work, anyway." He shrugged at her questioning stare. "Many jobs, remember? There was a private party at the Shamrock last night, so they didn't need me, but it's back to normal hours tonight." He reached for her hand, pulling her close. "I liked last night. A lot. I'd be happy to do it again. But not if you've got any doubts about what we're doing. The festival's only a month away. We're going to be working some long hours together. And then you'll be gone, because me and this place are too small for the likes of Whitney Foster." She opened her mouth to protest, but he talked over her. "My point is, whatever's happening between us is temporary. We have an expiration date, so we may as well be up front about it. The only question is whether we want to blow off a little steam together until then, with no expectations of anything more."

She didn't like summing up the sex they'd had as just "blowing off a little steam." It felt more substantial than that. But he was right about having an end date, and the need for similar expectations. He was being annoyingly logical.

"You're suggesting we sneak away for a little afternoon or evening delight whenever we can, but keep things the same between us other than that?"

"I'm not suggesting anything. This has to be a mutual decision. But afternoon delight is definitely an option." He winked. "We both like being together. And we both know there's no future to it. I'm not crazy about the friends-with-benefits tag, but…"

She couldn't resist staying in character. "That would require us to be friends first, right?"

He chuckled, then swept in for a smoking kiss that took away her snark as well as her breath.

"Sounds like a lot of pressure. I gotta run, but you think about it and we'll talk tomorrow."

Tomorrow? But that was so far away…

He left after she loaded him down with a large box overflowing with empty envelopes, useless pages and junk mail—all the refuse from the surprise boxes and bags. She sat at her computer and started entering data. Fortunately she could enter the numbers without a lot of thought. Her brain was busy trying not to think about Luke's proposal.

He was suggesting they keep everything the same between them, but hook up for sex when the mood arose. Judging from both their reactions today, the mood might arise a lot. No expectations. No complications. Just a month or so of really, *really* good sex, then they'd part ways as if nothing had ever happened. She'd salvage her career somewhere, somehow. He'd stay here at the winery, living in a town where he thought people assumed the absolute worst of him.

How could he handle the whispers and side-eyes? That was what chased her out of Vegas as a teen—everyone pointing at her mom and laughing or rolling their eyes. And Chicago became unbearable once Harold Carmichael started his whisper campaign against her. When she ran into her former coworkers, they looked at her with suspicion, or worse—pity. Leaving was the only way to escape. But Luke *stayed* here, working hard and ignoring everyone.

"How's it coming in here?"

Whitney jumped so high at Aunt Helen's entrance that her finger sent a row of 7s flying across twenty columns on the spreadsheet she was working on.

"Oh! You're back! I…um…it's good. I think the numbers are starting to make sense. I just need to finish the puzzle."

"Did Luke hook up with you?"

"Aunt Helen!" Whitney caught herself. "I mean… what?"

There was a quick flash of amusement in Helen's eyes, then she looked away toward the doorway.

"The boxes? Did Luke get the recyclables?"

"Oh! Yes. Yes. He was in and out…" Whitney winced. Helen coughed, keeping her eyes firmly fixed on the floor. Maybe this arrangement wouldn't be as simple as Luke suggested. "I mean…yes. He got the recyclables."

Helen didn't answer, just nodded and left the room. Hiding this no-strings relationship from Helen would be a chore. It meant lying to a woman she and Luke both adored. Maybe this was a sign that it was a bad idea. It was a high cost for a summer affair that had no hope of going anywhere. Sure, the sex was fun…

Who was she kidding? The sex was fantastic. But could they keep it all as simple as Luke suggested? A little tryst behind the wine barrels in the afternoon? A tumble by the falls at sunset? Sneaking into each other's rooms at midnight? And when they weren't trysting, they'd do their work as if nothing happened? It sounded impractical. Too good to be true. Unworkable. A recipe for disappointment and possibly flirting with disaster. No sex in the world was worth that.

"Oh, Whitney?" Helen called from the kitchen across the hallway. "If you have any more recyclables to go, it looks like Luke is getting into his truck now."

Luke was on his way to his job at the bar, not the county waste management center. Instead of telling Helen that, Whitney grabbed one of the bags, barely half-full of scrap paper. It was one way to see him before tomorrow, and maybe talk to him about *tonight*.

"Good idea, Helen! I'll run this out to him."

She cut across the yard. The truck tires slid in the

gravel when Whitney ran in front of it at the base of the driveway, out of sight of Helen's kitchen window. Luke jumped out as soon as it stopped.

"Jesus! I almost hit you. What's wrong?"

"Nothing. Or everything… I don't know. But…" She handed him the bag. He took it as if she was handing him a bomb. And there *could* be a lot of land mines waiting ahead of them. "Here's more recyclables."

"I'm not going…"

Before she lost her nerve, or maybe the moment she lost her mind, Whitney jumped forward and flung her arms around his neck. He dropped the bag to the ground and wrapped his arms around her, kissing her long and hard. They didn't stop until they heard a car coming up the road. They might be hidden from the house, but they'd be visible to anyone who drove by.

They jumped apart from each other. A little voice in Whitney's head told her this was no way to have a relationship, even as bed buddies. But the voice in her heart was stronger. Once the car passed, she gave a stupefied Luke a wink and wave.

"I'll be waiting for you on the porch when you get home tonight."

Her plan was to leave him speechless, but Luke turned the tables on her.

"Don't."

Her heart fell. "What?"

He tossed something in her direction and she caught it. It was a key ring.

"The big key is the tasting room. The small one's my place. It'll be a late night for me. If you're waiting, you may as well be comfortable." He turned to get in the truck. "My bed's pretty comfortable, don't you think?"

CHAPTER EIGHTEEN

THE ONLY INDICATION Whitney had taken him up on his offer was the soft glow of a lamp shining through the window when Luke parked his truck a little before two in the morning. He'd craned his neck as he drove up the driveway to see if there was a light there, and the sight made him grin like a schoolboy. He'd nearly sprinted from the truck to the door, in a ridiculous hurry to get up to the apartment. This wasn't his usual keep-a-safe-distance method of dating. He was giving her too much power. Hell, he'd given her his *keys*.

But the moment he opened the door upstairs, all second thoughts evaporated. Whitney was asleep in his bed, stretched out under the sheets. She was wearing one of his T-shirts again, her dark hair splayed across the pillow. In front of the bed lay his usually territorial dog. Molly raised her head and watched him enter, her little stub of a tail wagging furiously. But she didn't leave Whitney's side, almost as if she was afraid to wake her. He wouldn't have predicted his dog would switch loyalties that fast. Then again, none of this could have been predicted. A beautiful woman warming his bed, with him peeling off his clothes as quickly and quietly as possible to join her.

He turned off the light and slid between the sheets. Whitney sighed softly and moved her back against the warmth of his body, making a little kitten sound when he wrapped his arms around her and pulled her in. They stayed like that for a long time, with his face in her hair and his leg thrown over hers. It felt…right. Like he was coming *home*, coming to where he belonged. To a place he never dreamed he'd experience. Or deserve. But here he was, breathing in the perfect scent of Whitney, feeling her satin skin against his.

It had been a long day after too little sleep, followed by long hours on his feet at the bar. He'd given her his key so it would be easier. So they could have more sex like last night. But now? Now all he wanted to do was lie here and hold her, listening to her soft breath going in and out. He didn't want to break the moment by seeking more. He closed his eyes and gave in to peace that swept over him.

He didn't wake for another two hours. Neither of them had moved, but he heard the change in her breathing and knew Whitney was awake, too. He nuzzled the back of her neck, and sure enough, she let out another one of those kitten sighs and moved against him. His body responded instantly, no longer looking for peace. When she felt his erection harden against her, she started to grind her hips. He nipped her shoulder.

"Naughty girl." Another grind against him, causing him to bite back a groan.

Whitney let out a soft, throaty laugh. "You started it."

"Hmm. I'm going to finish it, too." He turned her in his arms. Her face was lit only with the soft moonlight coming through the window. She wrapped her arms around his neck and pressed against him.

"You're not going to finish it alone, are you?"

He kissed her, and nearly got sidetracked. Damn,

her kisses were good. He spoke against her lips, reluctant to let them go.

"One thing you can be assured of, sweetheart. I won't be finishing alone." His hands slid under the T-shirt, and she wiggled against him to remove it over her head. Killing him slowly in the process. "Whitney..."

"Right here, Luke." Her hand reached between them and slid lower. "Right here."

He sucked in a sharp breath as she reached her target, tempted to roll back and let her continue. But he'd made a promise, and he wasn't going to let her take control this time. Maybe later. But not now.

He moved to the side, away from her grasp, and slid on a condom. Then he rolled on top of her, covering her mouth with his and raising her hands up to rest on either side of her head. Their fingers intertwined, and her grip tightened fiercely as he sank into her. He didn't move at first, overcome with sensation. It was the same as it had been last night. Just as right. Just as perfect.

She whispered his name, so much pleading in the single syllable. He started to move, and her hips rose up in response. They were perfectly synchronized, moving in rhythm to some unknown beat. It was slow at first, then faster and deeper, until they were panting and moaning and sweating and making unintelligible sounds as the sheets twisted beneath them. He kept his promise—they came at the same moment. She cried out his name, while he moaned hers into her shoulder, pressing his teeth against her skin.

A word entered his mind that he'd never considered before, as he lay there on top of her and waited for his heart to stop thrashing in his chest. The word was... *forever.* He could see what forever would look like with

Whitney. Coming home to her every night. Forever. Waking up with her in his arms. Forever. Making love to her—because no way was it just sex anymore—forever. The idea should have sent him running, but instead, he kissed her skin and lifted his head to look into her eyes.

"Hey." Her voice was thick and husky.

"Hey, yourself."

"So…" She tried to move, then stopped when she felt him go hard again. "Already?"

"With you? Yeah. Always." *Forever.*

"Well, I hate to disappoint you, but I may need a minute." She shifted again, and he rolled to his side to give her space to breathe. But not much. He couldn't let her go yet. She snuggled up to him after he disposed of the condom, but he could tell her mind was somewhere else.

"What's wrong?"

"Nothing. I'm just…processing. I've never woken up in someone's arms like that. Sleeping together *before* sex. It was…different." Her body relaxed in his arms. "Why didn't you wake me when you got home?"

"I don't know. You were so beautiful…so peaceful… that I just wanted to hold you. It was pretty incredible to slide into bed after a long day and fall asleep wrapped up in you." He brushed his lips across her ear. "It's new for me, too, but I like it."

"Yes, I think I do, too." She moved her head to expose more of her long neck for him to explore. "But what does that mean? What are we doing?"

He traced a trail of kisses down to her throat. "Do we need to analyze it right now?"

A long sigh of surrender was her only answer. They made love again. Slowly. Tenderly. The only sounds were the shush of the sheets moving beneath them and their breathing. One would hold a breath, then the other, followed by a low moan as the breaths released. Fingers explored as hips rose and fell. It was a dance, and the dance was more intoxicating than any wine. He was lost in her. Falling for her. Throwing caution to the wind as he rocked into her and knew. He'd never be the same after this. Whatever was coming, good or bad, there'd be no recovery for him. This… Whitney…had altered his life in ways he couldn't see. It was frightening. And he didn't care, burying himself in her with a shuddering cry. He didn't care what was coming, as long as he could have this now.

Luke had no idea how much time passed before a movement woke him. Whitney was dressed, slipping into her shoes in the soft light of predawn. He reached out and touched her, almost as if to reassure himself she wasn't a dream. She turned and smiled, twisting her hair back into a knot. She was doing the same to his heart.

"The sun will be up soon." Her voice was barely above a whisper. "I don't want a repeat of yesterday morning, trying not to get caught by Helen."

He stilled, feeling a familiar sting of pain. It reminded him of being back in school, where even the kids who were nice to him in private would shun him publicly. They couldn't afford to be seen hanging around with a Rutledge boy.

"Luke? What's wrong?" She leaned over and pressed her lips to his.

"Would it be so awful if people knew we were… whatever?"

Now it was her turn to go still.

"I think the issue is the 'whatever' part of the equation. *We* don't even know what we're doing yet, and I think we should figure that out before sharing it with anyone."

She was right, of course. Practical Whitney, always looking at the big picture. The problem was, he didn't want to define what they were doing. Putting a label on it would make it…ordinary. Were they *dating*? Was she his *girlfriend* now? He was in unfamiliar territory here.

"Okay." He returned her kiss, resisting the urge to pull her back into bed and remove those pesky clothes she had on. "I'll walk you downstairs."

"I don't need a chaperone."

He sat up. "Bully for you. I'm still walking you downstairs." He tugged on a pair of jeans. "If we're up, Molly's up. And if Molly's up, she's gonna want to go out." The dog was already sitting, ears perked and head tilted, ready to go. Her energy was boundless, especially in the morning.

The three of them went down through the tasting room and out into the cool air. There was a hint of fall in the air already. Whitney gave him a quick kiss and turned to go to the main house. He should let her go. He had to let her go. Instead, he caught up with her with three long strides, spinning her around and tugging her up against him in the parking lot. Whitney moved into his arms without protest, resting her head on his shoulder. The predawn light was soft and blurry around them. She was right where she belonged. He rested his cheek on her head. "Is it weird that I don't want to let this end?" He wasn't sure if he was talking about the night or whatever this was turning into between them.

"If it is, then we're weird together." Her arms slid

around his waist and they started to sway. She looked into his eyes. "Are we *dancing* again?"

"Hard not to when they're playing our song." Right on cue, a couple of birds starting twittering in the trees by the carriage house.

She laughed, the sound blending perfectly with the birds' song. Luke had somehow stepped into an animated fairy-tale movie, where little bluebirds would soon be on their shoulders and forest animals would step up to watch their predawn dance. He knew for damn sure he'd never imagined *that* before.

She gave him a squeeze. "You like to dance, huh?"

"No." He kissed the top of her head. "It's you." She looked up in confusion as he told her the truth, unable to do otherwise when he was staring into her golden eyes. "It's *you* that makes me want to dance, Whitney. Anytime. Any place."

Her lips parted, but she didn't speak right away, just looked at him and weighed his words. Then she laughed softly, and dropped her head back down, moving with him to the rhythm of their own sultry slow dance. "Damn, you're good."

After a minute, he reluctantly stepped back. "You go on." She turned away, and he called her name. She looked over her shoulder. A smart man would say *never mind* and let her walk away. For good. This whole thing was bound to crash and burn. They'd both get hurt. But Luke had never claimed to be a smart man. "Will I see you tonight?"

She gave him a soft chuckle. "I'm game if you are."

"Okay, then."

She went around the back of Helen's house, where he knew she'd find the spare key under the mat and sneak upstairs before Helen woke. Like some lovesick teen, he wondered if he could sneak right up there behind her. That would be a bad idea on so many levels. Molly leaned against his leg, looking up with her tongue lolling.

"Yeah, yeah. I hear you, dog. There's work to be done. But first, a shower and coffee."

WHITNEY QUIETLY SLIPPED out the back door five nights later, ignoring her increasing guilt over keeping secrets from Helen. She'd been sneaking out like this all week. Tiptoeing down the stairs in the dark, going out the back, then running to the carriage house, where she'd usually find Luke waiting in the doorway.

Sleeping together night after night had definitely moved them into the relationship category. She was having a relationship with Luke Rutledge. In Rendezvous Falls. Where she was *not* going to be staying. Even if she *had* picked up another new client—Bridget at the pub had recommended her to Jeff at the beverage supply company, and he'd dropped off a shoebox full of spreadsheets, checkbooks and receipts yesterday. A little messier than the diner or the pub, but it looked pretty straightforward. She moved around the corner of the house. Picking up a few odd jobs while she was here wasn't really a commitment. But this thing with Luke? That was starting to feel very much like a commitment, and the shocking part was that she liked the feeling.

She was halfway across the parking lot when the door to the tasting room opened, sending soft light onto the carriage house porch. Luke stood in the doorway. She picked up her pace, then started jogging toward him. His arms opened and she actually leaped into them. She *leaped*. Into a man's arms. It was a first. Luke swung her inside and kicked the door shut behind her, kissing her senseless the whole time.

They were up the stairs, undressed and in bed in what seemed like less than a minute. Condom on, him on top and the deep connection that made them one. A blur of exquisite movement, a white-hot orgasm, followed by a long, trembling embrace. It was an addiction. She was addicted to making love with Luke Rutledge. And right now? As she lay in his arms trying to find her breath? She wasn't interested in a cure.

He rolled over on his side, and she could feel the vibration of his laughter.

"Did we even say hello?" he asked.

"I don't think we said much of anything." She kissed his chin. "Hi."

He gave her a warm smile. "Hi."

Luke shifted, taking her with him as he tossed the pillows into the corner and leaned against them. She ended up tucked snugly under his arm, and they had a beautiful view out the window of the moon rising over the lake far below. He gave her a little squeeze.

"Does it bother you? The no-talking thing with us? The way we avoid each other when the sun's up?"

Whitney hesitated. She was normally the one who analyzed things and sought out logic. But she wasn't sure she wanted to analyze what was happening here. She was a little afraid of what she might find if they pulled back the curtain.

"We talked a lot that first night."

"That's not an answer."

She craned her neck to look up at him. "You're the

guy who embraces the strong silent act. Now you're worried about our lack of communication?"

He let out a long breath. "That's *still* not an answer. I'm not saying we need to be BFFs, but it's beginning to feel like we're vampires. Like we only exist after sundown." He grinned. "Mind you, I like what happens after sundown, but…"

"Luke Rutledge, are you saying I'm making you feel *cheap*?"

He laughed. He'd been laughing a lot this week.

"Not exactly. But I want to make sure *you* don't feel that way." He ran his hand through his hair. "I just don't want to assume anything, if that makes sense."

Her chest tightened. He was worried about her feelings. A tremor went through her, and Luke tugged the blanket up around them. She was safe in this corner with him. She was home.

"Luke, I don't know what we're doing. On paper, this relationship makes no sense. But here we are, and it's…incredible. Shocking, but incredible."

He thought about that for a moment. "So…this *is* a relationship?"

"It's more than a one-night stand, so I guess the default definition is that it's a relationship. But don't ask me to define it in any more detail than that, because I can't." She nodded against his chest, knowing one of the things that was bothering them both. "We should let Helen know. I don't like keeping secrets."

"Agreed. That way I can kiss you in the sunlight, and I've really been wanting to do that."

She didn't answer right away, lost in wondering what that would be like—kissing Luke in the light of the day. They were entering dangerous territory now. Sharing their relationship, or whatever this was. Making it more than just sweet-hot sex in this bed. Making it *real*. Her stomach fluttered.

"I think I'd like that, too." She settled back against him with a sigh. "Helen told me how you came to work at the winery, after Tony caught you stealing from their garden."

Luke went still, then nodded against her head. "I was a punk-ass kid."

"You were trying to feed your family."

A rumble of low laughter went through him. "Great. I suggest we talk more, and the first subject that comes up is my bad behavior *and* my train wreck of a family."

"It wasn't bad behavior if it was for a good cause." Whitney was surprised to hear those words come out of her mouth. As an auditor, there was no excuse for bad behavior. Wrong was wrong. Period.

"Is Whitney Foster giving me a free pass? Are you feeling feverish?" He put his hand on her forehead and she swatted him away.

"You were just a kid. Kids are a lot more likely to get free passes than adults, who should be better problem solvers."

"Yeah, you'd think that." He went quiet, slowly running his hand up and down her back.

"You're thinking of your parents. That they should have done better?"

His hand stopped moving, then started again. "They did the best they could. That's what everyone kept telling me. It wasn't our fault. Our parents were doing the best they could. Blah, blah, blah. The problem was, their best was pretty bad."

"Is your father in jail for killing Doug's brother?"

It was hard to forget the words Doug and Frank had thrown at him last weekend.

"Man, I am *really* sorry I suggested talking." He took a deep breath. His words came out clipped and sharp, as if he wanted to get it over with. "No. My father's in prison for his third armed robbery. After my mom died, booze wasn't enough for him, so he moved on to stronger things. That did not help his already bad judgment. Didn't take long for him to gather up a third-strike arrest and catch a long prison term. He can rot there, as far as I'm concerned."

There were no words to make that story less awful, so Whitney just wrapped her arms around his waist and held on tight. He resisted for a moment, then returned the embrace, resting his head on hers.

"My brother and Doug's brother were in a car accident a few years back. They were both too drunk to drive. But Larry Canfield was the one behind the wheel when they went off Hilltop Road and barrel-rolled through a cornfield. He died on the spot. Zayne broke about every bone in his body, but he survived somehow. Too much of a miserable SOB to die, I guess."

"I take it you're not close? What about the rest of your family?"

Luke shrugged. "Zayne's even more of a loner than I am. I call him every month or so, but he doesn't always pick up. My sister, Jessie, calls once in a while from Florida. My baby brother, Riley, joined the army and I guess *that's* his family now." His father's crimes had scattered the family like the wind. Or like a bomb. "How about you? I don't remember you mentioning siblings?"

"Nope. Only child. Just not the spoiled kind."

"Because *you* were the one taking care of things."

"I still do, but I keep my distance to protect my sanity. I actually called Mom this morning, though, and had to listen to her raving about the new boyfriend and how he's gonna make a few calls and maybe she'll get an audition for some big TV competition next season and oh, my god, it never changes."

"An audition? That sounds pretty awesome."

She snorted. "Yeah, it always *sounds* awesome. But the reality is she's a lousy judge of men. She'll fall for anyone who promises to make her a star, and George is no different from all the others through the years. He'll get her hopes up, then he'll cheat her out of some money and get her to buy him a car or something, and then he'll disappear."

"Can she actually sing?"

Whitney smiled against his chest, remembering being a little girl and listening to Mom sing all day long in their house. "She's got a great voice. She's made a decent living as a wedding singer and lounge singer in Vegas. But it all goes back to those bad decisions."

"Are you worried about this George guy?"

"Nope. Most of Mom's money is safely invested in accounts she can't access without my permission. He can get *some* cash out of her, but not enough to hurt her financially."

He kissed the top of her head. "You're like a financial ninja, Whit. Using your money brain to protect the people you care about, like your mom and Helen and Evie. It's cool."

She'd never thought of herself as a warrior of any kind. He tightened his grip and moved her onto his lap.

"And I think we've done all the talking we need to do tonight."

She moved to straddle him, putting her hands on either side of his face.

"But what else is there to do?"

His mouth slid into a crooked smile.

"I'm sure we can come up with something."

And they did.

When she looked out the dining room window and saw him in the vineyard the next day, trimming leaves from the vines, she didn't hesitate to set her laptop aside and head out the door. Helen had left early for a hair appointment, so Whitney hadn't had a chance to talk to her about Luke. But she would. For now, she just wanted one of those daylight kisses he'd talked about in the dark last night.

He straightened when he saw her, watching as she walked toward him between the tall rows of vines. Molly sat up and barked once in greeting before settling back down at his feet. Whitney glanced at the trimming shears in his hand.

"Whatcha doin' up here?"

"Getting a little more sunshine on the berries."

Bright green grapes hung in large clusters on either side of them, fattening in the late summer sun. She reached for one cluster, then hesitated, looking at Luke.

"Can I try one?"

In answer, he reached over and plucked a grape from the vine, wiping it gently on his shirt before handing it to her.

"They might be a little bitter, but they're getting sweeter every day as we get closer to harvest. Hold it like this..." He held it up for her, the stem end against her lips. "The skin can be tough, but if you squeeze the bottom, the flesh will pop right out of the skin and into your mouth. Like this…" He pinched the end of the grape, and her mouth exploded with flavor. It was tart, but definitely grapey. She gave a low moan of pleasure.

"Can we afford to lose a few more grapes?" She reached for a bunch, but hesitated.

Luke reached over and clipped off four grapes. "If you yank on them, you might damage the others. And yes, we can spare a few grapes." His eyes darkened. "Especially if I get to see that expression on your face again."

She held up a grape and squeezed the end until the flesh popped into her mouth. "Oh, my god. It feels so… decadent. I feel like I'm suddenly connected to centuries of history. I can imagine Cleopatra plucking grapes and eating them like that. Give me one more…"

He handed her a grape, keeping one to eat himself. He didn't find it quite as delicious as she did, twisting his face. "Still sour. Wait a few more weeks, and then you won't be able to stop eating them. When they're ripe, each grape is like a sparkling sugar burst." A few birds flew overhead. "Pretty soon Steve and I will have to net the vines to keep the birds from stealing our berries."

"I think they're pretty irresistible now." She ate the last one, staring longingly at the heavy bunch hanging from the vine. Luke didn't answer, and she found him staring at her. This was a look usually reserved for his place after dark. His voice wasn't a daytime voice, either. It was low and rough and filled with desire.

"I think *you're* pretty irresistible." He stepped forward and gave her a playful wink as he tugged her against him. "Although you can be a little sour."

A laugh bubbled up in her throat. "Hey!"

That was all she was able to say before his mouth fell on hers. Gentle but demanding, his fingers wrapped around her hips and held her close. Hmm. A daylight kiss. A kiss that tasted of grapes and sex and…something. She couldn't describe the feeling at first, turning her head to give him better access. He growled and slid one hand up her spine to cup the back of her head, making it difficult to think. It was more than pleasure. It was more than desire. It felt like…falling. She was falling into this kiss, into his embrace, and into him. She was falling for Luke, without a safety net in sight. She wrapped her arms around his neck.

Helen's voice, coming from three feet away, jolted them apart.

"I brought some lunch home, if you think you can untangle yourselves long enough to come eat it." She stood there, arms crossed, with an amused smirk on her face as she looked back and forth between them. "Oh, please. I'm not an idiot—I've known all week." She turned toward the house. "I hope you two know what you're doing."

Whitney touched her lips. She hoped the same thing.

CHAPTER NINETEEN

LUKE'S DAYS FELL into a pattern he'd never expected to
see in his lifetime. Waking in the morning with a beautiful woman in his arms. Cooking her breakfast—on the
mornings they didn't join Helen—then going off to do
their own jobs. Whitney worked on Helen's books, along
with a few other businesses around town she was doing
bookkeeping for. He worked the winery. Sometimes
they saw each other at lunchtime, but if not, she'd come
up to the wine barn midafternoon with a bottle of water
and a ready kiss. The kiss quenched him more than any
water could. Her kisses were a salvation for his heart.

Dinners depended on whether he was working the
bar or not. If he was, dinner was early at his place.
Sometimes early enough to hop in the shower together
before he left her to wait for him. If he wasn't working the Shamrock, they had dinner with Helen. If he
thought Helen started smiling more when Whitney first
arrived, well…these days, that smile never left her face.

Tonight was no exception. Luke had done the cooking, but the three of them enjoyed the short ribs in
Helen's kitchen. The women were finishing up the
dishes as he enjoyed his coffee. That was the rule—
whoever didn't cook, cleaned up. In a couple short
weeks, they not only had a routine…they had *rules*. It
should have felt foreign and weird and uncomfortable,

but it didn't. It felt *right*. Like this was what he'd been looking for all along and he'd never even known it.

Helen hung her towel on the oven door handle. "Well, that was one of the best meals I think I've ever had. But now all I want is a nap!"

Luke met Whitney's gaze. Yeah, a nap. Or something else bed related. Helen didn't miss the change in atmosphere.

"Oh, good grief. You two are like a couple of horny rabbits!"

"Aunt Helen!" Whitney laughed, her cheeks turning pink.

Helen waved her off. "Bah, you know it's true. Enjoy it. There's nothing quite like the beginning of forever."

Luke and Whitney both went still, confronted with the word neither of them had discussed. The word *forever* had certainly floated through his mind more than once when he held her in his arms. But he had no idea what she was thinking. She'd talked about job hunting a few weeks ago. They'd said no strings attached. So why did he feel his heart was already ensnared?

"And speaking of rabbits, you don't always have to sneak off to Luke's tiny den out there." Helen put the last of the pans in the drawer beneath the stove. "When you and Tony converted the family room into our bedroom suite, Tony made sure there was insulation in the walls. If he was watching baseball out in the living room, he didn't want to keep me awake." She gave Whitney a pat on the back, then did the same to Luke as she walked by. "That means I can't hear anything that goes on upstairs, either. Just sayin'…" She headed out of the kitchen, but stopped to speak to Molly, lying at Luke's feet. "And yes, you can stay, too. Just leave Boots alone and remember this is *her* house."

He and Whitney stared at each other in shock for a moment after Helen left, then burst into laughter. Helen Russo never ceased to amaze him. She'd basically given them permission to go upstairs and do whatever they wanted. He stood and tugged Whitney into his arms, knowing they both wanted the same thing.

Luke had never been inside Helen and Tony's old bedroom. After Tony broke his ankle badly five or six years ago, they'd moved to a first-floor suite they'd created from the former family room. They decided they liked the convenience of being downstairs and stayed there. The upstairs suite Whitney was using was bigger than he'd imagined, with a nice sitting area inside the round tower extension. From there you could look down at the lake, where a few rooftops from Rendezvous Falls could be seen among the trees, or up to the vineyard.

"This puts the views at my place to shame."

Whitney walked over, sliding her arms around his waist. "I don't know. I kinda like the views I get at your place." She winked when he looked down at her. "Although it's nice to have all the clothes out of sight."

"Yeah, yeah, Miss Fussy Housekeeper. You've made it clear you don't approve of my organizational skills." He ignored her snort of laughter. "But I know where everything is in that place."

"Sure! Because you can *see* everything in that place. It's all right there in the open." She bumped her hip against his. "And appreciating things like dressers and cupboards and closets does not make me a fussy housekeeper. It makes me normal."

"Normal, huh? Do normal people keep lists and

spreadsheets for *everything*? Color code every task? I'll bet your closet's even color coded." He noted the way she glanced at the closet door. "Oh, my god. It is, isn't it?"

She tried to hold him back, laughing, but he made it to the closet. Sure enough, blue tops hung with blue tops, pink tops hung with pink tops, and so on.

"You *do* understand there's nothing 'normal' about this, right?"

"Maybe not, but it *is* efficient!" She slammed the door closed. "Now come over here and fulfill all those fantasies I've had of you crawling into *my* bed for a change."

He nudged her toward the large bed, covered with a blue-and-yellow-flowered comforter. "Are you telling me you've lain in this bed and fantasized about me?" The image made him so hard his jeans hurt him.

Whitney sat on the bed and ran her hand across the top of it. "Maybe. Back when I was sneaking back here at sunrise, thinking we were fooling Helen. I never could go back to sleep." She sighed. "I don't know if I'll ever be able to fall asleep without being in your arms."

Luke ignored the tremor of anxiety that rocked him. *Ever* sounded a lot like *forever*. Was it possible Whitney was thinking long-term, too? Or maybe she was just making casual conversation. Meaningless words. Nah, she was looking for that next big thing, and that certainly wouldn't be in Rendezvous Falls. It wouldn't be with him. She tugged her top up over her head, revealing the dark lace bra he liked so much, and his worries about the future evaporated.

When he woke the next morning, he found Whitney standing in the sitting area, with the comforter wrapped around her like a royal robe. He pulled on his jeans, but didn't bother to fasten them. He slid his arms around her and she leaned back against his chest with a sigh.

"Look at those colors, Luke. It's like the whole sky is celebrating the birth of a new day."

"Mmm-hmm. Pretty."

She glanced over her shoulder at him. "That's all you got? Pretty? That sunrise is gorgeous!"

Something about having her in his embrace always made him want to sway to unheard music. "What sunrise? I was too busy looking at you."

She rolled her eyes, swaying with him. They were silent for a moment before she softly asked a question he didn't know how to answer.

"Where is this going, Luke? You and I—what are we doing?"

What *he* was doing was falling in love. He knew it, but he couldn't bring himself to say it out loud. Not until he knew where her heart was. He wasn't ready to give her that kind of power over him. But he *loved* this woman, and he couldn't help wondering if that was the biggest mistake he'd ever made. After all, from the day she'd shown up at the winery, she'd accused him of all kinds of things. Had her suspicions about him evaporated? He kissed her temple.

"I don't know, Whit. I *like* whatever it is we're doing. I like it a lot. I hate to think about it ending, but…"

She continued to stare out the window, watching the sun rise over the hills across the lake, her head resting against him. "Does it have to end?"

Why was she putting this on him? "What do *you* think?"

"I think I hate the thought of it ending, too."

"But...?"

Her shoulders fell. "But I don't know how this plays out. I've never felt...anything like this. But I can't see how...unless I stay..."

Luke didn't react, but that word—*stay*—resonated in him like a bell. Could he ask her to do that? Would that be fair?

"Is that what you want?"

She opened her mouth, then closed it again, shaking her head. Was it possible she was waiting for him to ask? Damn, was this one of those *read my mind* moments married guys complained about? Was he supposed to know what she wanted without her saying it? If that was the game, they were in trouble. Because Luke Rutledge wasn't about to risk a bad guess. Not with his heart on the line.

That night, he and Steve Jenkins got to talking at the Shamrock. Steve didn't usually frequent the place, but he said his wife had kicked him out of the house for a few hours so she could have her girlfriends over to make salads in a jar, whatever that meant. Luke slid a local craft beer across the bar to his older, wiser friend.

"Did Linda come right out and tell you she wanted you to leave?"

Steve's brows shot up. They usually talked about wine and grapes and that was it.

"Oh, she made it very clear. I mean, it's not like she just ordered me out tonight. She told me last weekend I had to find somewhere to be Thursday because of this party. God forbid any man overhears the secrets women share once they get a few glasses of wine in them."

"So she didn't hint around and hope you'd know? Women don't really do that?"

Steve laughed so loud nearly everyone's head turned toward them. He wiped his eyes, then he slapped his hand on the bar and started laughing all over again.

"What the hell is so funny?" Luke growled.

"Oh, man…" Steve wiped his eyes again. "What's so *funny*? It could be the way you asked me that—like you were actually praying it was some silly rumor you'd heard. But it could also be the idea that *you're* asking about women!" He winked at Luke. "Let me guess—that niece of Helen's got under your skin?"

Luke glanced around to make sure everyone had gone back to their own conversations after Steve's outburst.

"Something like that, yeah. It's casual, though." There was nothing casual about his feelings, but no need to advertise if he was making a mistake.

Steve took a swig of his beer. "Pal, if you're asking me how women's minds work and the kind of head games they can play, you are *way* past casual. And to answer your original question… There are lots of times when women will expect you to know their thoughts. And they will be disappointed every time, because we're not freakin' mind readers. We will never know what they really want for their birthday, or where they want to go for dinner or how to answer the dreaded does-this-make-me-look-fat question."

"But then how do you…?"

"Survive?" Steve shook his head. "It's a mystery. But *trying* gets you points. And groveling when you get it wrong helps. And once in a blue moon, if you come out and ask them for a direct answer, they'll forget the women-rules and tell you."

"That seems like a lot of risk… I mean…work."

His friend sobered. "It's both. Risk and work. You each have to be ready to trust and forgive. A *lot*." Steve tipped his head and studied Luke. "But if this 'casual' relationship of yours ever gets serious, it's totally worth it. Marrying the right person is the best move any man will ever make on this earth. If you find the right one, figure out a way to keep her."

But how do you know? Luke shook his head and kept that question to himself. He'd already exposed more to Steve than he'd intended. And he was no closer to figuring out what to do about Whitney Foster.

He wiped down the bar. He'd always scoffed at marriage, but the minute Steve mentioned it, Luke could see himself spending his life with Whitney. But what was *she* picturing?

WHITNEY STARED AT the tall stack of bank statements. More accurately, she stared at *three* tall stacks of bank statements. Helen and Tony's personal account. The Falls Legend business account. And the other one.

The statements for the mystery account said "Falls Legend Winery" under Tony and Helen's names, but it wasn't a business account. It had been relatively inactive until Tony's death. But after that, there were fairly frequent withdrawals. Big ones. And deposits. The deposits weren't always big, but they were fairly consistent—two hundred one month, three hundred the next.

Those small deposits weren't enough to explain how there could be almost two hundred *thousand* dollars in the account. Helen's personal account was just enough to keep her afloat. The business account had been solvent two years ago, but was barely covering the bills now. But this mystery account held a small fortune.

And *someone* was writing checks out of it. Checks for thousands of dollars.

She could see where some of that money had gone—some of the bills had been paid from the account, and Helen swore she hadn't used it. There were mystery withdrawals taken out, then redeposited, penny for penny, a few days later. And the occasional cash withdrawal that *didn't* get repaid. She closed her eyes and massaged her temples.

Helen came in and sat, handing Whitney a coffee. "You're telling me we actually have money in this new account? Enough to pay our bills?"

After Whitney finished putting all the numbers together in a dozen different spreadsheets, she'd presented the data to Helen that morning. Her aunt swore she'd known nothing about the mystery account, and had no idea where a checkbook might be. She'd been shoving all the bank statements into boxes and bags for the past couple of years to avoid dealing with them, so she had no idea there was a third account.

"That's the thing, Helen." Whitney sighed. She didn't like mysteries. Especially when she was in the middle of an audit. Especially *this* audit. "There are a couple of recent bills from vendors that have overdue balances, but not that many, and not that much. It looks like bills have been paid, but not from the business account. They were paid from *this* account. But…I don't know where this money came from. Or who's been using it."

Helen shifted in her chair. Something about her body language caught Whitney's attention. Helen's hands had a death grip on her coffee mug, and her eyes were fixed on the far corner of the dining room.

"Aunt Helen? What aren't you telling me?" If her

aunt was hiding another box of papers somewhere, Whitney was going to lose it.

"I called Tom Garland at the bank after lunch." Helen fidgeted again, then set the coffee cup on the table and turned to face Whitney. "He said the account's been open for years, since before he got there. It looks like Tony deposited a chunk of money in there every year, usually in January. Tom said I'm on the signature card with Tony, but I don't remember it. Then again, Tony used to hand me stuff all the time to sign, and I didn't pay much attention. There's only one other signature on the account." Helen's fingers twisted together in her lap. "It's Luke."

She'd feared as much, even though she'd hoped it wasn't so. Once Helen made it clear Whitney and Luke didn't need to sneak around anymore, their relationship—for lack of a better word—had settled into a comfortable routine. They each did their own thing during the day, with perhaps a quick kissing session in the barn or out in the vineyard, and then they'd have dinner together. Sometimes with Helen, sometimes just the two of them. And then they'd spend the night, usually at Luke's, but sometimes he'd quietly slip upstairs to share her bed. It felt easy now. It felt like the type of thing that could grow into…more. Neither of them had said so, but it felt like love.

She gripped the edge of the table and closed her eyes, trying to hold back the burning tears. Her heart swelled and hurt at the same time. It was true. She was *in love* with Luke Rutledge. Head over heels for the man. Couldn't imagine her life without him in it. And his name was on a mysterious checking account with a small fortune in it.

None of this made sense. Not falling in love. And not the mystery account. There *had* to be an explanation for the money. And she needed to figure it out soon. Without having to ask him, if she could help it. Luke knew she believed in him, and that *meant* something to him. If she had to confront him about this account, it could shatter his fragile trust before she had a chance to tell him she loved him.

On the bright side, she'd found those rent checks he said he'd been paying. He'd been depositing them in the mystery account. But why hadn't he told her that? Why had Luke kept this all a deep, dark secret? Why was he withdrawing money from the mystery account? He wouldn't steal from Helen. That couldn't be what happened. But whatever he was doing, even if it was some crazy-but-well-intentioned scheme, she needed to know. She needed to fix it.

"It's not like Luke was hiding it from us," Helen pointed out. "I had all the bank statements right here in the house. I just didn't look at them. All that worry and we had money the whole time. This is my fault."

"That's true. I mean *not* the 'your fault' part…"

Helen snorted. "That's the most true thing of all. It's a miracle the place isn't in bankruptcy because of me."

"We've had this conversation already. We're not playing the blame game anymore."

Despite her words of reassurance, Whitney couldn't help thinking back to dealing with her mom's careless attitude toward money. Toward everything. Nothing was ever a problem. Nothing was worth worrying about. *Everything will work out fine, baby.* But they hadn't been fine. They'd been in a hole they almost didn't dig out of.

Why couldn't people understand that managing

money was the ultimate security? Knowing where the
pennies went meant knowing where the dollars went.
And dollars added up to mortgage payments and car
payments and groceries. The idea of not knowing where
her money was made Whitney's brain twitch. How had
her aunt *survived* it? What was Luke doing with that
money? Why couldn't her mom understand paying
some shady guy for music lessons at fifty-eight was
not going to make her the next winner of some TV competition? Why didn't people have any damn sense? How
could she possibly be in love with Luke Rutledge? It
all made her head hurt. She stood so quickly her chair
almost tipped over.

"I need to go for a walk."

The falls were noisy after the rain they'd had, but it
still wasn't enough to shut out all the questions whirling through Whitney's head. Were she and Tony the
only ones in the family with any money sense? With
any common sense? Why did it have to be *Luke* who
had been using the mystery account? There were thousands of dollars gone since Tony died that couldn't be
accounted for. Her heart insisted Luke would never help
himself to anything that belonged to Tony or Helen. But
her head reminded her that numbers don't lie.

"There's a pretty picture if I ever saw one." She'd
been so caught up in her thoughts that she never heard
Luke approaching. He sat beside her on the rock. "This
isn't the legendary rock where the lovers turned into
deer, you know. That's out there." He lifted his chin toward the flat rock centered in the swirling water.

"I know." She didn't even try to smile. She wasn't
ready for this conversation right now, but here it was.
Luke frowned.

"What's wrong?"

There was no easy way to do this. No way to sugar-coat it. Better to get it out in the open and deal with it.

"There's a bank account Helen didn't know about. One that you've been making withdrawals from." She finally met his gaze. Already she could see the walls coming up. "I need to know why."

"You think I'm stealing from her." It wasn't a question. He thought she'd assumed the worst of him. Because he thought everyone did that. Even her.

She blinked away. "I didn't say that."

"You didn't deny it, either." He stood and started to pace. She could see his anger growing. Or was it pain? She reached for him, but stopped herself.

"Luke…"

He stopped and scrubbed his hands down his face. "What?"

"I *don't* think you just took it without a reason. You would never hurt Helen like that. But…money *looks* like it's missing." She pleaded with him. "Just *tell* me. We'll juggle things around to make it right."

He turned away from her and shoved his hands into his pockets, staring at the water tumbling over the rocks. "Helen really didn't know anything about the account?"

"To be fair, there were a lot of things Helen chose not to know about. She wasn't looking at any of the records." She stood and joined him by the stream. "Whatever you've done, we'll deal with it together."

His head snapped around. "What I've *done*? So you've already decided I took the money. From *Helen*. You think that's possible."

"No-o." It wasn't a very convincing denial. She was so confused. Maybe he'd needed the money because

Helen wasn't paying him enough. She could work with that. She could fix it.

"Unbelievable." Luke gave a harsh laugh and turned away. He took a few steps as if he was going to leave her standing there. But he stopped near the trail, speaking straight ahead toward the trees. "It was Tony's 'rainy-day fund.' They'd had a harsh weather year a few years after the winery opened, and it nearly broke them. When things turned around, he started setting money aside, in case it happened again. He gave me the check-books the year I moved into the carriage house. Said I was family, and if anything happened to him or Helen, I should have access to it to keep the winery going. I figured Helen knew."

Whitney hated the distance between them. The distance in his voice. But she didn't move, knowing he wasn't finished.

"I forgot about it until the first bill collector called the business line six months after Tony died. It was the power company, threatening to cut us off if we didn't pay immediately. Helen was practically catatonic at that point, so I wrote a check out of the rainy-day account." He finally turned to face her again. "I had no idea what the account balance was. I just crossed my fingers and hoped there was enough to cover the check. I guess there was, since the lights stayed on."

"So all those withdrawals were to pay bills. Did you just wait for calls to come in?"

Luke rubbed the back of his neck and sighed, finally turning to face her. "Sometimes. But after a while I could recognize the dunning notices in the mail. You know, 'Urgent,' 'Time-Sensitive,' stuff like that. Instead of giving those to Helen and upsetting her, I'd pay them. I didn't have her PIN number or anything, so I never knew how much money I was playing with. I'd write myself a check, wait a few days to make sure it cleared, then put it back in and pay the bill. Sometimes they wanted instant payment, and I'd have to use my credit card to pay right then, and reimburse myself. Either way, if a check was going to bounce, it would bounce to *me*, not to one of our suppliers."

Whitney couldn't wrap her head around what he was saying. "You...took money out...waited...then put it back...and paid bills..."

Please don't let us be audited.

She'd never be able to explain that cash flow without it sounding like a money-laundering scheme. God save her from bad money managers!

Luke lifted his hands, then let them fall, shaking his head. "I tried to discuss it with Helen a few times, but she always shut me down. Told me there was nothing to worry about. But the calls kept coming. I'd make up some excuse about a miscommunication and pay them."

She should be angry. It was an accounting *nightmare*. She *was* angry, but the person she was angry with was dead. Tony had always managed his own books, and clearly he'd never taught Helen or Luke anything about his bookkeeping methods. That was a huge mistake. After his sudden death, Helen fell apart, and Luke was juggling the grape growing, the wine making and the bills.

"When Helen told you there wasn't enough to cover your pay, you must have thought..."

"I thought we were finished." Emotion roughened his voice more than usual. "I kept waiting for the money to run out."

She walked over and took his hand. He tried to pull away, but she wouldn't let him. Luke's plan to withdraw money to see if it was really there, then put it back and pay bills, was completely unorthodox, and possibly unethical or maybe downright illegal. She'd never heard of anything like it. But it was his way of making sure they didn't bounce a check to anyone, which would have seriously damaged their reputation as well as their credit. And it had worked.

"Luke, there's over a hundred and eighty thousand dollars in that account."

He went still as stone.

"Say that again?"

"Tony's rainy-day fund was big enough to cover a lot of rainy days. I don't think you ever had to worry about bouncing a check."

He shook off her grip, waving her off angrily when she tried to reach out again.

"Give. Me. A minute."

He walked back to the water's edge, bending over to put his hands on his thighs like someone knocked the wind out of him. He sounded stunned. "Every time I took money out, I thought it was the last time. You must think Helen and I are complete idiots."

Her heart broke for the pressure he must have been under.

"I think you were both doing the best you could under the circumstances."

He straightened and shook his head, staring up at the falls.

"Your little accounting brain must be ready to stroke out right about now."

She gave him a crooked grin. "It was touch-and-go

there for a few minutes. The only thing saving you and my aunt from a beatdown right now is the fact that you were both listening to your hearts. Hers was broken, and yours was in hero mode, trying to protect her." She moved closer, and he didn't back away this time. "It was definitely creative bookkeeping, and I don't *ever* want to explain it in a tax audit, but you pulled it off. I only have one question—where did the random deposits come from?"

"Me." His shoulders lifted and dropped. "I was so afraid the account would run dry, I shoveled any spare money I had back into it to keep us solvent. And, of course, my rent."

No wonder he'd been shell-shocked to hear the account was in six figures. He'd been working all those extra jobs because he thought he was paying the bills for the winery.

"What have you been living on?"

He huffed out a laugh. "As my mom used to say, I was living on dreams and beans. When you grow up poor, you learn how to make a dollar go a long way. I eat good food, but it's day-old bread. Generic brands. A turkey breast or pork roast can last me a week between sandwiches and meals." He gave her a sardonic grin. "And I steal fries from the kitchen at the Shamrock when Bridget's not looking."

"Ew!" She stepped up and slid her arms around his waist. He froze for a half second, then took her in his arms. It was the first fully released breath she'd let go of all day. She was home. Luke was holding her. His chin rested on top of her head.

But something had changed. He was holding back. Just a little.

"Luke?"

He took a deep breath, his voice catching. "You thought I'd stolen that money."

"*No!* I know you'd never do that." Her pulse quickened. They both knew she'd suspected him of something from the day she'd arrived. But that stopped once they fell for each other. Or had it? Was there a part of her that would never be able to trust *any* man? Not even the one she loved? She should tell him, but this didn't seem like the right time. It would sound false. Contrived.

"Don't lie to me, Whitney," he growled. "Even if it was just for a heartbeat, you thought I took it. Even if you thought I was doing something 'good' with it, you thought I took it." He stepped back, setting her away from him. Throwing up a wall between them. She could see it in his eyes. Hear it in his tight words. "You thought I was hiding things. Gaming the system. With *Helen's* money."

"Luke…" What could she say?

He turned and walked away, leaving her alone by the falls. She'd hurt him, and she wasn't sure how long it would take to repair that. Or if she'd ever repair it.

CHAPTER TWENTY

LUKE HAMMERED THE last piece of clapboard onto the front of the carriage house. The limestone pillars had been pressure washed. New rocking chairs were up in the barn, waiting to be set in place. Things were looking pretty good. He slid the hammer into the loop on his cargo shorts and started down the ladder.

A burst of female laughter came from inside the tasting room. Helen insisted this "Wednesday work party" would be a way to get some projects done before the festival. But Luke was wondering how much actual work would get done today. It sounded more like a social event, and that was okay, too. It had been too long since Helen had been surrounded with this kind of laughter.

The book club was repainting the tasting room, because Whitney had decreed the room too dark. It was an awfully big job, but he couldn't argue about the color. Tony had been gung ho for the Italian theme when the winery opened, but the dark green walls made the space feel small.

"Trying to avoid the hen party in there?"

Luke looked down from the ladder to see Rick Thomas. He didn't know the man well, other than knowing he was a professor at the college and a member of Helen's book club.

"Hi, Rick. Looks like you're avoiding them, too."

"I'm not exactly gifted with a paint brush. I'm much better with a hammer or rake, like you." Rick glanced up toward the off-kilter gate in front of Helen's still-messy garden.

Luke grimaced as he stepped off the ladder. "I wouldn't want to be the one caught messing with Helen's roses."

Rick clapped him on the back. It was an odd move for someone he barely knew. Usually the guy just nodded abruptly in his direction and quickly moved on. A lot of people in Rendezvous Falls did that. Treated him like someone who had to be tolerated. And now Rick was squeezing his shoulder affectionately. "You won't be the one caught. I will. And I can handle Helen—we go way back."

Luke didn't say anything. He didn't have to. Rick started laughing. "I know—*you* go way back, too. But you were working with Tony most of the time. Helen and I became good friends almost as soon as I got to Rendezvous Falls twenty years ago. In fact…" Rick's laughter faded to a fond smile. "We became *such* good friends, Tony came to my office one morning to have a chat about how much time I was spending with his wife. I hadn't outed myself to many people in town at that point, but I came rainbow-flag clean to Tony as soon as I saw the look in his eye and the set of his jaw."

"I'll bet."

Tony hadn't been a big man, but he was tough as nails. He probably could have beaten the tar out of most men. Especially if he considered them a threat to his marriage. But why was Rick sharing all of this *now*? Awkward silence settled between them, until Rick nodded toward the main house.

"I'll go tackle that garden, which is *criminally* neglected. I gave her most of those rose bushes, you know." Luke didn't know that. Rick studied him for a moment before continuing. "Look…of all people, *I* shouldn't be one to listen to gossip. But I did, for a lot of years. I made assumptions about you, because your family is…um…notorious around here."

Luke wasn't sure where this conversation was going, but any talk that involved his family was one he'd rather avoid.

"Yup. Sorry, but I have a lot of work…"

"My point is…" Rick moved to stay in front of Luke. "I owe you an apology. You took care of Helen after Tony died." Another burst of laughter came from the tasting room. "You stepped up long before any of us realized how bad things were. And I want you to know how grateful we all are. If you ever need anything, or if Helen needs anything…" Rick dug in his pocket and pulled out a business card. "You call me."

"Okay." Luke took the card, thrown off balance by Rick's unexpected apology and gratitude. He didn't have a lot of practice responding to either.

Rick chuckled. "You're not much of a talker, are you?"

"I… No, not really. But…" It was weird to be accepting an apology for something he hadn't even known had happened. For opinions half the town still had because of his name. He shook Rick's hand. "Thank you."

"No worries. I'll have that garden spiffed up in no time to look good for your customers." Luke once again had nothing to say. He watched Rick walk to the garden after pulling some tools from the trunk of his Lexus.

The door to the tasting room opened behind him.

"Hey, hot shot, you going to stand around all day or are you going to get some work done?"

Whitney stepped up beside him. He dropped his arm on her shoulder, but didn't pull her closer. Things hadn't been the same since their conversation by the falls. Whitney had been trying hard to get him past it with an extra sunny attitude and constant affection. He looked down into her hopeful eyes. She was trying *too* hard.

They were going to have to work this out sooner or later. But right now, rejecting that smile would feel like he was kicking a puppy. He gave her a quick kiss on the forehead.

"Hey, yourself. Aren't you supposed to be painting?"

She laughed—it sounded forced—and held up her arm so he could see the streak of bright blue paint on her skin. "I've learned I'm not the world's best painter. Good thing you made us put all that plastic on the floor before we got started."

Luke wanted to take that arm and kiss the tender skin there, working his way up from where her pulse beat at her wrist, past the blue forearm to her shoulder to her neck… But that would be a bad idea. That would lead to him taking her upstairs, and he couldn't do that. Not as long as there was a chance she still saw him as some loser to feel sorry for.

Whitney went up on tiptoe and kissed him, her lips soft and warm against his. He knew she was begging forgiveness. The thing was, he'd *already* forgiven her. He just couldn't forget. He tried not to respond to her kiss, but…who was he kidding? She was irresistible. His hand cupped her face and he kissed her back. Sweet, sweet Whitney. She had his heart right there in her hands, and she was probably going to crush it, but he couldn't save himself.

Molly woofed a happy greeting and came over to Whitney, bringing Luke to his senses. It was broad daylight and there was a work party going on. Sure enough, when he broke away and looked over her shoulder, several faces were pressed to the tasting room window, grinning widely. They scattered when they realized they'd been caught.

Whitney brushed her lips on his neck. "Please don't pull away. We...we have to figure this out. I'm sorry..."

He somehow found the strength to set her away from him.

"Whit, it's the middle of the damn day." His frustration with himself boiled over into his tone, and she recoiled a little. "I mean, we have work to do, and an audience." He looked up at the house, where Rick quickly turned away to start raking again. Her smile returned.

"Duly noted. Sorry." She said that word twenty times a day now, and it was getting on his nerves. Words didn't mean anything. Actions did. And when she'd had the chance to believe in him, she'd doubted instead. To her credit, she'd pictured him as some modern-day Robin Hood, but she still thought he took the money.

It probably *had* looked pretty bad, especially to an accountant. She was obviously sorry, but that didn't change what happened. He wanted her, but he couldn't help holding himself back, protecting himself. He rubbed his thumb on the dried paint on her arm.

"Is *that* the color you're painting the tasting room?"

She chuckled. "That's a highlight color for some of the trim. We want to keep the colorful spirit of the Rendezvous Falls Victorian houses in there, so there's blue, green and orange trim. Most of the room will be a silvery blue, though. Lena said it will look like the lake in the morning." Whitney shrugged. "She's the artist. Once we get the new wine labels, brochures and signage, it will all come together. A new look for Falls Legend."

"You're going to have all of that done by the festival? You know it's less than two weeks away, right?"

She nodded, her eyes sparkling at the challenge. She was back in her element now, feeling more confident. She was in charge. "It'll be tight, but we'll make it. Everything's on a hot rush, but we should have the new wine labels this Friday. They're extra thick, so they'll go right over the top of the labels we have. The signs should be here next week. A new road sign and new signs for inside." Her hands gestured as she warmed up to the subject. "And I ordered a statue for the float no one will ever forget!"

"You bought a statue?" Luke was picturing some marble monstrosity of the Greek god of wine or something.

"Well, not a *statue* statue, and I didn't *buy* it. There's a film supply warehouse that rents out props, and they had life-sized deer statues…figurines…whatever. I think they're fiberglass."

"They?"

"One of each—a male and a female. I ordered this water pump thing that will recreate the waterfall on the float, and then the two life-sized deer standing there. Get it? The legend? Falls Legend? I've hired Evie's brother to build the platform and frame for the float. It'll be the best one in the parade. Helen said there's a contest and I know we'll win—and most important, *everyone* will be talking about it. And if everyone's talking about the float, then everyone's talking about the winery!"

Luke couldn't stop the proud smile tugging at his mouth. This was the woman who'd captured his heart. Bright-eyed, confident and strong. Her plan sounded a little over-the-top, but she was right. Everyone would be talking. Which meant he had to get busy.

"Sounds ambitious. You and I both need to get back to work if we're going to have this place crawling with people in a few weeks." As much as he wanted to protect his heart, he tugged her in and gave her a quick kiss, because he couldn't *not* kiss her right now. "You're just the one who can pull it off, Whit."

"THOSE ARE NOT DEER."

Whitney blurted out the obvious, because no other words came to mind that she'd be willing to say in front of her aunt. They both stared into the back of the delivery truck.

"Is that…" Helen shook her head, as if doing so would change what they were looking at. "Is that… a moose?"

You're just the one who can pull it off, Whit.

Luke's vote of confidence, even after the rough patch they'd hit, had made Whitney's heart glow last week. Last week had been a wonderful time. Last week was before every damn thing had gone wrong.

"There's been a mistake." Whitney hoped the truck driver would tell her he opened the wrong crate and her two beautiful deer were right behind this massive moose.

He looked at his manifest and checked the packing

slip. "Sorry, ma'am, but this guy is all yours. And his lady friend on the other pallet. The model numbers match up. I'm sorry, but..."

She knew she looked horrified. Holy good lord, she *was* horrified! When he'd pulled a square of cardboard away to verify it was what she'd expected, Whitney had actually screamed. A life-sized moose may be majestic, but it was not exactly...pretty. And definitely not romantic, unless you were a female moose. His antlers were missing—the driver explained they were boxed separately and had a six-foot span. Great. His head was enormous, and fake greenery hung from his mouth at the bottom of his bulbous nose, as if he'd just lifted his head from some swamp.

"I can't use a moose. I can't use *two* mooses. Two moose. Whatever. He's bigger than the entire float!" Of course, the float didn't exist anyway, because Evie's brother broke his arm riding his dirt bike two days earlier.

Helen patted Whitney's arm. "Well, you wanted to get people talking. This will sure as hell do that. We'll make it work."

"We *can't* make this work! We can't make *any* of this work! I'm sure I ordered the deer. They sent the wrong thing. This is a disaster. *Everything* is a disaster." She turned away from the moose, who now seemed to be laughing at her. Yeah, him and the universe and whoever else she'd somehow pissed off.

Helen nodded at the driver. "You can put them up in the wine barn. There's a loading dock around back."

Whitney knew she was bordering on having a meltdown, but who could blame her?

"Helen, I don't want the stupid mooses! Moose.

What*ever*." Whitney threw her hands up in defeat. "What are we going to do? Now I don't have any deer for the float. Not that we'll *have* a float, since I have no one to build it. That means no parade for us. The signs haven't arrived yet—none of them. Not for the winery. Not for the festival booth. Nothing. The promo booklets have a misprint right on the front page, so *those* are useless. The wine labels came in the wrong color. This rebranding plan has officially failed."

Helen's face flushed in embarrassment. "I'm so sorry about the labels. You know how bad I am with computers, and I must have clicked on the green ones by mistake. But it's okay. We'll be plain old Falls Legend Winery at the festival, with our plain old trifold brochures and regular labels. We can gradually introduce all the new stuff afterward."

How could Helen be so calm? Whitney fought off the irrational urge to stomp her feet like a five-year-old.

"That won't work. I had it all planned. We need to make a splash. We need something that says 'look who we are now!' The festival is the perfect opportunity. If we miss it, all this planning, not to mention the investment, will be pointless."

Whitney's chest tightened, and hyperventilating was a very real possibility. So was bursting into tears, but she wouldn't let that happen.

Before Helen could respond to her outburst, Luke walked up, a bemused smile on his face.

"Would either of you ladies like to explain why there are two giant *moose* being unloaded in the barn? Molly just about lost her mind."

His question made the disaster feel that much more

real. This wasn't a dream. There were moose—mooses?—in the wine barn.

"It's a *mistake*, like every other damn thing this week. A mistake! The whole festival is ruined for us now."

He held up his hands to stop her. "Okay, why don't you just take a breath."

Whitney saw red. Her mom used to say that all the time. That and…

Luke finished her thought for her. "I think you're overreacting."

This was the story of Whitney's whole damn life. No one around her ever worried about a damn thing, even as she yelled out warnings about impending disasters. Why did everyone she knew seem like the kind of folks who'd rather rearrange the deck chairs on a sinking ship than try to save themselves? They had a chance to put Falls Legend Winery back on the map, and no one cared but her.

This time she *did* stomp her foot. "Damn it, why is everyone so mellow about all of this? Is no one paying attention to what's happening? Or should I say, *not* happening?"

Helen laughed. She *laughed*. "Honey, two weeks ago we all thought the winery was about to go under. Now we have that rainy-day fund *you* discovered. Take a moment to enjoy the thrill of surviving. Everything else will sort itself out eventually. And the place looks nice."

She gestured at the freshly painted carriage house with its refreshed front porch and newly stained deck overlooking the lake. There were baskets of flowers hanging all around, and a potted hydrangea sitting on top of an old wine barrel they'd put by the entrance.

The building had a fresh, vibrant look compared to when she'd arrived.

"Helen's right," Luke said. "Besides, throwing a fit when things go wrong doesn't help anyone."

Maintaining her happy-happy attitude around him while waiting to see if he was *ever* going to forgive her was beginning to take a toll on her self-control. She leveled a glare at him.

"I am *not* throwing a fit. Trust me, if I was throwing a fit, you'd damn well know it." She took a shaky breath, trying to steady her voice. "That account was good news, but it's not a golden parachute that can carry this business forever. We've already earmarked a big chunk of it for repairs and upgrades, including getting ready for the festival. Looks like *that* was a wasted investment."

Luke shook his head. "We're as ready as we're going to get. We'll make the best of it at the festival and pick up our sales the old-fashioned way, by selling good wine. It'll be fine."

And there it was. Luke's favorite word over the past week. *Fine.* Everything was freaking *fine*, no matter the subject. He was fine. They were fine. The winery was fine. Finances were fine. The festival would be fine. But nothing felt fine right now, especially between the two of them. The signs were subtle, but something had definitely shifted. Cooled. His eyes weren't quite as warm. Or if they were, he'd blink it away as if he'd caught himself in a weak moment.

His touch was cooler, too. He told her they needed "space" and suggested she not come to his place for a while. She hated it, but she gave him his damn space. Because she loved the man and wanted him to work through this and let her back in. She understood he was upset she'd questioned his handling of the rainy-day account. But she was an *accountant*. She read numbers like most people read thrillers. And the story had pointed her in the wrong direction. How long was he going to make her pay the price for doing her job?

And the roller coaster started up again. She was sorry she hurt him. She was also *angry* that he couldn't forgive her. She wanted him back. She also wanted to yell at him. Sure—he had family history. But so did she. And there went the carnival ride again. It was *her* family history that made it so hard for her to trust. It was *his* that made him think everyone was judging him. Their mutual family baggage was piling up between them, and she was beginning to wonder if they'd ever blast through it.

The surprise phone call this morning from Dallas had rattled her even more. She'd been cleaning up the tasting room when her phone rang with a job offer. A good one, with a clear path to partnership. Whitney sat at the wine counter and listened to what sounded like a dream job. Or at least, it *would* have been a dream job a few months ago. But now? How could she leave Rendezvous Falls when she was in *love* with Luke? She'd scribbled some notes on scrap paper as the recruiter talked, more out of habit than anything else. She'd let the guy ramble on, while her thoughts did the same. She'd heard something in the carriage room during the call, but figured it must have been Molly upstairs. When the recruiter asked what she thought about the offer, she'd hedged, saying the same thing she would have said two months ago—to email her more details. She'd give them the courtesy of at least *acting* interested.

"Whitney?" Helen touched her arm.

"What?" Her voice was much sharper than she'd intended, and Luke pounced.

"Hey, don't take your shit out on Helen."

Helen held her hands up, stepping between them.

"Okay, we're all tired and on edge." She looked back and forth between Luke and Whitney. "I don't know what's going on with you two, but you need to work it out. Now." She pointed to the carriage house. "That's an order. And once you've worked it out, go to dinner somewhere nice and get away from this place. That's an order, too."

CHAPTER TWENTY-ONE

LUKE FOLLOWED WHITNEY into the tasting room. Per Helen's orders, they were to "work it out." He wasn't sure how that was going to happen in their current moods, but Helen didn't give orders often, so he tended to listen to them. Whitney marched to the tasting counter and threw herself onto a stool with a huff. She was in full diva mode right now. He couldn't help smiling.

"Sounds like you're having a pretty bad day."

She shoved her hair off her face and barked out a laugh. "You *think*?"

He stood next to her, but she wouldn't even look at him. Very mature.

"Look, Whitney, you need to calm down. The moose are intense, but…"

"Did you just tell me to *calm down*?" Whitney's question didn't sound like a question at all. It sounded like a death sentence. Her head turned slowly, and he could almost hear her teeth grinding together. He raised his hand in innocence.

"I didn't mean it as an insult. I just meant…"

Her hand slapped the countertop. "We are trying to save this winery, remember? And the plan is falling apart. Nothing is going right. We have no signs, no brochures, no *deer* for the float! This isn't a joke to me, and it shouldn't be one to you."

Luke's eyes narrowed, thinking of the phone call he'd overheard earlier. "Don't take on that corporate lecture tone with me. I didn't even know we *needed* signs and brochures and deer to save the winery until you came along. I thought we needed good wine. We've got that." He let out a ragged breath.

Until she came along, he thought he had all *he* needed, too. A roof over his head. Work to be done. Simple, but enough. Then Whitney showed up and flipped it all upside down, giving him a glimpse of what *could* be. And like a fool, he'd thought for a moment he could have it. But she was never meant to be his. Never meant to stay.

If he really loved her, and he was pretty damned sure he did, he should let her go. "Look, you've worked hard for the festival. But Helen and I may have overstated the importance of this one weekend. We wanted to get the winery solidly back on the wine trail, and we'll do that." Whitney had spent hours visiting tour companies, liquor stores and restaurants. She'd said she wasn't a salesperson, but she sure knew how to hammer out a deal. He tipped his head toward her. "That was all thanks to you, Whitney. You offered specials and twisted their arms until they agreed to bring their groups to us, to buy our wines. We've got the winery in great shape..."

"Except we don't have signs."

He rolled his eyes. "We *have* signs. They're just not the signs you *want* us to have. But we'll get there..."

She shook her head. "And we don't have brochures."

He pointed at the boxes in the corner. "We *have* brochures. They just have a little typo. We'll use them up and—"

She threw her hands up in the air. "You can't 'use

them up,' Luke. The typo is in the *name*! We can't hand out booklets that say 'Falls Legund' with a *u*. It'll make us look like amateurs."

He couldn't hold it in any longer.

"Look, it's time for you to stop saying 'us.' Helen and I will deal with it, okay? You can stop worrying about this place and move on."

She folded her arms across her chest, her voice rising another octave.

"Excuse me? Move on to *what* exactly?"

Temporary. She was always going to be temporary. He'd made the mistake of forgetting, but she hadn't. She'd never changed her plans. He folded his arms, too.

"Move on to your new job. You've done what Helen needed—you figured out the bookkeeping. You can stop pretending you're actually part of this place."

She gave a slow, disbelieving headshake. "What the hell are you talking about? What new job?" Hurt flashed in her eyes. Yeah, well, he was hurting, too.

His mouth twisted. "Come on, Whit. Don't play games. I expect more than that from you. But I guess that's been my problem all along, hasn't it?" He'd prided himself on *not* having expectations. Until she gave him some weird sense of hope that made him act like an idiot. That made him fall in love with her. The least she could do was be honest about it. She owed him that much.

Her whole body recoiled at his words. High spots of pink appeared on her cheeks, and she swallowed a couple of times. The fight left her voice as her arms dropped to her sides.

"How do you know about the job offer?"

"I heard you talking to the guy on the phone."

She gave a bitter laugh, avoiding looking at him.

"Do those security cameras have microphones, too? Were you spying on me?"

"Sure, let's make me the bad guy. Again." She went completely still as he continued. "I was in the back room doing inventory. It's not like I had to put a glass up to the door or anything—you were talking loud and clear. And then you left your notes on the counter when you were done."

Her gaze snapped to his, fire in her eyes.

"And, of course, you took it upon yourself to read them."

"Are you surprised?" he asked, leaning toward her. Whitney's soft perfume almost rendered him speechless. His will had to be stronger than his desire for her. His voice hardened. "That's ironic, since you had no problem thinking I took it upon myself to take Helen's money."

"Luke…" His name came out in a breathy rush, as if someone had punched her. As if *he'd* punched her. *Damn it to hell.* This wasn't what he wanted. They could do this like adults. Without hurting each other. *Too late.* His pain was a living, breathing part of him now, but he didn't have to inflict it on her. He ran his fingers through his hair and stared at the ceiling.

"The notes were sitting there on the counter in plain sight. And yeah, I read them. What difference does it make? It's not like anyone ever thought you were going to stay, including you."

He'd been foolish enough, for a little while, to *hope* she'd stay. It had always been a pipe dream to think he'd be reason enough, and he knew it. That didn't make it hurt any less to see her go.

"But, Luke, I'm not…"

"Don't." It was his own damn fault for thinking he could hold her forever. He shook his head. "It's okay. You always said you were leaving. And that's for the best, don't you think?" He tried again to smile, then gave up, glancing at his watch. "Helen doesn't give orders often, and she'll hound us if we don't grab some dinner. I know I'm probably the last guy you want to be with right now, but we both have to eat. I'll pick you up at the house in a half hour." He started to turn away, then stopped. "For Helen's sake, let's get through this as peacefully as we can. She wants us to be team players, and that's what she'll see, okay?"

He headed for the stairs, feeling beaten. Her soft, sad laughter stopped him cold. He turned to see tears shimmering in her eyes. He got it. Goodbyes hurt, even when you knew they were coming. She walked over to him, her scent wrapping around him again like a warm blanket. Christ, he was going to miss this woman.

"You accused me of already making my mind up about you when I found the rainy-day fund. Now you're doing the same exact thing, Luke." She raised a finger to point at his face, and he noticed she was trembling. Her eyes narrowed at him. "You've already decided you know my heart, but trust me—you don't. This conversation isn't over."

WHEN THEY GOT to the restaurant an hour later, Whitney slammed her car door a bit harder than she'd intended. She lifted her hands in defense when Luke looked back.

"I didn't mean to do that. Honest."

"You okay?"

She huffed out a laugh. "Oh, yeah. Definitely okay. Couldn't be okay-er."

He waited for her to catch up, then walked on without touching her. He did stop to hold the door to the Marina Bay Bistro open for her. She gave him a bright smile and thanked him. She'd thought if she pretended long enough that everything really *was* fine between them, it would come true. Fake it till you make it, right? But after the week she'd had and the confrontation in the tasting room today, her faking-it button wasn't working very well.

Her mind was in freefall. Luke had heard her talking to the recruiter about the job in Dallas. Sure, she'd asked them to email more details, but she wasn't seriously interested. How could Luke think she'd accept a job in Texas without even *discussing* it with him? She knew the answer to that. Luke figured *everyone* lived their lives without considering him. The realization made her both sad and angry. He should have known she was different. Before she'd doubted him over that damned bank account, he *would* have known.

They sat by the windows, opting for an indoor table to avoid the heavy clouds moving in from the west. He held her chair, then sat across from her, and they silently watched a large cruiser pull into the docks. Marina staff scurried to grab and secure the lines. The waitress made both of them jump when she set their water glasses on the white tablecloth and delivered their menus.

This was supposed to be a relaxing night out, per Helen's orders. A chance to heal whatever was broken between them. But neither of them were at all relaxed as they read the menus. She *hated* this. Hated the hurt she saw in Luke's eyes. Hated the thought she'd somehow managed to destroy any chances of fixing things. She couldn't give up. Not yet. She pasted on her biggest, happiest smile.

"Wow, everything looks good! I haven't been here before. The lemon pepper haddock sounds amazing. I know you're a steak guy—are you thinking the prime rib?"

"Whitney...stop." He set his menu down, frowning at it before looking up at her. "Give the 'happy' routine a rest, okay?"

She managed to keep her smile in place, but it trembled a little.

"You don't want me to be happy?"

He leveled his eyes at her, not saying a word. She cleared her throat and blinked away from that look that told her he was retreating to a point where she might never reach him. She absently rearranged the silverware in front of her, then moved her water glass and wiped the water ring it had left. *Fix this!* Her vision blurred with tears. She didn't know how, other than to tell him what was in her heart.

"I just want to help you feel better about things. About us. *I* want to feel better about things. This tension isn't good for either of us, or for our relationship."

The waitress stopped at the table with a bottle of Chianti, and they placed their meal orders. Luke stared out the window after that, his chin rigid under his beard. Sadness hung over their table like a cloud. She gave it another try.

"Things were *good* with us." So good that she'd fallen in love with him. "I get it. I hurt you with what I said about the money. I'm *sorry*. Are you really not going to forgive me?"

"It's fine." His lips barely moved as he spoke, and he was still staring out at the boats.

Her wine glass hit the table so hard, some of the wine sloshed out and splashed her fingers. Luke's right brow arched.

"Let me guess—you *accidentally* slammed your glass, too."

She sucked in a breath through her teeth, reminding herself they were in a public place and she couldn't scream, no matter how tempting it might be.

"No. I did *that* on purpose. And you know damn well you are not *fine*." She leaned forward, her voice low but sharp. "Nothing about us is fine right now, and I seem to be the only one trying to *fix* it!"

"Running away is a funny way of fixing things."

"I'm not *running* anywhere, you idiot!" She couldn't if she wanted to. Not without him.

They glared at each other for a moment, and Luke was the first one to blink away. "Like Helen said, we're both tired. It'll be—"

"I swear to god, if you say the word *fine* one more time," she hissed, "I will break this fucking wine bottle over your head!"

Luke scowled, then gave a harsh laugh. "You've been hanging around me too long. You're starting to sound like a Rutledge."

"Seriously? The Rutledge thing again? Don't you think it's time to leave that behind?"

His eyes narrowed. "I don't have that luxury, Whit. It's my goddamn *name*. It's who I am."

She waggled her forefinger back and forth. "No. Those two statements don't automatically go together.

It is your name, but you can decide how much of its baggage you're going to carry. You've opted to carry it all."

Their food was delivered, and they ate in sullen silence. Outside, the rain that had been threatening finally arrived. It swept across the docks and restaurant deck, sending people scurrying for cover. A rumble of distant thunder rattled the windows. The gloominess of it all matched the mood at their table. Her fork clattered when it hit the edge of her plate. Luke glanced at the fork, avoiding her eyes until she spoke.

"That one was accidental."

He nodded solemnly, then set his own fork down and stared at her. Was he finally going to open up?

"Are you guys interested in dessert?" Their waitress still hadn't managed to pick up on the tension at the table. Whitney and Luke both shook their heads. "Okay, then! I'll get your check!"

The restaurant was quiet tonight, but the bar was filling up with a noisy Friday night crowd. It was a mix of jeans-and-T-shirt locals and chino-and-polo-shirt tourists. Funny how she could see that after just two months here. How she identified with the locals, not the outsiders. Evie and Mark walked in, hand in hand. Evie was laughing, reaching up to push a strand of bright blue hair behind her ear. Mark leaned over and kissed her. Whitney smiled. Looked like Evie was going to get that happy ending she hadn't believed in.

"If that number you scratched down is your starting pay, you'll be sitting pretty."

She blinked back to Luke. "What?"

"The job? In Texas? Big bucks. Sounds perfect."

"Yeah. Perfect." She shook her head. "Luke, did you

really think I'd accept a job without talking to you? To Helen?"

His jaw was tense, despite his Joe-Cool act. "We both knew we were temporary."

"Did we?"

Had it always been temporary to him? No. She didn't believe it. Not after the nights she'd spent in his arms. Nothing felt temporary about that. She couldn't have misread him so badly. She knew in her heart he had feelings for her. Maybe not love, but there was *something* there.

"Look, we had fun." His eyes hit her hard and hot. "A *lot* of fun. But your real life isn't in Rendezvous Falls. It's in a corporate office somewhere, where you can crunch numbers on a computer and boss people around. You don't belong someplace where audits are done on the dining room table and things don't happen the way you ordain them."

"And where do *you* belong, Luke?"

His eyes went wide. "Right where I am."

Her heart clenched. He was right. He *did* belong here. But why couldn't he see what was right in front of him? She reached for his hand.

"And what if I belong wherever you are?"

He leaned forward, his eyes dark and shining. He started to say something, but here came their Perky Patty waitress again with her disastrous timing.

"Okay, here's the check. No hurry, guys."

Luke sat back and tossed his credit card on the table. The waitress snatched it up.

"I'll be right back!"

His walls were up again, and he fixed Whitney with

a hard look. "You don't *belong* here. I was your summer fling on the vineyard. But summer's over."

Her hurt battled with her fury, and fury won. She almost came across the table at him, and he sat up straight as if he knew it. Her voice was low but sharp enough to carry. "How *dare* you make me sound like some heartsick teenager having a crush at summer camp! I'm a grown-ass woman, and I'll decide where I belong—"

"Okay!" Perky Patty was back. "The top receipt is ours, the other two are yours, and here's your credit card. Anything else I can do for you?"

Whitney dropped her head, letting her hair hide the tears on her face. Luke signed the receipt and tucked the card in his wallet. She brushed the back of her hand across her face, but not quickly or efficiently enough.

"Christ," Luke muttered. "Don't *cry*. Come on, let's go."

"This isn't over. We're not done talking."

"We are for now."

She didn't trust herself to answer. They *couldn't* be over. She wouldn't let that happen. The rain was still coming down hard, so he gestured toward the bar entrance, which would give them the shortest walk to his truck. She kept her head down, wiping her face again and hoping no one would…

"Whitney! Oh, my god, I can't believe you're here!" Evie jumped up from a bar stool. "Look at what Mark gave me tonight! It's his high school ring—he saved it all these years for me!"

The ring hung from a heavy gold chain around Evie's neck. Whitney pasted on her brightest smile, which felt thin enough to break.

"Evie! Mark! Wow, that's great. You two finally got

your act together, huh? I'm happy for you!" Evie showed
Luke the ring, and he nodded absently. Asshat. If Whitney could act civil, so could he. She nudged her hip hard
against his, and he got the message, holding his hand
out to Mark with a gritty smile.

"Glad you two worked it out, man."

"I wasn't going to take a chance of letting her get
away again. I wasted so much time trying to be someone I was never meant to be. When I think about how
I could have lost her forever... Well, I wasn't going to
give up when I loved her so damn much. When you love
someone, you fight for them, right?"

Luke gave some strangled grunt of a response, looking everywhere but at Whitney. Damn it, she wasn't
giving up on love, and neither was he, whether he knew
it yet or not.

She gave Mark a quick hug, then turned back to Evie.
"We have to run, but I definitely see a girls' night out
in our future. I want to hear all the details."

Evie studied her face closely for the first time.
"What's wrong?"

"Nothing! We're just working ourselves ragged getting ready for the festival. And we still have more to
do tonight..." Luke wasn't any help. His attention was
focused elsewhere. Doug Canfield was walking their
way. She grabbed Luke's arm. "Let's go."

But Luke didn't budge. Doug stopped in front of
them, glaring at Luke but speaking to Whitney.

"If you were dating this loser, Whitney, all you had
to do was say so that night. I wouldn't have come within
ten feet of you if I'd known you had that kind of taste."

"I wasn't dating anyone—"

Luke talked over her. "It's none of your business who she dates. Just know it'll never be you."

Whitney held up her hand. "Okay, we've already had this conversation once." She glanced over her shoulder at Luke with a pointed glance. "And I'm perfectly capable of speaking for myself."

Doug wasn't as drunk as he'd been that night at the farm. But he was well on his way. He puffed out his chest, making his already-too-small black T-shirt stretch nearly to bursting.

"I know you're still new around here, but you shouldn't be seen around town with a Rutledge. It's not good for your reputation."

Mark stepped forward. "Go home, Doug. You're drunk."

Doug brushed him away. "Step back, Hudson. This ain't about you."

The mood in the bar was shifting fast. People were backing away, and the bartender had his phone to his ear. Mobile phones were coming out to record the scene. Luke was behind Whitney, silent but vibrating with emotion. She tried again to defuse the situation.

"Doug, I'm sorry things didn't click between us, but that has nothing to do with Luke." And then her mother's words fell from her mouth. "Let's all take a breath, okay?"

Luke's chest brushed up against her back. She planted her feet and stood firm against him. He couldn't get involved. As much as she hated the stupid "Rutledge" business, if he got into a fight in a public place like this, he'd be playing right into the gossip narrative.

"Nothing to do with him?" Doug looked Luke up and

down, his voice rising. "He punched me in the face at Falls Legend Winery!"

There was a collective gasp in the bar, followed by low murmurs. She was living in a soap opera scene. Doug was intentionally adding fuel to the Rutledge legend. And now he was trying to throw shade on the winery, too. Her voice amped up a notch. Two could play that game.

"Yes, he did punch you, Doug. After you manhandled me and wouldn't take no for an answer. Remember that, Doug? When you slammed me up against your truck and Luke rescued me from you?" The fresh gasp from their audience let her know she'd evened the score.

"Whitney…" Luke's voice was low and tight. "Get the hell out of my way."

She ignored him. He was mad. She got that. But she wasn't moving.

Doug sneered. "That's cute, Rutledge. Your little woman's fighting your battles for you now. Must be a family trait—hiding behind people instead of admitting guilt."

With a hand on each arm from behind, Luke firmly moved Whitney aside, but she wasn't giving up that easily. She scrambled to get back between them, shrugging off Evie's attempts to pull her away. A bar fight was the last thing Luke needed. There wasn't much space between the two men, though. They were eyeball to eyeball. Luke's voice was hard.

"You need to think real hard about what you're doing, Doug. Both our brothers were shitfaced that night, but *your* brother was driving the car. He's dead and my brother will never walk without pain again. Haven't we all paid enough?"

"If he hadn't been hanging around with your family of losers, Larry would still be alive." Doug chest-bumped Luke. "The Rutledges are why he's dead."

No wonder Luke felt the way he did, if all he ever heard was this bullshit from the people in this town. She grabbed Doug's arm.

"Stop it! He's more than just a last name, damn it!"

"Whitney, get back." Luke's voice cracked like a whip.

"No! This isn't fair! People can't keep blaming you or your family for every damn thing that happens. It's stupid."

The bartender's voice cut in. "I've called the cops, guys. Break it up or take a ride."

The two men glared at each other. Then Luke stepped back, lowering his head and raising his hands.

"I'm done."

But Doug wasn't ready to let it go.

"Oh, sure, go hide behind her skirts." Doug looked at Whitney. "Careful, girl. I don't know what your auntie sees in this asshole, but he'll end up ripping her off, if he hasn't already. He can't help himself. It's in his fucking blood."

Many things happened at once as that last sentence fell in the tensely silent bar.

Luke let out a curse and stepped forward.

Doug told Luke to "bring it."

The door opened behind Doug and two police officers walked in.

Doug cocked a fist and took a swing.

Whitney tried one last time to get the men apart.

At that point, everything went into slow motion. She saw herself jumping forward—to fight Doug, to protect

Luke, to stop a disaster—who knew? A fist coming forward. Luke's hand grabbing her arm. People shouting. And finally, a thundering impact on the side of her face that turned her world silent and dark.

CHAPTER TWENTY-TWO

"LUKE, SHE'S OKAY. I promise." Helen's hand rested over his to stop his fingers from drumming on the kitchen table. The sun had come up two hours ago, and two cold, empty coffee mugs sat in front of them. There were a million things that needed to be done to get ready for the bottling truck. To get ready for the festival. To get ready for the harvest.

Luke didn't give a gold-plated damn about any of it.

Helen sighed. "Why don't you go up and check on her this time?"

Whitney had refused to go to the hospital last night, insisting she was okay. The EMTs didn't argue hard enough to suit Luke. They agreed she probably had a mild concussion at most. But how could they know for sure? They told Luke to make sure she was woken every couple of hours for the next twenty-four hours to make sure she was still coherent.

"Luke? Go on upstairs and check on her. You need to look at her and see her breathing so you can relax."

That's the last thing he needed. He already had the night's events running on a constant loop in his head. Seeing her would make it that much worse. But he couldn't tell Helen he was afraid. He cleared his throat. Twice. "It's not about what I need, Helen. I'm the last person *she* needs to see."

"You're the first person she asked for, Luke. Go on—"

"*No*, damn it." He grimaced, eyes tightly shut. He didn't intend to raise his voice against Helen, but he wasn't going to change his mind.

Helen stood slowly, her voice resigned. "Okay. I'll go. But honestly, she's—"

"Don't tell me she's fine, Helen. She got *punched* in the *face* because of *me*."

A soft voice came from the doorway.

"I got punched in the face because I tried to stop a fight. I just didn't intend to use my face to do it." Whitney gave them a half smile. "My first ever bar fight."

Luke jumped to his feet and pulled out a chair for her. Looking at her nearly brought him to his knees. The left side of her beautiful face was swollen. Circles of angry red and purple bruises were already forming around her eye.

"Jesus…"

She huffed out a quick laugh. "That pretty, huh? I was afraid to look in the bathroom mirror."

Helen got up and reached into the freezer. "Here, honey. Frozen peas make the best ice packs." She handed the green-and-white package to Whitney. "I'm taking you to urgent care this morning."

Whitney had barely opened her mouth to reply before Luke jumped in.

"You're going. No argument."

A spark of defiance glimmered in her eyes, even the one that was bloodshot and half-closed. Luke breathed a little bit easier, knowing she still had some fight in her. Maybe she wasn't hurt that bad after all, but only a doctor could say for sure.

"I'm fine. Just a little—"

Luke struggled to keep his voice from rising. Every word came out like a full sentence.

"You. Were. Punched. In. The. Face." He scrubbed his hands down his own face, trying to erase the knowledge that it was his fault. "You were out cold."

He couldn't stop reliving it. The sickening sound of Doug's fist hitting Whitney's face. The feel of her as he caught her dead weight in his arms. The blessed sight of her eyelids flickering open less than a minute later.

"I know. I was there," Whitney said. "I was out for a split second. And I barely even have a headache. Luke…" She waited for him to meet her steady gaze, only partially obscured by the bag of peas she was clasping to one side of her face. "I really am okay. I promise. Helen said Doug was arrested?"

Luke walked to the window, his legs heavy. He was lost between wanting to run from the kitchen or run to Whitney and hold her safe in his arms. He pinched the bridge of his nose tightly. As much as he wanted to keep her safe and happy, he clearly wasn't capable of it. No wonder she'd been job hunting. He'd only bring her pain—maybe not physical pain like she'd received last night. But she'd forever suffer the sharp looks and knowing whispers of anyone in town who believed the Rutledge hype Doug and his pals had spread. The thought made his chest burn, and he buried his clenched hands in his pockets. He didn't want that for her.

"Luke?" Whitney asked. "Last night? Doug was arrested?"

He cleared his throat. "That tends to happen when you punch a woman in the face in front of the police and twenty cell phone cameras."

"But he wasn't trying to punch *me*…"

He closed his eyes, feeling the direct hit of her words.

"No. He was trying to punch me. But you stepped right in front of his fist."

She adjusted the bag on her face. "Not on purpose, believe me. Will I have to testify or anything?"

Was she worried about having to hang around town?

"If Doug has half a brain, which is questionable, he'll plead guilty. The whole bar saw him take the swing. The police saw it, and it's on video. It's not like he can deny it."

The only reason Luke hadn't swung first was that he was determined not to be *that* Rutledge. Tony used to tell him a man should never live *down* to other peoples' expectations. He'd walked away from a lot of fights to prove that point. It didn't matter, though. He was a trouble magnet. And Whitney got hurt because of it.

"I know Doug's father," Helen said, "and Doug Sr. isn't going to want this to drag out any longer than it has to. It doesn't reflect well on his 'family-focused' flooring company with all those ads featuring sweet little babies sitting on their floors. His oldest son hitting a *woman*?" She tsked, then gave a little laugh. "He'll do everything he can to make it go away fast."

Whitney set the peas on the table. "Meanwhile, we have a lot of work to do. I need to call the movie prop company and figure out what to do with the moose. Mooses. Whatever. The replacement wine labels came in yesterday, and, assuming they're the right color this time, we need to get them on a bunch of bottles before the festival. I'll see if I can come up with some temporary trifold brochures locally to replace the misspelled booklets. They won't be as impressive, but it'll work. We need a new idea for the float. And—"

"And you're not doing any of that today." Helen's voice was firm. "You're going to the doctor, and then you're going to rest, young lady."

"There's no time for that, Helen. We have to—"

Luke pushed away from the window. Between the talk about that asshole Doug and discussing Whitney's head injury, his nerves were starting to fray and twitch. He hadn't let Whitney play make-believe with him yesterday, and he wasn't going to let her play make-believe with Helen. "Helen's right. The winery is *our* problem, not yours."

Helen's eyes went wide. "That's not what I said—"

Whitney's eyes narrowed. "What the hell is that supposed to mean?"

His agitation was making it hard to think straight, so he stopped thinking and blurted out the words.

"Didn't Whitney tell you, Helen? She's taking a job in Dallas."

Whitney sat ramrod straight. "I never said I was—"

He talked over her. "The winery problems are *ours* to solve. I don't know about you, but I don't give a damn about some stupid float, or booklets, or stupid signs we don't need. I only care about the wine. We'll bottle the rest of the Legacy blend on Monday, and the pinot, too." He was on more solid ground discussing grapes and business. "We also have a harvest to get ready for."

Helen was staring at her niece across the table. "You're leaving?"

Whitney's mouth opened and closed a few times. "I haven't accepted any job offers. Yet." She shot Luke a quick glance. "But… Helen…" she stammered. "Look, when I came here, it was supposed to be…temporary. But then I…"

Those words hurt more than any look ever could.

It was supposed to be temporary...

If only she'd let his heart know before he'd lost it to her.

Whitney's voice turned icy. "Luke's made it clear I have some decisions to make."

Who was she kidding? She'd already made her decision. And it was the right one.

Helen sighed, speaking almost to herself. "Stubborn hearts and foolish brains." Luke wondered if maybe he should have that tattooed on his chest. Helen nodded toward Whitney. "You're not making *any* decisions today. You're going to the doctor, then you're sitting your butt on the porch and doing nothing." Helen held up one finger to stop Whitney's objections. "And that's *that*. As for you..." Helen took that finger and pointed it at Luke. "*You* are going to get our wine ready for bottling and our grapes ready for harvesting. Out!" She gestured toward the door, and he didn't hesitate to make his escape. The farther away from Whitney Foster he was, the better.

WHITNEY TIPTOED PAST HELEN, who was asleep in her recliner with the cat curled up in her lap, and slipped outside. The sun had set, but the sky above the vineyard was still a riot of oranges and pinks. After an entire day spent sitting or napping, she couldn't take it anymore. She had to see Luke. She tried the tasting room first, then his apartment. Both were empty.

Molly's bark caught her attention as she walked across the driveway. Luke was coming out of the barn carrying the old tool bag, and he didn't look happy to see Whitney standing there. Molly, on the other hand, came galloping over, tongue lolling out, big doggy grin on her face. She'd managed to win the dog over just in time to lose the man.

"You're supposed to be resting." Luke's voice was painfully neutral, as if he was talking to some stranger. It hurt her more than anger would have.

"I'm not headed out for a jog or anything. I'm just standing here."

He looked down at the lake, avoiding her eyes. Avoiding the bruises he'd decided to blame himself for. "Helen told me the doctor said you were going to be okay." He gave her a quick glance, as if he couldn't help himself. "But that you should stay off your feet and rest."

He'd spoken to Helen about her. That showed he cared, right?

"*I* told you I was going to be okay this morning. And the doctor said I should listen to my body and not push myself. But if you want me to sit, you could join me on the tasting room porch." She gestured to the four new rocking chairs sitting there.

"I've got a lot of work to do."

"Helen told me you barely slept last night, and you've been working all day. You can sit for a few minutes. We either have this conversation while I trot around behind you as you work, or we have it sitting down."

His mouth thinned to an angry straight line. "There's nothing to talk about."

"And yet, here we are. Talking. Your choice—sit in chairs or I chase you around the vineyard. Either way, there *will* be a conversation."

He stared at the ground for a moment, then tossed the tool bag aside and stomped his way onto the porch. They were getting off to a great start. She bit her tongue and followed, sitting and gesturing for him to do the same. He gave a sharp shake of his head and leaned against the railing instead, arms crossed.

She cleared her throat. "I know we've never put a label on what happened between us, and I'm as guilty about that as you are. We've both danced around it, not wanting to admit what was growing there. We didn't expect it. We didn't want to jinx it. Whatever. But you know what we have is *real*. It's not going to go away." She paused, hoping he'd make eye contact, but he stared straight ahead at the carriage house wall, stoic and silent. "I told you last night I belong where you are, and you belong here."

"I don't *belong* here. It's just where I happen to be." He gestured toward the town below. "You've seen what everyone here thinks of me. How can I *belong* someplace like that? This is a dot on the map, and I'm standing on it. There's no deep message to it."

"First, it's not *everyone*. Doug Canfield and his crowd don't count. But if you really feel that way, why have you stayed?"

He finally made eye contact, but she wished he hadn't. His eyes were hard and cold, and she was relieved when they slid away to take in the house and the vineyard.

"I made a *promise*, okay? I told Tony I'd take care of Helen if anything ever happened to him. And this is the only real damn home I've known! I won't cut and run like you. When I give my word, it sticks. *I* stick." He struck his own chest. "For good. But you wouldn't know anything about that, would you?"

His words hit hard. *I stick. For good.* His word meant something, not only to him but to the people he gave it to. And he'd never once given his word to her. She'd never asked for it, either. A flicker of doubt pulsed through her. Had she been the only one falling? She had to know.

"I'm in love with you, Luke."

His mouth dropped open, then snapped shut again. He didn't melt at the words. He didn't say them back. His face hardened.

"Bullshit."

There was a sudden, painful tightness in her throat. Was he saying it because he didn't believe her, or because he didn't want to know? She pushed back.

"You know it's true. And I think you love me back."

There was a heartbeat of hesitation, just enough for her to notice, before he looked her straight in the eye.

"Nah. That was temporary, remember?" He pushed away from the rail and stepped off the porch, grabbing the tool bag as he strode by it. "If you really…care… about me, you'll take that new job and leave me alone to do mine. I'm no good for you, and you're sure as hell not good for me."

He walked away without a second glance. Without any apparent feeling at all. Her hands clenched and unclenched a few times, then she rubbed them on her jeans and turned away, unable to watch him any longer. His defenses were too high. And she was fresh out of fight.

SHE WOKE FUZZY HEADED and cotton mouthed the next morning. It wasn't as much from her concussion as it was from crying herself to sleep. Yes, her head hurt, especially if she rolled over without thinking and touched the left side of her face to the pillow. But it didn't hurt anywhere near as much as her weary heart did.

As she showered, got dressed and went down to the kitchen, she started building some defenses of her own. Her pain morphed into white-hot anger. Ah, yes—this was better than numbness or sorrow. Anger worked for her. Caffeine refined the glow of her rage. Sharpened the edges of it. Yes. This was definitely better than weeping and feeling sorry for herself. This was taking control. Being angry meant her heart was protected from any more breakage. She could work with anger.

By the time Helen came into the kitchen, Whitney was positively glowing with superhero control. She even mustered up a wide smile, which was a mistake because it hurt. Luckily Helen went right to the coffeemaker without looking at her, so she could let the grin fade to a manageable level.

"How are you feeling this morning?" Helen turned, took a good look, coffeepot in one hand and mug in the other. "Oh, boy. You'd better grab that bag of frozen peas and put it over *both* eyes, girl. Unless you want everyone to know you spent the night crying."

Whitney's fingers touched her face lightly. The areas under both eyes were like squishy water balloons when she pressed. Damn it, why couldn't she be a pretty crier like in the movies? As happy as she'd been to be headache-free this morning, the image in the mirror had set her back on her heels. The bruise ran from her left temple to her cheek, with colors ranging from nearly black to purple, blue and a tinge of yellow. Her left eye had a dark crescent beneath it.

"It could be from the injury, you know."

Helen laughed, filling her mug and setting the coffeepot back on the counter.

"A—I'm a woman and I know what crying eyes look

like. B—I have ears. You angry-cried all the way up the stairs and into your room last night." Helen sat across from her. "Let me guess—Luke told you he's no good for you?"

"How did you…?"

"He spent all night Friday telling me the same bull. He's bad for you. He's bad for me. He's bad for the winery. He's tainting everyone with the family curse, blah blah blah. He's worked himself into a regular lather this time."

"This time?"

"Oh, we've gone through this before. When his sister got pregnant in high school and left town. When his dad went off to prison. When his brother was hurt in that wreck." Helen sighed. "He's always in such a hurry to carry his family's problems around. When something like this bubbles up, he frets about it affecting our business, as if tourists have any clue who he is or what the local rumor mill says. He convinces himself he's tainted by his name, and that he taints everyone he's in contact with."

Whitney's chest went tight. Luke didn't *have* to shoulder that burden. He was a *good man*. He just refused to see it. Her anger reminded her that maybe she couldn't fix everything. If Luke couldn't see the obvious, why should she keep fighting to change his mind?

"You can't help someone who doesn't want to be helped, Helen. He's determined to push me away, and it's working."

Maybe she should focus on controlling what she *was* able to control. Like the Blessing of the Grapes Festival. She straightened.

"But you know what?" She looked at Helen with

renewed resolve. "We have a festival to get ready for. Luke made it clear what he cares about, and that's the wine. Great. But *I* care about the brochures and labels and…"

Helen's expression stopped her. "About the labels."

Oh, no. "You said they arrived Friday in the right color. Please don't tell me there's a typo on those, too!"

"No. But…" Helen looked at the kitchen counter, and Whitney followed her gaze. Several bottles stood there, sporting the new labels. The plan was to order enough poly labels to place right over the existing ones, figuring there was no time to peel and replace the ones already on dozens of cases of wine. The labels were beautiful, in pretty shades of blue, with Lena's sketch of the falls and the deer. What was Helen worried about? They looked perfect. Except…what was that dark shadow in the center? She walked over to inspect them.

No, no, *no!*

"The old label is showing through! The printer said that wouldn't happen! He said they could use a poly material that would…" She pulled a handful of labels out of the box. They were *paper.* Paper couldn't hide the dark Russo family crest on the old labels. They were useless. Just like the booklets. Just like the gigantic moose up in the barn. Just like everything else she'd tried to control…er…accomplish.

"That's it, then. No new labels. Probably just as well, since we don't have any marketing materials to support the new design anyway."

"I'm sorry, Whitney. I definitely ordered the thicker ones, but this is what they sent. We could try to peel the old labels off?" Helen sounded so hopeful. But, if nothing else, Whitney was a realist. It was her strength, even in the face of defeat.

"Peel the labels off *hundreds* of bottles? In a *week*? Forget it, Helen. I never should have tried to make this work. Any of it." She turned to face her aunt, and caught a glimpse of Luke outside, driving the tractor up the hill. She wasn't going to make *them* work, either. "I let you down. I'm sorry."

Her aunt moved to stand at her side, putting her arm around Whitney's waist.

"Any more talk like that and I'll take you right back to the doctor to have your head reexamined. First, you couldn't let me down if you tried, because we love each other. Second, you not only straightened out the bookkeeping nightmare I created, you *found* a small fortune I didn't know we had. You saved this damn winery!"

Whitney shook her head, still watching Luke. He was twisted on the tractor seat, watching both the direction he was headed and the sprayer behind him. The pose pulled his shirt tight across sinewed shoulders. His beard was dark against his tanned, weathered skin. Her heart warmed. He was doing what he always did—what needed to be done. Calm and steady, unperturbed at the thought of her leaving. Honoring his promise to Tony.

"I didn't save the winery, Helen. Luke did."

He was sticking. And he'd already decided she wasn't. He knew she'd originally suspected him of taking advantage of Helen when she arrived. After they'd ended up in each other's arms, sharing kisses and stories and building what felt like a future, she'd questioned what he'd done with the mystery account. His belief in himself was fragile enough, and she'd ripped a gaping hole in it.

She took a deep breath. "Your books are in great shape. If you have any accounting questions, Mark Hudson would probably help you out, as long as it doesn't interfere with his art business."

"You're talking like you're not going to be around."

"Maybe that job offer came along at the right time, Aunt Helen." She shrugged halfheartedly. "Maybe it was meant to be. I'm going to give them a call."

"So you haven't accepted yet?"

She shook her head. She'd had no real intention of accepting when they'd called. She'd only humored them because she'd been distracted by everything that had gone wrong here. At the time, it had been impossible to imagine walking away from Luke. Little did she know *he'd* be the one walking away. She loved him. She loved Helen. Much to her surprise, she loved this town. She'd been warming up to the idea of setting up her own business here.

Evie told her the nearest CPAs were in either Geneva or Watkins Glen. There was an opening for her to create a solid foundation of local clients, then she could use the internet to find consulting jobs anywhere. Two weeks ago, she'd been happily jotting a business plan in her journal. Luckily for her pride, she hadn't told anyone else her ideas, not even Luke. No one would know her leaving meant she'd failed to achieve something she desperately wanted. A *home*.

She loved a man who refused to let himself love her back. Her chin rose. She deserved better than that. He didn't want her here. And she wasn't going to fight anymore. It was time to move on.

"I haven't accepted it yet. But I'm going to."

Helen puttered restlessly around the kitchen. She

stopped at the sink and stood for a long time, as if her mind was a thousand miles away.

"Do you have to call them right away?"

"No. Why?"

"Wait until after the festival—" Helen ignored Whitney's attempted protest and said the one thing she couldn't argue against. "I *need* you. I know you think the plans are a mess, and maybe they are, but that just makes me need you more." Helen took a ragged breath, looking back at Whitney with large, sad, shimmering eyes. "Tony always took care of the festivals. I don't know how. I can't do this without you. Please."

Whitney frowned. She'd assumed Helen had been helping Tony all those years with the festival. They did everything together, didn't they? Her aunt took another trembling breath, staring out the window, her shoulders rounded in defeat. Guilt started whispering at Whitney again. Whispering that she hadn't come to help when Helen asked for it. When Helen needed her. How could she say no now? But still…

"It's not like the new job will start next Monday. I could stay for the festival if you really want me to, then leave." She didn't *want* to stay. She didn't think she could bear working that closely with Luke for another week. "But I was thinking I could go to Dallas early and find a place to live?" She knew better than to make a statement in the form of a question, and Helen pounced on her hesitation.

"But you don't *have* to do that. You don't *have* to call them this week." Helen moved slowly toward the table. Was she limping? She rubbed her lower back with her hand, then sat down with a sigh. "I'm so tired, Whitney.

We've all been so busy and with all the drama and then you got hurt and scared me to death..."

Helen had been concerned, but she hadn't seemed *traumatized*. Or maybe Whitney had missed it because she was too busy battling with Luke. Just as she'd missed how exhausted her aunt apparently was.

"Okay, Helen. I won't leave early." She saw a glimmer of a smile on Helen's face, then it was gone. "I'll tell them I'll be there in two weeks. I can always stay in a hotel while I'm apartment hunting."

Helen's face fell. "Oh, but do you have to call them at all? Can't you wait?"

"But...why?"

Helen shrank in the chair. "Maybe just to humor an old woman?"

Whitney never considered her aunt an *old woman*, but she looked like one now. Sad and small and...was her lip trembling? Oh, god, was she going to *cry*?

"Why are you so upset? I mean... I told you I'd be job hunting. I was only going to be here for a few weeks. Yes, that turned into a few months. But you knew it was temporary, right?"

"Yes, that's what you said. But then you made friends, and got some work in town, and you and Luke..."

"There is no me and Luke anymore. I'm sorry." The words cut her heart like a rusty knife. And Helen physically recoiled from hearing them, putting her hand on her throat. *My two favorite people...* It hadn't occurred to Whitney until right now how much Helen had invested in Whitney's ill-fated romance with Luke. Her aunt gave her a trembling smile, tears pooling in her dark eyes.

"I know, honey. But can't you do it for a silly, romantic old woman?" What was up with this "old woman" business? Helen's voice took on a pleading tone. "This week is going to be so hard for me. Can't you give me a glimmer of hope for you and Luke? I swear, if you want to take the job after the festival, I won't say a word, but please wait to make the decision. Help me get through this week without having to deal with the thought of you leaving. Let me play make-believe."

Whitney stared hard at her aunt. Helen had never in her life been a make-believe sort of person. She'd preached hard work and honorable ethics as the key to success. She'd refused to take Whitney to a Disney movie when she was a little girl because she didn't want Whitney thinking some white knight would come save her. She and Tony both told Whitney she should be ready to save her own damn self.

Helen's bottom lip quivered again, and Whitney caved. Helen had been through hell and back over the past couple of years. If she wanted Whitney to wait a week to accept the job, she'd wait a week.

"On one condition." Whitney held up her index finger, and Helen nodded. "If you need to have hope and play make-believe, that's fine. But I won't. Luke made it clear he doesn't want me, and I'm not going to throw myself at his damn feet. I'm *not* going to pretend he and I are okay. I can't." That was the truth. It would kill her. "I'll tell Dallas to expect my decision the Monday after the festival. Have all the hope you want until then, but manage your expectations, Helen. I'm staying for you, not to win him back."

"Oh, Whitney!" Helen grabbed a fistful of tissues from the box that always sat near the table and wiped at the tears on her cheeks. "You've made me so happy! We'll have so much fun at the festival together..."

The older woman put her face into the tissues held in her hands, and her shoulders shook. This was more emotion from her aunt than she'd seen since she'd arrived. Did it mean Helen was getting better—processing her feelings instead of stifling them? Or was she hitting another one of those "clocked out" phases Luke talked about?

Whitney looked back out the window, but he was out of sight. A cloud of dust rose from over the ridge where he must still be working. Staying so close to him and not being able to love him would be more painful than she could imagine. But if Helen needed them to be a team for one last week, then she'd figure out a way to make it work.

CHAPTER TWENTY-THREE

"SHE FELL FOR it hook, line and sinker." Helen smiled proudly, taking a sip of brandy-laced tea. "I gave her crocodile tears and everything. It was the best acting job of my life."

Rick took a seat next to Helen at Vickie's dining room table. They were having an emergency meeting of the book club. "You really think your niece will hold off on accepting the job?"

"She promised she'd wait. You should have seen her face when I gave her that little lip tremble. I had to bury my face in tissues so she wouldn't see me laughing! She folded like a house of cards."

Lena chuckled. "Why you little devil! I'm proud of you, Helen. But now what? Why this urgent gathering?"

"Wait!" Cecile put her hand up. "First, tell me how she is. Did Doug Canfield really punch her in the face? Is she okay?"

"Technically it was an accident—he was swinging at Luke. But she's okay. It looks awful, but she just had a bit of a headache. The doctor said she needs to take it easy, though—not a lot of activity or stress."

"So naturally, you went all Joan Crawford on her about staying and played on her emotions." Rick chuckled. Helen flipped him the bird.

"What I *did* was prevent her from making a huge

mistake when she's not thinking straight. We said we wanted to be matchmakers, right?" Helen looked around the table as the others nodded. All except Jayla.

"Just because we *wanted* to doesn't mean we were very good at it," Jayla said. "None of our matches worked, and mine was a total disaster."

Helen shook her head. "You had no way of knowing Kyle would stand her up that night, or that Doug Canfield would get involved. That wasn't your fault." Helen shrugged. "Let's just consider it a good lesson for the future." She grinned. "But right now we have a sure-thing love match. And it was right there under our noses the whole time!"

Vickie cleared her throat delicately, picking at the cuff of her sweater. "Helen, are you sure you want to—"

"Victoria, I swear to god if you're going to use the Rutledge name with any kind of criticism or waggling eyebrows, you can get up and leave right now." Helen stared down her friend, which didn't take long. Vickie blushed deep pink and started to stammer.

"I wasn't going… I just… You can't order me to leave my own house… Oh, *fine*. I'm shutting up now."

Lena nodded. "Good. Because honestly, it's time we brought all of this gossip about him to an end in this town. If Luke Rutledge wanted to date my daughter, I'd embrace the hell out of that. He'd certainly be leaps and bounds ahead of her current choices!"

Cecile joined in, blond curls bobbing. "Father Joe told me Luke is one of the best men he's ever met, and Luke's not even Catholic!"

Rick shook his head. "I can't believe we didn't know they had that kind of chemistry."

"Those two are *blistering* hot together," Helen said,

pretending to fan herself as the others laughed. "But it's more than chemistry. Those two *love* each other. They're both so stubborn, they'll end up throwing it all away if we don't do something."

Cecile gave a dreamy sigh. "Never let it be said that I don't love a love story. But what are we supposed to do?"

Helen waited to respond, watching as Vickie refilled everyone's cups. "The festival is this weekend. The three of us have been working on it for weeks. Starting right after the festival, the winery will be open six days a week. It's our chance to put Falls Legend back in the big leagues. It's also our last chance to get Luke and Whitney back together for good. She's going to give up and take that damn job if we don't, and she'll be gone."

"O-kay," Vickie answered as she sat back down. "But I still don't know what you want us to do. We've painted the tasting room, and Lena designed a new logo for the signs and labels, right?"

"The signs are just one of the issues we have to deal with." Helen sighed. "Guys, everything that *could* go wrong, *has* gone wrong. The signs are late, the booklets have a typo, the float isn't done and the wine labels were printed on the wrong paper, so they don't cover the old labels. I kid you not, we have two *moose* statues in the wine barn that were supposed to be deer!" She shook her head. "And I have dozens of cookies to get baked for our booth, which at this point will just be a tent and a card table. I'd call it a comedy of errors, but Whitney isn't laughing. She sees it all as a giant personal failure. We have to fix this."

Cecile leaned forward. "But none of that is her fault, is it?"

"No. But it's all stuff she thought she had under control, and my Whitney likes control. It's thrown her off her game. And then add the trouble between her and Luke, and the poor girl is feeling like Rendezvous Falls might be cursed."

"And we're here to reverse the curse?" Lena was sketching something in the small notebook she always carried. "I have an idea…"

Rick nodded. "Me, too. Is the float still up in the barn? I'll talk to the theater director at school and see if she wants to get the freshmen involved in a 'community project.'" He made air quotes with his fingers. Helen locked her fingers together tightly in front of her, trying not to let her new-found hope run away with her.

"Where are the booklets?" Vickie asked. "I had to make a last-minute fix to some misprinted programs for a charity function a few years ago, and I'll bet the same idea would work here." She leaned over to spy on whatever Lena was drawing, then smiled.

Cecile pulled her phone from her bag and started scrolling. "I saw something on Pinterest about removing labels from wine bottles. I think they used baking soda. How many do we need to change over before the festival?"

A buzz of energy filled the room. Jayla took Helen's hand. "I love to cook. I have an easy almond cookie recipe. Or give me *your* recipes and I'll make them." Her head tipped to the side. "But how is this matchmaking? How will this bring her and Luke back together?"

Helen blinked back unexpected tears. For nearly two years now, she'd been pushing these dear friends away. And here they were, each ready to jump in and help her. She couldn't recall the words in Italian, but one of

Tony's favorite phrases translated to *we can't have a perfect life without friends*. How true it was.

"You guys absolutely *rock* right now. I can't tell you what this means to me." She brushed away a tear that broke free. "As for how this will bring Luke and Whitney back together? I haven't completely worked that out yet, but the festival will force them to spend time together, and I think we're all pushy enough to make sure *something* happens, right?"

They laughed in agreement. Rick laid his hand in the center of the table.

They all put a hand over his, waiting for his rallying cry before lifting in unison.

"Matchmakers Unite!"

WHITNEY WAS SITTING on the front porch of the main house Tuesday morning. She'd heard back from Dallas, and they'd agreed to wait on her decision, providing she could let them know as soon as possible. She promised not to keep them waiting more than a week or so. Going to Dallas too early would be a mistake anyway, since her bruised face was bound to be a distraction to her employer.

She was apartment hunting on her laptop. Originally, she figured she'd want to be close to the corporate offices, but everything looked so sterile and covered with cement. The past few months of greenery and the scent of furrowed earth may have spoiled her for city life. It was probably a temporary condition, but for now, she'd try to find something outside the city. Something that had trees and grass and maybe a place to go for walks. Maybe even a waterfall. She snort-laughed, then looked around quickly to make sure no one had heard.

The clanking hum of the wine bottling machine carried across the lot from the barn. She was curious about how it worked, but she didn't think she could handle the noise of the bottler. She still had a dull headache. Besides, Luke was up there. A headache was one thing. A heartache was another. He'd shut her out completely, making it clear he didn't want to be anywhere near her between now and the time she left Rendezvous Falls. Her eyes narrowed as he and Molly came out of the barn. He moved as easily as always, as if he hadn't been hard at work for days on end. As if breaking up with her hadn't left a hole inside of him. Like nothing had ever happened.

She wanted to *demand* he look her in the eye and tell her that he didn't love her. Didn't want her. Forget the nonsense about what was right, or smart, or whatever he was trying to tell himself. She knew those nights together had been as life altering for him as for her. She *knew* it. But she didn't leave the porch. If she was wrong, she wouldn't be able to bear hearing it from his lips.

Instead, she went inside to finish clearing the dining table. Helen and Luke would need to maintain records themselves once she left, and they'd need written instructions. The system she'd created would do all the calculations and reports for them once they plugged in the figures. And the worksheets were set up to be shared, so she could always take a virtual peek at them once in a while from Texas.

They'd be fine—her favorite word. Everyone would be just fine. They'd all make the best of it. For one more week, she could make Luke think he didn't matter. She could hold in her tears and anger until she was behind closed doors.

She was halfway through typing up her color-coded instruction sheets when a red Mercedes drove past the house to park at the tasting room. Vickie Pendergast got out, dashing into the tasting room. Another car pulled in, and *three* older women exited and went into the carriage house. Whitney recognized them as Helen's book club buddies.

She'd barely sat back down from looking out the window when a dark Lexus went by the house, followed by a beat-up old Jeep filled with what looked like college kids. They went straight up to the barn. Maybe they were helping with the bottling, but she could have sworn it was Rick Thomas from the book club driving the Lexus.

Whatever they were up to, it wasn't her concern. She went into Tony's office and filed a few more tax documents before reorganizing the bookshelves. It was just busywork, but that was okay. It kept her in the house and away from Luke. It was lunchtime before she went back into the kitchen and checked outside. All the cars were still there. Curiosity got the best of her, and she headed outside.

The carriage house was a beehive of activity, smelling of paint and buzzing with low conversation and bursts of laughter. Vickie was at the tasting counter, with papers spread out from one end of it to the other. There was a much older woman working with her, sitting on a stool. That woman looked up and spotted Whitney.

"Wow! What a shiner!" she exclaimed. "How's the other guy?"

"Shush, Iris!" Vickie scolded. "And pay attention to

what you're doing. Make sure you get them on straight or it will look too obvious!"

"I'm not an idiot, Victoria. Leave me alone." Iris rolled her eyes when Vickie looked away to focus on what she was doing, then winked. "Hiya, honey. Excuse her lack of manners. I'm Iris Taggart from the B&B in town. Your aunt's back in the kitchen with Cecile."

"Nice to meet you, Mrs. Taggart—"

"Bah—don't call me Mrs. I kicked the Mr. to the curb a long time ago. You call me Iris."

Whitney gave an absent nod. "Aren't these the booklets I put out in the recycling bins?"

All those expensive, stapled, useless booklets with the misspelled name. But wait. She picked one up from the end of the counter. *Falls Legend Winery.* The winery name, no longer misspelled, was inside a square of darker blue. She ran her finger across it, feeling the slight ridge.

"Are you...*gluing* the right name on there?"

Vickie picked up a square of dark blue paper with the name printed on it, flipped it over on a piece of waxed paper, running a glue stick along the edges. She lifted the square and placed it carefully over the misprinted name on the brochure, pressing the patch firmly in place.

Iris nodded as she reached for the glue stick. "Not bad, right? You can't tell unless you look close."

"You can tell if someone puts them on crooked. Iris..." Vickie sighed. She looked up at Whitney again, and her eyes went wide. "Oh, dear. If that black eye isn't better by the weekend, I've got some makeup that'll cover it up for the festival. Does it still hurt?"

Whitney shook her head. "It looks worse than it feels. What are you two doing?"

Vickie turned back to the job, gesturing for Iris to do the same. "You've already said it. We're gluing the right name on the brochures." She glanced up and smiled. "I had a similar 'disaster' years ago for an event, with no time to put new programs together with the right sponsor's logo. We printed a bunch of logos on contrasting paper, cut them out and glued them over the wrong ones. It looks like an intentional three-dimensional effect."

Iris flashed her a quick, conspiratorial grin, her blue eyes twinkling. "Don't tell anyone, but Rick printed these at the college yesterday, then we all took some home and cut out the squares last night."

Whitney watched the two women working together in amazement. The repaired brochures were perfect. Vickie was right—it looked as though the raised square with the winery name was designed that way.

"But…I ordered fifteen hundred brochures…"

"Yes, I know." Vickie gave her a stern look. "Remind me later to talk to you about printing small runs before you decide to get a year's supply."

Whitney straightened, feeling stung. "It's not a year's supply. I was hoping we'd go through at least half of them at the festival."

Vickie shrugged, not looking up. "I suppose you could, if the weather's perfect and all the stars line up just right."

Vickie glanced over at Iris's work and sighed. "Iris, for god's sake, you need to pay attention to what you're doing. That one's crooked!" She looked up, exasperated. "I'm sorry, Whitney, but if we're going to get these done today, we need to focus."

Iris stuck her tongue out behind Vickie's back, making a choking motion with her hands. Whitney managed not to laugh and give her away. Vickie made it clear that Q&A time was over. Whitney recognized a bit of herself in the woman's organizational zeal. She headed back to the event room, where she could hear Helen laughing with someone as bottles clinked together.

Lena Fox was up on a stepladder, with an array of small paint cans and jars on the ladder tray. She was dressed in a brightly colored tunic worn over leggings. The tribal pattern swirled across the cotton fabric as she moved, her bracelets jangling on both wrists. Her head scarf was of the same fabric. She gave Whitney a bright smile.

"Hiya, honey!"

"What are you doing in here—oh!"

This blank wall facing the windows was where Whitney had intended to hang one of the nonexistent new signs. But not anymore. There was a large image sketched onto the wall, with swaths of color starting to appear. It was the new logo, and then some. The falls were there, surrounded by large trees. The stag and doe were at the bottom of the falls. At the top of the falls, a Native American man and woman gazed down at the deer. Behind all of it, a rainbow arched across the sky. Next to the forest, rows of grapevines marched up the hill.

"Lena..." Whitney breathed, still trying to comprehend what she was looking at. "It's beautiful! But... why? And how? And...it's *beautiful*."

Lena nodded. "Yes, it's looking pretty good. Mark Hudson came over this morning and sketched it out for me to help with proportions. Wall murals aren't my thing, but turns out they're one of his specialties!"

"I don't understand." Whitney watched as Lena dipped a brush in bright green paint and started stippling leaves into the trees. "Why are you doing this? I'm not complaining, believe me! But...why?"

Lena continued tapping the brush along the tree branches. "Helen told us about all the trouble you had with the signs and stuff, and I figured a mural might be better than a boring old sign anyway. So here I am." She glanced at Whitney. "Child, you look like you took on a whole bar full of brawlers instead of just one guy. How are you feeling?"

"It looks worse than it is." That was Whitney's new mantra. A fresh burst of laughter came from the doorway to her right. The kitchen consisted of a couple of deep wash tubs and a long stretch of counter space, with a microwave on a cart in the corner, next to a refrigerator and freezer. Plates and crystal were stacked on shelves above the sink. The counter was almost invisible under dozens of dark wine bottles. Helen and Cecile were elbow deep in sink water.

"Be careful!" Helen scolded Cecile. "You have to keep a firm grip if you're going to rub that hard."

Cecile giggled. "That's what *he* said!"

"What? Oh, you. Honestly, are you going to make jokes all day or get that thing peeled?"

"That's what *she* said!" The blonde was laughing so hard she was crying.

"Ce*cile*!" Helen couldn't hold a straight face, and joined in the laughter. Whitney did, too.

"Aunt Helen, what are you *doing*?"

Helen grinned at her over her shoulder. "Hey, girl! Oh, it looks like the swelling has gone down today."

Cecile turned, her pink mouth forming a perfect O when she saw Whitney's face. "Wow, you're wearing your very own rainbow."

"Um…yeah, I guess." Maybe she should take Vickie up on her offer to cover up the bruises for the festival. "What are you two doing in here?"

"We're peeling labels!" Cecile held a bottle up out of the sink, dripping water and void of labeling.

"Why?" Whitney couldn't believe how many times she'd asked the question in the past hour. What the hell were these geriatrics up to?

"Because it needed doing, dear." Helen handed another bottle to Cecile. "The old labels showed through the new ones, so we're getting rid of the old labels."

Another of Helen's friends appeared in the doorway behind Whitney. This was Jayla, the elegant doctor. Her dark hair was swept back into a twist, and she was wearing trim cotton trousers and a crisply pressed dark red top. Her voice reminded Whitney of whiskey and honey.

"I have all of the labels organized on the back table. You can start bringing the clean, dry wine to me. Pinot noir is first, right?"

Helen nodded. "Yes, this is all pinot. We'll need to get it out of the kitchen before we peel the Legacy blend bottles, so we don't mix them up. Whitney, can you roll that cart over here?"

She helped them stack the gleaming, unlabeled bottles on the metal cart, then carefully rolled it out to the table near the windows, where Jayla had the labels stacked and ready. They transferred the bottles—several cases' worth—to the table. Jayla calmly began the process of attaching new labels to the bottles. She was using one of the horizontal iron wine racks they sold in the tasting room to hold the bottles level.

Whitney tugged Helen into the corner. "*What* is going on?"

"Well, your plans for the festival ran into a few glitches last week. And glitches are exactly what friends are made for. After all, if you can't rely on a friend to help fix a glitch, then why have friends at all?"

"Damn straight!" Lena called out from her perch on the ladder. Jayla nodded in agreement as she scowled at a bottle, trying to determine if the label was on straight. Vickie walked in from the tasting room and handed Cecile a bottle of water.

Cecile raised the bottle in a mock toast. "Couldn't have said it better myself, Helen. Friends do more than cheer from the sidelines. They get on the field and fight with you. For you. Ugh, you know what I mean!"

Whitney still couldn't wrap her head around it. The festival was days away. Their efforts were sweet, but…

"There's no way you can hand peel and replace labels on hundreds of bottles."

Helen rolled her eyes. "If we had to, we'd make it happen. But I realized we only need to relabel enough bottles to have at the festival, and to have some on display here in the tasting room. And the only bottles we need to display are the ones actually in the competition—the pinot, the blend and the chardonnay. The thicker replacement labels will be here in another week or so, but that's a work party for another day." She nodded toward the mural taking shape on the wall. "The winery looks completely refreshed. We'll hand out your fancy booklets to everyone who walks by the booth, and..."

"But we don't *have* a booth." Whitney had barely spoken the words when Vickie started to tsk.

"You're right, Helen. She *is* a Negative Nancy, isn't she?"

Whitney bristled. "It's not being negative when I'm just pointing out the facts."

Vickie raised one shoulder. "Before you walked in here, you thought it was a 'fact' that you didn't have any brochures or signage. You thought it was a 'fact' that you were going to have to deal with the old labels not matching the new logo. So are you *sure* you're stating a 'fact' about the booth? Or maybe even a float?"

The older women were all smiling at her like the conspirators they were, and her mouth dropped open. She'd stepped through the looking glass and was surrounded by silly Cheshire cats.

She threw her hands up in defeat. "Okay, I give up. Who's working on the booth? Rick?" He was the only one missing. She shook her head in disbelief. "And a float, too? But how...? Oh, never mind. Clearly I've underestimated you all."

"Happens all the time." Lena turned back to her painting. "Comes with the gray hair. People assume we lose our intelligence when we lose our natural color."

"Hey, speak for yourself!" Vickie patted her champagne hair, winking at Whitney. "Some of us still have our natural color!" She ignored Lena's snort. "Rick has some kids from the theater department's stage crew helping him with the booth display and the float."

Oh, no. "*Please* tell me they're not using the moose... mooses...whatever."

"No!" Helen laughed. "But we *are* putting them to use for the festival. Sylvia over at the garden center always does a corn maze to raise money for the town's festival fund. This year's big attraction will be Mr. and Mrs. Moose at the center of the maze. Anyone who finds them can pay to get their picture taken with them, and it's already getting lots of buzz." Helen grinned. "Both of the moose will be sporting grape vine wreaths around their necks, with a sign that says 'courtesy of Falls Legend Winery.'"

Whitney couldn't help returning her aunt's proud smile. "I'm impressed!"

For the first time in days, she felt a flutter of hope in her chest. If they could do all of *this* that she'd declared impossible, what *else* might happen for the festival? She looked up toward Luke's apartment, and Helen gave her arm a squeeze.

"Nothing's impossible, sweetheart. You have friends here. You have work here. And you have a man who loves you, even if he's too afraid to admit it at the moment."

Iris Taggart came into the room, her white hair gleaming and her blue eyes sharp. Whitney had a hunch not much got past Iris, who looked at her now and arched a brow.

"I used to be the president of the Rendezvous Falls Business Owners Association, you know." She smoothed the front of her blouse. "In fact, the organization was my idea a few decades back." Whitney glanced at Helen, who nodded toward Iris as if telling Whitney to listen. "Meg McAllister is the president now, and I spoke to her yesterday. She said the town *desperately* needs an accounting firm since Harold Lightner passed away. The business owners group would do whatever was necessary to make sure a new enterprise like that succeeded. You know—marketing, grants, networking opportunities, whatever." She started to turn away. "Just in case you're interested, dear. After all, even the stupidest men come around eventually."

Whitney stood there, mind whirring with possibilities. Was it possible? Could she win Luke back if she stayed? Lena pointed her paintbrush at Whitney.

"That's right. Helen said you're good with plans, so come up with one. In the meantime, get busy. We need all the hands we can get."

Whitney watched Jayla studiously apply a label to a bottle. It would take her all day just to do the pinot at this rate. She shook her head in disbelief at what she was going to say. "Okay, ladies. You've got me thinking, that's for sure. While I'm doing that, I'll help Jayla. With two of us, it will be easier to keep the labels straight. And faster. We need all the fast, easy and straight we can get."

Cecile had turned for the kitchen, but she stopped and held her hand up.

"That's what *she* said!"

Everyone answered in a unison groan.

"Ce*cile*!"

CHAPTER TWENTY-FOUR

LUKE WAS TOO tired to care about whatever had been going on in the tasting room. Vickie and Cecile were still in there tonight, fussing over papers on the tasting counter. He barely acknowledged them as he went by. It was probably something for the festival. That was the problem with the Blessing of the Grapes. The damn thing fell right at the beginning of harvest time, when grape growers were already balls-to-the-wall trying to get everything done.

Watch the weather. Bottle the previous years' vintages to make room for the new harvest. Bring in the grapes. Crush the grapes. Start the wine. Deal with the sharply increased tourist traffic. And, oh yeah, take an entire weekend out of that manic cycle to throw a parade and have a freaking wine party in town. He tossed his jacket into the corner so hard that Molly jumped from her bed.

"Sorry, girl." She trotted over to accept his apology ear scratch. "I've been in a mood."

Helen, Whitney and their little posse of helpers had been annoyingly busy around the place. Rick Thomas had some college kids hammering away on some ridiculous float right in the middle of the wine barn. They covered the trailer with fake grass and fake trees and what looked like a giant bottle of wine lying on its side

above a waterfall. It was tacky as hell. And it was probably going to win the stupid float contest.

He'd made it clear to Helen that he wanted no part
of the festival preparation, and she'd been surprisingly
willing to honor that request. She'd simply nodded and
told him it was for the best. That wasn't like Helen at
all, but…gift horse and all that.

He was only going to be grunt labor for the festival,
lugging wine cases and setting things up. Considering the crowd of helpers Helen had scurrying around
this place, she probably wouldn't need him working the
booth at all. Which was fine. Totally fine. It was time
for Helen to become the public face of the winery now
that Tony was gone. That was never going to be a job
for Luke. Having a Rutledge front and center would be
bad publicity in this town.

He made himself a quick dinner of rosemary and
basil chicken with new potatoes. It had been one of
Whitney's favorite meals. The thought, creeping over
the boundary wall he'd erected in his mind to keep
her memory away, weighed on his shoulders like fifty-
pound bags of sand. Everything he did, everywhere he
looked, it reminded him of her.

The empty kitchen chair across from him, where
she used to sit and eat, laughing and gesturing with her
hands. The battered leather chair, where they'd cuddled
together to watch old movies. The bed in the corner,
where they'd made sweet love, and hot love, and every
kind of love in between. He hadn't changed the sheets,
unwilling to give up the scent of her that still lingered
there. Twin dressers stood at the foot of the bed, holding all the clothes that used to be stacked semineatly
on the floor.

He'd surprised Whitney with the dressers—and a clean apartment—before everything went to hell between them. It hadn't been as big a deal for her as he'd thought it would be. After all her initial griping about his lack of organization, he figured she'd be thrilled to see him leave his Neanderthal ways behind. But she'd turned the tables on him, asking him how *he* felt about the place looking more like a home. And damned if he didn't blurt out that it felt like the home he'd always wanted, but didn't figure he'd deserved. What he didn't realize at the time was that it was *Whitney* who made it feel that way, not a few pieces of furniture.

His food sat on his plate so long it grew cold. Same thing had happened every night this week, ever since he'd told her they were through. He'd pretend everything was normal when he came up here and cooked a meal. Then he fell down the rabbit hole of Whitney memories and Whitney regrets.

He hadn't been wrong to end things. If she didn't take the job in Dallas, she'd take another one. And he was obviously no good for her. Even before the disaster at the Marina Bay Bistro, they both knew that. She kept saying the whispers and stories about his family didn't matter, but if that was true, she never would have thought he'd take Helen's money. And she *had* thought that, no matter how briefly or reluctantly. No matter that she thought he did it for a "good reason." No matter how sorry she was. She'd looked at him with those sad eyes, and said she could help him "fix it." And that was the killer right there.

She'd felt *sorry* for him when she thought he'd used Helen's money. It ripped his insides to shreds. He was used to people fearing him because of his family. He was used to people suspecting him. He was used to people laughing at him. But *pity*? That was the last thing he wanted, especially from the woman he'd fallen in love with.

He let out a low curse and set his plate on the floor for Molly to finish for him. His appetite had vanished again. Of *course* he'd fallen in love with Whitney. She was smart and sassy and strong and beautiful. And the chemistry between them was on fire. It was more than the sex, although that was great. Really great. He glanced at the bed again. Who was he kidding? It was the best sex of his life, and he'd never top it. Ever. But that wasn't it. It wasn't the talking, and the laughing, and the arguing and then laughing again.

It was the way she'd looked at him. She'd looked at him like he was a man she *respected*. Like a man she trusted. Like a man who was her equal. She'd looked at him like she saw forever in his eyes. She made him feel, however briefly, like a man worthy of her love. And then he'd destroyed it all.

That's what Rutledges did. They destroyed things.

A soft tap at the door brought Molly to her feet, barking as she ran across the room. Luke opened the door and stepped back in surprise.

"Father Joe!" The good father had never been to Luke's apartment. They usually had their chats at the bar, or standing around outside the rectory after Luke finished mowing. Joe walked past Luke, looking around the place and nodding.

"Not so different from my room at the rectory." He nodded at the dinner plate, still on the floor but shiny clean. "But I don't have a four-legged dishwasher like you do. How are ya', girl?"

Luke scrambled to get the plate off the floor and into the sink while Joe bent over to greet the dog. Molly threw herself on her back for a belly rub.

"Joe, is everything okay?"

"Sure, lad. Nothin' to worry about. I was visiting with Helen and thought I'd stop over."

"Is Helen okay?"

Joe gave him a quizzical look. "Luke, I'm a priest, not the Angel of Death. Just because I appear at your door, it doesn't mean there's something wrong. I thought you might have a drop o' whiskey handy?"

Luke chuckled. "Sure, Joe. Have a seat and I'll pour you a shot."

"That'd be grand. Pour one for yourself while you're at it."

"Yes, sir."

The two men sat at the table and sipped their whiskey in silence for a few minutes before Luke dared ask another question.

"Why *were* you checking on Helen?"

"Well, we just got her comin' back to Mass, then she and Cecile and Jayla all missed choir rehearsal last night. I was curious about what would keep that group of troublemakers away."

"And?"

"Turns out it was a good deed keeping them busy, so I gave her my absolution."

"Good deed?"

"That lovely young niece of Helen's…what's her name? Whitney?"

Luke went still. "Yes. Whitney." It hurt to say her name out loud.

Joe didn't seem to notice Luke's change of mood.

"Ah, well, after that little donnybrook at the bar last weekend, Helen said Whitney was distressed over a few things that hadn't gone her way while getting ready for the festival. Helen and her friends decided to pitch in and cheer her up, good folks that they are." Joe tipped his head to the side and gave Luke that calm I-know-all look of his. "I was surprised you weren't mentioned as part of the effort."

"You know damn well why I'm not part of it." Luke turned toward the window. "She was hurt because of me."

"Which hurt are you taking responsibility for exactly?"

He frowned. "I...what?"

Joe sighed, draining his shot glass and gesturing to the bottle. He didn't start to speak until Luke refilled the glass.

"Are you taking responsibility for her outside hurt or the inside one? And if it's the inside one, are you taking responsibility for yours, hers or both?"

Luke lifted his glass to his lips, but was so busy trying to figure out Joe's riddle that he forgot to drink, setting it down still full.

"Don't play head games with me, Father. I'm tired, and I didn't ask for a shrink session."

"That's two things I am not, lad. Neither Angel of Death nor shrink. I'm just a simple village priest making small talk."

Luke barked out a harsh laugh. "There's nothing *simple* about you, Father Joe. And there's no such thing as 'small talk' with you, either. You have something to say, so...out with it."

"A few weeks ago you asked me about love, Luke. It was Whitney you were thinking of that day, yeah?"

Joe didn't wait for a response, saving Luke the pain of having to either agree or deny. "And now you're letting her go. Tell me about that."

This was the last thing Luke wanted to talk about, but he knew this stubborn Irishman wasn't going to quit.

"She was always going to go. I forgot that for a little while. My bad."

"Helen seems to think Whitney was going to *stay*. Maybe even start an accounting business here. She thinks Whitney may have fallen in love with some guy in town. Any idea who that might be?"

"Damn it, Joe…"

"Ah, this is good whiskey." Joe calmly took a sip. "The incident at the bar wasn't your fault, you know. The only one who thinks so is you."

Luke's fingers tightened on the shot glass. Molly appeared at his side, as if she knew he was hurting. Hurting so damn much.

"I don't care what anyone else thinks of me, Joe. Never have." He stood and started pacing, ramming his fingers through his hair. "But she got *punched* in a *bar*! You think that would have happened if she wasn't with me?"

Joe's voice was steady. "It's my understanding that was an accident."

"Ha! Yeah, she took a punch meant for me. Some accident." He stopped, unable to keep from asking. "How is she?"

"I didn't see her, but Helen says she's fine. Other than the broken heart."

Luke was pacing again, waving off that last comment. "Give me a break. Her heart's fine. She'd already decided to take that new job in Dallas."

"Did she?"

"She'd be an idiot not to. Huge money. Fancy title. Big city. It's everything she had in Chicago."

Joe nodded. "But she's not in Chicago anymore, is she?"

Luke shook his head. "Only because she had trouble in Chicago." She'd told him the story one night as she lay in his arms. "But you know what I mean, Joe. She's meant for the big life. Tenth floor apartments and an impressive title after her name. It makes perfect sense that she's leaving."

"Did you ever ask her to stay?" Joe's voice was soft, but the words fell on Luke like hammer blows. He *hadn't* asked. Didn't want to hear her tell him straight out that he wasn't enough to change her mind. He stopped pacing, jamming his fingers through his hair with a growl.

Whitney *told* him that she loved him. And what had he done? He'd thrown it right back in her face. Told her he didn't believe it. Now she was leaving. Was it possible he was the world's biggest idiot? Yes, it probably was.

His eyes closed tight and he grimaced. "Why are you so invested in this, Joe? Can't we just drink whiskey together and let that be that?"

"Ach, you're a good lad, Luke. I wish *you* could see that." Joe tapped his empty glass on the table a few times. "I've had all the whiskey I can handle for tonight, so I'll leave you alone to think about things." He walked to the window where Luke had stopped, and put his hand on Luke's shoulder. A still came over the room, and over Luke's troubled heart. Joe gave his shoulder a squeeze. "You are your own man, Luke Rutledge. You are not your father. Not your brother. Not your name. You are a man, and it's okay for you to love someone. To be loved. That's why you're here. It's why we're all here."

Luke had more than a little trouble getting his voice to work. He wanted to argue with Father Joe, but he couldn't seem to clear the heaviness clogging his throat. Joe chuckled softly and headed for the door.

"Have a good night, lad. You'll need your rest for the weekend you've got coming."

ON SATURDAY MORNING of festival weekend, Luke's worst fears were realized. He knew Helen had been too easy on him all week about not putting in more time on the festival preparations. This morning she'd knocked on his door and told him she'd woken up with a "head-ache" and thought the festival would be "too much" for her. As if.

And all her little book club cronies, who'd worked all day Friday to set things up, were mysteriously suffering from various ailments, too. He could either leave Whit-ney on her own in the booth on a perfect September af-ternoon when the festival would be wall-to-wall people, or go stand in that confined space with the one person who had the power to destroy what was left of his heart. Who was he kidding? There wasn't anything left.

He got to the booth before she did, because she was off collecting the first prize trophy for Best Parade Float. It was no surprise the Falls Legend Winery float won. It was so over-the-top ridiculous, everyone wanted to take a selfie in front of it. And damned if they didn't come looking for the Falls Legend booth right after that. He was quickly overwhelmed with customers tasting— and buying—their wines.

When Whitney finally arrived, she didn't say a word to him, just jumped in to help handle the crowd in front of their booth. Her hair was falling free around her face in soft, dark waves. She was wearing snug jeans and a silver-blue sweater that matched the new wine labels and sign. Even with the small crescent bruise still visible under her eye, she was stunning. She didn't seem annoyed to see him there. She didn't even seem surprised.

They fell into a natural rhythm, moving around each other smoothly, handing each other whatever wine a customer requested. When she passed behind him, she'd rest her hand on his back, taking his breath away every single time. She was acting as if he hadn't ended things between them. As if they were still together. It was killing him, because he *wanted* that to be true more than anything. She wore a smile he couldn't quite define, and the mystery of it had him looking her way every chance he got.

She seemed relaxed and confident. Not like a woman who'd been dumped. Her smile was…serene. That made sense, because she was probably off to Dallas soon, and that fancy job and new life that wouldn't include him. Good for her. She greeted more people by name than he expected, laughing with them as if she belonged there. Her happiness rubbed on him like sandpaper, and his mood spiraled. The day he told her to take the job and go, she'd acted as if he'd crushed her. She'd bounced back pretty quickly, though. And Father Joe thought Luke had broken her heart. Looked like the good padre didn't know *everything*.

Luke tried to ignore her, but a fresh burst of her happy laughter made it impossible not to look. She was talking to Meg McAllister from the Rendezvous Falls

Business Owners Association, and Whitney gestured
toward something Meg held in her hand. She'd been
handing out Falls Legend Winery booklets left and right
all afternoon, and bright blue business cards, too. It
wasn't until now that he realized people were talking
about the cards more than the wine or the booklets.
Meg shook Whitney's hand, congratulated her and took
about a dozen more of the business cards. What the...?

Whitney was handing a card to Steve Jenkins when
Luke intercepted it, snapping it up to read for himself.
In an instant, the noise, the crowds, the sweet smell of
the grape pie stand next door simply vanished. He was
pretty sure the ground under his feet vanished, as well.
What he read made him feel like he was falling without
a net to catch him.

Whitney Foster, CPA
Bookkeeping-Auditing-Taxes-Consulting
A Local Accountant with Global Experience

When he was finally able to tear his eyes from the
card to look at Whitney, she was wearing that serene
smile again. She gently arched a brow at him, waiting
him out. In the meantime, Steve had moved into the
booth and was manning the counter in Luke's place,
chuckling to himself as he poured wine for customers.
It took another minute for Luke to gather his wits together and find his voice.

"You're *staying*?" It didn't compute for him. Why
would she stay in Rendezvous Falls?

"Looks that way."

"But...why? What happened to Dallas?"

She shook her head, laughing softly.

"Luke, I *never* intended to go to Dallas." She hesitated. "The only reason I started considering it was because of what happened between us. I didn't *want* the job. I didn't want to leave. How could I? I was already in love with you."

"You're not." She couldn't be. Shouldn't be.

"Oh, I definitely am. And I realized something this week, watching the book club pitch in to save things and listening to their stories. To Helen's story." She reached for his hand. "What I heard was that love is hard. Messy. Contentious. Frustrating. Painful." She squeezed his hand. "And worth it."

Steve laughed out loud behind Luke. He'd basically told him the same thing that night at the bar. Luke worked his jaw back and forth, ignoring the tiny spot of warmth growing in his chest. It felt a lot like hope, but that would only hurt him at the end of the day.

"This isn't the time for this conversation—"

"You love me, too, Luke. I know you do."

Luke wondered how he could still be upright when he couldn't feel his legs. But he could sure as hell feel his heart. It was thrashing around in his chest like a terrified animal trying to break free. His teeth ground together. He wasn't going there. Not today. Not ever.

"That doesn't matter. We're busy here, and we need to get back to what does matter. The winery."

He saw the flash of pain in her eyes, and his hand rose to touch her face. He stopped before he got there. He didn't want to hurt her feelings. That's why he was trying to keep her away—to *protect* her from being hurt. The truth crashed into him with so much power his knees nearly buckled again. It wasn't about protect-

ing Whitney. He was protecting *himself*. He closed his
eyes tightly, trying to banish that traitorous thought.

Her hand rested gently on his, and she moved it the
rest of the way to her cheek. Her skin was soft, and wet.
She was crying. He'd made her cry. He opened his eyes
and was surprised to see her smiling brightly up at him.

Her voice was triumphant. "You didn't deny it."

"What?"

The booth had gone eerily quiet. Over her shoulder,
he noticed the crowd was still there—growing, even—
but everyone was completely enthralled with what was
happening between him and Whitney. His hand was
still on her face, with hers holding it there.

"You didn't deny you love me. You gave me some
BS about it, but you didn't deny it."

A few women chuckled from the peanut gallery that
had gathered. They always stick together. Wait—was
that *Helen*? Miracle cure, much? He needed to end this
game, before everyone's hopes got too high. Before he
allowed himself to hope at all.

"I don't…" He stopped. The words wouldn't come.
He tried again. "I don't… Whit… I…"

He looked into her eyes, and he was lost. No—he
was *found*. She was smiling up at him, so sure of herself. So sure of *him*. She wasn't pushing. Just patiently
waiting for him to catch up.

He shook his head and started to smile.

"You're really staying."

It wasn't a question this time.

"I'm really staying. No more running for me, Luke.
I told you I belong wherever you are, and you belong
here. Not because of promises you made, but because
this is *your* town. Your place." She glanced at the people

watching them. Father Joe and some of the book club members were among them. "These people care about you more than you know. *You.*" She put her other hand over his heart, and it leaped in response. "They care about the man you are. The man I love." The warmth of hope was spreading now, filling his entire body, making him feel lightheaded and terrified. Whitney went on her toes and brushed his lips with hers.

"I love you, Luke Rutledge. And I'm staying."

CHAPTER TWENTY-FIVE

WHITNEY FOUGHT TO keep her body from shaking. She'd laid everything on the line. With an audience. And now she waited, one hand holding Luke's hand to her face, the other feeling the erratic pounding of his heart. There were distant sounds of festival revelry and rides and music, but the immediate vicinity of the Falls Legend Winery booth was silent. *Everyone* was waiting.

Sure, she'd played it cool and confident to Luke, but it was all an act. What if he *didn't* love her? What if he wouldn't *let* himself love her? The man had been hurt. She'd been one of the many who'd hurt him. And now she'd pushed him into a corner and challenged him to admit he loved her in front of half the town. What if he wouldn't trust her again? What if...

His fingers moved against her cheek, so slightly she wasn't sure she'd felt it. There. He did it again. She released his hand and closed her eyes, praying. He pushed her hair behind her ear, then slid around to hold the back of her head. His mouth moved against hers, almost reluctantly. He was fighting it. He was fighting loving her. He spoke against her lips.

"Open your eyes."

She did. He was right there, eyes dark with emotion.

"I want you looking at me when I say this. I want to be sure you understand."

Oh, god. He was going to turn her away. She was going to lose him. Her heart stopped.

"I love you, Whitney. God help me, I do. I love you."

He kissed her hard and deep, and she thought she'd faint with relief. She grabbed his shoulders and held herself up, kissing him back as much as she could between crying and laughing and listening to the cheers of the crowd that had gathered. He pulled her into his arms and buried his face in her shoulder, crushing her in his embrace. She felt the wetness of his tears on her skin and started crying all over again, overcome with emotion.

"Okay, folks, the floor show is over!" Helen's voice rang out from inside the booth. "And if you'd like to know the magic recipe for all of this lovey-dovey stuff, Luke's favorite wine is the pinot noir he harvested with my late husband, and Whitney's is our unoaked chardonnay from the steel tanks Tony invested in. Both are finalists in the wine competition today!"

Luke and Whitney lifted their heads and watched in amusement. Helen continued her spiel, laughing with renewed life as she and Steve started handing out samples of the two wines as fast as they could pour them.

"It's as if my Tony is still looking over us today. As Tony used to say, '*Vivi con passione. Ridi di cuore. Ama profondamente.*' That means live with passion, laugh out loud and love deeply." Helen turned to Luke and Whitney and raised a glass in a toast. "To love!"

The crowd cheered again, repeating the last two words loudly. Helen shooed Luke and Whitney out of the booth and told them to "go be in love somewhere out of her way." Vickie and Cecile stepped into the booth to help Helen, as they'd planned when they'd cooked up this idea in the carriage house the other day.

As they worked their way out of the crowd, people were clapping Luke on the back and congratulating him. He nodded absently, a baffled smile on his face, hardly saying a word. He'd never let himself trust people enough to learn that not *everyone* was judging him. It would be a while before he'd let himself believe it, but she'd help him get there.

They moved away from the festival madness and walked up Main Street, their arms around each other's waists, moving in unison with each other. Having a little more space and a little more quiet helped them both breathe easier. Her phone chirped with an incoming text. She fished it out of her pocket without letting go of Luke.

"It's from Evie." She read the message and gave a little whoop of excitement. "Luke, we won!"

"Yeah, I know. You won me and I won you."

She smacked him on the shoulder. "No... I mean yes...but that's... Oh, never mind. I'm talking about the *winery*! The Legacy red won a silver in the reds, and the chardonnay won the gold medal for whites!" Another text came in. "And best overall for the festival! Oh, Luke! You did it!"

He swung her around, lifting her feet right off the sidewalk. "*We* did it, babe." He set her down and kissed her. "Helen's right. We make one hell of a team. Let's find her and celebrate."

They turned down the hill toward the festival, and he glanced at her with a grin as they walked. His delicious, relaxed, light-filled grin. She blinked back fresh tears.

"What's that look?" he asked.

"This is what love looks like, my friend." She nudged her hip against his. "I hate to break it to you, but you're wearing the same goofy expression."

He barked out a laugh. "Goofy, huh?" Then his smile faded. "You decided to stay without knowing how I felt?"

"Well, I had a pretty good idea, but yeah. I printed the business cards on Helen's printer yesterday. I'm done running, Luke. I decided to stay and fight, because we're worth it."

They walked on as he digested that.

"I feel like a schmuck for *not* fighting for us. Thank god you never gave up."

She pulled him to a stop. "No. We're not doing that. We're not putting blame on ourselves or each other or our names or our families or anything else."

He stared at her, his eyes dark with emotion. "You know, I can't imagine I could have really let you go in the end, Whit. You're…you're everything. You're my world."

"I don't think either one of us could have gone through with it, but we came awful close, didn't we?" The thought sent a tremor of panic through her, and he saw it, pulling her close.

"I swear, Whitney, I will *never* let that happen again. I can't promise to be perfect, but I promise I'll never let you go. I will *always* fight for you. For *us*."

Her heart swelled with love. "We've both made mistakes. But nothing that happened in the past matters anymore. This is us, and we start today. Right now."

He gave her a slanted smile, then a mock salute.

"Yes, ma'am."

"Now you're getting the idea!" She turned, but he grabbed her by the waist and pulled her back.

"Nice try, Miss Bossy Pants." He kissed her until her head spun. "There's only one way you're getting away with making the rules here."

"Yeah? And what's that?"

"You're gonna have to tell me you love me a lot." His brows gathered. "I mean, not that you love me a lot, but you have to *say* it a lot."

Whitney put her hands on either side of his face. "Here's an idea. What if I do both? Because I do love you a lot and I'm happy to say it a lot. I love you."

He stared at her in wonder. "I love you, too, Whitney. And I'll tell you that every damn day until the end of time." His arms wrapped around her. "That's another promise. And you know what it means when I make a promise."

She smiled against his lips.

"You stick."

"Forever."

EPILOGUE

December 21

LUKE'S ARM WAS firm around Whitney's waist as he led her, blindfolded, up the stairs to his apartment. She trusted him completely. Even so, it was scary to go up the steps in pitch darkness. Her fingers dug into his arm until he let out a hiss.

"Easy, woman. I'm not throwing you from the damn tower."

"How would I know *what* you're doing? I can't see anything!"

"That's how surprises are supposed to work. Stop being so paranoid."

"But it's not Christmas yet!"

"Close enough. Stop complaining. Hang on…"

They were on the landing now. He leaned forward. Opening the door? Yes, she heard the lock turn. She felt Molly rush past her leg and into the apartment. Luke didn't even *live* up here anymore. He'd officially, and permanently, moved into her…*their*…upstairs suite in the main house over a month ago. What could be so interesting about this space in the carriage house? He turned her to the right, his breath warm on her neck.

"Ready?"

"More than," she assured him. But when he pulled the folded scarf from over her eyes, she was speechless.

The apartment had been transformed. The kitchen was partially walled off, creating an actual *entrance* at the top of the stairs. Hanging on the wall was a sign of some sort, but it was concealed under one of Helen's white linen tablecloths. There was a round table in the center of the room, surrounded by comfortable-looking chairs. Beyond the table, where the bed used to be— oh, the times they had on that bed—was a cherry desk with an antique bookkeepers lamp on the corner of it. Whoever sat in the sleek leather chair could easily turn to see the sweeping views of the Seneca Valley. In front of the desk were two tufted green leather chairs.

The wall that once held the wooden pegs that had acted as Luke's closet was now lined with built-in bookcases. A long, low sofa sat along the opposite wall.

Her mouth had fallen open the instant Luke removed her blindfold, and she only managed to close it now because she had to speak. But words didn't come easily.

"What…? Why…? Who…?"

Luke gave her a wide smile as he ticked off the answers on his fingers. "What? Your new office. Why? Because Helen would like her dining room back. Who? Me. With a little help here and there."

"I can't even… When did you *do* this?"

He shrugged. "While you were working on all that new business you've been raking in, I was up here with a hammer and a saw."

She narrowed her eyes at him. "You told me you were working in the barn."

He gestured around the room. "Welcome to the barn."

She turned a full three-sixty, taking it all in one more time. "It's...perfect. But you didn't have to..."

Luke tugged her into his arms—forever her favorite place to be. "Yeah, I did. Every time I think about how I almost let you walk away..." He rested his forehead on hers, eyes tightly closed. "If you hadn't..."

She put her hands on his face and waited for him to look into her eyes and hear her. "Don't go there, Luke." The corner of her mouth lifted. "Besides, you're pretty stubborn, and I can totally see you hiding my car keys or locking me up here so that I couldn't leave."

His soft laughter blew warm across her skin. "Not a bad idea. I wouldn't have let you walk away. You'd be taking my heart with you." His shoulder lifted. "And you know I'm kind of a last-minute sort of guy."

"Exactly." She grinned and pressed her hand on his chest. "That heart of yours was trying to do the right thing. You were standing back, even though you loved me, because you thought leaving was best for *me*." She kissed his lips, then smiled against his mouth. "I think the last-minute guy would have come to his senses eventually, even if it was after I'd already packed my car full."

He laughed out loud at that, then kissed her, hard and deep, squeezing her tight. "I think you're right. And I *know* I love you. More every day."

Her heart fluttered in her chest. Their love was as much a miracle to her as it was to him.

"I love you, too, but...what does that have to do with building me an office?"

"Come here." He led her back to the wall by the front door, and tugged on the linen tablecloth that covered the sign. It was made to look like the bottom of an oak barrel, but the round center was a smoked mirror. There was one line of script lettering in gold leaf.

Whitney Rutledge, CPA

She couldn't breathe for a moment. *Rutledge?* Was he…? She turned, and Luke answered her question by dropping to one knee. *Oh. My. God.*

"I want you to stay here, Whitney. Forever. As my wife. So what do you say? Ready to marry a Rutledge boy?"

Her laughter bubbled up. "I've heard rumors about those Rutledge boys." She sobered when he took her hand and held up a delicate diamond ring.

"So…will you?" One brow rose in question.

When I give my word, it sticks.

"Do you promise to love me forever?" she whispered. The warmth in his eyes told her he knew what she was asking.

"You have my word. I'll stick, Whitney. For good."

"Then…yes!"

He slid the ring on and leaped to his feet, lifting her in the air and spinning her before letting her slide down his chest. They kissed—sweetly at first, then it deepened and she wound her fingers into his hair. There was a nice, big sofa right over there, and she tugged him toward it.

"No can do, babe." His voice was pained.

She pulled back, confused.

He chuckled and shook his head. "One more surprise—there's a party waiting for us downstairs."

She cocked her head. Sure enough, she could hear laughing voices below.

"Who…?"

"Everybody." He rolled his eyes, then glanced at the

ring sparkling on her hand and shrugged. "You're not the only one who can conspire with those gray hairs in the book club. It's part engagement party and part open house for your new office."

"Hmm. Engagement party, huh? Pretty sure of yourself, weren't you?"

"Let's call it *hopeful*. Hope is kind of a new thing for me, and I'm liking it so far."

She kissed him, then turned and tugged him toward the door.

"Okay, let's go party. But when everyone leaves, I'm *hopeful* we'll come back up here to try out that sofa."

He let out a bark of laughter, glancing back at the sofa over his shoulder. "You have my word we'll get naked on that sofa soon. And often. But first, I want to show off my fiancée to our friends."

She headed out the door, amazed at the change in Luke since the festival. He had hope. He had love. And he finally realized he had *friends* here in Rendezvous Falls. They were all waiting at the base of the stairs—Helen and the book club cohorts, Father Joe, Evie and Mark, Steve Jenkins and others from town—cheering and raising their glasses high.

Their friends. Their family. Their hope. Their beginning.

* * * * *

*Read on for a sneak peek at the next book in
Jo McNally's charming, funny and heart-tugging
Rendezvous Falls series,* Stealing Kisses in the Snow.

Piper Montgomery was plunging the toilet in room twelve of the Taggart Inn when her four-year-old daughter announced she wanted to dress up as Deadpool for Halloween.

It wasn't even ten o'clock in the morning, and this was already turning into one of *those* days. Piper was pretty sure she already knew the answer to her next question, but she asked anyway.

"Lily, where did you even *hear* of Deadpool?"

Lily brushed her white-blond curls from her face with a big smile. "Ethan told me! He said Deadpool was a superhero and he wears red and red's my favorite color, so it's perfect!"

Piper sat back on her heels on the marble bathroom floor. Mr. and Mrs. Carlisle would be finished with breakfast soon, and they'd expect their bathroom to be fully functional when they got back. But Lily's grandparents would have some expectations, too. She could just imagine the look of horror on Susan Montgomery's face if Lily dressed up as a foul-mouthed superhero.

"But Grandma Montgomery already bought you that pretty butterfly costume, remember?"

Lily's face scrunched. "Ethan says butterflies are stupid. He says…"

"Yeah, Ethan says a lot of things." Her grip tightened

on the wooden plunger handle, wrinkling the rubber gloves she was wearing. She had no doubt this whole Deadpool idea was her thirteen-year-old son's payback because she told him he might be too old for trick-or-treating this year. Or it could be payback for her working three jobs. Or for moving into the house he claimed to hate. Or it could just be payback for the fact that Piper was his mother, which seemed to be on the top of his resentment list lately. "I think Ethan was teasing you, honey. He knows you're too young to be Deadpool. It's not appropriate."

"Oh! I know what 'appropriate' means!" Lily, often light-years ahead of her age, loved big words. "It means what people expect, right? So people wouldn't expect me to be Deadpool and they wouldn't like it?"

Piper could think of one person who definitely wouldn't like it. "That's right, honey. Let's talk about this later and we'll come up with something for you to wear that will make everyone happy." Except Ethan, of course, but making her son happy seemed a lost cause these days.

She put her frustration into her plunging efforts, and was relieved when the toilet drained with a whoosh. Lily clapped her hands and started dancing. Victory dances for toilets that flushed. *Livin' the good life.* Piper wiped down the bathroom, then shooed her daughter out to the hall.

Plumbing wasn't normally her responsibility at the B&B. She usually just handled cooking breakfast and some cleaning for the owner, Iris Taggart. But Iris broke her hip a week ago, so Piper was, as the only employee, the Woman in Charge. Iris was eighty, so "temporarily" could last awhile. And as long as Piper was in charge, she was not paying a plumber a hundred bucks for a job she could handle on her own.

She'd just peeled off her rubber gloves and tucked them, and the plunger, into the hallway closet when Mr. Carlisle came up the stairs. Just in time. She doubted the guests she'd served salted caramel pancakes to forty minutes earlier would want to see their cook with a toilet plunger in her hand. She gave him a bright smile as she grabbed Lily to stop her from twirling and singing about toilets.

"Your room is all set, Mr. Carlisle. So sorry for any inconvenience. If you'd like, I can box up some of those cookies your wife liked so much so you'll have a snack while you tour the wineries today."

"That was fast. Then again, you probably have a plumber on call with a place this ancient." He looked around the hallway, with its bold floral wallpaper, and wrinkled his nose. Piper had been campaigning for a while now to get Iris to update the decor, but the old woman had built this business and decorated it herself, and she wasn't a fan of change. Mr. Carlisle shook his head as he put his key in the door. "No offense, but the wineries and this place are my *wife's* idea of a good time, not mine. But I've heard there's a distillery around here, so I'm hoping that'll be worth the drive from Phillie."

"Eagle Rock Distillery? Oh, you'll love it. Ben Wilson has done a great job up there, and the views this time of year are spectacular. And if your wife likes wineries, you'll drive right by one of my favorites on the way up there—Falls Legend Winery on Lakeview Road." She moved past him toward the main staircase. "That way you'll *both* have a good time today!"

Lily nodded solemnly, precocious as ever. "Yes, the views at Ben's are spectac-alar this time of year."

Mr. Carlisle chuckled, leaning down to the little girl's level. "So you've spent a lot of time at the whiskey distillery, have you?"

Lily's blue eyes were shining at being talked to like an adult. She was in way too much of a hurry to grow up.

"Oh, yes! Grandma and Grandpa take me there. Mr. Ben has a donkey named Rocky, and I feed him carrots. Mr. Ben was my daddy's best friend, but my daddy's dead, so Mr. Ben says he's *my* best friend now."

Piper had to give John Carlisle credit. He hid his shock well, his smile barely faltering as Lily info-dumped all over him. Meanwhile, Piper was adding *talk to Ben* to her to-do list. Ben Wilson was a great guy. Her in-laws adored him, and she'd already suspected Susan had decided he was the "anointed one" to take over Paul's role as husband and father. But, like so many other things, that wasn't Susan's—or Ben's— decision to make.

"Come on, peanut. Momma has work to do." She tugged Lily toward the stairs. "Enjoy your day, Mr. Carlisle!"

Once downstairs, Piper started clearing the dining room. There were only three rooms occupied last night, but the weekend ahead was fully booked. Not only was it the peak of leaf-peeping season, it was also Harvest Fest weekend in Rendezvous Falls. The festival would take place downtown, just a few blocks from the Taggart Inn. Iris usually had the porches decorated and set up for folks to enjoy tea and spice cookies to showcase the bed-and-breakfast. But it was already Wednesday and Piper had no idea how she would get the decorating done in time, much less the food.

"Look, Momma! I'm an Iroquois princess!" Lily had grabbed a garland of brown-and-gold silk leaves from the bannister of the formal staircase and wrapped it around her head like a crown. Piper had been reading a children's book aloud to Lily about the rich Iroquois history in the Finger Lakes region of New York, and the many legends handed down through centuries.

"Very pretty, Lily. Just be careful not to pull those down by accident, okay?" At least Piper had managed to get some autumn decorations inside of the inn, even if it was mostly pumpkins and gourds and silk leaves. Iris had been hauling out the boxes of decorations when she took the fall that led to her broken hip. Thank god Piper had been cleaning a room on the second floor and heard the awful thud and Iris's cry of pain from above. Another half hour and the elderly woman would have been lying up there the whole day before anyone knew she was hurt.

"Momma, I'm going to go feed Mr. Whiskers, okay? Because I'm responsible for him." Lily had been thrilled when Iris pronounced her the cat's caretaker while she was recovering.

"Just be sure not to let him out of Iris's apartment, and lock the door when you leave." Lily started to skip away as Piper called out one more order. "And no playing in the guest areas!"

The Victorian mansion, built in the late 1800s, had three floors plus a full attic and a creepy basement. The first floor held several common rooms for guests to enjoy, a large dining room, the kitchen and Iris's living quarters in the back. When Piper bought the house next door, she'd started helping Iris part-time, eager for any job she could find. The elderly woman had gradually added more duties to Piper's list, and she was glad for the extra hours. Even better, Iris didn't mind her bringing her daughter with her. She didn't have live-in babysitters these days, unless you counted Ethan. But he was barely a reliable babysitter in the afternoons, much less in the early mornings. Lily bounced out of bed every day raring to go, but Ethan was more of a don't-talk-to-me-until-noon kid.

Iris insisted she didn't mind the endlessly active girl being around while Piper worked, as long as she didn't disturb the guests. Of course, Lily *did* that on a fairly regular basis, but most of the time the guests were charmed by her. She was so much like her father, with her ability to make people just like putty in her hands.

Piper loaded breakfast dishes into the commercial dishwasher sitting on the stainless steel kitchen counter. The big kitchen was the one area in the inn where Iris didn't mind a modern look. There was stainless steel everywhere, including the oversize appliances and backsplash. It was sterile enough to be a hospital operating room. Piper had made sure of that, spending her first month here scrubbing every surface until it gleamed.

"Momma!" Lily's shriek as she ran into the kitchen startled Piper so much she almost dropped the platter she was holding. She should be used to the child by now, but tell that to her heart that just tried leaping out of her chest.

"Lily! *Please* don't scream like that. There are guests…"

"But, Momma, I saw a *giant*! He was walking right down the hall—a real live giant!"

Piper probably had Ethan to thank for *this*, too. He

tried to tell Lily the inn was haunted by monsters. Luckily, her fearless little daughter loved that idea, so his plan to scare her had failed. But Piper was going to have yet another talk with him. Seriously? *Giants* now?

"Lily, it's not nice to tell stories." She talked over her daughter's objection. "I know, your brother loves tall tales, but we should always tell the truth, okay? Did you take care of Mr. Whiskers? Did you lock Iris's door?"

"Yes, but, Momma, that's when I saw him! A big, shaggy giant dressed in black!"

Piper slid the door open on the dishwasher and rolled the steaming tray out onto the counter. She glanced at her watch. Damn, she was going to be late to the insurance office if she didn't get moving. They'd been understanding of her need to help Iris more, but Piper still needed both jobs. She humored her daughter to move things along.

"Okay, Lily. If you see that giant again, you bring him to me so I can tell him to stop hanging around here during the day. That's bad for business."

Lily giggled and dashed out of the kitchen before Piper could tell her they were leaving soon. She put away the last of the dishes and tossed the dishrag into the bin to be washed. She was mopping up the last corner of the floor when she heard the kitchen door open again. Good—Lily hadn't wandered far.

"I'm glad you're back, sweetie. I'm almost done, so—"

"Momma! I found the giant! Isn't he humongous?"

Piper turned and froze, clutching the mop handle tightly. Lily was standing in the doorway, holding hands with a stranger. Well over six feet tall, with straggly wet hair hanging to his shoulders and a scruffy beard, the man was clothed entirely in black leather, including leather chaps on his long legs. He had the deepest-set eyes Piper had ever seen, shadowed under heavy dark brows. With his size and overall menacing appearance, it was no wonder Lily thought he was a giant.

And he was holding her daughter's tiny hand.

Piper bristled, brandishing the mop handle in front of her like a sword as she went toward him. "You let her go right this minute! And get out of here! I'm calling the police…" She fumbled to get her phone out of her back pocket while still aiming the mop at him. Her voice was fast approaching a scream. "You get the hell away from my daughter and get *out*!"

Logan Taggart had been thrown out of plenty of places in his lifetime, but never by a pretty little pony-tailed momma wearing a yellow apron. He managed to squelch his amusement, knowing it would be a mistake to laugh.

The golden-haired munchkin clutching his fingers right now was clearly the woman's daughter, and he probably looked like an ax murderer. He gently freed himself from the child and stepped back, raising both hands and modulating his voice carefully.

"I'm sorry. The little girl said she wanted me to go to the kitchen, and I was heading here anyway…"

The woman was flummoxed for a moment. Her chest rose and fell rapidly, her blue eyes wild. She raised the mop higher with one hand, then dropped her phone on the counter with the other so she could snatch her daughter's hand and tug her to safety behind her. She waved the mop again, as if that would really protect her if he posed a threat. He was a foot taller and close to a hundred pounds heavier than she was. The biggest danger to him was in her other hand—the cell phone she'd picked up again.

"Please don't call the police," Logan said, trying to sound as reasonable as possible. "It'll upset the guests and I haven't done anything wrong."

The woman hesitated, glancing back at her daughter. Mama bear had saved her cub. She swallowed a couple times, then gestured to the door with the mop. Her voice shook. "You need to go."

"I'm sorry I startled you. I've had a long-ass..." He glanced at the kid and grimaced. "It's been a long trip, and I got caught in a rainstorm just south of here. I haven't eaten since dinner..."

Her eyes softened a fraction, even as she held the mop out firmly. "The Methodist church three blocks over has a food pantry, and the Catholic church does soup and bread every Wednesday for whoever stops in. Father Joe might be able to help you find a place to sleep. But you can't stay here."

Logan couldn't stop his bark of laughter, even though it made her jump. She thought he was *homeless*? He couldn't decide if he was offended or impressed. Clearly scared out of her wits, she was still kind enough to offer him a chance at hot food and a bed. Yeah, definitely impressed. It was no surprise she worked for his grandmother, who was also a tough-as-nails woman who cared about others far more than she ever let on. Her eyes started to narrow again, and he leveled his voice. Again.

"Actually, I *can* stay here."

She lifted the cell phone, so he rushed to explain.

"I'm Logan Taggart. This is my grandmother's place. I know I look like Sasquatch right now, but I'm honestly just here to help my grandmother." There was certainly no other reason he'd ever come to Rendezvous Falls with all its frou-frou festivals and Gran's kitschy old inn.

The woman froze. "You're *Logan*? But Iris said…" She looked him up and down. "Iris said you were a big shot in oil." Her eyes narrowed. "And she didn't tell me you were coming."

He rolled his eyes. Leave it to his grandmother to exaggerate his job description for her friends.

"She didn't know I was coming. She told my sister and me not to, but we knew she'd need help, and I was the lo…the lucky winner who had time to come to Rendezvous Falls." The truth was, he'd lost the bet with Nicky a week ago, and had no choice but to uproot his own life, stuff it into a duffle bag and ride his Harley from Alabama to New York. He rolled his bum shoulder and tried not to groan. All so he could be threatened with bodily harm by a woman half his size. "I assume you work for Gran. Nice to meet you, Mrs.….?" He held out his hand and waited. The woman was pretty in a fresh-scrubbed, wholesome way that had never been his style. But there was something about her that was…interesting. She stared at his hand in suspicion before her shoulders dropped a fraction and she let out a long breath, lowering the mop at last. She reached out to take his hand, but she clearly wasn't happy about it.

"Piper Montgomery. I work for Iris part-time, and a little more than that now that she's laid up. I'm sorry, Mr. Taggart… I…"

"Your reaction was one hundred percent understandable. And please, don't ever call me 'Mr. Taggart' again. It's just Logan. And *I* should be the one apologizing for frightening you and your daughter…"

The girl jumped out from behind her mom. They were so much alike—long blond hair, big baby blue eyes and porcelain skin. The girl flashed him a toothy grin.

"*I* wasn't scared! I knew you were a real giant, and Momma didn't believe me. But now she does! My name's Lily, and I'm gonna call you Logan the Giant, 'kay?"

Oil rigs were no place for kids, so he didn't have much experience talking to them. And he was still wary of Lily's mom, who'd just released his hand to hold Lily back. Either she didn't believe he was Iris Taggart's grandson, or that fact didn't automatically make him "safe" in her book. She shook her head at the little girl.

"You will call him Mr. Taggart…" She glanced up at him. "Or maybe Mr. Logan?"

He nodded. "As nice as Logan the Giant sounds to my ego, Mr. Logan is probably the better choice. It's nice to meet you, Lily." He extended his hand to her, and she grabbed his fingers and shook up and down with a great deal of enthusiasm, making him grin.

"Hi, Mr. Logan! Are you staying at the inn? Miss Iris lives in the back. I can give you the key. But you'll have to watch Mr. Whiskers if you stay there, because he likes to escape. Or are you going to take a room? Or you could stay with us! We live right next door and there's a bedroom in the attic that my brother wants but I bet he'd let you have it…"

Piper held up her hand to stop the seemingly endless flow of words. "Mr. Logan is *not* staying with us.

You can't just invite strangers into our home, Lily. Why
don't you go to the library and find a book to read while
Mr. Logan and I have a chat?"

Uh-oh. Whenever a woman said they wanted to have
"a chat" in that tone of voice, it was rarely a friendly
conversation. She may not think he was homeless anymore, but she wasn't giving off a "welcome to the Taggart Inn" vibe, either. She picked up her phone, shaking
her head at his look of concern.

"I'm not calling the cops on you. Yet. But I do have
to make a call." She tapped on the screen and turned
away from him.

"Sandy? It's Piper. Look, I have a bit of a…situation…
to deal with at the B&B. Is it okay if I work noon-to-four
today instead of ten-to-two?…Yeah, everything's fine…
No, no need for Pete to stop by…" She glanced over her
shoulder quickly. "Unless he wants to meet Iris's prodi-
gal grandson…"

Logan grimaced. Great. That's just how he wanted
the locals to think of him. She noted his expression and
for the first time, he saw a glint of amusement in the
eyes that had been icy until now. She'd said that just to
goad him. He liked her sass.

"Yeah, you heard right…Well, he's…scruffy…" She
laughed at something Sandy must have said. Her laugh
was light and soft, and he couldn't help thinking that
it fit her somehow. "He seems fine, I guess. I just have
to get him settled, then I'll drop Lily off and come to
the office, okay?…Thanks."

He seems fine…I guess? So he hadn't exactly won
her over with his charm yet. She turned back to face
him after the call ended. Her voice was brisk now, and
all business.

"Okay. Let's figure out some logistics. How long are you staying? And where?"

Logan scrubbed the back of his neck. Probably would have been nice if he'd thought that far ahead.

Don't miss Stealing Kisses in the Snow
by Jo McNally!

*After escaping her abusive ex, Cassie Zetticci is
thankful for a job and a safe place to stay at the
Gallant Lake Resort. Nick West makes her nervous
with his restless energy, but when he starts teaching her
self-defense, Cassie begins to see a future that involves
roots and community. But can Nick let go of his own
difficult past to give Cassie the freedom she needs?*

*Read on for a sneak preview of
A Man You Can Trust,
the first book—and Harlequin Special Edition debut!—
in Jo McNally's new miniseries, Gallant Lake Stories.*

"Why are you armed with pepper spray? Did something
happen to you?"

She didn't look up.

"Yes. Something happened."

"Here?"

She shook her head, her body trembling so badly
she didn't trust her voice. The only sound was Nick's
wheezing breath. He finally cleared his throat.

"Okay. Something happened." His voice was gravelly
from the pepper spray, but it was calmer than it had been
a few minutes ago. "And you wanted to protect yourself.
That's smart. But you need to do it right. I'll teach you."

Her head snapped up. He was doing his best to look at her, even though his left eye was still closed.

"What are you talking about?"

"I'll teach you self-defense, Cassie. The kind that actually works."

"Are you talking karate or something? I thought the pepper spray…"

"It's a tool, but you need more than that. If some guy's amped up on drugs, he'll just be temporarily blinded and really ticked off." He picked up the pepper spray canister from the grass at her side. "This stuff will spray up to ten feet away. You never should have let me get so close before using it."

"I didn't know that."

"Exactly." He grimaced and swore again. "I need to get home and dunk my face in a bowl full of ice water." He stood and reached a hand down to help her up. She hesitated, then took it.

Don't miss
A Man You Can Trust *by Jo McNally,*
available September 2019 wherever
Harlequin® Special Edition books and ebooks are sold.

www.Harlequin.com

The countdown to Christmas begins now!
Keep track of all your Christmas reads.

September 24

- [ ] *A Coldwater Christmas* by Delores Fossen
- [ ] *A Country Christmas* by Debbie Macomber
- [ ] *A Haven Point Christmas* by RaeAnne Thayne
- [ ] *A MacGregor Christmas* by Nora Roberts
- [ ] *A Wedding in December* by Sarah Morgan
- [ ] *An Alaskan Christmas* by Jennifer Snow
- [ ] *Christmas at White Pines* by Sherryl Woods
- [ ] *Christmas from the Heart* by Sheila Roberts
- [ ] *Christmas in Winter Valley* by Jodi Thomas
- [ ] *Cowboy Christmas Redemption* by Maisey Yates
- [ ] *Kisses in the Snow* by Debbie Macomber
- [ ] *Low Country Christmas* by Lee Tobin McClain
- [ ] *Season of Wonder* by RaeAnne Thayne
- [ ] *The Christmas Sisters* by Sarah Morgan
- [ ] *Wyoming Heart* by Diana Palmer

October 22

- [ ] *Season of Love* by Debbie Macomber

October 29

- [ ] *Christmas in Silver Springs* by Brenda Novak
- [ ] *Christmas with You* by Nora Roberts
- [ ] *Stealing Kisses in the Snow* by Jo McNally

November 26

- [ ] *North to Alaska* by Debbie Macomber
- [ ] *Winter's Proposal* by Sherryl Woods

Harlequin.com

XMAS0319BPA